DØ725176

**A STAR SHELL BURST ABOVE THE BUILD-
INGS TO THE NORTH. THE SKY LIT UP
LIKE DAYLIGHT.**

Bascom was startled by the light, but not nearly
so startled as when he swung his gaze to the two
men in greatcoats waiting among the sandbags.
They had turned their faces upward to stare at
the hissing Russian flares. One, as Bascom suspected, was the same high-ranking Gestapo officer he had seen enter the Chancellery garden at
midday. The other, face frozen in icy calm, eyes
vivid and alert beneath the downturned brim of
his slouch hat, was as familiar to him as his own
reflection in a shaving mirror.

Bascom felt his blood turn hot—for there, standing not forty feet away, calmly gazing at the midnight sky in the middle of a burning, dying city,
was Adolf Hitler.

Also Available from Dell

THE NINTH MAN

The Thirteenth Hour

JOHN LEE

A DELL BOOK

Published by
Dell Publishing Co., Inc.
1 Dag Hammarskjold Plaza
New York, New York 10017

Dell ® TM 681510, Dell Publishing Co., Inc.

ISBN: 0-440-18751-6

Reprinted by arrangement with Doubleday & Company, Inc.
Printed in the United States of America
First Dell printing—September 1979

For David and Tina Rubin,
with pleasant memories of Row T,
Seats 14, 16, 18, and 20.

THE THIRTEENTH HOUR

PROLOGUE

Friday—March 12, 1954

It was a sunny March morning, hinting teasingly of the warm spring that would come, when Sidney Longland made his long-delayed personal pilgrimage back to Berlin. It wasn't the first time mere duty had made it necessary for him to revisit the now divided city since the end of the war, but he looked at it this morning with a new awareness.

The city had undergone great regeneration in the past nine years. Sheep grazed once more beside the runways of a rebuilt Tempelhof aerodrome. Bomb-shattered buildings had been torn down with ruthless efficiency and new glass-and-concrete structures had risen from the ashes. In the inner city, as Longland knew, the Reich Chancellery was gone, with nothing but an empty field left in its place, a no-man's-land between an East and West Berlin. The underground bunker where Hitler spent those final days had been dynamited years back and was now only a grass-covered hump in the center of the field. There were four new landscaped hills in Berlin, created from the collected debris of World War II. One, a four-hundred-foot colossus in the Grunewald, had been named *Trümmerberg*, Ruin Mountain, while another in the borough of Schöneberg just west of Tempelhof was known as *Der Insulaner*, The Islander, a nickname that isolated West Berliners now applied to themselves. Two more such mounds existed in East Berlin, the largest of which bore the imposing name Mount Klamott. Under these four man-made mounds lay fully a third or more of what had once been Berlin.

Longland approved of the new feeling of spaciousness

the city now had, but he had to disapprove of the rate at which Berlin was rebuilding. Poor old London still sported boarded-up ruins everywhere one looked. He frowned at the building cranes and bricklayers that his embassy-provided limousine passed in the British sector, the frown deepening two furrows the years had plowed between his eyebrows. He had to admit that he, too, had changed since the war. Heavier now. Not yet much gray in his hair, but the hairline itself seemed to be rising. His slightly pointed ears perhaps were more prominent, and his once-mischievous eyes had dulled with the disillusionments of peace.

Disillusionments. How would it be with the nameless, nationless man he had come to see today? Would the man even recognize him after all these years? It wasn't as if they had been great friends. If anything, they had been enemies. Or at least rivals. Perhaps he should have stayed in London, let it pass. But then, someone ought to be on hand when the man crossed over. And it was unlikely any of the others would bother.

He dismissed the limousine near the Friedrichstrasse checkpoint, a major crossing station on the East-West border, and limped on to the designated tram line. There was a *Kneipe*, a little workingman's bar, a quarter block from the tram stop, Longland noted with satisfaction. It would offer a quiet place to talk, once he greeted the man. The bar looked dingy, but the proprietor had set several metal tables out front on the sidewalk. Two young Germans had already occupied one of the tables and stripped off their shirts, exposing torsos the color of fish bellies to the sunshine. East Berliners or West Berliners? They crossed back and forth constantly on the trams to work in one another's sectors. Maybe not forever. The Russians had proved to be increasingly contentious when it came to an exchange of commerce and communication across the East-West line, and it wouldn't surprise Longland if one of these days they found a way to block human traffic, as well.

Longland liked sunshine, even though he was British enough to prefer keeping his clothes on when confronted with it. He moved a few feet from the tram stop to a slash of sun hitting a brick wall and leaned there, waiting patiently until he saw the approach of the tram. Six men, all dressed in heavy, hideously fitted woolen suits, parting gifts from their jailers, got off the tram with an escort, a stolid-looking infantryman with a rifle slung over his shoulder. The infantryman passed out a set of papers to each man, then went back to wait for the return tram to the East. The six men hesitated, as though uncertain what to do with their new freedom or bewildered by the unceremonious manner in which it had been handed to them. Then they broke apart and began to walk away in different directions.

Good Lord, which one? The tall one? Thin as a leather whip, short-cut hair, and the worst-fitting of all the suits? Could the man have changed so much? Longland limped hurriedly forward.

"Bascom?" he said.

The tall man's greenish eyes touched him, then coldly looked beyond him, as if assessing the area. It took only a moment. Then the tall man said quietly, "Hello, Longland."

"I wasn't sure at first," Longland said. "If I hadn't been expecting you, I might have missed you entirely."

The green eyes roamed across Longland again, then glanced back at the infantryman, and Bascom stood quietly, waiting.

Deflated, Longland nevertheless had to laugh. "Bloody hell, Bascom, aren't you even going to ask how I chanced to be here?"

"I imagine you'll tell me if you want to," Bascom said.

Even the passage of years couldn't account for the profound change Longland sensed here. He was glad he had the nearby bar and a drink to suggest, for he was suddenly uncertain how to manage a welcome that would be even slightly suitable for this distant, quiet man. He was even less certain how to offer the excuses he had rehearsed, or how to ask the questions he had worded and reworded mentally at odd moments over the years.

In front of the bar, with the warm metal chair biting into his shoulder blades and the hot metal table warming his hands, Longland regained some of his aplomb. "What will you have?" he asked Bascom. "Schnapps? Or shall I check to see if they have any whisky?"

"I haven't had anything to drink for a long time," Bascom said. "Make it schnapps."

Perhaps he'd lost the taste for it, or the head for it, Longland concluded, for when the glasses arrived, Bascom took only two cautious sips, then set his glass quietly aside.

"Did they treat you badly?" Longland asked.

"Not as badly as some of the others."

"I'm glad for that," Longland said.

"Are you?" The green eyes were flat, noncommittal.

"Goddamn it, Bascom," Longland burst out, "I had nothing to do with it, you know. I had hell's own time even finding out when you were due to be released."

"I'm grateful," Bascom said, although he didn't sound it in the least.

Longland could feel his pointed ears growing red. To cover his embarrassment, he said, "I suppose you'll want to go home now. I've brought you some money. Quite a lot of it, in fact. And a passport." He took a thick roll of dollar bills and an American passport from his inner coat pocket and put them on the table in front of Bascom. "The money is real," he said. "The passport isn't, but it should get you home. San Francisco, isn't it? I'm told you're officially dead, but I'm sure you can straighten that out."

Bascom let the money and the passport lie, but the evidence of the forged passport was apparently not lost on him. He nodded at it and said, "I take it you're still with the same old shop?"

How could a smile, the first that had appeared on Bascom's face, look so cold? "You might say that," Longland admitted. "In fact, now that Mumford has retired, you might say I'm the new Mumford. Not that I call myself that. Sounded a shade too classy for me. My people refer to me as Mr. Yapp."

He thought that might bring a genuine smile, but the man across the sun-washed table seemed to walk among his words, choosing only the few that struck him as interesting. "Mumford has retired?"

"Yes. Forcibly, if you want the truth of it. Gone into manufacturing ladies' dresses, of all strange things."

"Doing well?"

"Not very, I understand."

Bascom's lean body relaxed a fraction, and only then did Longland realize how tense, ready, the long muscles under the heavy suit still looked. "And Holley?" the American asked.

The face was cold, almost wolflike. For the first time, Longland remembered the buried killer that used to stir behind Bascom's eyes, and for the first time now, he saw that the killer wasn't buried any longer. "Um," he said. "Um, he's back in London, as it happens. They sent him to—oh hell, I don't remember. Singapore? Then somewhere else. Then finally back to London."

"He's still with the OSS?"

"There isn't an OSS anymore. It was disbanded after the war. You have something new now. The CIA. On a somewhat bigger scale, of course. Holley is a charter member, I understand, and a rather big man on the organization chart. Bigger than when you last saw him, I regret to say."

The green eyes flickered with interest, and behind them the killer lurked, hating. Longland instantly put himself on guard. Bascom had every right to be resentful, even bitterly angry. But there was more than simple anger sheltered behind those cold, steady eyes. Someone, Longland saw, was going to die, and Longland's automatic response was care that it should not be he.

He knocked back his schnapps and signaled for another. In God's name, how was he to reach this man? There were so many questions he wanted to ask. What had happened during those frenzied last weeks of the war? Longland couldn't vouch personally for a fraction of what Bascom had apparently undergone. Nor could anyone else, unless Bascom was willing to share it.

Nine years ago. Was that when this strange mutation

had begun? Was Bascom thinking about it even now, his eyes hooded and the sun streaming across hands that looked ready to clench upon the instant into fists? Possibly. It wouldn't be easy to forget. The war finally winding down. Nazi Germany folding in on itself like a squeezed tube of toothpaste. Russian armies poised on the Oder River, just miles east of Berlin. The Americans rampaging through shattered German lines to the Elbe. The hurried plans taking place in Mumford's London shop. And then, on a glorious April day, much like today, that sudden, premature Russian attack . . .

ONE

The Storm

1

ВПЕРЕД! ПОБЕДА БЛИЗКА!

"Forward! Victory is near!"

—slogan on Soviet military poster

1

Two hours before dawn on the morning of Monday, April 16, 1945, twenty thousand heavy Russian guns opened up in one of the most extensive artillery barrages of World War II, blasting German positions along a seventy-five-mile front in the Oder Valley. Three massive Russian Army groups waited behind the guns. Their ultimate goal, Berlin, lay only thirty-six tantalizing miles away.

It was an awesome barrage. The noise was so severe that blood ran from the ears of Russian gunners. Forests across the Oder River dissolved. Villages and outlying farmhouses were leveled in an instant. A cloud of dust and debris rose to a height of more than three thousand feet. Explosions, stuttering so closely together that they fused into one unending roar, rocked the earth for forty minutes.

Then, as the barrage lifted and rolled forward, one and a half million Russian soldiers raised their voices in a chilling cheer and followed Red battle flags into the smoke. Only five hundred thousand weary, outgunned, outmanned German troops stood between them and the tottering capital city of the Third Reich.

"Fortress Berlin" was by now a bomb-shattered city inhabited largely by women. Because of continuous Allied air raids, they spent most nights huddled in cellars, leaving the deserted streets to the desperate, the determinedly carefree, and the dogs, which were officially banned from the shelters. Dogs in the eastern suburbs howled in misery at the first rumble of the distant guns, and many women

awoke. Most thought what they heard was only far-off
anti-aircraft fire. Most sank back into exhausted sleep to
await the coming of what would be an incongruously radi-
ant spring day, for amid the rubble and death, the season
celebrated new life. Tulips and lilacs were in bloom. Those
few apple trees that had survived the bombing raids were
on the verge of breaking into rosy blossom. Poplars and
maples already flaunted small, acid-green leaves. Although
the long-range weather forecast called for thunderstorms,
clear skies were expected for this day's dawning.

Spring had also come, in the form of a vase of golden,
sweet-scented crocus, to a set of dreary, cramped underground quarters in the heart of Berlin. This was the Führerbunker, a small concrete world of artificial lighting, gray
walls, and stale air, buried below the ruined garden of the
Reich Chancellery, from which the crocus had been sal-
vaged. The obsessed leader of the German people had long
since gone to earth here, complaining he could neither sleep
nor work efficiently in the upper rooms of the Chancellery
due to the interminable air raids. But even protected by
fifty feet of packed soil and reinforced concrete, Adolf
Hitler worried about direct hits. His greatest concern was
characteristically peculiar: What if he were killed while in
his nightclothes? To avoid the undignified possibility, he
usually slept only in the predawn hours, during the brief
hiatus between the nightly RAF raids and the daytime
American raids, which came later each morning, and he
was sleeping when the Russian bombardment began.

Hitler, still remembering the disaster that had befallen
the German Army in Russia when it allowed itself to be
tempted by Moscow's proximity, had not believed the Russians would be so foolish. He was convinced they would
not attack Berlin. If they did, he was equally confident
Berlin could withstand siege. His loyal troops along the
Oder, he insisted, would fall back before the Russian forces,
inch by inch, to form a steel ring around the city, a trap
into which the Russians would stumble after stretching
their supply lines to the snapping point. It would be Stalin-

grad and Moscow all over again, but this time it would be fanatically determined Germans fighting on home ground.

When the attack began, the thunder of guns and the wolflike howl of Russian rocket launchers did not carry across the miles to the center of the city, and Hitler's adjutant did not disturb him with the bad news. Eva Braun had arrived only the night before. The Führer's fifty-sixth birthday would be celebrated Friday. The once dynamic, dramatic leader who had roused the German populace to dreams of world conquest badly needed his rest.

The clock was ticking for the crumbling Third Reich even before the attack began. Only the day before, on April 15, 1945, Lieutenant General William H. Simpson, whose Ninth Army had seized a bridgehead across the Elbe fifty miles to the other side of Berlin, had sent an urgent request to Supreme Headquarters, asking for a green light to close the gap and storm Berlin before the Russians could get there. The road was wide open, he reported. Only isolated pockets of resistance stood in the way. His American troops could be in the outskirts of the city in twenty-four hours.

When the light flashed in response to Simpson's request, it blinked not green, but red. General Omar Bradley delivered the bewildering message personally: "I'm sorry to have to tell you this, Simp, but you can't go any farther. You have to stop on the Elbe. Berlin is out."

Simpson was staggered. "Where the hell did you get that?"

"It just came from Ike."

Simpson tried to argue, but it was pointless. General Dwight D. Eisenhower, Supreme Commander of the Allied Forces, had already decided that Berlin was not a military target, but only a political target on which he was unwilling to waste lives. As far as he was concerned, the Russians could have it.

Eisenhower's decision, one which maddened the British, was based in part on a troublesome rumor, a rumor that

spoke of a great German National Redoubt, an unapproach-
able, impregnable mountain citadel supposedly situated in
the icy heights of the German and Austrian Alps, to which
Hitler and the remnants of the German armies would soon
retire, to fight to the last. Eisenhower worried that if the
Germans were allowed to slip away to the South, to enclose
themselves in nature's towering fortress, the war might be
prolonged indefinitely and additional oceans of Allied blood
might still be shed. He considered it more important to
shift the focus of the Allied attack southward, to bypass
Berlin and drive across the shrinking waistline of Germany
in order to slice the country in two, thereby blocking access
to the suspected Redoubt.

He even sent a coded cable to Soviet Premier Joseph
Stalin, informing him of the Anglo-American military intentions. Eisenhower asked that the Russian spring offensive, scheduled to begin in the middle of May, be co-
ordinated to meet the Americans in the area of Dresden,
insuring the division of Germany. The Russians acknowledged the message, but they believed not a word of it.
Convinced that Eisenhower was deliberately lying to keep
them off balance and convinced that British and American
troops would still try to beat them to Berlin and Hitler,
they accelerated their attack plans by a full month, for-
warding their jump-off date to the predawn hours of the
sixteenth of April.

By the time the sun came up over the advancing Russians on that first morning of the attack, the 744 heavy
German guns along the Oder line—plus some 500 flak
weapons rushed from Berlin to substitute for artillery—
were already running short of ammunition.

Seventeen-year-old Helmut Geisler, an apprentice Luftwaffe mechanic who had been pressed into service as an
infantry private, watched in bewilderment as his fellow
mechanics and hospital attendants and cook's helpers suddenly panicked in the face of oncoming Russian tanks and
fled from their trenches. Geisler stayed behind for one
clock's tock of time, then threw down his only weapon, a

rusting Norwegian rifle recycled from captured stores in a German military warehouse, and fled after them.

The thirteenth hour had begun.

2

Henry Bascom first learned of the sudden Russian offensive when one of the fishermen aboard an aged Swedish fishing boat picked up a report from Stockholm on the wireless and rattled Bascom's coffee cup with jubilant shouting. Feeling elated and a little self-conscious, Bascom joined in the cheers and back-thumping that greeted the news, but Nils Frychius, the Swedish newsman accompanying him, translated only garbled bits, and Bascom found it deeply frustrating to know so little about the attack. After the wireless fell silent, they both went up on deck to wait for the German coastline to appear. The elation gave way to a state of extreme uneasiness that had plagued Bascom since daybreak, without his quite knowing why.

He kept sorting through the possible reasons and discarding them. Perhaps it was only being at sea. He'd never felt really comfortable on boats. To listen to the vibrations of the boat engines and sense the cold, heavy presence of water all around him—how small it always made him feel. The thing was, the sea didn't give a damn. It could drown a man without knowing, without even a murderer's zest in killing.

The vague, gray outline of land loomed on the southern horizon, but the strange uneasiness stayed with Bascom. He didn't think it was because of what he was about to do—land voluntarily under German guns to be taken to the local Gestapo headquarters. Even though this was his first behind-the-lines assignment in a three-year intelligence career, he was reasonably confident that the guarantee of safe conduct for himself and the Swedish newsman at his side would be honored. Yet, at the very beginning of his OSS training, Bascom had encountered the unofficial operational motto, "If anything can foul up, it will," with sundry

variations of the salient verb. To fall into the hands of the
Germans with the war only days from ending . . . Nice
thought. It took only seconds to die.

As the boat chugged onward, the North German port of
Rostock took clearer form two points off the starboard
bow. Bascom couldn't stop worrying. Perhaps his state of
confusion had nothing to do with the sea or this sub-rosa
business with the waiting SS officer from Berlin. Perhaps
the real reason he was so on edge was this new threat of
impending peace. The unexpected news of the Russian attack. Maybe with the Russians on the move, they'd have
to set up a new timetable back in London. For a moment,
Bascom wished himself there, where you only had to step
into the hall to get the latest communiqués, well laced with
rumors, on any aspect of the war. It wasn't that he dreaded
the war's end. Good God, no. He hated the whole mud-
dled, gory business, just like everyone else. But if it ended
too quickly, might this whole Rostock business turn out to
be a waste of time? He felt sure he could handle this or
any other assignment supremely well, but he didn't like to
waste his efforts.

Bascom looked up and saw that the Swedish newsman
was watching him. Forgetting that he had been thinking,
not speaking aloud, he asked the tall Swede, "Do you think
it's really about to end, Nils?"

"It can't go on much longer," Frychius said without surprise. "A month, perhaps. Two at the outside. I look for
the Germans to surrender about the end of June. Perhaps
earlier, unless Hitler pulls another *Kaninchen* out of his
hat."

Bascom nodded. "What are you going to do when it's
over?"

"Cover the peace conference, I suppose. And you?"

"I'm not sure," Bascom said. "I haven't had much time
to think about it." He liked the dry, intelligent newsman,
but they were scarcely intimate, and Bascom was normally
reticent about his own affairs anyway.

Reticent about his affairs. He winced. Perhaps that was
what really bothered him this morning. The shameless way

he'd taken advantage of a certain Ann Christy, just so he could crowbar himself into this meeting with one of Hitler's top aides. Ann was a driver for one of the masterminds in British intelligence, a man called Mumford. Bascom had met her a pair of years before, delivering a set of classified files from his own would-be mastermind, E. Wilson Holley. She was tall and black-haired, with eyes like deep lake water, and he had been smitten instantly. They'd hit it off pretty well in the bedroom, though she had an irritating policy of sharing the wealth. But she was determined not to get serious, since, as she put it, "All the nice young men go off and get killed." The fact that he never went off and got killed seemed to puzzle her.

Even so, he never should have told Holley what she'd said about the British raid. She'd feel justifiably betrayed if she knew he'd gone straight to his office the next morning and blabbed the whole thing to his boss. Well, not the whole thing. He'd let Holley think his information was the result of some careful probing at the British officers' club.

"There are officers waiting for us," Frychius said, gesturing toward the approaching docks and three gray-uniformed figures standing at the end.

Again, Bascom had the uncomfortable feeling Frychius had been tapping his thoughts, so he quickly flapped a cape to distract him. "Is Fegelein with them?"

Frychius leaned forward with a myopic scowl, as if the three or four extra inches would make a difference. "I doubt it," he said. "He isn't likely to show himself in public outside of Berlin. Those are probably just local representatives of the Gestapo."

Bascom's uneasiness deepened. As cover, he had been assigned the role of a neutral Swedish journalist, like Frychius, only in his case he was to be a photographer, neatly set up with a bulky Swedish view camera and a case full of film holders. But his forged papers weren't half so neat. In fact, they'd looked damned shoddy when he'd been handed them by the agent authentication expert back at OSS/Stockholm before setting off for Malmö and the fishing boat with Frychius.

The papers. Bascom seized upon that one worry almost
with a sense of pleasure. Maybe it was just the papers that
had been eating at him all morning. The gap of water between them and land was narrowing rapidly, but Bascom
dug the phony Swedish passport out of his coat pocket for
a last, hasty look. Frychius watched with wry amusement.
Why not? Frychius had nothing to worry about. His papers
were real.

"Don't worry," said the Swede, mind-reading still. "Perhaps they won't check too carefully."

But two of the Gestapo officers did, just as soon as the
fishing boat tied up and Bascom and Frychius swung up to
the dock. They collected both passports and studied them
minutely. Bascom clutched the camera bag and sweated
in a light brown raincoat supplied him, like all his clothing,
by an OSS specialist in Stockholm to avoid any obvious
look of London tailoring. He peered apprehensively over
the shoulder of a Gestapo lieutenant at his own passport
photograph. The photo, he decided, seemed as suspect as
the job of forgery. He looked nothing like the picture. The
casual observer might have found something appealing in
the face gazing out of the passport, with its broad forehead,
its widely spaced, intelligent-looking eyes, its guileless
mouth, but Bascom had never noticed anything pleasing
about his features. Too, there were lines on the real face
that weren't reflected in the black-and-white image, lines
around the eyes and mouth that shouldn't have appeared
for years yet, maybe even until he was thirty or thirty-five.

The young Gestapo officer glanced at Bascom with open
mistrust and carried the papers to a bored-looking captain.
The captain surprised both the lieutenant and Bascom by
snapping the passport shut and saying, "It doesn't matter."
To Frychius, the captain said, "You will come with me.
I have been asked to drive you to headquarters in all haste.
Our visitor from Berlin awaits you there. As his time is lim-
ited and you are already a half hour late, your photographer
may as well stay with the boat. I'm sure there will be no
time for picture-taking."

They spoke in German. Frychius said quietly, "No, it's

better that my photographer accompany me. Specific arrangements were made. Naturally, everything must be as the visitor from Berlin expects."

"Naturally," the captain agreed, accepting correction with no visible annoyance. In the German pecking order, one's superior officer was always right. "You will both step this way to my car, please. Your photographer can ride in front with the driver."

Bascom had looked forward to a potentially useful scrutiny of the little coastal town. It served as a naval base, and it was bound to be bristling with guns. But they drove so fast and the streets were so empty that he saw little but a gray blur of buildings. Where were the people? Inside, probably. Listening to sanitized German radio pronouncements about the Russian bombardment along the Oder. After five years of strident propaganda seldom borne out by the facts, had they learned to read between the lines? If so, there would be a lot of long, depressed faces behind those closed shutters.

The car stopped in front of a plain, two-story brick building, and both Bascom and Frychius were hustled up the steps beneath the red, swastika-bedecked banner of Nazi Germany. Bascom swallowed. He felt tense but ready, the way he'd sometimes felt at the top of a ski run or the tip of a diving board. An overwhelming odor of disinfectant and stale air, the smell of public buildings everywhere, assaulted his nostrils as the captain ushered them through the front rooms to what was probably his own office, expropriated that morning by the brass from Berlin. A short, worried-looking man with a large nose and a receding hairline, dressed in an immaculate black SS uniform with the silver collar tabs of a Gruppenführer, stood waiting inside with his back to a shuttered window. The Gestapo captain snapped a stiff-armed Nazi salute at the high-ranking SS officer, spoke Frychius's name, then backed out into the hall and pulled the door shut.

The man from Berlin nodded gratefully at Frychius and turned a searching expression on Bascom. "You may introduce yourself," he said.

"Broome," Bascom said. "Major Robert Broome. United States Army." He saw Frychius cover a smile. The false name was part of his OSS concealment, but the rank was a last-minute decision. Though he was officially listed in classified files as a captain, OSS personnel habitually assigned themselves any convenient rank, from private to general, depending on what would most impress the person to whom they were speaking. For this particular German, Frychius had suggested Bascom promote himself to brigadier, or at the very least to colonel, but Bascom had chickened out, figuring he looked too young to get away with it.

"I am SS Gruppenführer Hermann Fegelein," the German said stiffly. "You are late, Major Broome. Your delayed appearance has already jeopardized these negotiations. Another five minutes and I would have departed."

Bascom's eyebrows went up. The man had taut nerves. Strain cut deep lines into his smooth, youngish face, and his big nose, matched by big ears, was pale around the nostrils. Frychius hadn't mentioned the nervousness during the hurried briefing last night in Malmö. Arrogant, yes. Crafty, maybe. Glib. But this new note was perhaps important. A man ought to be played according to the way his strings were wound. "I'm glad you waited," Bascom said politely. "It would have been a pity to waste the trip."

Fegelein cocked his head. "Your German seems adequate," he said. "Will we need Herr Frychius as an interpreter?"

"That's up to you," Bascom said.

For a man who was in a screaming hurry, Fegelein seemed slow to make decisions. He spent several minutes discussing "confidentiality," before finally apologizing curtly to the Swede and sending him to wait in the hallway. Then he spent even longer telling Bascom he could give him very little time.

"It was difficult enough, disguising my schedule so that I could slip away to Rostock unnoticed," the German assured Bascom. "Even now my plane is being refueled for the return trip to Reichsführer Himmler's headquarters in Hohenlychen. I must report to him the results of our discussion and drive back to the city before I am missed. Though you may not have heard, Major Broome, the Russians launched their long-awaited attack on the Oder this very morning, and I am expected at a meeting with the Führer and his military advisers this evening. I cannot afford to raise suspicion by being late."

Fegelein then said it all over again, with particular emphasis on the necessity of avoiding suspicion. It gave Bascom time to assess him. That prominent mention of the Führer was undoubtedly meant to impress Bascom with Fegelein's importance, but Bascom wasn't buying. True, the man was the equivalent of a two-star general in the American military system, but both Holley in London and Frychius last night had been careful to describe him as a toothless cog in Nazi machinery. A one-time jockey, they'd said. A former riding instructor who had risen in Hitler's personal court primarily because he'd married the sister of Hitler's companion, Eva Braun. In effect, he was merely a social conduit between his boss, Reichsführer Himmler, and the boss of them all, Adolf Hitler.

There, was he finally getting on with it?

"I am thankful to Herr Frychius for transmitting our proposal to you," he was saying. "I trust you have brought good news for the Reichsführer? When and where is the meeting with General Eisenhower to take place?"

Belated, but right to the point. Bascom dithered an instant, considering the proper way to handle the man. There was to be no face-to-face meeting between Heinrich Himmler and General Eisenhower. Himmler, apparently eager to gain some kind of official postwar sanction from the Allies, had cautiously offered to use his offices in bringing the war in the West to a close, but Allied policymakers were determined not to conduct any piecemeal peace negotiations. Nevertheless, just because Himmler's tentative proposal via Fegelein had already been rejected was no sign a productive use couldn't be found for its promoters, Holley had emphasized. So the world wagged.

Bascom decided to copy Fegelein's direct approach. "I bear no concrete decision at all," he said. "My superiors have asked me to inform you that certain revisions are necessary before we can consider Reichsführer Himmler's terms."

Fegelein seemed taken aback. "What revisions?"

"I am not authorized to discuss them," Bascom said. "My function is to appraise your willingness to co-operate and to arrange a private conference between you and a suitably high-level Allied negotiator."

Fegelein blew up. "Conferences!" he spat. "Why do you think I am here today? Conferences indeed! You Americans think nothing of arranging meeting after meeting while the Russians hurl themselves at Berlin. I must tell you, sir, the Reichsführer will be deeply disappointed when he hears of this further delay. No, he will be furious! How dare your government send me a man who is not authorized to carry these proceedings forward!"

His eyes openly and angrily appraised Bascom's ragtag raincoat and borrowed woolen suit, and Bascom realized he'd made an error in judgment by not following Frychius's advice on claiming an even higher rank. This self-important ex-jockey, restricted to social duties or not, was looking down on him.

Bascom held his temper. Holley had given him a specific program of instructions to follow, but none of it would be possible unless Bascom stayed in control. He would have to knock the hard edges off the man's hauteur, and quickly. He said coldly, "I take it, then, that you decline to meet with our negotiator. Your position will be relayed to the proper authorities as soon as I return to Sweden."

He turned toward the door. It was risky, but it seemed to work. Fegelein said quickly, "Wait. One moment, please."

Bascom stopped, hand on the doorknob. "I see no point in carrying this further," he said. "Please convey my government's regrets to Reichsführer Himmler for the time and risk he has undergone." Let the man sweat a bit. Let him think about Himmler's wrath if he allowed the negotiations to break down.

The German began to hedge instantly. "Please, Major Broome. You don't understand . . . another meeting. I can't abandon my duties again. I would be missed. It's too dangerous."

Bascom let his hand fall from the knob. "My instructions are to arrange the meeting as close to your duties as possible," he said. "It will take place in Berlin."

Fegelein gulped air. "What? In Berlin? You must be joking. Our military situation may be critical, but you surely can't expect to enter Berlin at will."

That part puzzled Bascom, too, but Holley seemed to think it could be done. "It will be arranged," he said.

"It . . . it would have to be very soon," Fegelein said.

"It will be. Can you make yourself available on Friday? Four days from now?"

The German looked dubious. "Friday is the Führer's birthday. We will be expected to be on hand through most of the afternoon to welcome well-wishers. It would have to be quite late."

"I've been directed to arrange a late meeting, for security purposes," Bascom said. "We have no desire to endanger you. Shall we agree on Friday night, at eleven o'clock?"

"Where? Even late, I can't be away from the Chancellery for any length of time."

"For your convenience, my superiors suggest that the meeting take place at the edge of the Tiergarten, near the Chancellery. The discussion need not be lengthy. No longer than one would spend on an evening's stroll. You will chat for a few minutes. It can appear very casual."

"Evening strolls have not been very common since the air raids began," Fegelein said sadly. "But perhaps that could work to our advantage. The streets should be empty. The park will surely be empty."

Fegelein seemed to accept the necessity, so they quickly worked out the details and the exact location of the meeting. They settled on an intersection near the east end of the park, where Bellevue Strasse crossed Tiergarten Strasse to form a pie wedge. The site was less than a half mile from the Chancellery, and Fegelein began to look more comfortable with the whole idea.

"You will, of course, come alone," Bascom said. "Our

negotiator will appear sometime between eleven and eleven-thirty. He will greet you by your first name."

Fegelein nodded agreement. "Yes, that is acceptable. It can be done. Will you be there with him?"

Bascom was startled. "Me? No. You will have no need for my presence."

"True," the German said. A trace of the earlier arrogance crept back into his bearing. "Very well, Major Broome. Eleven o'clock this Friday at the edge of the Tiergarten. But a final decision must be reached that night if it is to be reached at all. The Russians will not wait. Neither will Reichsführer Himmler."

"I understand," Bascom said. "And I will so inform my government."

"See that you do. And now, as my time is short, I will have you and Herr Frychius escorted back to the boat."

The German bowed him out with hurried courtesy, and Bascom was glad to go. He wasn't sure just what he had accomplished, but he had followed Holley's program to the letter. Presumably the Tiergarten meeting would be useful somehow.

The Gestapo captain was waiting in the front hallway, where their passports were returned, then Bascom and Frychius were led outside to the car. Frychius, apparently not at all put out about being banned from the meeting, confined himself to nice-day-isn't-it platitudes until they were safely back on the fishing boat and their three Gestapo escorts drove away. Then he smiled at Bascom and said, "Well, what did you think of Gruppenführer Fegelein?"

"You didn't tell me he would be so nervous," Bascom said.

"Wouldn't you be?" Frychius said. "He lives in dread that Bormann or one of the others in the Chancellery clique might find out what Herr Himmler has put him up to. Cause enough for tension, eh?"

The firm line of Bascom's mouth relaxed into a youthful smile. "I see what you mean. Still, it's a bit contagious. I found myself getting jumpy, too."

"If you think he's nervous here, you should see the way he acts in Berlin," Frychius said. "Even with me. Not that it's necessary. After all, I'm a neutral. And a journalist. The Germans allow me to come and go almost as I please. Nor is it at all unusual for me to contact German functionaries. Yet the Gruppenführer is so cautious that he won't even allow me to telephone him at the Chancellery."

"Then how have you managed to keep in touch with him?"

Frychius shrugged. "Only with difficulty. If something comes up and I want to see him, I'm forced to go through a tiresome rigmarole. Code words. Countersigns. All that."

"What kind of code words?"

Frychius gave him a sly look. "Planning a trip to Berlin?" he asked. "Come, Captain Bascom, give. I've had the feeling since meeting you that something is in the wind. What is it? More than just these negotiations, isn't it? Are the Americans going to try to beat the Russians into Berlin after all? Are they sending in agents in advance?"

For a moment Bascom was jolted. Had he let some hint of the British raid or Holley's interest in it slip? No, surely not. It was just the journalist's sensitive antennae, the chronic inquisitiveness of the newspaper reporter—and the spy.

The two men looked at each other, both knowing a standoff when they met one. Frychius smiled and apparently decided to prime the pump. "In answer to your question," he said, "whenever I want to see the Gruppenführer, I take a room at the Adlon Hotel a few blocks from the Chancellery and seek out the assistant manager. He's an amiable man. Robeus is his name. So I tell him I am seeking opera tickets at the Kroll. That's my part in the rigmarole. He then calls the Gruppenführer at the Chancellery and says something ridiculous about having received a shipment of choice albacore or a few tins of Cherbourg *pâté*, and the Gruppenführer then sneaks to the hotel and creeps up the back stairs to my room. I suppose it would be amusing, if I didn't find it so exasperating. Do you know the Adlon?"

"I stayed there once."

The sly look came back. "Recently?" Frychius asked. "Since the start of the war?"

Apparently the Swede felt he'd earned a trade on miscellaneous wartime information. Bascom said, "No, this is the closest I've been to Berlin since '38. I've done most of my time in France and Italy, working with the resistance."

The Berlin part was true, but he hadn't been to Italy since he was a bewildered eleven-year-old, carted along by his new foster mother to a spa specializing in kidney-stone complaints, her illness of that particular summer. He felt a little ashamed of himself for the truth-stretching. But a series of implied incidents among French and Italian partisans sounded much more interesting than the duller reality, which was a few half-assed courier assignments to France and Portugal, but even more paperwork in London. Besides, an experienced OSS officer was expected to obfuscate as a matter of principal, to assume false backgrounds and identities as easily as one changes socks. And even though Bascom knew he didn't really qualify as experienced, he always tried to do what was expected of him.

Didn't qualify as experienced? Bascom blinked with sudden realization. Who said he didn't qualify? He'd done what he'd set out to do, hadn't he? and quite successfully, too. He'd braved German guns and carried out his mission right under their noses. Now it would be fishing boat to the southern coast of Sweden, feeder flight from Malmö to Stockholm, a guarded debriefing at the embassy with full details to be saved for Holley, then RAF Mosquito back to Scotland. It would be midday tomorrow before he reached London, but word of his success would precede him, perhaps even early this afternoon. He'd been instructed to send a one-word radio message, if the meeting with Fegelein went as planned, as soon as the fishing boat reached open sea. Perhaps Holley would be so pleased that he would give Bascom tomorrow evening off, and he could add to his travel itinerary a cab to Ann Christy's flat in Kensington, and a bottle of something warm and fierce or cold and bubbling to celebrate a very neat piece of chicanery.

Would he tell Ann about it? Probably. There was no way she could make the connection between Fegelein and the British raid, he was certain. He wasn't sure he understood himself what Holley was up to, nor how it tied in. Besides, it might be pleasant to have something worthy of a little quiet bragging for a change. It might even warm her embraces, now that he'd gone out and faced death like a good little boy.

He felt so buoyed up by the prospect that he forgot the uneasiness that had gadflied him through most of the morning, nor was he apprehensive about the upcoming hundred miles of return trip across the Baltic. He leaned on the deck railing, smiling to himself, and watched the fishermen prepare to cast off.

"Well, at least you appear to be in better humor now," Frychius said. "I take it you got what you wanted?"

"I think so," Bascom said. He listened to the ancient fishing boat engines as they coughed and sputtered. Then his good humor deepened. Sure he had what he wanted. A job well done. One moment of adventure, one quick glimpse of the clandestine dangers for which he'd been trained. With peace just around the corner, there wouldn't be time for any more. But it was enough. After all those stifling years of waiting in the wings, Bascom's war, brief though it was, was now over. And he didn't mind a bit.

3

An hour after Bascom's message was relayed to London, Adrian Courtney, a British SIS planning specialist known to his peers as Mr. Mumford, stood at his office window pondering the refinements a small brown spider had been making on a rather extensive web, and simultaneously pondered the presence of the man seated comfortably behind him. An American accent intruded smoothly upon his thoughts as his late-afternoon visitor said, "I may as well tell you right now, Mumford. We know about this raid you're working up."

Courtney stiffened. He could feel the American's eyes boring into his back, so he didn't permit himself to turn around. He puffed his pipe and peered more closely at the web. He had only once succeeded in catching a glimpse of its maker. Stalling, he murmured, "Raid? My dear Holley, I don't know what you're talking about."

Holley, his OSS counterpart, said, "Oh, you know all right. But what you don't know is that I sent an agent into Germany this morning to meet with one of their top-level officers. The information my man is bringing back could be very important to you."

Courtney cautioned himself to proceed with care. Still stalling, he said, "I can't imagine what possible use a meeting with some German could do us."

"That depends on the German," Holley said. "This one is a general in Hitler's own private staff. My man has been feeling him out on points that might prove vital to your assault team."

"We have our own sources for that," Courtney said.

"Maybe," the voice said smoothly, "but this German is close to the decision-making process. He'd be one of the first to know if Hitler decided to pull out of Berlin. What's more, he knows his way around the Chancellery."

"Interesting," Courtney said. He puffed again. "May one inquire as to why this German has offered his assistance to the Allies?"

"He hasn't," the American admitted. "He has other things on his mind, and he thinks we can help him. We won't, of course. But we've dangled a bit of bait in front of his nose, and insisted on another meeting. In Berlin. We thought maybe about eleven o'clock this Friday night near that big park in the center of the city—if you get what I mean."

Courtney's eyebrows went up before he could stop them, and he was glad he had his back still turned. The fellow was deucedly well informed. Courtney looked past the spider web to a corner of St. James's Park, where a pretty girl in a blue uniform waited in the fading light beside a parked limousine. She was his own driver, Sergeant Christy, and in a way she was involved in the cat-and-mouse game he was now playing with Holley, but she was off on loan today. From the moment the news came in that the Russians were on the move again, there had been a steady stream of chauffeured traffic in and out of the soot-encrusted arches of this quiet old building. But, then, small wonder. The PM was no doubt beside himself with frustration. According to all the staircase reports, beating the Russians to Berlin had been seductively uppermost on his mind for weeks now.

Courtney glanced surreptitiously at his watch. Should he play his first card yet? No, Holley was obviously trying to wait him out in their little game of nerves, and it wouldn't do for him to give in too quickly. Allowing the silence to lengthen, Courtney focused his concentration on Sergeant Christy. He never looked at her closely in the office, but now, from a distance, he noted that she had an alluring ass. No doubt that was partially what was so appealing to all the younger intelligence men.

A tall, bony man with sandy hair and pale gray eyes, Courtney had always enjoyed remarkable success with the ladies himself, although he had never figured out just why. All dalliance was conducted very carefully, of course, which was why he had left the wooing of the nicely contoured Miss Christy to other comers, among them his own top operations man and one of Holley's OSS people. He preferred his own liaisons far removed from the intelligence community. One simply never knew when a colleague might notice and get ideas. Queer, that intelligence types so relished any sort of intrigue.

The silence had gone on long enough. Mustn't let Holley get too cocky. Time to score one for the home team. Courtney said mildly, "Even if we were planning the, um, event you mentioned, what makes you think your General Fegelein would be of any use to us?"

Holley responded, as Courtney had hoped, with his own shocked silence, then hesitantly said, "How do you know his name?"

"You have your sources, I have mine," Courtney said.

Holley seemed to regain his confidence. "Then you must realize how valuable he could be as a guide through the Chancellery."

Courtney mused aloud, "Guide? Now, whatever for? Assuming there were to be a raid, perhaps all we want are a few pertinent documents, or to snatch a few members of the German General Staff."

"Bull," Holley said. "Hitler's the target, and you know it."

"Even if that were so, why would we need this guide of yours?"

"Oh come on," Holley said. "You don't even know exactly where the damned Führerbunker is. I know you've only had a couple of weeks to chew on this Redoubt business and get ready, but you've hardly managed a thing on the research end. Admit it. A handful of aerial photos of the Chancellery grounds, that's all you've got. And they don't tell you a damned thing about what's buried there, or where."

Courtney took a last speculative look at the window, not at the girl but at the spider's web, then turned with poised composure to regard his visitor. Holley was dressed in civilian clothing, a very tweedy, very British country suit. He wasn't British, of course. Nor was he a civilian. An officer in the American intelligence branch, Holley was merely affecting yet another British mannerism, something he apparently delighted in doing. Courtney decided it was irritating. "All right, damn you," he growled. "Just what is it you want?"

Holley blinked brown eyes that looked the way chocolate does when it melts in the hand on a warm day. "I'm just trying to lend a helping hand," he said. "I thought we could talk some kind of a deal."

Courtney crossed to his desk and sat down. "Holley, I

won't ask you how you found out what we're up to," he said briskly. "Obviously there's a leak in my system. But I must ask you to keep it quiet. If the Russians discover we're out to beat them to Hitler, they'll raise such a political row that we might never get off the ground."

"That's no problem," Holley said. "There'll be no need for me to say anything to anyone—if you and I can come to terms."

"That sounds like blackmail."

"Now really," Holley said. "I'm offering something extremely valuable, a German who knows every nook and cranny of the Chancellery building and the Führerbunker, every stairway, every guardpoint. All I ask in return is a piece of the pie."

"You're aware of the risks?"

Holley shrugged. "I know you can't get official sanction from the boys at SFHQ. From what I hear, the most they're willing to offer is unofficial co-operation on logistics."

"And skimpy co-operation at that," Courtney said. "If this mission fails—and the chances for failure are quite high—they've made it clear that the ax falls on my neck alone. Are you sure you want a piece of that?"

Holley hesitated. "I recognize the risks," he said. "But the rewards if you succeed . . . good God, have you thought about it? You'll be a goddamn hero. I definitely want in."

Courtney tried to keep his face from looking as disgusted as he felt. "How far in?"

Holley began to smile. "For one thing, I've got some pretty good men sitting on their asses, doing nothing. I want some of them to go along."

"How many?"

"Let's say twenty."

"Out of the question," Courtney snapped.

"Far from it. You've got four transport gliders and not nearly enough top-rate SOE people available to fill them," Holley said. "It's hard to line up good men this late. I understand your operations chief only has about thirty-six so far."

"You're quite wrong," Courtney said. "Major Longland has nearly the full complement. At most, I might be able to send five of your OSS people."

"Make it fifteen."

"What makes you so sure Fegelein will co-operate?"

Holley's smile ripened into a grin. "What choice will he have? When he shows up for that meeting and finds a full assault team waiting for him, he'll co-operate. I guarantee it. But let's not change the subject. My price also includes some responsible leadership in the mission. I want one of my people as pathfinder. I've got just the man for it."

"I couldn't think of it. Major Longland is in charge, and he's already assigned our Lieutenant Formoy as pathfinder."

The smile turned hard. "Maybe you should reconsider. The man I have in mind is the agent I sent to Germany, the only one for sure who can lure Fegelein out in the open. His name is Bascom. Henry Bascom."

"Bascom?" Courtney's bony nose wrinkled in surprise, and he picked up his pipe and sniffed it, trying to cover up. "I've heard of him. He's quite short on experience, isn't he?"

"Oh hell no," Holley said quickly. "Where'd you hear that? Hell, Bascom's a crackerjack OG man, one of my best. Done jumps all over the place. More important, he knows Berlin like you know the wrinkles on your balls. Lived there a couple of years before the war. Speaks fluent German. I tell you, he's perfect for the job."

"I'm afraid there's a problem you apparently don't know about," Courtney said. "Something between your Captain Bascom and my Major Longland."

Holley's eyes shifted. Courtney made another mental mark for himself on the gamesmanship scoreboard, enjoying Holley's obvious resentment at being told there was anything he might not know.

"What kind of a problem?" Holley demanded.

Courtney glanced toward the window, below which Sergeant Christy presumably still waited. "It seems Longland and Bascom have both been dallying with the same girl," he said, "each over the extreme objections of the other."

Holley guffawed, a quick burst of genuinely amused laughter. "Well, hell, nobody cares about their love lives. Anyway, how do you know?"

"The lady in question is an employee of mine," Courtney said. "I've seen them both in her company. I've also seen the way the two men look when they come face to face. Best to keep them separated."

"Stuff. They'll just be that much more determined to outdo each other in the field." The American's eyes narrowed. "Besides, I'll have to insist."

The implied "or else" was clear enough. Courtney wondered what compromise could be effected and instantly decided. "The most I can offer is to let Captain Bascom accompany Formoy in the pathfinding plane. No matter how you regard the man, I can't afford to put the whole mission in the hands of an unprepared, inexperienced agent."

"He goes as an equal," Holley said stubbornly. "I don't care who does the work. This Formoy guy of yours can run the show, but he does it as Bascom's equal partner. Agreed?"

"Have you told young Bascom what you have in mind?"

"Not yet. What difference does that make?"

"None, I suppose." Courtney sighed in defeat. "Very well, an equal partner."

The intercom buzzed, and Courtney glanced at his watch again before thumbing it. "Yes, Colonel Norman?" he said impatiently.

The voice of his elderly aide quavered, "I'm sorry to interrupt, sir, but Major Rutherford's office inquires if you've forgotten your six-o'clock appointment."

"Oh damn," Courtney said. "All right, sorry. Tell them I'll be there in five minutes." He slumped back in his chair and pinched the bridge of his nose as if a small, buzzing insect had established residence inside and he was trying to squash it. "I must go, Holley," he said. "The next time you decide to indulge in interagency arm-twisting, please don't just barge in without an appointment."

"Now, now," Holley said. "No need for hard feelings. Besides, my people will be damned useful. Don't you agree?"

"Have you left me any option?"

Holley's voice purred with comfortable certainty. "No."

Courtney didn't rise as the American whistled his way out of the office. Courtney banged the dottle from his pipe and refilled it from a silver box of tobacco, and he only glanced up and continued tamping the tobacco as his aide entered and began his slow journey across the floor. Colonel Norman was seventy-two years old. He suffered severely from arthritis and crept around only with the use of two walking sticks, yet he peered at Courtney with unquenchable enthusiasm from beneath bushy white eyebrows, companion pieces to his white cavalry mustache. Courtney admired the fragile old fellow. The Army wouldn't have him back, of course, but Norman was determined to do his share in this war, and Courtney had taken him on without a qualm. The old boy and his equally antique wife seemed grateful for the addition of the SIS salary to his tiny Service pension. Besides, everyone else of Courtney's rank and status had eager young lieutenants as aides. Courtney enjoyed the contrast.

Arrived at last, Colonel Norman leaned comfortably on his sticks and studied Courtney's face. "Well, sir, how did it go?" he asked eagerly.

Courtney smiled. "Perfectly. Just as we thought it would."

"Splendid!" Colonel Norman said. "How many men will he give us?"

"Fifteen. He offered twenty, but I didn't want to seem too eager. I was afraid for a moment I might be forced to bargain him down to ten, but he proved to be even greedier than I expected." He lit his pipe in the leisurely manner of a man who had no appointments whatever on his afternoon's calendar, and the room began to fill with a fruity haze of Navy Cut De Luxe. "Tell Longland he can come up now, would you? I'm afraid he'll have to make up the difference any way he can."

"Yes, sir. And Sergeant Christy? Would you like to see her too?"

"What on earth for?"

"Why, to thank her, sir. It seems she must have done a good job on young Bascom."

"Good heavens, no," Courtney said. "I shouldn't want her to think we've been using her. Women get very touchy about that sort of thing. I'd prefer she think she's merely been passing along odd bits of friendly chitchat." He puffed hard to get the pipe going. "By the way, it's a pity I didn't ask you to buzz sooner. I had to agree to take Captain Bascom along on the pathfinding plane, as well. I shouldn't mention his role in this to Longland just yet, if I were you. I'll have to do a little tactful preparation first."

"Yes, sir. Is there anything else, sir?"

Courtney thought of tea, then thought of the colonel's two walking sticks and the difficulty he always had with the tea cart, and decided to do without it. He said, "Yes, you might as well open a permanent file for our operation. Now that we've managed to acquire Holley's help, it looks as though it will definitely be on."

His aide's faded blue eyes lit up. "Yes, sir. For what it's worth, I've thought of a name for the mission that seems to fit rather nicely. Considering the fact that our boys might be bringing out some rather unusual prisoners, what would you think of EXPORT?"

Courtney repeated the name thoughtfully, as if tasting the sound of it, then tried to look enthusiastic. "Excellent," he said. "Perhaps we'll use it."

And so he would, he decided while watching Colonel Norman smile. Left to his own devices, Courtney probably wouldn't have come up with anything half so good. Unless, possibly, a plan to land a dangerously small force right in the middle of the foe's lair should have been labeled Operation SPIDER WEB.

2

Tuesday—April 17, 1945

This is the site of
THE INFAMOUS BELSEN CONCENTRATION CAMP
Liberated by the British on 15 April 1945
10,000 unburied dead were found here,
Another 13,000 have since died,
All of them victims of the
German New Order in Europe
And an example of Nazi Kultur.

—sign erected by the British at Belsen

1

The Germans called him Rösselsprung, when they spoke of him at all, but that wasn't his name. His real name, taken from him four years earlier when the Gestapo came to his messy flat in Antwerp and arrested him, was now buried in an underground vault on Prinz Albrecht-Strasse in Berlin, along with millions of other names from all over Europe, disused, forgotten, filling the acres of underground filing cabinets below Gestapo headquarters.

That Tuesday morning, a full day after the Russians fired the opening salvos in their Oder offensive, Berlin buzzed like a disturbed wasp's nest, but Rösselsprung's world was hermetically sealed, and he heard nothing of either the previous day's attack or any ensuing disturbance. Instead, he listened closely as a man in a white medical smock said over his head, "He's looking paler today. Have you done something new?" Rösselsprung noted that the man's mouth didn't pull down at the corners as he spoke. A good sign. When the man's mouth didn't pull down, his hands were gentler. Quick, efficient, professional.

The two young Gestapo men who had brought Rösselsprung to this place glanced at their superior, as if to see whether he wished to reply. The officer, a thin-chested, grim-faced man wearing the Knight's Cross with Swords around his neck and bright silver leaves on his collar tabs, compressed his slashlike mouth and remained silent, so one of the younger men said, "We took the sun lamp out of his cell."

The man in the smock said, "That's good. Of course, it isn't my department, but you were getting a little too much improvement in his color." He turned to select instruments from a drawer. Usually he had things already laid out. Rösselsprung was surprised. The Gestapo officer must have noticed the lack of preparation too, for now he did speak, impatiently but with icy politeness.

"Can we get on with this quickly, please? I have a busy schedule this morning."

The man in the smock gave the officer a cold look. "As do I. If I'm a little late today, you can blame the Russians." He was a dentist, a tall German with a balding dome, and on his lapel he wore the gilded swastika of a high Party official, but who could tell whether he was as important as the officer? Take no chances. Irritate neither of them. Take your place in the dental chair and don't wait for them to gesture you into it. Since the very first of the weekly visits, over three months ago, he had stopped struggling when confronted by the chair. He had always been frightened of dentists, with their horrible drills and probes. But no longer. Or, anyway, not very much.

The chair was in a second-floor dental office on the Kurfürstendamm, and he stared out the window at the ruined tower of the Kaiser Wilhelm Memorial Church, and tried to give the impression he wasn't listening to the voices that began to rise edgily in back of him. His eyesight had never been good, but he knew what the church clock said. Seven-fifty. It never said anything else. It must have stopped at precisely seven-fifty during one of the Allied air raids. He would have liked to know for sure, but he had always been afraid to ask.

He would also have liked to interrupt and ask what the Russians had to do with making the dentist late, but naturally he didn't dream of it. Were the Russians advancing again? He hoped not. He already knew a little English and therefore preferred to be liberated by the British or the Americans. If liberation was really on the way. The Berlin streets had looked completely normal as the Gestapo men had transported him at dawn from his cell to the dental office. A few early streetcars running. Women already lining up in front of the bakeries. Of course, they did that even when unexploded bombs left over from a night raid were still being detonated by cleanup crews throughout the city. Business went on as usual.

"I'd like to complete this soon," the dentist said. "I plan to leave the city, like the others, to join my family."

"You know it is forbidden?" the grim-faced officer said.

The dentist sighed in reply. "My dear Müller." Something new. A name, to be stored carefully away.

"I could stop you," the officer, Müller, said.

"Of course. But to what point? They'll want soldiers, not dentists. And as to our patient here, well, I *could* tell you that after this morning I'm through, finished. All the bridgework done. All the enamelplasty completed. Then I could leave. But am I telling you that? No. I wish to allow at least another week's time for the use of the dentition to improve facets and remove burr marks before I can say it's perfect. A conscientious man could do no else. But I would like your honest opinion on one point. Do I have that one more week?"

The Gestapo officer nodded slowly. "Yes, I think so. The Russians have bogged down near Seelow. If the Fourth Panzer Army can hold them one more day . . . yes, yes, we'll have the week. I'm sure of it."

"Excellent," said the dentist. He switched on the high-intensity lamp over the chair. "And now to work. Hold his head to the light, please."

It had been unnecessary to hold him since that first time, but they always did it anyway. Back then, they had roughly clamped his head with black-gloved hands while the dentist probed and tapped and made marks on a chart. They spoke around him, never to him. But he had heard the dentist express satisfaction at the end of the visit and say he would begin treatment the next time they brought him. He had reflected on this when they took him back to his cell, and found, within himself, not fear but hope. It came only in a faint glimmer at first. But as he reached into his memory to re-create the dentist's every comment, every nuance, the hope blossomed and grew, filling a vacuum, no, a chasm, emptied by four hopeless years behind barbed-wire enclosures.

"I think we'll do some gumwork around the incisors before delivering the lower bridge," the dentist said today. "Too much neck mustn't be exposed. I don't want to take any chances."

Such care. It was strange that they would take such care. He was an unimportant man, as historians measure humanity. He admitted it freely to himself. Unimposing in stature, he stood only five feet, eight inches tall when he stood tall, and his time in the camps had long since stooped his shoulders and frostbitten his heart. His blue-gray eyes, once lively in spite of a severe case of astigmatism, had dulled. He was too thin, but they had improved his diet since removing him from the camp, and he was slowly regaining some of the flesh he had thought forever lost to him.

The dentist filled a needle from a small bottle and thrust it behind his lower front teeth. It went in deeply, a sharp, hot prick, then pressure as the fluid was forced in. It didn't feel good, but he was grateful, as always, to this man for deadening the greater pain that would otherwise have come. The needle bit again, in front of the teeth, but already he could feel his lip going numb.

He had once been an artist of sorts, back in the days when he had a name of his own. Even at that he had been undistinguished. Twenty years of painting, broken by intervals of sculpting, acting, drumming in a jazz band, playing the violin for tea dancing at an Antwerp hotel, then back to painting again. A lucky few of his friends had risen to the point of selling paintings regularly. But not him. He had been only mediocre in a career in which second-best can't earn a decent living. The only thing he had ever done well was to survive without money. He was not without charm, and he had taken an almost innocent pleasure in pitting his wits against the landlady with her hand out for the rent money, the acquaintance who had sworn he'd never make another loan, the hostess who had no intention of including him with her other artistic friends in a party invitation. It may have been a party that was his downfall, celebrating, as it did, the escape to Spain of a Jewish sculptor hours before the Gestapo came to arrest him. A week later he himself was picked up by the Gestapo.

Now the dentist was scraping energetically with one of his tools. Rösselsprung could hear it grating against bone, far below the gumline. He looked stolidly out the window, trying not to think of it. Usually a flock of garrulous sparrows cheeped and made their own grating sounds around the clock tower. Odd, that there were no sparrows this morning. He'd first started listening to them during the early visits, over the horrible sounds the dentist made then, pushing and rocking his teeth, loosening them, before extracting the bad ones. More recently, he had listened to the sparrows during lulls in the interminable drilling the dentist did on his remaining teeth. Amazingly, there had been little pain. The dentist had deadened his mouth every time. He was lucky.

At first, he hadn't been that lucky with Germans. They sewed a red felt triangle on his pajama-style prison garb, marking him as a political offender. They shaved his head and put him in with other prisoners, each wearing his own colored badge to identify his crime—the other red triangles for political truants, the green for convicted criminals, pink for homosexuals, black for undesirables and loafers, and the double yellow triangles, one superimposed on the other to make a star of David, for the Jews. As he moved from camp to camp, from Vught to Flossenburg to Sachsenhausen, the badges remained, but the differences in minor transgressions and major ones seemed to fade, like his name, into the background, first ignored, then forgotten. After that, all prisoners were treated the same.

The dentist took another tool, a tiny, long-handled scissor of some sort, and began to snip along his gums. It made a worse sound than the grating, right there in his mouth, *snick, snick,* cutting into his living tissue. He stopped watching for the sparrows and closed his eyes.

He had taken tool in hand himself at Sachsenhausen. Like the others, he starved at mealtimes. Like the others, he struggled to his feet each day and took pick in blistered hands and broke clay in trenches until it seemed his back would also break. He never knew what happened to the clay after it was carted away. No one ever told him. He never dared ask questions of any kind.

The nasty little *snick, snick* sound continued. His neck muscles tightened.

Because he was quick-witted and already knew some German and worked hard to pick up more, he had an advantage over the others. The others frequently misunderstood orders. They would just stand there stupidly, and often they were clubbed for it. Not him. When he was told to move or stop, he obeyed instantly. Even more, he listened carefully to the guards when they bantered among themselves. Soon, if one complained to another of the heat, he was able to fly unbidden to the nearest water barrel, fetching a cooling dipperful to the surprised guard. His lifelong training in ingratiating himself with people now was of utmost importance.

The noise in his mouth stopped, and the dentist stepped away. He opened his eyes to see what was happening, saw the two plaster models of his teeth now sitting on the dentist's tray. Another gold-and-porcelain bridge winked on the phantom lower jaw. This one appeared to anchor on both sides. Good. The dentist apparently hadn't been able to anchor the upper bridgework on the right side, and it was painful sometimes, the way it rubbed up and down when he chewed. He closed his eyes again.

Eventually the game with the guards paid off. When one of the violinists in the camp orchestra died of pneumonia, he overheard a guard speaking of it. Camp musician was an enviable position. There was less work. He had approached the guard quickly and offered himself as a re-

placement. He was an accomplished violinist, he said. The
guard had developed a tolerance for him, and he soon
found himself struggling out of his filthy bunk each day
and taking not pick, but violin, in hand.

He was one of twenty-one camp musicians. He had
played softly among the others, hoping his sour notes
would go unnoticed. Like the others, he played every
morning as the camp prisoners moved out to work. Like
the others, he played on Sundays when the work schedules
were shortened. Like the others, he played whenever and
whatever he was told to play as part of the grand Nazi
concession, even in a concentration camp, to culture. Like
the others, he played for his life. And so, for the first time,
he had use for his one great accomplishment: By using his
wits, he continued to survive.

A pungent odor suddenly caused him to open an eye.
The dentist apparently was mixing cement. He didn't understand a great deal of the man's talk of crowns and plates
and retainers, but when the upper bridgework had gone in
there had been a severely painful moment as a little gold
cap had been cemented in place. Yet, all that gold. And
surely he'd be able to chew better, since he had only five
of his own lower teeth left. He shut the eye again.

In the fourth year of his living death, wonder of won-
ders, had come The Day. A team had appeared at Sachsenhausen, SS officers who spent a week going over the camp
records, then called for certain select prisoners to be
brought before them. Of the thousands wasting away at
Sachsenhausen, only a few hundred were summoned. He
was one of them. They had led him before the camp doctors, who had measured his head, peered into his mouth,
listened to his heart, compared his complexion to a color
chart, poked and prodded him like a side of beef. It took
them three days, even with the most cursory of inspec-
tions, to check the prisoners they had selected. And at the
end of the three days he was one of four men still of interest to them.

Camp rumors were that the selection process was to
find men for some secret medical research, and that usu-

ally meant the end. A quick or slow death, depending on the experiment, but nearly always excruciating. He and the other three from Sachsenhausen silently bade farewell to life and left with the SS men who took them by car to a special compound north of Berlin. When they arrived, they were taken swiftly through a large cell block to individual cells. It was here they discovered that men from other camps had also been brought.

The dentist's soft footfall told him the man was approaching with the cement. He opened his eyes and prepared to open his mouth wide.

He never knew for certain how many other men were at the compound north of Berlin. He guessed there were perhaps thirty or forty men in all, but there might have been more. There had been detailed tests at the special compound. The doctors seemed as puzzled by the process as did the prisoners. They measured heads more minutely. They examined and X-rayed teeth. They fluoroscoped chests. They treated open sores. And all the while, as they answered long lists of questions on innumerable forms, they made mild jokes and tried to guess what they were doing. It was surely some new form of *Wunder Waffe,* they suggested. One of the miracle weapons so long promised to a discouraged German public. The war had been going quite badly, it seemed, and something special was needed to put the Allies in their places. One of the doctors murmured that he had heard the answer. They were going to pick out some man whose brain waves were perfectly compatible to a new automatic calculator of some sort and strap him to a massive bomb and shoot him through the heavens toward New York. The man, controlled by the calculator mechanism, would guide the bomb to its target.

Because he could understand German he overheard the doctor's remark and was terror-stricken. It caused his blood pressure to shoot up so violently that he was almost rejected by the doctors out of hand.

An aspirator was in his mouth, sucking bits of bloody tissue and saliva and pulling cold air around the sensitive teeth to dry them. The dentist was humming now, as if he enjoyed his work. It was not a tune that the prison musicians had ever played. Too lively, too gay. At least the camp supervisors had been sensitive enough to avoid asking for anything gay.

The results of the tests at the special compound were forwarded to Berlin. It took time, but in January, when the snows were on the ground and the Russians were sweeping across Silesia toward the German frontier, a final decision was made: The little Belgian one-time would-be artist was the winner, or loser, of whatever contest had been conducted. He never saw the other prisoners again. He never saw the doctors at the compound again. He was whisked to a cell in Berlin, where a new and puzzling life began. They filled his cell with comforts he had forgotten. Toilet paper. Even a radio, though it was frozen to one station. When air-raid sirens began to scream, as they did almost daily and nightly, special guards hurried him from his cell and down a back stairway to a secluded shelter. They cared for him between air raids, looked closely to his health. One doctor now, the same doctor all the time, tending his body, just as the one dentist, the same dentist, always tended his teeth.

"Now hold him still," the dentist said, dabbing his horrid cold cement into the waiting crowns. Anything hot or cold now made his remaining teeth hurt. And God, how icy the cement was, oozing against all the most sensitive spots, excruciating pain that he would have jerked away from if he could, but the two young Gestapo men held his head, and the dentist held the bridgework in place with both thumbs hooked under his chin, and the pain drilled coldly into the very bone.

Pain was frightening to him, but no more so than the fear for his own life. But his life had improved. There was no doubt about that. And finally, after the years of being known only by a number, he had a name again. Not his own. Rösselsprung. He heard it whispered guardedly when his keepers spoke of him to the grim-faced officer outside his cell. They never used it openly. But he came to think of himself as Rösselsprung. Any identity was better than a number.

The dentist told the officer cheerfully, "Almost through now. I must only check the bite, but it should be perfect. Now, the gumwork I've done today presents a small problem. The area must be kept clean so the gums will heal properly, but, contrarily, we don't want to interfere with the natural buildup of tartar. Also, we'll want him to chew. He'll be able to now. Give him meats. And see that he rinses after eating with warm salt water, but no tooth-brushing for at least two days, and then let him brush only once a day."

And that was what had given him the most hope. They had obviously discovered that his teeth had been damaged by the terrible camp food, the watery, rotten, starvation diet. They had been bringing him secretly, by gray dawn, to this dental office, where a real professional dentist could treat him.

The pain was ebbing. Only one more visit, perhaps, from what the dentist had said, and he'd have a full complement of teeth, some golden, some porcelain, some his own, in his head again.

That meant something, didn't it? They wouldn't work so hard on his teeth if he were destined only to become a piece of machinery, a robot part in some new destructive weapon. Surely, after four years of wondering, despairing, he was to survive. They wouldn't spend so much time and care on him if he was to die.

Would they?

2

Shortly after the Belgian called Rösselsprung was escorted back to a Berlin cell, a black limousine rolled through a set of open gates at an estate named Gut Harzwalde, preceded by a motorcycle escort of six SS men. There was a touch of cold in the early-morning air. The eastern sky, rosy with a promise of daylight warmth, held no hint of the horrors taking place beneath it, the second day of non-stop fighting and dying in the Oder Valley, only some thirty miles away.

A mild-looking man with a pale face and pudgy hips sat silently in the rear of the limousine. His blue eyes, flecked with chips of gray, gazed through steel-rimmed spectacles. His mouth, thin and bloodless, turned down slightly at the edges beneath a small, prissy mustache. He could have been mistaken for a high-school teacher or a minor district official had it not been for the gold braid on his crisp black uniform and the silver death's head of the Schutzstaffel above the narrow visor of his military cap. Unremarkable in appearance, unpretentious in demeanor, he was Heinrich Himmler, infamous Reichsführer of the German SS.

On this particular morning, his face was even paler than usual, and he looked a bit frightened. And with cause. With the war skidding to a rapid and unsatisfactory conclusion, his seat of power had heated up uncomfortably, making him a prime target of the Allied scorekeepers and scoresettlers. A timid man by nature, fanatically devoted to cleanliness and efficiency and administrative paperwork, he had allowed his passion for organization and office discipline to be twisted into a worldwide reputation as history's most productive executioner, and now that reputation hung over his neck like a headsman's ax.

As the limousine curled up the driveway, he spotted SS Brigadeführer Walter Schellenberg, his chief of espionage, waiting on the front steps, breath forming frosty wisps in the chill air. Schellenberg. It was Schellenberg's fault that he was here this morning, instead of in the cozy warmth of his suite of rooms back at Dr. Gebhardt's sanatorium in Hohenlychen. A quiet, isolated hideaway some seventy-five miles north of Berlin, the sanatorium had lately become his favorite resting place, a kind of unofficial headquarters, far from the chaos of war and the incessant nattering of aides.

But no, Schellenberg had insisted on setting up yet another meeting with Folke Bernadotte, the Swedish count who kept flitting in and out of Germany as a Red Cross

representative. Schellenberg was only one of several people who had lately been pressuring Himmler to take steps
to arrange peace terms. The Minister of Labor had added
his whining voice to that of Schellenberg, privately encouraging Himmler to treat with Bernadotte; the Führer's Minister of Finance suggested a different approach, prompting
him to seek peace through the Pope; even his personal
doctor, at whose country estate this meeting was to be
held, kept after him relentlessly about the Jews and concentration camp inmates. Nags. All of them, nags.

Himmler listened to them all, professing interest, but
carefully pretended not yet to have made up his mind. It
was better, of course, to treat with the Allies in secrecy as
he was attempting through Gruppenführer Fegelein. Were
he to follow their advice and go through outsiders like
Bernadotte or the Pope, everyone would soon know about
it. And that could be fatal.

Though Himmler had been careful not to tell Schellen-
berg or anyone else about his own secret approach to the
Allies, he did not actually consider it an act of disloyalty.
Unless he took it upon himself to treat with the British and
Americans, nothing would be left but a country in flames.
Certainly the National Socialist Party had made mistakes.
He had made mistakes himself. But even though he sometimes had to act contrary to his own true convictions, he
wanted only what was best for Germany. Besides, surrender was inevitable. And someone—preferably a man
dedicated to efficiency and sound administration—had to
lead the government after surrender.

No sooner had the limousine pulled to a stop than
Schellenberg was blathering about Folke Bernadotte.

Himmler sighed and started up the steps. "Did he say
what he wants this time?"

"I thought it impolite to inquire," Schellenberg said, "but
I believe it concerns the concentration camps."

"Always the camps," Himmler said. "Doesn't he realize
how difficult it is to arrange anything about the camps?"

Schellenberg shrugged. "Also, Herr Reichsführer, about
the proposed conference with the representative from the

World Jewish Congress, I've talked to Dr. Kersten and he says the man will arrive at Tempelhof on Friday. I would suggest you meet him here at Gut Harzwalde after the Führer's birthday celebration and—"

"I don't want to meet with a Jew," Himmler said.

"It might be wise to talk to him, Herr Reichsführer," Schellenberg said. "I'm thinking only of your future welfare. If you agree to release two or three hundred Jewish women from the Ravensbrück camp, it might go a long way toward proving your deep concern for their unfortunate plight. Such a humane gesture would not go unnoticed by the world press."

Himmler looked up sharply, then thought about it for a moment. "Perhaps you are right," he said. "It's time to clean the slate between me and the Jews. Frankly, Walter, if I'd had my own way, things would have been handled differently with the Jews. You understand that, don't you?"

"Of course," Schellenberg said.

Himmler stared at him. Cynicism? A hint of disbelief? It didn't matter. He peeled off his gloves and his military cap in the entry hall, then followed Schellenberg.

In the dining room, Folke Bernadotte and Himmler's physician, Dr. Felix Kersten, were waiting over coffee. Bernadotte, son of the royal brother of King Gustav V, was a dark man in the uniform of the Swedish Red Cross. He was a genteel, gentle man, but he had the dark, burning eyes of a religious fanatic or an ax murderer. This morning there was a dark, whiskery shadow across the man's lower jaw. He was a hemophiliac, Himmler had been told. Did he never shave closely? Perhaps not. A simple shaving cut might bleed for days.

Kersten quickly excused himself, and Bernadotte leaned forward, a sign that he was eager to get down to cases. "Herr Reichsführer, I've come to speak to you this morning about a subject that the Swedish Red Cross considers vital. We are eager to obtain authorization from you to work in the concentration camps, particularly those in which Norwegian and Danish citizens are interned."

Himmler glanced at Schellenberg. These meetings with Bernadotte were dangerous. Still, his pipeline to the Allies through Fegelein was tenuous at best, and could easily break down. Perhaps it would be wise after all to keep Bernadotte happy. He might be useful later, if the Fegelein approach failed.

He smiled graciously at Bernadotte and said, "That would probably be very helpful. I will give my official permission immediately. Now tell me: How else may I aid you in these difficult times?"

One must do what one could to prove to the world that one was no monster.

3

Sidney Longland was tired of the war, tired of responsibility, tired of being tired. His leg ached, the result of a knee injury in Greece in '42 on which he had postponed surgery, and he was tired of the ache, too. The only pool of pale sunshine available to him was two feet from a dustbin outside the officers' mess, but Longland ignored the stench of kitchen refuse and the pain and dreamed of Spain.

Basking, leaning against the splintery prefab wall, he had only to feel the sun caressing the backs of his hands to be pleasantly far away from this dingy Royal Air Force airstrip in Leuchars, Scotland. Instead, he was walking beside a narrow Spanish river where wild iris grew along the banks. Before he reached the sea, he would see a farmer plowing blood-red dirt with two oxen and a wooden plow. Gulls followed the plow, he remembered. Gobbling worms or grubs. Farther downriver, a party of village women always came to wash clothes and gossip while their sheets bleached on the rocks. Odysseus among Nausicaa's maidens. They fluttered like the gulls when a stranger appeared.

Longland sighed happily, remembering. He heard the two-engined drone of an approaching Mosquito, but he refused to open his eyes. That would be Bascom, most likely. A bit early. Too bad. But the plane wasn't yet in the landing pattern, and Longland was a man who seized even seconds of pleasure. The proximity of a dustbin didn't matter if spring was cracking through the tedious obscenity of war. Longland was stony broke as usual, or he'd probably be inside the officers' mess, like Philip Formoy, with a pint of bitters in his hand, but a pint didn't matter as long as he could enjoy a phantom glass of straw-colored sherry in an Andalucian village, seen years ago, where sea and river met.

Longland listened to the plane bank and circle toward the field, and wondered if he should go back to Spain for his first postwar holiday. He needed the rest. Of course, with that old devil Franco still in power, the Spanish might not be too eager to see British tourists right away, not with their German allies freshly beaten to their knees. And given Spain's own brutal war, the civil one, the village might have changed drastically.

Longland sighed again, this time wistfully, and this time he opened his eyes. War. One could never get far enough away from it. It was hard to concentrate on sunshine and purple bougainvillea cascading beside an outdoor table when he might never survive to see any of it again. Sixty-eight men. Pitifully few for the raid Mumford had thrust on him, but the most he had been able to lay on at such short notice. A handful of them were familiar faces. Good, solid men like Formoy, Granville, Parsons, men he knew he could trust. Another handful whose reputations were known to him, even though he'd never worked with them personally. But an unsettling number would be strangers. Particularly the Americans.

It was an iffy damned raid at best. Too little time to train, inadequately supplied. He'd spent most of last night arguing for more transport to get them out, but Mumford said the logistics people had nixed it. One three-quarter-ton American Ford truck, that's all they could efficiently deliver to the target area. He'd have to use that for the prisoners, if there were any, and the assault team would have to walk. Well, bugger that. He'd think of another way to put his men on wheels, even if it meant stealing every vehicle within two hundred yards of the assault point.

Then there were the uniforms, someone's bright but useless idea. They were all to be British khaki or American olive-drab, with British and American markings, but they would be cut and shaped to look German in the moonlight. Stiff collars, jodhpur trousers, and high knee boots for the officers. Baggy field blouses and pants, with three-quarter-length hobnail boots for the lower ranks. The theory was that the raiders could pass for German troops if anyone spotted them in the darkness before they reached the target area, yet still be protected by international conventions if, God forbid, any of them were captured.

Waste of time, as far as Longland was concerned. Everyone knew the German position on behind-the-lines raids. Hitler himself had set the pattern. Any enemy taken in the commission of a commando action, whether in uniform or not, whether armed or not, whether fighting or in full retreat, was to be slaughtered out of hand. Longland was sure his men knew it. They might as well be outfitted with legitimate German uniforms and be done with it.

But the thing that bothered him most was that last callous reminder from the American, Holley, before Longland and Formoy left for Leuchars this morning. The man was only in this operation by Mumford's sufferance, and already he was sounding off as though he were in charge. "Just remember," Holley had told them sternly as they climbed into the C-47, "the primary purpose of this thing is to keep that murdering sonofabitch from flying south to his Alpenfestung. You make sure your boys understand that. If anything goes wrong and it looks as though you may not be able to get him out, he's to be killed. Instantly and without a qualm. He is not to fall into the hands of the Russians. Am I right, Mumford?" Mumford, looking pained, had murmured agreement. Not a word from either of them about the disastrous consequences such an action was likely to bring on the raiders. It would be difficult enough making their way to safety with prisoners as hostages. If they had to kill the man and flee without him, every German in the countryside would be after them. It was as though Holley had given them orders to commit mass suicide.

The Mosquito, popping smoke from its twin-engined exhausts, settled on the runway and ran out its string, then turned and taxied back toward the operations building. Time for business, and for a dour American bastard named Henry Bascom. Longland anticipated enjoying this particular encounter to the full. "Formoy," he called, "look sharp. Our man is here." Then, without waiting—Formoy, a fellow operations specialist from Mr. Mumford's London shop, had never been known to rush a pint of bitters—Longland limped forward to meet the plane.

Yes, there was Bascom, in the cockpit, leaning over the pilot's shoulder. Longland waved and smiled sunnily, and was rewarded with a look of frowning surprise. Now it would begin. Bascom probably thought the C-47 warming up on the adjacent apron was there to take him on to London and Ann Christy's chintz-curtained bedroom. The plane was for him, all right, but it wasn't going to London. How delightful to be the one to tell him of the change of plan.

The pilot and a yawning copilot were first out of the Mosquito. They made straight for the mess and their favorite tipple, sidestepping Formoy, who was finally on his way to join Longland. The tall American dropped from the plane, moving much slower, and Longland relished the frown on his face. An odd mix, Bascom. While there was something almost shy-looking about his eyes and mouth, the set of his chin always seemed to proclaim a kind of churlish defiance. He probably had his good points, otherwise Ann wouldn't have had anything to do with him, but Longland had been unable to fathom any thus far.

Longland didn't really believe in astrology, as Herr Hitler and his German henchmen were rumored to, but he'd wondered the first time he ever saw Bascom—while leaving Ann's flat in a slightly rumpled state, only to encounter the American coming up the stairs—if the fellow were a Taurus. He'd known from reports that Bascom was a steady, hard-working organizer, supposedly devoid of fractiousness. A good, unimaginative dog, somewhat of the shepherd type. But there'd been a sudden look in his eyes, during that momentary meeting on the stairway, that said a predator's temper rattled around somewhere beneath that quiet exterior. No, perhaps the American wasn't a Taurus. A temperamental Pisces? No one would ever know, apparently. Longland had sneaked a look at Bascom's private dossier and had discovered that he was, of all odd things, a foundling. There was no birth date on record.

Longland ordinarily had little use for any of the OSS intelligence types. The "Oh-So-Social," as it was known among most experienced British SOE agents, since it largely recruited what in America appeared to pass for an upper class. Or such peculiar types as movie stars and American football players. Bascom apparently was recruited because of a facility with languages and a prewar familiarity with Europe, something only snobbish, rich Americans usually had. Bascom had his faults, certainly, but unlike the others, Bascom couldn't really be accused of being either snobbish or rich. What an embarrassment that must have been to his superiors.

But the real reason Longland didn't like Bascom was simply because Bascom so obviously didn't like him. Longland and the rest of the world usually regarded one another with mutual tolerance, and, often, warmth. He even got along well with old Formoy, a short, shaggy bear of a man whose only two interests in life, beer and archaeology, so preoccupied him that he often seemed barely aware there was a war going on, with him in the thick of it.

Formoy shuffled up with his typical rolling gait and stood blinking at Longland and the approaching American as if he'd never seen human beings before but doubted they were relevant to his field. Longland waited until Bascom was within reach, then limped forward, with a typically foxy smile, and shook the American's hand heartily, just to see him squirm.

"Welcome home, old lad," Longland said. "Allow me to introduce Philip Formoy. We've been waiting for you.

Sorry we can't give you a few minutes for a drink, but we're taking off immediately for France."

The American's frowning surprise deepened. "Is this some kind of a joke?" he asked.

"Certainly not," Longland said innocently, but he knew that his slightly pointed ears, his fox-red hair, and the mischief that rarely left his eyes invariably made any assumption of innocence suspect. "You've been chosen to go with us on the raid, old lad."

The buried killer flickered for an instant, peering from Bascom's face. "What the hell are you talking about?" he demanded.

Longland hadn't heard anything as delightful all day. He cautioned himself to stop clowning, but he couldn't resist. "Why, it seems your man Holley was so enraptured with your maiden venture into the art of espionage that he's persuaded Mr. Mumford to sign you on as copathfinder with Formoy here for the landing. It's your reward, I gather. So we're off to France to join the rest of the assault team. Rush, rush, you know. You mustn't miss the final briefings. They'll be especially important to you as a pathfinder. Muck up, and we're all in trouble."

Bascom looked outraged. "Holley set this up?" he said through gritted teeth. "Without even telling me? Are you serious?"

"Yes, indeed. Shoved his way in, if you want the truth of the matter. He's anxious that you Yanks get a share of the glory. You'll be happy to see quite a number of your men when we get to France. Some of them, I'm told, even know which end of a gun to point."

"Forget it," Bascom said. "I'm going to London to talk to Holley."

"I'm afraid I can't permit that, old lad. Security, you know. You'll be quite busy the next two or three days, boning up on what's expected of you."

Longland watched contentedly as Bascom appeared to struggle with himself. Apparently Holley's personal ambitions were not unknown among the London OSS people. But whether or not Bascom realized he'd been swapped about like a piece of merchandise, he succeeded in wiping all expression from his face, except for a trace of anger, mixed with resignation and perhaps fear in his gray-green eyes. That made sense. Longland was none too eager, either, to risk getting killed with the war so near over.

He felt a pang of sympathy for his victim, but Bascom scotched it by saying, "Okay, Longland, I'll go with you. But if this turns out to be one of your goddamned practical jokes, you'd better learn to sleep with your eyes open."

The American strode off toward the C-47. Formoy scratched his shaggy beard and seemed to come awake. A crafty look came over his face, and he peered back over his shoulder at the mess building. "Must go to the lav," Formoy boomed in his deep, growling voice. "I'll be right after you."

"No, you don't," Longland said. "No more beer. Come along."

"Hell and damnation," grumped Formoy. "A man can't even go to the lav?"

Formoy rolling, bearlike, and Longland limping, they followed Bascom to the plane. Longland had to sigh again. Now Formoy would be out of sorts, and Bascom was already furious, and he wouldn't have anyone to talk with through the long, dreary flight to Epernay. Ah well, he could always go back to planning his postwar holiday. If the Mediterranean countries proved to be too war-torn, perhaps he could beg a pittance from the most indulgent of his three elderly aunts and go to some sunlit country that had seen no war at all. One of the islands, perhaps. Or Mexico? Delightful. Perhaps he'd even have the postponed surgery done on his gimpy knee before he went, and then he could take a walking tour. Was Mexico all cactus? Surely not. There would be a river. And warm sea. Palm trees?

As the plane took off minutes later and headed toward the gray North Sea, Longland's imagination had already provided wild orchids and the metallic burring of cicadas to break the silence of a tropical spring. It was hard to wrest pleasure from a war. He felt so weary that it was hard even to feel very playful about it. Thank God for the occasional sobersided ass like Bascom to tweak and tease, and for visions of . . . yes, why not? . . . a sunny, charmed prewar life which, if one could live through this day and the next, just might become a sunny, charmed postwar survival.

4

Captain Alexei Pavlovich Volkov jumped from the sidecar of his motorcycle and ran for a ditch as German shells fluttered flatly overhead. His driver, a young Kazakh sergeant with high cheekbones, dived for the ditch first, and Volkov tumbled in after him just as one of the shells impacted about forty meters behind them, spraying a rain of dirt and clods across their shoulders.

The ditch was already occupied. Two fur-capped enlisted men wearing the infantry patches of the XXIX Corps, startled by the sudden appearance of Volkov and his driver, turned wild, red eyes and leveled weapons on them. Volkov spoke quickly, identifying himself, and the rifle barrels sagged.

"Sorry, Comrade *Kapitan*," one of the infantrymen said. He ducked his head guiltily.

"Our fault," Volkov said. He looked away. The infantrymen shouldn't be here. The XXIX Corps was supposed to be at least two miles beyond this point, staging for an assault on the Seelow heights. Deserters, most likely. Or shirkers. Not that one could blame them. German resistance had been murderous here on the approach to Seelow.

The Germans, fighting furiously for the second day in a row, were dug in along the top of the hills overlooking the Oder Basin. Spring floods had rendered the Haupt Canal, which ran along the valley at the foot of the Seelow hills, all but impassable to Soviet tanks and self-propelled guns on the first day, and Russian infantrymen, forced to assault the heights without mechanized support, had been driven back twice already. Now the tanks were across and moving once more, but the Germans still held the high ground.

Another shell whistled in, this one even closer, and the ground shook beneath them as it exploded a few meters to their left. Both infantrymen buried their faces in their arms with practiced efficiency. As another stinging shower of pebbles and earth peppered Volkov, he understood the wisdom of their apparently reflexive actions. "Damn!" he said. "Has it been like this for long?"

A pair of eyes peeped from crook of elbow, waiting to see if another shell would follow, then a young infantryman with crooked teeth raised his head. "Off and on since yesterday," he said shakily. "They haven't let up yet."

"They'd better let up soon," Volkov said. "I've got to get to corps headquarters. Do either of you know where it is?"

"There's a farmhouse up forward," the youth said, "beyond the near ridge. It's sheltered in a defile. They might be there."

The other infantryman, a dark-skinned older man, gave the youth a warning look and said, "He's guessing. We wouldn't know. We've been pinned down here since yesterday. We have no way of knowing what's forward."

"I see," Volkov said. He studied them both for a moment, but got only sullen looks in return. He decided not to press the point. No sense in getting shot by a pair of nervous deserters.

He crawled to the front lip of the ditch and raised his head cautiously. Geysers of dirt and black smoke erupted with regularity across the fields as shells continued to slam down. Volkov squinted, trying to make out the German gun positions. A haze of smoke and powder fumes clung to the distant heights. He slipped a pair of wire-framed glasses from his tunic pocket and slid them over his ears. The distant image sharpened, and he could see the torn earth and the spindly trees, blackened and scraggly against the hillside, but he still couldn't spot the guns. His eyesight was far too weak.

He removed the glasses. Fortunately, good vision wasn't

a prerequisite for his line of work. He wasn't a combat
soldier. An intelligence officer assigned to front-line duties,
his job was to study captured German documents and to
question prisoners of war, from monocled generals down
to the lowliest Schütze, and extract from them tidbits of
military information that could be siphoned to field officers
in his sector. It was tedious work, often with negative results, but Volkov took it seriously. He worked hard to
sharpen his command of the German language, and had
long since taught himself to be a good judge of people and
their motives. He felt he could tell, with almost 100 per-
cent effectiveness, whether a man was answering questions
truthfully, or only saying what he thought his questioner
wanted to hear. He had a good record of success, and field
commanders who knew of it usually trusted his information. Perhaps that was why he had been summoned to corps
headquarters. They must have someone unusual under
guard, a top-level German general perhaps, someone ripe
for his special talent.

He dropped back to the bottom of the ditch and looked
at the two trembling infantrymen. Poor bastards. He produced a box of cigarettes and offered them around. The
two infantrymen accepted them suspiciously but gratefully,
and rolled the cardboard mouthpieces between thumb and
forefinger to round them out.

"Were you on the line during the big barrage?" Volkov
asked.

The younger infantryman nodded. "We were in the first
wave," he said. He leaned toward Volkov for a light, then
said, "God, it was loud. I thought I'd go deaf."

"It was a farce," the older man said. "They had searchlights strung out along the line. They were supposed to
turn them on when the artillery opened up. A hundred of
them—big, powerful searchlights. Our lieutenant explained
it to us. The lights were supposed to blind the Germans
and expose their positions. A farce."

The young one giggled, his crooked teeth shining. He
sounded on the verge of hysteria.

"Why a farce?" Volkov said. "What happened?"

"What do you think happened?" the older one said. "The guns opened up and tore the countryside apart. There was so much dirt and dust in the air that the searchlights couldn't penetrate. All the damned lights did was bounce back and hit us in the face. It was we who were blinded, not the Germans. Generals. They ought to have their heads rammed up their rectums so their brains would have company."

Volkov frowned. "The Germans have generals, too," he said. "Perhaps their people are just as bitter."

"I don't think the German generals could be as stupid as ours," the old soldier said. "This was supposed to be a walkover. That's what the officers told us. And it was, at first. We came across the valley there. Our tanks went through them like shit through a goose. Most of them turned and ran without even firing back. Then all of a sudden, wham! Those guns on the hills opened up. I thought our barrage was supposed to wipe them all out. I hope the officers can figure out what happened. I damned sure can't."

Volkov stubbed out his cigarette. "Don't worry," he said. "There'll be a flank assault on the heights soon. Once those guns are silenced, you should be able to move up."

The youngster's eyes jerked toward Volkov. The idea was obviously appalling to him, but he swallowed and said, "I hope so."

His older companion looked away in disgust. "Not me. I've done my part. I've been fighting Germans for five years. Let someone else do it from now on."

Volkov's driver reached over and tugged at his arm. "Captain, I think we should move on. The guns are quieter now. Maybe we can make it."

"I wish you luck," the older soldier said. He folded his arms resolutely and leaned back, determined not to move.

Volkov followed the Kazakh driver over the rim of the ditch, zigzagging across ground to the motorcycle. As soon as they were moving, the Kazakh said, "If we'd stayed much longer, that old bastard would have started shooting. He was getting pretty edgy."

"I don't think so," Volkov said. "He's just tired. I imagine there are thousands like him out there. Maybe hundreds of thousands. On both sides. I feel a little of it myself."

The farmhouse, when they reached it, was a two-story white stone building of modest appearance, tucked in a fold of the foothills near the southern outskirts of Seelow, less than a mile from the front. There were other vehicles surrounding the farmhouse, dusty command cars, motorcycles, Lend-Lease Jeeps.

Volkov stepped over a clutter of blankets and field kits, and followed his ears and nose through the building. The quiet sound of hushed voices seemed to come from a room on the right, and there was an unmistakable odor of tobacco, spirits, and unwashed bodies flowing from it.

When he looked in, he saw twelve or fourteen officers, all dirty and tired-looking, standing over a map table. The room was filled with cigarette smoke. A captain was passing a wine bottle back and forth.

"Colonel Klimenko?" Volkov asked.

A sweat-stained lieutenant colonel looked up from the huddle of officers. He had shaggy black eyebrows and a sun-darkened face. "I am Klimenko," he said.

"Captain Alexei Volkov," Volkov said. "You sent for me?"

The colonel looked blank for a moment, then nodded. "Yes, of course," he said. "You're the one who speaks fluent German."

"My German is workable," Volkov said.

"Good. Come with me."

He led Volkov to the rear of the farmhouse. Volkov was still expecting to be taken to a special prisoner, so he was surprised when they reached the kitchen and the colonel seated himself behind a rough-hewn table. There was a cold chicken on a tin plate.

"Sit down," Klimenko said. "I assume you've not had much time for food?"

Volkov shook his head.

"Share my meal with me," Klimenko said. He brushed flies away from the chicken and tore off a chunk for himself, then pushed the plate to Volkov. "I've heard a lot about you," he said. He stuffed white meat into his mouth. "Go on, eat. Eat."

"I'd rather see the prisoner first," Volkov said.

"What prisoner?" the colonel said, chewing. He licked his fingers and reached for a bottle of cognac. "French," he said. "We found it under the floorboards." He uncorked it and handed it to Volkov.

"You have no prisoner for me?" Volkov said. "I assumed I was brought here to question someone."

"Ordinary prisoners are no longer your primary duty," Klimenko said. "As of today, you have a new assignment."

"Sir?"

"Comrade Volkov, we have come to the heart of Germany for one purpose: to smash the government of the Nazis for all time. We will soon enter the barricaded streets of Berlin, perhaps even before the week is out. Our priority mission is to capture the major war criminals and process them for immediate removal to Russia."

"Of course, sir. But what has that to do with me?"

"A great deal," Klimenko said. "Our No. 1 objective, of course, is Adolf Hitler. He is to be located and taken prisoner, or his body found and identified. If alive, he must be removed to the Soviet Union for punishment. If dead, his body must be taken from the city and his remains placed under Soviet guard. We cannot have his bones treated as sacred relics and passed from generation to generation. Nor do we intend to share him with the Western Allies. Do you understand?"

"Yes, sir. Of course, sir."

"You aren't drinking," Klimenko said. He took the cognac bottle and wiped the rim with his hand and tilted it to his lips, as though to show Volkov it was permitted. When he was done, he said, "You, Comrade Volkov, have been chosen for special duty. You are to head one of the special teams that have been set up on the orders of Marshal Zhukov himself. From now on, you will have one purpose in life, and one purpose only: to locate and apprehend the criminal Hitler."

Volkov stared at the lieutenant colonel for a few seconds, then reached for the cognac. He drank deep and long. When he lowered the bottle, his eyes were watering.

Klimenko grinned. "I take it you accept the assignment?"

Volkov clenched his teeth and nodded. "With the deepest of pleasure," he said.

3

Adolf Hitler ist der Sieg!

"Adolf Hitler is Victory!"

—slogan scrawled on Berlin wall

1

Henry Bascom's part in the Export mission began three nights later when a black-painted C-47 throttled back its engines and headed toward the center of Berlin, carrying its two passengers—a bearlike Britisher and the reluctant Bascom—to their drop zone.

Feeling uncomfortably cramped in his tight parachute harness, Bascom groped his way through the darkened plane to one of the rectangular side windows and stared down at a blacked-out city he hadn't seen in seven years. Streams of RAF bombers droned through the night sky to the northeast. Thin searchlight beams clawed upward like pale, frantic fingers, probing for them. Beyond the center of the city, among the worker's tenements in the Prenzlauer Berg district, bomb-ignited fires burned out of control. Strings of explosions flickered across the black cityscape as more bombs fell, and bright green and red tracers arced upward in answer. Here and there, flak bursts blossomed in the sky.

It was like nothing Bascom had ever seen or ever hoped to see, and he shuddered in spite of himself. Berlin was quaking beneath its 362nd air raid of the war. Allied bombers, striking with demoralizing regularity since late 1943, had come in increasing numbers these last months, until the wave upon wave seemed almost continuous. Below, the beautiful old imperial city of Berlin, once peacefully criss-crossed with tree-lined avenues, canals, dotted with cool green parks and lakes, lay smoldering in the darkness. More than seventy-five thousand tons of incendiaries and high explosives had rained down on the city since the beginning of the raids, with the American Eighth Air Force dumping bombs by day and the Royal Air Force Bomber Command continuing the destruction by night. Some forty thousand Berliners had died in the attacks. Another million and a half were homeless, forced to live in cellars, to take refuge in packed public shelters, or to crowd in with more fortunate friends and relations. By now every third building had been reduced to rubble or was so severely damaged that it was no longer habitable.

Though Bascom had no way of knowing it, this night's raid was the next-to-last raid of the war. Tomorrow morning, at ten o'clock, American B-17s would hit the city for the last time, then Allied bombing co-ordinators would decide the Russians were getting too close to risk any more strikes. Had Bascom's darkened C-47 been higher, he might have seen the reason himself in the form of red flickers on the horizon, a tank battle raging only ten to twelve miles from Berlin. German Army Group Vistula, overwhelmed by superior numbers and with no reserves to bolster sagging lines, had fought without rest for four days. But it wouldn't be able to hold out much longer.

As the C-47 homed in on the drop zone, one of two lights, a red one, blinked on above the door to the pilot's compartment. Formoy, his shaggy beard barely visible in the blackness, came to Bascom's window and gripped him by the arm. "Time to hook up!" he yelled above the muffled roar of the engines.

Bascom swallowed and fastened his static line to the overhead cable. Taking turns, Formoy first, Bascom second, they checked each other's equipment—the chute packs, the special silenced Stens slung over their shoulders, the hooded signal flasher hooked to Bascom's harness, the small "22" radio beacon strapped to Formoy's leg. Satisfied, they gripped their static line clasps and guided them along the cable, inching their way to the jump door on the port side, where the British jumpmaster calmly waited for them.

As Bascom looked out over the shorter Formoy's shoulder into the wind-whipped darkness, he felt the first tightening of the solar plexus and the testes, a giddy rush of blood that left him feeling weak and limp. He braced himself and closed his eyes. A normal reaction, he told himself. No soldier ever went into battle without being scared to death, at least not the sane ones. It happened to beginners and hardened veterans alike. At least that's what he told himself. But he wasn't sure it was true.

Formoy was in jump position, and Bascom leaned closer to the doorway and forced himself to look down. The sprawling Tiergarten, black on black, loomed up in the darkness below the left wing, 630 acres of trees and duck ponds and broad walkways, a long east-west rectangle of uninhabited parkland dominating the very center of Berlin. Faintly visible buildings crowded blackly to the edges of the park, and he could see quiet streets around the perimeter. It reminded him vaguely of Manhattan, the way Central Park might look in a power failure.

But this wasn't Manhattan, and the Tiergarten no longer resembled Central Park. Even through drifting smoke he could see splintered tree trunks stretching upward like shattered telephone poles in the feeble moonlight. Cratered clearings apparently had once been stands of luxuriant oak and beech. Finding a suitable flat area for the landings would be damned difficult.

It was a bleak sight, appallingly different from the last time he had seen the Tiergarten. That was a hot, sparkling day in '38, toward the end of his twenty-eight months in Berlin as an undistinguished student, desultorily studying medieval literature. He had gone to the zoological gardens, over in the southwestern corner of the park, with a girl named Karola to visit Rosa the hippopotamus. He and Karola had lunched on the restaurant terrace, and he'd been so lazily happy for a change, that it had been hard work to look properly sad when Karola, Karola of the long legs and the deeply dimpled buttocks, had told him she was going to be married. Hadn't her fiancé lived somewhere out of the way? Brazil, was it? He hoped she had long since left Berlin.

The green light came on. The British jumpmaster thumped Formoy on the shoulder, and the squat man lurched through the door. The jumpmaster gestured Bascom forward and gave him a thumbs-up sign. Bascom hesitated only an instant, then took a deep breath and stepped after Formoy into the blackness. The slipstream caught Bascom and yanked him from the plane, and the static line ripped his chute pack open. Folds of black silk rustled out and billowed above him, popping noisily, and he felt the shock as his harness dug into his crotch and armpits.

And then he was swinging in the void. The C-47 engines droned beyond him and faded. A wave of loneliness as tangible as seawater swept over him, and he dangled limply, waiting for it to go away.

The wave, as waves will, subsided, and he turned his attention to the ground below. He thought he saw Formoy's black chute dropping beyond a stand of chestnut trees that had somehow escaped the destruction, and he saw with apprehension that the wind was carrying him directly into the trees. He tugged at his lines, spilling air, aiming at a narrow meadow near one of the smaller waterways. He was suddenly desperately aware of the sounds, the continuing clamor of war, the far-off *crump, crump* of high-explosive bombs thundering in the distance, and a closer, more rhythmic answering sound, the steady *bam-bam-bam-bam* of German anti-aircraft guns, probably from the top of the twin flak towers over by the zoo, less than a mile and a half away.

He came in silently, legs together, knees bent. His feet jarred when he hit, and he allowed himself to roll forward, tumbling across the ground, and bobbed up gathering in his lines and the waving black silk. Then, arms filled with the folds of his collapsed chute, he dived behind a cluster of robinia bushes and waited.

As he crouched in the bushes, he was astonished to hear the faint, coughing roar of a lion, sad beyond measurement and so forlornly wild that the hairs on the back of his neck tingled. A lion? He'd thought surely the animals would have been evacuated from the zoo by now. Apparently they had not. Apparently the animals and birds were still locked in their cages below the flak towers, screaming in the darkness while the anti-aircraft guns thundered above them. Poor damned lions. Poor birds. Poor, terrified creatures, trapped in a wasteland of war.

Footsteps approached stealthily through the darkness and Bascom cringed back, hugging the ground. The park was supposed to be empty. Gruppenführer Fegelein had told him so. Particularly with the RAF rumbling overhead. Longland had said the same thing at the briefings. German civilians would all be in shelter, keeping their heads down. Even if a few fools stayed out in the raid, they wouldn't be anywhere near the park. The footsteps came closer.

But it was only Formoy, darting with the surprising agility of the stout person through the jagged stumps. Bascom breathed again and raised his head. Formoy angled over to join him. "What are you doing back here?" Formoy whispered.

"Listening," Bascom said. "I thought I heard something."

Formoy lifted the night shield on his wristwatch and studied the radium-green glow of numerals. "We'd better get a move on," he said. "I think I spotted a fair-sized clearing up that way."

"Wait," Bascom said. "What if there are people? Shouldn't we wait until we're sure?"

Formoy stared at him in the darkness. "We've got less than thirty minutes to locate an adequate landing site," he said. "If they don't hear the beep of my radio beacon by the time they reach the release area, the mission will be aborted. They'll all turn back. That means you and I will be left here. Alone."

The thought chilled Bascom to the marrow. He shrugged quickly out of his parachute harness and stuffed it, along with his armload of black silk, into the bushes. Then he hurried after Formoy into the splintered trees.

The first complement of British and American assault team members drifted behind tiny points of light flaring from the engine exhausts of a Dakota tow plane, twenty-five silent men, faces daubed with dark blue grease, bodies lurching with each windborne shudder of the big Horsa transport glider. Behind them, stretched out at two-minute intervals, three more Horsas wallowed fitfully in the wake of their twin-engined tow craft, carrying the remainder of the attack force.

Sidney Longland waited rigidly in a jump seat behind the pilot and the copilot of the lead glider, listening to the rustling sound of wind beating against the wooden fuselage and the subdued rumble of the Dakota at the other end of the three-hundred-foot nylon tow rope. He could hear the pilot and the copilot clearly above the wind, which was no consolation, for the pilot had been sighing huge, heavy sighs ever since they spotted the ragged silhouette of Berlin and skimmed over the outskirts at a height of six hundred feet.

The copilot jerked his chin up and said, "I hear it. I hear it. I've got the beacon."

The glider pilot sighed again and shifted his hand to a central console. "Hang on," he said. "We're going down." He tugged the release lever, and the tow line fell away.

Longland's stomach dropped sickeningly, and so did the silent, vibrating Horsa. The parent Dakota, feeling the sudden acceleration as its load lightened, wheeled away and climbed, nylon rope flapping in its wake.

The glider wallowed on soundlessly, nosing up, nosing down, and the air speed fell off to about a hundred miles an hour. The whisper of wind slackened. Streets merged with ruins below them, partially obscured by drifting smoke, then the tops of buildings gave way to the wide, winding coils of the Spree River, flowing through the heart of the city. A flash of moonlight sparkled from the dark surface of the water as they hurtled overhead.

They seemed to be on target. Next would come the broad pavement of the Charlottenburger Chaussee, with the shadowy form of the upthrusting Siegessäule column as a last aiming point, then the dark fringes of the Tiergarten.

"There's the flasher!" the copilot shouted. "Over there!"

The pilot sighed once more and locked in on the blinking light and tugged another lever on the console. The big landing flaps rattled down, and the lumbering Horsa slowed to ninety, to eighty, to seventy miles an hour. "Everyone hold tight!" the pilot yelled. "This is apt to be a bit irregular!"

Longland gripped his Sten and watched the ground pumping up at them. Even as he braced himself, he could hear the pilot's voice rise shrilly above the rustle of wind, babbling, "Oh bloody hell, the trees! Too many trees! Look at all the bloody tree-e-e-e-e-s-s-s!"

Charred trunks and brittle branches flayed the glider, and Longland felt his body jerk against the seat belt. The Horsa lurched against the earth and rebounded, then careened sideways across solid ground. Something thudded heavily outside the fuselage, and the glider slewed to the left and yanked to a stop.

An instant of awesome quiet swept over them, punctuated only by a few muttered curses from the shaken men in the rear; then Longland's frozen brain urged him to his feet. He unhooked the loading hatch and let it slam to the ground. The last thing his ears picked up before boots began to shuffle on the plywood flooring was a final relieved sigh from the pilot's compartment.

The left wing had sheared off completely, sliced away by one of the larger trees. One of Longland's section leaders quickly took stock and reported. The men could have been in better shape. Two complained of back pains from the rough impact, and an American OSS sergeant had broken a knee when his seat belt gave way. They would have to be left at the truck with the noncombatant pilots and copilots during the raid. Still, it could have been worse. Glider landings in the dark were touchy at best.

Longland used hand signals to send men out into the trees surrounding the clearing, then hurried with his section leader to the tail of the glider. The ground was rougher than he had expected, covered with upturned tangles of roots. Craters gaped everywhere. A low warning slipped from the section leader's throat. From the darkness at the edge of the clearing, someone ran toward them, hunched over as though under fire—Formoy and Bascom, most likely; at least they had bloody well better be. Longland gripped his Sten carefully until he was sure.

They hurried up breathlessly, two figures, one short and bearded, the other tall and clean-shaven. The bearded face whispered, "Sidney?"

"Over here," Longland said.

Formoy and Bascom ducked under the intact wing. "Good to see you," Formoy panted. "Damned lonely down here for a while there."

Longland glanced at the flasher in Bascom's hand and said, "You could have picked us a smoother landing site."

"That was my doing," Formoy said. "We found a clearer spot just north of here, but I didn't think it was large enough to handle all four gliders."

"You should have looked harder," Longland said. "We've already lost the use of three men. No telling how many more we'll lose before they're all down."

Bascom snorted. "Formoy's choice was the best possible," he said. "If you think this is bad, you should have seen the rest."

Longland turned away without answering. He moved into the open to watch for the next Horsa. Moonlight fell across the clearing, but it was dark as a grave under the decimated oaks where the perimeter men had taken position, and Longland could see only the occasional glint of an eyeball or a tooth as greased faces twisted around to peer at the sky.

Two minutes passed, though it seemed longer, and Formoy's deep voice murmured behind him. Longland glanced around and saw Bascom aim his flasher and begin blinking the light. A dark shape sighed toward them over the jagged treetops to the north. Glider No. 2. Right on schedule.

The wide wings took shape as silently as an apparition, settling, settling, skimming through the darkness. It touched, bounced, and skipped several yards before touching again, then rolled into the stumps. The wheels seemed to sink into soft earth, and the Horsa trembled to a stop, nosing gently forward. As it dropped back to its belly, the side panel plopped open, and dark figures hurried out with several large bundles. Those would be the inflatable boats. Later, with luck, it would be those boats that took them down the Havel, on the first leg homeward.

The rest of the men piled out into the ashes and dirt. Only twenty this load, due to the extra weight of the boats and the inflation canisters. There would be another twenty men in the next glider, bringing the tanks of knockout gas, then the three-quarter-ton American truck with a crew of four in the final glider. The truck, which would be left among the trees with the noncombatants until the mission was done, would then be used to transport the boats and the more important personalities in their bag of prisoners to the Havel staging point.

Longland's third-in-command, a bandy-legged, excitable little Londoner named Granville, was the last man out of the No. 2 glider, and Longland saw him jogging across the clearing with his pilot and copilot. He was spitting with rage when he reached Longland. "We almost missed the breakaway point," he grumbled. "Bloody damned smoke was too thick coming over Moabit. You'd think the idiots in ops would think to check the bloody wind direction before setting up their bloody bombing patterns."

They waited again. Two minutes dragged slowly by. And then it came, glider No. 3, flaps down, scraping across the trees. It rustled darkly above them and headed for the ground beyond. Longland smiled in relief. For a mission with so many built-in difficulties, things seemed to be going remarkably well.

Neither wishing to confess anxiety to the other, E. Wilson Holley and his British companion, the man they called Mr. Mumford, had lingered late over dinner. It was 11:03 P.M., Berlin time, as they finally strolled out of the gray darkness of Trafalgar Square and onto the fabled thoroughfare of Whitehall. Holley was dismayed to hear the plunging basso voice of Big Ben begin to strike the hour, three minutes late. Although all evening he had sneaked only occasional peeks at his wristwatch, he now forgot himself and looked at it openly. Then he saw that Mumford had noticed his preoccupation with the time, and he flushed with embarrassment. Holley was in love with all things British, but to save face he had to make a disparaging remark: "Looks like your famous Big Ben can't keep time tonight."

Mumford raised sandy eyebrows in a long, humorous face, and Holley cursed himself silently as he suddenly remembered being told that Big Ben was the bell that tolled the hours, not the clock. But Mumford replied only, "Mmmm," and puffed at his pipe.

While Holley rarely walked the half mile down Whitehall without congratulating himself on having drawn the assignment to London, his mind wasn't really on the city tonight. It was on Berlin, where the most dazzling coup of the war was taking place at this very moment—Mumford's coup, to be honest about it. But he had every intention of siphoning off as much of the credit as he could. It wouldn't be easy. Mumford, he divined, was hungry for success, and Holley himself was hungrily certain that success would have to come now. The clock was moving. Everybody kept saying the war would be over in a matter of weeks, unless . . .

It amused Holley that everyone had his own favorite "unless." British and American intelligence had been shooting teams off in all directions, checking out the various rumors of new secret weapons. There was even some kind of top-secret OSS group poking around in the Hohenzollern area of southern Germany, where the Nazis had supposedly shipped all their top physicists to put together some kind of super new disintegration bomb. Holley didn't believe it, any more than he believed the silly scuttlebutt about the U.S. physicists working on some new secret bomb of their own to use against the Japanese. As well believe the reports that the Germans had developed, of all damned things, a new gun that could shoot around corners. The Germans were on the ropes. Nothing could save them now. But he thanked God nightly that there sat Ike off in France worrying about his National Redoubt. Without that particular myth, this great opportunity might never have dropped into his lap so close to the end.

Holley stretched his arms, using the motion to sneak another look at his watch. Eleven past. The assault team should be making contact with Fegelein any minute now, if they hadn't already. That was the clincher. Mumford would never be able to explain Fegelein away. The word of Holley's contribution was sure to get back to command level. Let Mumford try to wriggle out of that.

Maybe Bascom would do something courageous. High visibility, that's what Holley needed from his people. In his mind's eye he saw Bascom, a good American kid, sneaking out into the open to latch onto Fegelein. Then they would force the German to lead them along a street much like this one, only its name would be Wilhelmstrasse, instead of Whitehall. Damn it, he should have talked to Bascom before letting Longland take him to France, given him a pep talk or something. Bascom should lead the way, until they reached the Chancellery. Longland's Britishers would cut the telephone wires, then a team would move into the garden out back to feed the sleeping gas into the underground ventilating system. Ten minutes, the scientific guys said. Ten minutes to put every German in the Führerbunker to sleep. Then Bascom, bless his all-American heart, would make Fegelein guide them right down into the underground passages to the deep vault where Hitler and all his pansy generals would be sprawled over chairs and tables, unconscious and ripe for plucking. It would be like shopping in a supermarket. Bascom could poke around at his leisure and pick up as many prisoners as he wanted. Well, Bascom and Longland. Give the British some due. They could bag them all, maybe—anyone unlucky enough to be sucking around the Führer on his birthday.

It would take an hour or so to transport the captives to the Havel, but that wouldn't matter. That gas was supposed to keep them asleep for two or three hours. Then Bascom and the others could shove them into the rubber boats, spend another couple of hours navigating quietly down the western fringes of Berlin and out to open counery, and arrive at the designated airlift sector just about daybreak, in time to beam a radio signal to the two planes circling above the clouds. Only the top prisoners would be flown out, of course. Maybe with Bascom along to ride shotgun. The rest could walk out with Longland and the other guys in the raiding team. It was only a day's march, more or less, to Allied lines on the Elbe, and the Germans would be far too busy coping with confusion and the Russians to come chasing after them.

Holley smiled in anticipation. Like the notes of a mighty bell, like Big Ben, the names of prisoners they might bring back pealed in his mind. Göring, Goebbels, Speer, Himmler. Maybe some of the big military guys: Kitel, Guderian, Dönitz. Even that little chippy of Hitler's, Eva Brown or whatever her name was, if she was unlucky enough to be there when the gas hit the fan. But most important, the big cheese himself, the fanatic little bastard with the Charlie Chaplin mustache and the blood of millions on his hands. Adolph Goddamn Hitler.

Holley glanced at Mumford, then chuckled to himself. Ike wanted the Redoubt stopped? Hell yes, they would stop it. They would stop everything. When historians looked back at the war in Europe, they would have to pinpoint April 20, 1945, as the day it all came to a screeching halt.

And there might even be room in a footnote for the name of one E. Wilson Holley.

4

At 11:43 P.M., the rendezvous point still stretched out before them, two empty streets meeting in a broad, angular wedge. It was a deserted landscape filled with gutted houses and brick rubble. Waiting patiently, Philip Formoy scratched his beard behind a row of prickly hawthorn shrubs and regarded it all with interest. Though the Bronze Age was his favorite culture and fragments of red-and-black pottery were the most fascinating things in the world to him, he liked all rubble. He moved his scratching fingers to his shaggy hair and wondered, not for the first time, what future archaeologists might make of the war's debris, were they discerning enough to excavate an undisturbed site. His brother and sister-in-law had bought it in London's East End in '41, during the final months of the blitz. Brick rubble, like Berlin. A crushed aluminum pot. Scraps of wallpaper, but they would rot quickly, of course. Shards of his sister-in-law's prized Wedgwood plates. Formoy had looked, both in sorrow and habitual scholarly distraction, but he hadn't found much else.

Glimmers of light, like heat lightning, flashed on the tops of buildings across from the Tiergarten as another distant string of bombs cracked down in the Prinzlauer Berg and Weisensee districts to the northeast. Formoy shifted his Sten and stared upward at the jagged walls of what had once been buildings filled with the artifacts of a pleasant, peaceful existence. Of course, the archaeologists of a few centuries hence wouldn't find much that was helpful from it all. The toilets, perhaps. Like pottery, would porcelain endure? Wood rotted, metal corroded, stone crumbled, but pottery lasted forever. Formoy began wondering about his sister-in-law's Wedgwood and its composition, but movement beyond the shield of shrubs caught his attention. Faintly visible in the intermittent bomb flashes, a figure emerged from the shadows: Longland's American adversary, Bascom. Still alone.

Formoy looked both ways down the line of nervous men, some sixty strong, hugging the earth at the edge of the park. The blasted German contact hadn't come. Two sweeps of the street already, now a third, and still no sign of him. What in God's name was keeping the man?

Even Longland, sprawled out to his right, seemed upset about the delay. Good old Longland, usually so full of pranks back home, though always strictly business when on an operation. It was as though the man checked his emotions before jumping off, along with his cigarettes and items of personal identification. But tonight, for some reason, Longland had brought his nerves with him, and with them apparently had come worry, even irritability.

The American hurried across the street. "No luck," he reported. "I covered the area thoroughly." He looked suffused with guilt, as though he were personally to blame for the German's not showing up.

Longland's jaw muscles worked.

The American glanced over his shoulder at the dark street. "Look," he said, "what if we were to take to the ruins somewhere and hide out for the night? I think I could get to him in the morning by going through the Swede's hotel contact. We could set it up again for tomorrow night."

"Fine," Longland snapped. "And what do you suggest we do with the gliders? Disassemble them and take them with us?"

The American winced. "Oh. I wasn't thinking."

"Start," Longland said. "Once the Germans spot those gliders, we've had it. No, we have no choice. German or no German, it's tonight or never."

Earlier, the American had been quick to come to Formoy's defense, so Formoy spoke up in order to deflect Longland's spleen. "If we're going to have a go without a guide, we shall have to make some adjustments," he said. "You'll need recon teams to check the layout once you get inside the Chancellery. Would you like me to turn the vehicle search over to someone else and help out?"

Longland shook his head. "I'll need you even more on transportation. We may have to move fast once we're finished. I'll assign some of the OSS people to reconnoiter the bunker."

"I'll take a team," Bascom volunteered, still sounding contrite.

"No you won't," Longland said. "You're staying outside. That's an official order."

He didn't offer any explanation, and Formoy couldn't help wondering if the crackle in Longland's voice had something to do with that pretty bird for whose attentions both seemed so actively to compete. Perhaps a way of dulling the American's chances for any luster that might accrue from tonight's business? If so, it seemed a petty approach, not like Longland. Not like him at all.

Formoy whispered to the American, "Don't worry, lad. I'll be glad to have you along. We'll steal only the best. You can swipe all the Mercedes you see, and I'll take Daimler-Benz. We'll leave our mark on the city."

But the American turned on him and bit, like an insecure animal one reaches to pet. "What the hell are the two of you trying to pull?" he demanded in a furious whisper. "By God, you dragged me along on this thing. What makes you think you can keep me out of the Chancellery?"

"My rank and my position as leader of this expedition," Longland said. "If you refuse to take a direct order, I'll place you under arrest and arrange an escort to take you back to the truck to wait until the mission is done. Is that what you want?"

The American clamped his mouth shut. Longland checked his watch and said quietly, "All right, let's get going."

As the word passed, dark figures rose all about Formoy, and there was an instant outpouring into the rubble-strewn street of keyed-up men who were ready to get under way. Formoy knew it didn't matter to a single one of them that they were moving half blind. Anything was better than sitting still in the darkened citadel of the enemy; just get on with it, get moving. There was no orderly march. Treading on one another's heels, they hurried out of the park and into the flickering darkness.

Formoy rolled out with them, trying to ignore a fluttering in his stomach. He watched Longland and Bascom begin to drift apart, each consciously allowing figures to come between them, as though neither wanted to be near the other. Well, the devil with them. Formoy had his own skin to think of. He forced his mind to less worrisome matters, concentrating on the ruins and shadows that towered above them. As they rushed deeper through the heavily damaged streets, his nervousness ebbed. He couldn't see much, given the lighting, but he could see enough to keep his mind occupied. What utterly fascinating rubble.

5

"I'll want five or six men, the best we've got," Longland whispered to Granville. "Preferably people who can *sprechen* a little *Deutsch* if called upon to do so."

"I'll pick them myself," Granville agreed softly. He cradled his Sten and moved back toward the agents strung out in the shadows behind them.

Directly ahead lay the center of the German universe, the Chancellery complex. The key building, a yellowish brick-and-marble structure called the new Chancellery, ran the length of Voss-Strasse, all the way from Hermann Göring Strasse, on which they now stood, down to Wilhelmstrasse, some 450 yards farther east, where it joined the southern edge of the old Chancellery building to form a massive L shape. Now, Longland knew, would come the difficult part, finding their way through the dark oaken doors and the endless corridors. Without Bascom's German general to guide them, God only knew where the doors would lead.

A few feet away, Philip Formoy shifted uncomfortably,

a confused expression clouding his bearded face. Poor bastard, probably wondering why Longland had stuck him with the job of nursemaiding Bascom. Longland couldn't tell him. On a job like this, every man was expected to do his part, and how could Longland explain he was giving Bascom special treatment just because he was afraid of what might happen if Bascom were killed or injured under his leadership? Damn it all, Ann would never believe he hadn't purposely shoved Bascom right into the roughest go. Better to keep him outside safe and sound than to have to face her back in London with bad news and lame excuses.

Granville returned, leading six men, a pair of whom Longland thought he recognized, even though their faces were blackened. "These are first rate," Granville whispered. "If you get in trouble, let them do the work. The rest of us will follow to the mouth of the street. Once we get your signal, we'll come on the trot."

Formoy rumbled, "Shall I be off with my band of car thieves then? Looks like time to get our feet wet."

Suddenly, sharply, Longland's mind focused on the job at hand. "Yes, good," he said to Formoy. To Granville, "Send the phone teams off to do the line-cutting, then be sure to give us a couple of minutes before you bring the main body forward." He unlimbered his Sten and motioned for the six men to follow him.

In quick, darting scampers, they hurried around the corner onto Voss-Strasse and headed for a spill of brick rubble. Longland lingered a moment in the darkness, nursing his knee, and took stock. There were at least two impressive entrances visible in the tall, sleek structure, one only about fifty yards ahead, near this end of the street, the other much farther down toward Wilhelmstrasse. The edges of the street were badly clogged from end to end, filled with uneven mounds of stone, which had gushed from a string of collapsed houses across from the Chancellery.

Longland gestured at the closer entrance, and they began to slip forward, alert for signs of sentries. He wasn't expecting much of a guard, not during an air raid and in a place where no trouble was expected, but it was always wise to be prepared.

Square pillars, tall and white in the faint moonlight, rose from a flight of broad steps leading up to a massive door. Above the pillars, etched in stone, a spread-winged eagle clutched a sculpted swastika. The building had taken a few bomb hits, but nothing as severe as the houses opposite. A water cart, parked at the foot of the Chancellery steps, gave evidence that the Chancellery plumbing had probably been knocked out during one of the air raids.

All clear? It seemed to be. But as they edged forward, one of the agents touched his elbow and whispered, "Someone at the top of the steps. Near the second column."

Longland dropped behind a brick pile and peered. A soft red pinpoint of light arced upward and brightened. The tip of a cigarette. Someone inhaling back in the shadows of the entryway. The glow lingered at mouth level, then faded and dropped back to its original waist-high position.

"How many?" Longland whispered.

"Can't tell yet," the man whispered. "We'll have to get closer."

Longland nodded. "All right, three of you take the Chancellery side of the street. The other three on the opposite side, along the row of houses. I'll take the middle. Don't start anything until we're sure we've got them all spotted. Understood?"

The agents vanished into the shadows. Longland waited briefly for them to get into position, then limped to the next mound of rubble.

He moved quickly until he was within twenty yards of the Chancellery steps. Then, just as he was about to slip to the cover of the next mound, something clicked to the pavement on his right—a loose stone or brick, probably dislodged in the darkness by one of the houseside agents.

The cigarette tip jerked nervously and dropped. A figure stirred from the shadows at the head of the Chancellery stairs. "Who's there?" a voice called in German.

Longland froze, cursing softly.

The figure took another step, and moonlight touched his shoulders. He was a tall, well-built young man in a black SS tunic, wearing a white ceremonial belt and high, polished boots. One of the elite Hitler Guard. "Who's there?" he called again. He came down four steps, unslinging a Schmeisser machine pistol from his shoulder.

There seemed to be another to the right of the big dark doors. Longland decided to show himself before one of them got excited and started shooting. He stood up and stepped into the open.

The German swung his machine pistol toward Longland. "What are you doing here?" he called. "This street is forbidden without a pass." He eased down three more steps, keeping Longland covered.

"I have a pass," Longland called back.

The German wavered, then let the barrel of his machine pistol droop a few inches. "Show it to me," he said.

Longland groped left-handed through the pockets of his German-cut tunic, as though searching, and moved hesitantly toward the steps. When he was within ten feet of the German, the man saw the Sten with its bulky silencer tube dangling from Longland's right hand. His eyes shot up to Longland's face, then to the symbol on his military cap— not the stylized German eagle, but a British lion. The German's entire body twitched as though someone had applied an electrical shock, and he started to swing his weapon up.

Longland lurched at him, but two of Granville's agents came out of the shadows and got there first. One had a knife in his hands, produced so quickly that Longland never saw where it came from, and he raked it across the German's throat from left to right in one sweep. The German sagged, a look of surprise still frozen on his face, and the other agent caught him at the armpits and held him up.

Longland quickly turned his attention to the second German, at the top of the Chancellery stairs, and stitched three hushed shots, *phut, phut, phut,* across the man's midsection. Stens from the shadows on the far side of the street opened up as well, adding their own silent firepower to Longland's. Bullets fizzed around the German from both angles, knocking chips from the stone wall behind him, and he pitched forward, his machine pistol skidding across the top of the steps.

Longland beckoned the others, and rushed up the steps, looking for more Germans. There were none. Two of the nearest agents clattered up behind him and he said, "Let's get inside, fast."

They burst through the wide double doors, weapons ready. There were three more German SS men in the gallery, lounging against the far wall, collars undone and sharing a cigarette over a sputtering candle. They started to rise when Longland and the two agents rushed into the room, but quick bursts from the Stens cut them down.

Longland and his two companions dropped into a crouch, waiting. There was no sign of life other than the guttering candle; no sound except for the soft approach of many feet out in the street. It was dark in the long gallery. Some of the bomb-shattered windows along the streetside wall had been taped over with cardboard, deepening the darkness, but enough moonlight threaded through the remaining windows to create patterned patches of light along the lengthy corridor. Thick dust and chips of ceiling plaster layered the polished marble floor. There were no rugs, no wall hangings. What little furniture that remained had been shoved back against the walls and covered with canvas. The long Chancellery gallery, 480 feet from end to end, looked forlorn and disused.

Combat boots scraped up the outside steps, and the rest of the assault party poured into the vast gallery, instantly seeking concealment. Two groups kept moving. One, the OSS team assigned to search out the underground labyrinth that was the bunker, prowled quickly into the inner corridors to seek the stairwells leading downward. The other group headed through the building toward the Chancellery garden, carrying the gas canisters. The ventilation shaft would be at ground level, they had been told by aerial reconnaisance experts, covered with a wire grating. It would take only a matter of minutes to feed the knockout gas into the underground air system of the Führer-bunker.

As quickly and noisily as the gallery had filled, it was now silent and seemed to be empty. Longland knew his men were there, if he listened closely could even hear the subdued rustles as bodies shifted, the quiet ratchet of snaps as cloth pouches were tugged open and gas masks came sliding out. But the only human forms he could see were the three dead SS men, lying awkwardly at the base of the wall where they had fallen.

Crouching on the Chancellery floor, Longland waited an eternity as planes droned and flak pounded outside. Years passed. He grew old and died. The next moment he wrinkled his nose at the sharp smell of sweat. His own, or that of the silent agent lying prone beside him?

Then movement caught his eye, and the search team streamed silently back into the gallery from a porticoed doorway at the western end. The team leader was an American OSS lieutenant whom Longland knew slightly. Both bored, they had once left a party at the same time, then ended up making a night of it. Part of an early morning, too. They'd played *bocce* with two ancient Italian men, out at sunup and hoping wistfully for a game, before yawning off on their separate ways. What was the lieutenant's name? Moldvay? Longland saw that he looked excited. He waved him over quickly.

"I think we found it," Moldvay said. "There's a long hallway beyond that door, with a deep staircase at the end. We went down far enough to hear ventilators humming, then got the hell back up. I think I heard a couple of guards talking at the bottom."

"Good, good," Longland said. He would expect guards to be protecting the bunker passageways, but the gas would soon take care of them. "We'll follow you down as soon as the gas team reports back."

But the gas team was slow to appear. When it did return, its leader looked less than enthusiastic. Longland hurried to him. "Trouble?" he asked.

The SOE man shook his head. "Sorry. The damned

garden is like a battlefield. Nothing looked like the pictures they showed us."

"The ventilation shaft. Did you find it?"

"Oh, we found it. Finally. It was right there above us the whole time. They've put up a silo to protect it. The thing is ten feet tall. That's what took us so long."

Longland breathed easier. "But you did get the gas into the system?"

"Yes, sir. It should be taking effect just about now."

"Good. Mask up. We're going down."

They moved through the back corridors of the Chancellery, a long procession of crouching figures, faces obscured behind grotesque black rubber gas masks, following the leader of the search team. The stairwell, when they reached it, was narrow and deep, dimly lit by low-wattage bulbs. Boxes of canned provisions crowded each landing, forcing Longland and his men to string out in single file. The gray concrete walls were cold and damp, and the footing seemed treacherous.

As they neared the bottom, Longland heard quiet voices speaking in German. He touched Moldvay on the shoulder, but the search team leader had already heard the voices. They paused on the stairs above the last landing, and the long file of men closed in behind them, hugging the wall. Voices? There shouldn't be voices. Not anymore. The gas should have taken care of that. Something had obviously gone wrong, but what? The air system was working. They could hear its low buzzing whine in the background. But just as obviously someone was conscious on the landing below them.

Longland motioned for Granville to come forward. He held a finger to his gas mask, then pointed at his ear. Granville listened. His eyes, visible behind the celluloid eyepieces, widened.

Granville held up his Sten and gestured to that of Moldvay, the American search team leader, and asked silently with a jerk of his head for permission to precede the assault force to the landing. Longland hesitated, then nodded. The pair crept down the last five feet to the edge of the landing.

Longland held his breath as Granville and the American lieutenant swung into the open at the head of the landing, shoulder to shoulder. Someone below them spoke sharply; then Granville and the American opened up with the Stens, raking the bottom of the stairway. Even with the silencers, the popping Stens sounded loud in the narrow confines of the stairwell. Shell casings clattered against the walls and tinkled noisily down the steps. Thumps, like two sandbags falling, echoed upward.

Granville and the OSS man rushed on, disappearing around the corner and the long file of raiders hurried after them, filling the vacuum. When Longland reached the landing, he saw Granville and the American hunched over a pair of SS guards, shoving them out of the way of a huge steel door there at the foot of the stairs, cartons of canned goods stacked on both sides.

Granville looked up, waiting for a sign, one hand poised over the handle of the steel door, the other clutching his Sten. Longland leveled his own Sten and nodded. Granville wrenched the door open.

From his position on the landing, Longland could see the sight beyond: not the rooms they had expected to make up the Führerbunker, but one large drab concrete room that seemed to go on forever—an underground dormitory of some sort. Bunks lined sweating gray walls. On the bunks, in various stages of undress, lay muscular young members of the elite SS Hitler Guard. Sixty or seventy of them. One nearest the door, a stocky blond giant with a cleft in his chin, jerked upright, his bare legs swinging abruptly to the floor.

For a heartbeat, Granville and the young blond SS man stared at each other. Then, as the Germans scrambled for weapons, Granville ripped the gas mask from his face and shrieked, "It's the wrong bloody bunker!"

6

The machine gun was only in his mind, but Bascom wielded it expertly, drawing a bead on Sidney Longland's mid-section and opening him up the front, like a suit of long johns. Blood splattered in slow motion and Longland toppled forward, frame by frame, red hair standing on end, bad leg buckling, silly grin turning into a grimace of agony.

Someone leaned through the window of the abandoned Kübelwagen and said, "This one ready yet?"

Bascom, who was hunched awkwardly under the dash-board, jerked his head, thumping it against the steering column. He sat up, rubbing the tender spot. Through the window leaned Formoy, Longland's bearded SOE buddy.

"Almost," Bascom said. He indicated the tangle of ignition wires. "Damn things are all screwed up. Looks like someone tried to get it going before."

Formoy frowned in the darkness. They were on Voss-Strasse, about a hundred feet east of the Chancellery entrance, and the shadows were deep and eerie. "Best hurry it up," he said. "We've about milked this street dry."

"Any luck?" Bascom asked.

"Some. Most have been pranged in the raids, but I found a Mercedes about twenty feet back. I've put one of your OSS people, chap named Weston, on it. He's doing up the engine now."

"Where do we try next?"

"Back on Hermann Göring Strasse, I suppose. I've sent most of the team along to poke about. As soon as you and Weston finish, we'll off and join them."

Bascom ducked his head and fumbled for the ignition wires again. Silly, wasting his time daydreaming in the middle of the night in a place like this. Besides, he wouldn't shoot Longland. Bare hands. That was the thing. Get a good, solid grip on his throat and . . . The machine-gun fire rattled again, only this time it was different. Distant. Sporadic. Like hands clapping at the bottom of a well. The sound filtered into his consciousness and touched a chord of alarm.

"What the hell?" Formoy whispered.

He'd heard it, too? Bascom eased himself from beneath the cramped dashboard and peered up Voss-Strasse, toward the Chancellery entrance. It was growing louder. Someone was shouting. What the devil was it?

"Holy Mary!" Formoy gasped. He ducked down beside the small car.

Bascom blinked in amazement as members of the raiding team came pouring out of the Chancellery entrance, scattering in all directions. On their heels, firing Schmeisser machine pistols, came a whole flood of German SS men, some still in their underwear.

Almost without thinking, Bascom flung the car door open and rolled out beside Formoy. He pressed his face to the cobblestones, Formoy's breath gusting at his ear, and watched with one eye through the crook of his elbow.

The incredible vision unfolded through the cramped undercarriage of the Kübelwagen. Like droplets of water in a hot skillet, the emerging raiders fled, skittering back and forth in confusion, bumping into each other in the darkness, falling, rising, running. Several figures crumpled under a steady stream of fire from the Chancellery steps. Wounded were scooped up and helped, staggering, stumbling to the corner. A few of the raiders dropped to their knees and fired back, guns winking silently in the night, only to be cut down in seconds by the loud, unsilenced German weapons. A grenade lit up the street, and Bascom thought he saw Longland—a fleeting glimpse of a limping man hurrying along the side of the street, dragging a wounded comrade, Sten firing back wildly from the hip.

"Holy Mary," Formoy murmured again in Bascom's ear.

Some of the fleeing raiders made it to the corner of Hermann Göring Strasse and ran into the night. Others, acting on split-second impulses, made the mistake of turning up Voss-Strasse toward Bascom and Formoy, in the direction of Wilhelmstrasse, but it kept them in the German line of fire too long, and they all went down, one by one.

It was a burst of Schmeisser fire directed at one of these men that got Formoy. The slugs raked the running figure, then danced across the pavement, kicking up chunks of cobblestone. Bascom heard bullets tear into the Kübelwagen, and one of the tires blew. It wasn't until the wild burst stopped and the German SS man spun toward Hermann Göring Strasse that Bascom realized that Formoy had rolled over, clutching his eyes.

Bascom tried to pull the cocking handle of his Sten into firing position, but Formoy clawed at him, moaning. Bascom pushed his hand away. By the time he got the Sten primed to fire and swung it into position under the Kübelwagen, the street was empty, except for the bodies of assault team members, which sprawled in heaps in front of the Chancellery building. They lay in incredibly contorted positions, as if they had been flung from the sky. Others had escaped. The Germans had streamed after them, chasing into the darkness.

There was a soft, scraping sound behind him, and Bascom jerked around, aiming the Sten at the darkness. A gangly OSS man, white eyes and white teeth showing, threw his hands out and whispered, "Don't shoot. It's only me."

"Only me" was no one Bascom could recall, but he assumed it was the man Formoy had called Weston. Bascom dropped the Sten barrel and gestured for the OSS man to come ahead. The man did, crawling behind the Kübelwagen, next to Formoy.

"What happened?" the OSS man whispered. "What went wrong?"

Bascom had no answers. He rolled back to his belly and swung the Sten toward the Chancellery entrance. A pair of German stragglers, one barefoot and wearing a white undershirt, came down the steps and poked among the bodies, checking for signs of life. More gunfire erupted beyond the opening to Hermann Göring Strasse, two quick, loud bursts. Someone yelled in German, "There goes one!" The two stragglers hesitated, then pattered down the street to join the chase.

Bascom felt his breath gush out. He lowered the Sten, trembling uncontrollably. He waited until the tremors subsided before he sat up. The OSS man, eyes still wide, was probing Formoy's tunic.

"How is he?" Bascom whispered.

"I think he's hurt bad," the OSS man said. "What happened? How did he get hit?"

"I don't know. Ricochet, I guess. We'd better get him out of here." He glanced toward the Chancellery steps and the bodies littering the pavement, then said, "We'll go that way." He pointed in the opposite direction, toward Wilhelmstrasse.

"We oughtn't to get separated from the others," the OSS man said. "They'll all head for the Havel."

"We'll circle around once we get clear," Bascom said. He hooked the Sten over his shoulder and pushed to his feet.

Formoy was a hefty man, short and stockily built, but they managed to get him on his legs. Each looped an arm across a shoulder and they took off, half stumbling, half running, up the darkened street. Formoy helped at first, driving his thighs drunkenly in an effort to keep pace with them, but after the first bouncing strides, he objected, "Leave me alone for a minute. I'll catch up. Leave me alone." When they hauled him onward, he began to sob like a child. Bascom was relieved when Formoy seemed to pass out, head lolling on his chest, although he was a dead weight between them.

But they weren't able to circle back. They allowed their flight to be dictated by the sounds behind them. Even after they reached Wilhelmstrasse, gunfire rattled repeatedly from the westerly direction of the park—distant, sporadic bursts as the Germans tracked down scattered survivors. Nor could they circle to the north, not while the bombs and the ack-ack continued to thump away. So they let themselves be driven eastward and southward, turning at every intersection, getting farther and farther from the safety of the Havel.

They covered about a mile, dragging Formoy bodily.

Formoy regained consciousness once and tried to pull loose, but they held him until he sobbed piteously once more and his head dropped back to his chest. The OSS man moaned too, though Bascom couldn't tell whether it was from shock or sheer exhaustion.

Finally, when they reached Moritzplatz, an intersection that fell roughly between the inner Berlin districts of Mitte and Kreuzberg, Bascom called for a rest. They lowered Formoy to the pavement in front of a relatively undamaged apartment building, and sagged gratefully beside him, gasping for air.

The area, except for their oddly unscathed apartment building, had been heavily hit in recent raids, and the streets stretched out emptily before them. Storefronts long since boarded up. Street signs twisted and scorched. Maimed trees dangling ragged branches over water-filled bombholes.

"We've got to turn back," the OSS man said. "If we miss the boats, we've had it."

"I know," Bascom said. He laid his head back against the bricks of the apartment building and closed his eyes, trying to think. Odd. Though his life, all their lives, probably depended on it, he could barely persuade his brain to function. Subconsciously, he wanted nothing more than to dive into the nearest hole and pull the earth in over him, waiting for it all to go away.

"Oh hell!" the OSS man suddenly said. There was alarm, perhaps even pain, in his voice.

Bascom's eyes popped open. "What's wrong? What is it?"

"He's left a trail. Back there, the way we came. Look. He's bled all over the pavement."

Bascom wobbled wearily to his feet. A thin trail of dark red spots trickled up the street and around the corner, staining the concrete and cobbles.

The OSS man's shoulders sagged. "Now all they have to do is wait till daylight and they can track us easy," he said. "What's the use? We might as well give ourselves up."

"We've got to find something to stop the bleeding," Bascom said. He looked up at the apartment building behind them. "Come on, we'll try in here."

"He's going to die anyway," the OSS man said. "He's bound to die. Didn't you see his wounds?"

Bascom linked Formoy's arm around his neck and tugged him up. "Let's go," he insisted.

The OSS man rose even more slowly to his feet. "What if there are people?" he objected.

"They'll be in shelter," Bascom said. "Come on, take his other arm."

The entry hall was black, and the corridor beyond was even blacker. They stumbled to the first door, and Bascom knocked. No answer. He knocked again to make sure, then kicked the door in. It wasn't as dark in the apartment. Pale window squares along the far wall admitted gray moonlight. They wrestled Formoy across the threshold and lurched through the gloom, bumping against furniture, until Bascom felt the softness of a couch. The OSS man helped him ease Formoy down. Then the OSS man sagged beside the Britisher, sighing.

Bascom crossed to the windows and felt around until he located the black-out curtains. He tugged them shut, one by one, until the gray light disappeared, then struck a match and looked for the light switch. He flipped it, but nothing happened. Before the match died, he spotted a pair of candles, half burned, on a mantel. He struck another match and lit them.

It was a modest apartment, filled with dark, heavy furniture. A color lithograph of Adolf Hitler held the place of honor over the mantel, flanked by framed black-and-white family pictures. In addition to portraits of an older man with a Kaiser mustache and an elderly woman with soft eyes, there was a candid shot taken during a picnic. A young woman with "Gretchen" braids stood looking adoringly at an enlisted man wearing the gray field uniform of the German Wehrmacht.

Bascom carried both candlesticks to the couch and set one in front of the OSS man. "Look him over," he said, gesturing at Formoy. "I'll see if I can find any medicines."

He went off to prowl the apartment, cupping the flame of his own candle. He passed a kitchen, small and bare, off to the right, and entered the bedroom, a cramped rectangle dominated by an ancient four-poster and a heavy dresser with a cracked mirror. He put the candle down and looked through the dresser drawers. The apartment apparently belonged to the young woman with the braids atop her head, for the clothing, though well worn, was youthful, full of color. There was also a drawer filled with a man's work clothing, carefully folded and tucked away, as though awaiting the return of the wearer. Good. They could get out of these telltale uniforms and into something less noticeable for the cross-city trip.

He tried the bathroom next. There was a gravity-operated commode and a big porcelain tub on lion's-claw legs. No medicine chest on the wall, but a small wooden stand with drawers and folding doors down beside the sink. He bent over the chest and located antiseptic and a roll of gauze. He also found a half-filled bottle of aspirin—not much in the way of pain-killer, but better than nothing. He carried them back into the living room.

The OSS man was sitting quietly, eyes staring vacantly across the room, and his face looked gray in the candlelight. Still in shock? Or just bushed? Bascom's own body ached in every bone, and he was suddenly aware that he was extremely thirsty.

"We'll take off as soon as we get Formoy patched up," he told the OSS man, trying to sound confident. "See if you can stop the bleeding. When you're done, come on back to the bedroom. I found some men's clothing back there. We'll have to get Formoy out of that silly damned uniform, too."

The OSS man sighed quietly. "It won't matter. He'll be dead soon."

Bascom frowned at the man and returned to the bedroom. He picked out a pair of wool trousers and a gray work shirt for himself and changed, then added a black sweater and looked into the cracked mirror. He still didn't look very European. He rummaged through the drawer again and found a cloth cap. He pulled it low over his eyes and looked in the mirror again. Better.

It might be a long, slow trip to the Havel, so he pulled a pillowslip off one of the big downy pillows, thinking it might make a handy carry-all for the first-aid supplies, just in case Formoy's wounds opened up again. He considered his Sten briefly. He wanted to take it, but a British weapon would be as bad as the uniforms when it came to being spotted, so he broke it down into four parts—body, barrel unit, stock, and magazine—and stuffed it under the four-poster bed.

Next he unsnapped the emergency survival packet from his discarded uniform belt and opened it, just to see what might be useful. The British had provided a wad of German Reichsmarks, enough to last for two or three days, and a handful of gold coins worth about a hundred dollars. He tied the gold coins in his handkerchief and slipped the money into his pocket. There was also a forged identity card stating that he was a French laborer named Henri Cadiot, assigned to the Krupp und Druckenmüller tank factory at the edge of Tempelhof. The forgery job was much neater than the one the OSS had done for him only a few days earlier. Foreign identity papers could help explain his accented German if anybody stopped them, providing it was someone who couldn't tell the difference between a French or American accent. He wished the British had checked with him before making the card out to a Frenchman. In spite of what his dossier said, his French was lousy. He added it to the money, anyway.

Finally, wrapped in cellophane, was the ubiquitous "L" tablet, just in case he was captured. He started to pocket it, then hesitated. Why bother? There was no way he could ever bring himself to bite into the damned thing, no matter how rough it got. He wasn't the type. If the Germans caught him and decided to torture him, they'd just have to torture away. He carried it into the bathroom and dropped it in the commode.

The OSS man still hadn't come to the bedroom to change, so Bascom grabbed up extra bits of clothing for both him and Formoy and carried them, along with the pillowcase, out to the front room. Formoy was breathing shallowly, his wounds still untended, blood still seeping through his tunic. The gauze and antiseptic lay untouched on the floor. The OSS man, head back against the couch cushions, hadn't moved an inch. His eyes were closed.

Bascom felt momentary anger. "Dammit, get with it," he growled. "We've got no time for resting."

The OSS man didn't stir. Bascom blinked foolishly and leaned over for a closer look. The man's teeth were set in a possumlike grin. He wasn't breathing.

Bascom made a noise of wordless pain. He tried the man's pulse, but there was nothing, nothing. What could have happened? Frantically, as though there were a life that could still be saved, he tore open the man's shirtfront, seeking signs of a wound. Again, nothing. He shifted the OSS man forward.

Then he saw it. A gaping hole in the flesh of the man's lower back. Bits of bone and tissue adhered to the ragged edges of his uniform blouse. There was surprisingly little blood.

"Oh my God," Bascom whispered. "Why didn't you tell me? Why didn't you say something?"

He sat quietly for a moment, trying to get command of himself. What to do? Even if he abandoned the OSS man's body here, in the apartment, he'd never be able to get Formoy all the way to the pickup point. Not by himself. The man was too heavy.

Should he leave Formoy, too? The most he might manage otherwise would be to get Formoy on the street and keep moving until he found a hiding place among the ruins. And what good would that do either of them? After all, the bearded Britisher was bound to die. The poor damned OSS man had said it himself. Formoy would die, and if Bascom wasted time waiting for it to happen, he would lose his chance at the Havel, his chance to link up with the others and get out of here. There would be nothing left; nothing but sitting in the darkness and waiting for the end to come. Formoy would die, and he would likely die as well.

But even as he considered it, he knew he would never

be able to go off and leave Formoy while the man was still breathing. The act was taboo. He'd never to able to live with it. He would always wonder.

He set his teeth and moved a gate-legged table close to Formoy to hold the candle, the gauze, and the antiseptic. The heavy bleeding seemed to be around the left shoulder, but as Bascom tugged at buttons with shaking fingers, he found another wound in the left side of Formoy's neck, one near the navel, one in the right arm, and the legs—my God, my God, there were wounds everywhere.

He stopped looking and slumped back, shaking his head helplessly. He stared at a tongue of wallpaper hanging loosely from the far wall, and tried to block out recurring images of the Havel, of escape, of safety beyond the Elbe. Then, with a deep, rending sigh, he began to work on Formoy's shoulder.

4

Saturday—April 21, 1945

Alle Halbheit ist taub.

"Half measures are no measures."

—German saying

1

The first gray tendrils of dawn stained the black wall of
sky behind them. Longland turned dull eyes and watched
the other two boats struggling to keep up. Oars dipped with
gurgling irregularity. Blank, dazed faces took shape in the
early gloom, riding silently above the low profile of the
inflated rubber dinghies. The sun would soon appear. Another ten or fifteen minutes and they would have to get off
the water and take refuge in the trees.

He looked away from the slackly hung jaws, the unsee-
ing eyes, the hunched shoulders. They seemed so thoroughly beaten. No one spoke. Those who could, helped with
the oars. Others, wounded, exhausted, one or two perhaps
even dead by now, huddled together in the centers.

A disaster. There was no other word for it. Longland
had managed to make it to the Havel staging point with
the truck and the injured from the glider landings, along
with a half dozen survivors from the Chancellery raid. They
had waited as long as they could. Another four made it on
foot. Then six, two of them severely wounded. They had
stalled another hour, hoping more stragglers would come
in, but none had. They left two of the boats sitting on the
shore near the Pichelsdorf Bridge, just in case, before
shoving off for the long, dangerous trip down through the
southwestern extremity of Berlin, with the suburbs of
Gatow and Kladow crowding the banks on one side, and
the wooded parklands of Grunewald and Wannsee on the
other.

Nothing had worked. Not even the escape route. Not the way it was supposed to. The city was wide open, they had been told. German troops had all been rushed to the East to face the Russians. Yet the last couple of miles before they reached the Pichelsdorf had been crawling with uniforms. True, the troops manning roadblocks along the Kaiserdamm were mainly kids from the Hitler Youth and oldtimers in Home Guard outfits, and the roadblocks faced outward, not inward, as though they knew nothing about what had happened in the center of the city behind them, but their very presence had forced Longland's small band of survivors to detour through winding streets and put them far behind schedule.

Then, after waiting and waiting, hoping others might make it, they had started down the Havel only to find more signs of military activity where none should have existed. Figures, dimly seen, patrolling the west bank near Gatow, probably guarding Gatow airfield. A full garrison occupying Potsdam. Guard dogs barking in the night from the shore. Thank God for the heavy smoke that all but obscured the moon. They might never have sneaked past otherwise.

A wounded SOE man coughed in the gray darkness beside Longland—a wet, tearing sound. Lung-shot, probably. He would need medical attention as soon as they could find a quiet place to take cover. It would help if they could reach the airlift sector, get the wounded out, but there was no chance of that. Not any more. They were too far behind schedule. Even if they had been close enough, Longland's two radio men were among the missing. Without them, there was no way to contact the planes, no way to summon them down.

No, they had no choice. The only thing left was to take cover before the streaking sky gave them away. They would rest through the day, tend their wounded, bury their dead, gather their strength. Perhaps he might leave someone here, near the river, just in case one or both of the other two boats came tagging along. At least for an hour or so. Then tonight, when it was dark enough and safe enough

to travel, they could start the difficult trek westward, toward
the Elbe.

Unless the Germans found them first.

2

Heinrich Himmler, finally back in his suite of rooms at the
Hohenlychen sanatorium after a long day and night of
motoring to and fro in the countryside, paused by a mirror
to examine his eyes, his tongue, the pallor of his face. He
didn't look at all well. So much gone wrong these days,
and now illness on top of everything else?

So much pressure, never letting up. Incessant appointments through most of yesterday and last night. His nerves
were worn thin. First he'd been forced to leave the safety
of Hohenlychen once more and drive to Berlin in order to
extend his best wishes to the Führer on his fifty-sixth birthday. It hadn't been a lively celebration. More like a funeral.
All the long faces, the low voices, murmurs and inquiries
about the progress of the Russians. And the Führer in that
ghastly concrete bunker, left arm hanging limply at his
side, eyes vacant, still trying to convince all his well-wishers
that the Russians would shortly absorb their most humiliating defeat at the gates of Berlin.

Then, with his duty call to the Führer out of the way, it
was back to the torn roads and the ever-present danger of
strafing by RAF Mosquitos and American Mustangs just
to keep his promised appointment with that Jew from the
World Jewish Congress. God, what a nightmare. The ob-
stinate fool. Himmler had graciously offered to evacuate a
hundred Jewish women to Switzerland, just as Schellenberg
had suggested, but the fool had wanted to bargain, so typical of his merchant-minded race, insisting on thousands,
not hundreds, of evacuees. The Jew didn't seem to recognize the temper of the times. To give in to his demands
might well cost Himmler his life. The Führer would be
furious if he found out about it.

On top of everything else, he'd been forced to undergo

another tiring session with that busybody Swedish count, Folke Bernadotte. Himmler hadn't wanted to talk to Bernadotte again this soon, at least not until he heard the result of last night's meeting between Fegelein and the Allied negotiator, but Schellenberg had insisted. Apparently the count had called yesterday from the Swedish legation in Berlin and said he would be in the area only another twenty-four hours. So after that grim celebration at the bunker and the wasted hours with the argumentative Jew at Gut Harzwalde, he had been forced to undergo, until just thirty minutes ago, another prolonged and useless diatribe from the suave Swedish count at Hohenlychen. No one seemed to mind that it had left him no time to sleep.

A soft knock sounded at the door, and he moved peevishly to answer it. A man named Reinhelm, one of Dr. Gebhardt's assistants, stood in the corridor, a ridiculous, fawning smile on his face. Himmler detested the man. He always seemed on the verge of flinging himself at one's feet.

"I've come to escort you downstairs," the man said. "Dr. Gebhardt and Brigadeführer Schellenberg were just about to sit down to breakfast, and they thought you might wish to join them."

Himmler fixed the man with cold eyes. "I will decide without your help when I am ready to take breakfast," he said. "I'm tired, and I must rest."

Reinhelm blanched. "Of course, Herr Reichsführer. I didn't mean to be presumptuous. They felt only that you would wish to know."

Himmler nodded wearily. No point in spoiling the man's entire day. He considered going on to the dining room and taking a few bites, along with twenty or thirty minutes of polite conversation. It wouldn't delay his rest so very much. But not immediately. His stomach had been sour for hours. Perhaps if he took something for it, settled his nerves a bit, he would make better company.

"Yes, all right," he said. "Inform Dr. Gebhardt and the Brigadeführer that I will be down in a few minutes. Ask Dr. Gebhardt to come to my rooms first, if he has the time to spare." That would be best. Gebhardt could prepare one of his effective medicinal concoctions for Himmler's seemingly chronic stomach condition.

When Reinhelm was gone, Himmler turned back to the mirror. The flesh below his eyes was puffy. He touched it gingerly with a finger, then opened his mouth and turned his head to let the light fall into his throat. It looked red and raw. Was he coming down with a cold?

He hurried into the bathroom to gargle, wondering miserably what would go wrong next. Everywhere he turned, people picked at him. Couldn't they understand that others made the rules, and that as a loyal soldier, he had no choice but to obey? Surely no state could survive without strict obedience and discipline. Posterity would probably overlook his loyalty and heap blame on him for things done by others.

His medicine cabinet, stuffed with bottles and pills and green and brown liquids, yawned widely at him as he reached for a mouthwash and poured an inch into the bottom of a glass. His private telephone began to ring in the front room of the suite, but he ignored it. Let them answer it downstairs. It could only be more bad news, another minor crisis at Gestapo headquarters in Berlin or a problem of signatures on some unimportant document. Amazing. The country trembled on the precipice of disaster, yet the paperwork went on as though nothing had changed.

He gargled twice, then chose an assortment of pills, a pair for an incipient headache, one for liver bile, another for blood pressure, a last for excess uric acid content. He took them one at a time, washing them down with delicate sips from his mouthwash glass, hesitating between pills to study his pale complexion in the bathroom mirror.

He was considering a cold compress when someone rapped at his door. That ass Reinhelm again? No, this was a more authoritative knock. Probably Gebhardt. Good. And about time, too. His stomach felt as though it contained a family of frightened birds, pecking and fluttering to get out.

But it was Schellenberg, not Gebhardt. Himmler looked at him woefully. "I said I'd be down shortly," he complained. "Can't you give me even a moment's peace?"

"My apologies, Reichsführer," Schellenberg said, "but there is a phone call for you. I thought you might wish to take it up here."

"I'm not interested."

"It's from the Chancellery," Schellenberg said. "They've been trying to reach you since midnight, but apparently there was some trouble with the phone lines. It's just now been repaired."

"The Chancellery?" Himmler said. His pale face turned even paler. "Is it . . . ?"

"No, it isn't the Führer," Schellenberg said. "It's General Fegelein. He says it's urgent."

Himmler considered the options. An urgent call? From Fegelein? Perhaps it was good news for a change. Perhaps the Allies had finally consented to the meeting between himself and General Eisenhower. But was he ready for such an eventuality? Once committed to meet with Eisenhower, there would be no turning back.

He said, "Yes, thank you, Walter. I'll take the call." He stepped to the telephone, then paused, waiting for Schellenberg to depart. But Schellenberg, possibly curious to know why Fegelein was calling at such an early hour, made no move to leave. Himmler thought briefly of dismissing him, then decided that might make him suspicious, perhaps even suspicious enough to go downstairs and listen in on the other line. He lifted the phone and said cheerfully, "Yes, Hermann? What is it?"

Fegelein's voice said, "Herr Reichsführer, are you alone?" The tone was wrong. Hollow. Even frightened.

"Not exactly," Himmler said. "But it doesn't matter. Have you news for me?"

"Yes," Fegelein's voice said tremulously. "Bad news."

Himmler closed his eyes briefly, but kept smiling for Schellenberg's benefit. "The men didn't come?"

"Oh, they came," Fegelein said. "How they came."

"I don't understand," Himmler said. "Are you telling me the response was negative?"

"I . . . I must assume so," Fegelein said. "I was a bit late for the meeting. There was an air raid. I thought . . . I felt it would make no difference if I waited a few minutes, just until the attack slackened. But they came anyway. A whole army of them."

They? An army? Himmler frowned impatiently. What was the man talking about? "They came where?" he asked.

"To the Chancellery, Reichsführer. An entire army. They stormed in just before midnight. I think they were after the Führer."

He sounded terrified, making no sense whatever. "Get a grip on yourself," Himmler said. "What are you trying to say?"

"There were so many of them. Gliders in the Tiergarten, near where I was to meet them. They came directly to the Chancellery and forced their way in. They had gas masks and some kind of sleeping gas. They fed it into the ventilating system. The Führer, his staff, everyone in the main bunker, passed out."

Himmler felt the blood draining from his face. He turned his back to Schellenberg and gripped the phone tightly. "Did they . . . did they get him?"

"No. They made a mistake. They broke into one of the guard bunkers by accident. I don't know how it happened. But they were driven off. It was practically a slaughter."

Himmler was silent for a moment, trying to marshal his thoughts. "What is the situation now?" he asked.

"Desperate," Fegelein said. "Most of them were killed, I think, but some managed to slip away in the darkness. A detachment of Chancellery guards is out searching for survivors now. If they take prisoners and it gets out that we—"

"Where are you calling from?" Himmler interrupted. By his own order, Gestapo personnel were monitoring telephone calls from Berlin on a spot-check basis. If someone chanced to be listening in while Fegelein raved, their lives would quickly be forfeit.

"It's all right," Fegelein said quickly. "I'm on the direct line. I . . . I think we can speak freely."

"Then the solution seems obvious," Himmler said. "If the . . . experiment . . . was a failure, and most of the perpetrators are dead, it would appear that the matter has taken care of itself. As an SS officer, you have the authority to instruct Chancellery guard units to shoot all survivors on sight."

"It may be too late for that," Fegelein said. "There were wounded at the scene. At least one of them appears to be an officer. If he lives long enough to be interrogated, he may mention names."

Himmler chewed nervously at the tip of his thumb. "Who would do the questioning?" he asked.

"I don't know," Fegelein said.

"Find out," Himmler said. "If it's one of our SS people, I'll call and sound him out."

"No, Reichsführer, you can't do that. No one but the guards and the Führer's personal staff know about it. Secretary Bormann has ordered all traces of the attackers removed and the gliders burned. He says it is to avoid a public panic, but I fear his motives may be more complicated. He may even suspect collusion. If you call, they will wonder how you learned of it."

"I see," Himmler said. "Very well, then you must handle it. I suggest you find out where any possible interrogations might take place, and arrange to be there."

"But . . . but Herr Reichsführer, what excuse can I give? I'm not normally present when such things occur."

"I'm sure you'll think of something," Himmler said tightly. "We must know what is said. A great deal may depend on it. One might even call it . . ." He glanced over his shoulder at Schellenberg. "One might even call it a matter of life and death."

There was a moment of wretched silence, then a shaky, "Yes, Herr Reichsführer. I will see to it."

For Schellenberg's benefit, Himmler lightened his tone and said, "Thank you for calling, Hermann. Let me hear from you again if anything comes up."

He cradled the telephone and stared at it for a moment, lips tightly compressed. An attack on the Chancellery? God in heaven, he'd never intended anything like that. Had the Allies misunderstood his proposal? Or was that their way of expressing their rejection?

"Trouble?" Schellenberg asked.

Himmler forced a smile and shook his head. "Oh no. Just a small problem with one of the new experimental weapons. It, ah, blew up during a test and killed a number of technicians. The Führer suspects sabotage. They may have to interrogate some of the scientists."

"What has that to do with the SS?"

"Well, the Führer thinks we may have been lax in preparing background dossiers. You know how he is these days."

"Yes, suspicious of everything," Schellenberg said. "Practically paranoid. Shall I look into it?"

"Oh no," Himmler said quickly. "Do nothing. It's supposed to be very hush-hush, according to Gruppenführer Fegelein. We don't want anyone wondering how you heard about it. Someone might get curious and ask questions and find out about our recently departed Swedish visitor."

"Yes, of course," Schellenberg said smoothly. "I understand."

Did he? Himmler stared at him briefly, then he buttoned his tunic collar and said, with forced cheer, "Let's go on down now and see what is being offered for breakfast."

As soon as they reached the stairs, Himmler moved ahead and allowed his facial muscles to sag. An attack by glider? Right in the heart of Berlin? And only hours after he had left the bunker himself? God, what arrogance. What if the prisoners said something, implicated him? What could he do?

His stomach, already sour and jittery, was seized with sudden cramps. He pressed his hand to it and said, "Walter, I've been thinking. Perhaps you are right about Bernadotte. Perhaps I have been too cautious. I think it is time we had a serious talk with him about seeking an honorable peace."

Schellenberg, apparently surprised by Himmler's abrupt about-face, nevertheless pressed his advantage quickly. "Excellent, Herr Reichsführer. He is scheduled to be in Lübeck day after tomorrow. I will call him there and make arrangements."

Himmler nodded. He kept his hand on his stomach and walked down the stairs, two steps ahead of Schellenberg, hiding his pain, hiding his fear.

3

Sirens wailed like tormented souls. Bascom felt his neck hairs stand on end, and for an instant he looked wildly around the musty coal bin he had chosen as a refuge for himself and Formoy. Then understanding flooded in: an air-raid warning, most likely. American bombers coming in from the west to take over where the British had left off last night.

The thought was warming. Curious to see the raid form, Bascom crept up the cellar stairs and moved cautiously toward the front wall. Or what had once been a front wall. The ground floor of this building looked as though someone had taken a wrecking ball to it. No signs of fire: just a great gaping hole where the front wall had been, and a spill of bricks leading down to the pavement. Possibly he could have found a sturdier place, but with the adrenaline pumping and the Germans scouring the city for them last night, all he'd thought was to hide. Get to cover. Drag Formoy from block to block, seeking a building too battered to harbor full-time inhabitants, yet sound enough that it wouldn't topple on them at the slightest vibration.

Most of the rooms on the ground floor had been hastily cleaned out, presumably by the previous owners before they moved on, though it was possible that scavengers had done it. There was a hallway leading to mangled rooms in the rear, some clobbered furniture that hadn't been worth salvaging, and a dark stairway that snaked upward, but beams and bomb debris had fallen from the upper floors to block it, and Bascom hadn't yet had time to see if he could force his way through the mess.

He dropped to his hands and knees as he approached the breached wall and crawled past a smashed piano. A piece of sheet music, warped and water-stained from exposure to the elements, lay pinned beneath a smashed light fixture. Its title was *"Wenn ein junger Mann kommt."* He shook it loose and stared at it. Fleeting visions of the former occupants drifted through his imagination, family gathered around the piano, warm glow from the fireplace, laughter and song. Well, a pair of young men had come, but from the wrong army. He wondered how the family would have reacted had they known their walls now sheltered two enemy soldiers. With righteous wrath, no doubt. The bombers had given them no reason to think kindly of British or Americans.

He tossed the sheet music aside and crawled closer to the street. The sun was about midmorning high, shimmering through patches of clouds with a sickly yellow glow. A curtain of smoke from the fires of last night's raid hung above the buildings, sifting the light. The pavement was about six feet below the jagged edge of the wall, but by stretching his neck, he could see the slow and anxious movements of a few people on the street, civilians, the first he had seen since tumbling out of the jump plane almost twelve hours earlier. Women bundled in threadbare coats, carrying empty shopping baskets. A frail old man, picking through the wreckage of a house across the way, as though hunting some cherished possession. A soldier at the far corner, eyes scanning the sky. Fifty yards to the south, in front of a plank-boarded butcher shop, a line of women fidgeted, waiting for the door to open. From time to time, their chins jerked skyward, like the soldier, but they held their ground, determined not to give up their places in the line.

Bascom pressed his cheek against cool stone and frowned in confusion. He'd liked Berliners, and even now it was hard to think of them as the enemy. He thought he knew Germans, understood them. And yet there had been ugly rumors of death camps and wholesale extermination spread across the German landscape. Only ten days ago the rumors had become substantiated fact when the British liberated a place called Belsen, and the facts had been compounded four days later, when American troops reached a camp called Buchenwald. The savagery they had uncovered was still almost beyond belief. There were pictures and outraged stories in the London papers, but they told only part of the story. Bascom had seen some of the photographs judged too graphic for public print, and had been so sickened that he'd understood General Patton's reported reaction when inspecting Buchenwald: He'd thrown up. God only knew what other horrors would be uncovered before it was over. Could those people down on the street be a part of such a thing? Could they allow it?

Next to the butcher shop, a little girl sat in a doorway, the picture of innocence, which she surely was. A skinny cat with spiky fur nestled on the stoop beside her. She stroked it with one hand, while with the other she poked bits of something into her mouth. A muffin or a cookie, it looked like. He was too far away to be sure, but his imagination filled in the details, made it a blueberry muffin, made it good. He watched greedily until the last muffin morsel disappeared into the little girl's mouth, then swallowed. He realized with sudden longing that he was damned hungry. Why hadn't he thought to raid the larder back at that apartment last night, instead of just contenting himself with a few futile medical supplies? It might be a long time between meals, unless he could find a food source for Formoy and himself.

He was suddenly aware that the sirens had stopped, and he glanced upward, wondering why. An ominous line of gray storm clouds had formed to the north and appeared to be coming this way. There would probably be a cold, driving rain within the hour. He could almost smell it on the wind. Maybe the city would weather in and the planes wouldn't come. Was that it? Had the planes turned back? But then, like a finely regulated drumroll of thunder, came the distant hammering of flak as guns opened up on the northwestern fringes of the city.

The women down by the butcher shop heard the hammering as well, and grew more restless. They stood stolidly, but chins rose apprehensively skyward more often. More flak, nearer to the center of the city, joined in. One of the women pointed across the rooftops to the north. Bascom craned his neck, wanting to see. High above the hanging veil of smoke, sparkling like hundreds of silver pellets, flight after flight of tightly formed B-17s rumbled in to begin the 363rd aerial raid on Berlin. One part of the sky was already full of them, high and steady, drifting across the city. Long, slender contrails, like white fingernail scratches across patches of cold blue, stretched out behind them, visible through breaks in the gathering clouds. Black flak puffs opened up soundlessly below and around them, pimpling the sky with shrapnel.

It was an incredibly beautiful sight, and Bascom smiled, feeling good for the first time in hours. Then he heard a series of discordant whistles, the shriek of wind through tail vanes, as countless bombs cut through the air and tumbled downward. He froze, the half smile still on his face, and realized with sudden terror that he was somewhere near the bombing pattern. The shrieks increased in volume, louder, louder. He buried his face in his arms, expecting to be blasted to bits at any moment.

The explosions, when they came, were at least a half a mile away, but his bombed-out building shook beneath him, and the sound battered his eardrums. Nor did it stop. The bombs marched across the horizon, ripping through buildings, tearing up streets, sending columns of smoke and flame shooting into the sky. The first wave of planes droned past, only to be followed by another, with more discordant shrieks wailing toward the ground, more thundering explosions.

When Bascom raised his head, gasping, he expected the street to be empty, the people scattered at the first explosion. Some had. The old man was gone. The soldier had disappeared, too. But not the women. Life had to go on;

their families had to be fed. Most of them held firmly to the line in front of the butcher shop, thinking beefsteak and pig's feet, not war. At least one had come prepared. The fourth woman in line slipped a water pail over her head, a kind of ersatz helmet, and stood with arms folded, waiting for the butcher to open his doors.

Bascom couldn't take it. At the first lull, he ducked away from the torn front wall and retreated down the cellar steps. The cellar was extensive, and he didn't feel remotely safe until he reached the stale, dust-moted coal bin. Even then, he sat cringing in a corner, feeling every shock wave as the bombs continued to fall. He thought of the storm clouds and prayed for them to move in, to close over the city and shut off the attack.

Formoy moaned, perhaps disturbed by the shaking floor, and Bascom grabbed at the distraction. He crawled over to the Britisher, thinking at first that he was unconscious, but then Formoy's foot twitched and his eyelids fluttered half open. Pupils moved. Last night, Formoy's eyes had been flecked with what looked like red brick dust, but today they looked clear, though glazed and unperceiving. Bascom suppressed a groan of his own. It had been like this most of the night. Formoy drifting between insensibility and semiconsciousness, never speaking, never seeming to gain ground. At least he seemed no worse. The bandages were mostly dry, so the bleeding hadn't started again. Tough bastard. He obstinately refused to die.

A treacherous thought bubbled up in Bascom's brain: Hurry up. Hurry up, man who is but a stranger to me, and die. Then as quickly, Bascom rejected the idea. He was shocked at himself. In an effort to make amends, he tried to think: Was there anything he could do for Formoy? Maybe somewhere in the city, if he puzzled over it hard enough, would be an old friend, someone from the old days, someone he could trust to find medical help. Not too likely, of course. Things had changed. People had changed. He was now the enemy. Even if he was lucky enough to track down some acquaintance, any good German would almost certainly turn him over to the authorities.

Formoy's wandering eyes closed. Bascom crawled back to his own corner. He didn't want to feel sorry for himself. There was no percentage in it. But he couldn't help it. He felt so damned helpless against Formoy's pain and jeopardy. If only he'd made a different decision last night. Probably he should have left Formoy in the open somewhere, out in plain sight where the Germans could find him and give him expert medical care. It would be his fault if Formoy died.

He stayed like that, curled in his corner, for almost an hour, until the bombs stopped. Finally, gratefully, out of the silence, he heard the raindrops begin to fall.

4

While two German enlisted men held the prisoner, a third unstoppered a bottle of nitric acid with a rubber-gloved hand and held it out at arm's length, nose wrinkling at the fumes, and let the colorless liquid fall, drop by drop, like raindrops, on the American lieutenant's bare leg. The acid splattered against the skin and bubbled, and the leg twitched. The American wrenched his body, trying to thrash loose. A deep, muffled scream welled up from his chest and flooded past the gag stuffed in his mouth. Several of the German clerks stopped typing and glowered at SS Hauptstürmführer Franz Schedle in silent protest.

Schedle, a blond young officer with a cleft in his chin, pointedly turned his back on the clerks and said, "Again. The other leg."

All three enlisted men turned their heads and gulped for air; then the one with the bottle tilted it once more and dribbled drops on the prisoner's left thigh. Again the skin blistered brightly and burned. Again the unclothed body wrenched. Again the throat swelled with a long, stifled scream.

Schedle waited until the scream subsided to a series of choked moans, then said, "That's enough. Remove the gag."

They were in a cramped underground corridor some fifteen feet below the southern edge of the ruined Chancellery garden, surrounded by desks and filing cabinets which, because of the extensive bomb damage done to overhead Chancellery facilities, had been carted underground months earlier and squeezed into the crowded bunker passageways. Most of the uniformed clerks and typists had stayed at their desks, creating unnecessary distractions with their clattering machines and continuous movements along the hall, and Schedle resented it. As captain of the elite SS bunker guard, he knew the clerks had duties to perform, and duty was not a word that Schedle took lightly. Still, he would have preferred privacy for the interrogation sessions. He took an almost perverse satisfaction in the growing discomfiture of the clerks to the muted screams, the choking fumes of the corrosive nitric acid, the smell of disintegrating flesh. Next time they would know better and would move on.

The prisoner, held down on a wooden office chair near a sweating concrete wall, moaned through puffy lips as the gag was removed. His chin dropped feebly to his chest. Tears, whether from pain or from the fumes rising from his blistered bare legs, rolled freely down his cheeks.

Schedle put a finger under the American's chin and raised his head until they were looking into each other's eyes. How much longer could the man last? Not only had his wounds of last night been left untreated, but he also bore a rash of red welts about the face and shoulders and rib cage where he had been beaten before being subjected to the acid treatment. He would probably die soon, and the prospect bothered Schedle. Not because he felt sorry for the man. He didn't. After all, seven of his own SS troopers had been brutally murdered last night by savage British and American commandos before the alarm was given. Nevertheless, he hated to lose an interrogation subject, even when the fault was not his own. Someone should have given at least superficial treatment to the more severe wounds before sending the man down to the corridor.

"I will ask you again," Schedle said. "Where were you to take him?"

"Please. I told. You. I. Don't know," the American said. His mouth was swollen, and several teeth were missing. It was hard to understand his words, though they came slowly.

"We can continue the treatment with the acid," Schedle said. "Would you prefer that?"

"No," the prisoner said. "No. Please. No. More."

"Then answer my question."

The man had difficulty breathing, and his words and phrases came in jerks and starts, with long pauses between each. Schedle had to listen closely to catch what he was saying. "I told. You. Field. There. Were to. Be planes. I don't. Know. Where. I. Hurt. Doctor? Please?"

"When you have told me everything I want to know," Schedle said. "Where did the others go? We know some got away. Did they go to meet these planes?"

"I. Don't. Know. I. Swear. Things went. Crazy. When we. Hit. The wrong. Bunker."

"What about the German you say was to help you? Was he to leave on these planes as well?"

"I. Don't know. I was only. Added at. The. Last minute. I. Did what. I. Was told."

"Why now?" Schedle said. "Why did you come at this particular time? Was there a special reason? Are the Anglo-Americans planning to join the Russian assault on Berlin?"

The prisoner's head sagged again. Schedle nodded, and one of the enlisted men slammed a bar against the American's bicep. The man's head snapped to the side, and he cried out.

"I ask again," Schedle said. "Why now? Why did you come?"

"We. Heard. Hitler. Might not. Be. In Berlin. Much. Longer. We. Had to. Come. Now."

Schedle frowned. "Are you certain? Is that all? Are you sure the Anglo-Americans don't plan to attack across the . . ."

Schedle's three assistants suddenly snapped to attention.

Behind him, the clerks all stopped working at once and jumped up from their desks. A hush filled the corridor. Schedle glanced at his rigid guards, annoyed at the interruption, then twisted around to see what had caused it. Coming down the hallway at a rapid clip, hands clasped behind their backs, were two men in crisp uniforms. The first was slope-shouldered Deputy Party Leader Martin Bormann, wearing brown with gold trim. A step behind him, outfitted in a gray dress uniform and wearing the Knight's Cross with Swords at his neck, strode Gestapo chief Heinrich Müller, a thin-chested officer with a tight, expressionless slash where his mouth should be.

Schedle jumped to his feet and sucked in his stomach. He stood at attention until the two men reached him, then snapped a stiff-armed salute. Bormann returned it limply and murmured, "You may relax, Captain."

Schedle immediately spread his legs to a parade rest, but his muscles trembled alertly. Reichsleiter Bormann looked more like an aging athlete gone to pot than the second most powerful man in all of Germany, but his presence commanded complete concentration.

"You have managed to make him speak?" Bormann asked curiously.

"Yes, sir," Schedle said.

"That's good," Bormann said. "We caught three more of them this morning, hiding in a field near the Olympic Stadium."

"Shall I question them as well, Herr Reichsleiter?"

"That won't be necessary," Bormann said. "They were only enlisted men. I had them shot."

Schedle blinked, but said nothing.

Bormann and Müller studied the prisoner briefly and exchanged whispers, then Müller turned to Schedle and said, "Would you please tell us what you have learned so far, Captain?"

"Not a great deal," Schedle admitted. "This is the only one who has told us anything beyond name, rank, and serial number. The others refused to say anything at all. And this one, I fear, is none too well informed. He seems to have some basic knowledge, most of which we have managed to extract, but on specifics he is quite weak. I assume only a few of the commando leaders were thoroughly informed."

Müller frowned. "Perhaps he knows more than he is telling."

Schedle hesitated. He didn't want to contradict the man who was chief of all the Gestapo, but he felt he should give both men the clearest picture possible. He said carefully, "I don't think so, sir," then paused, watching Müller's face for signs of displeasure. There were none, or at least none that he could see. Encouraged, he went on. "This man was one of the first officers we took, down in the stairwell. He is severely wounded, as you can see, and he is still in a state of shock. I don't think he is capable of lying, at least not convincingly. He tried to bluff his way at first, claiming he was merely a member of a bombing crew shot down in last night's air raid. He said they were all seeking shelter and simply had the misfortune to choose the wrong building."

"Ridiculous," Bormann murmured.

"My point exactly, Herr Reichsleiter," Schedle quickly agreed. "He's in no state to create an acceptable lie. There were at least fifty men with him on the stairs. It would take a sizable bomber to carry such a crew." He smiled wryly, but neither Bormann nor Müller appeared to share his amusement. He straightened his face and went on rapidly. "We managed to break him without much difficulty. This one reacts more favorably to pain than the others. We were not gentle with any of them."

"Has he admitted that they were here to assassinate the Führer?" the Gestapo chief asked.

"It appears to be more complex than that," Schedle said. "They were apparently instructed to take captives."

Müller cocked his head. "To what purpose?" he asked.

"They intended to spirit as many high-level people as possible out of the city and make their way back to Allied lines," Schedle said. "Conceivably with the aid of waiting planes. The prisoner hasn't been too clear on that yet."

He paused and looked at Bormann. "Herr Reichsleiter, there is something of note that I should tell you. According to this prisoner, the commandos apparently expected help from someone here in Berlin. A German general, it would seem."

Bormann looked up alertly. "A general? Has he said who it was?"

"No, sir. I don't think he knows. The general, if there was one, failed to keep an appointment at the rendezvous site. I've already questioned the prisoner extensively on the matter, but he insists that only one or two key men were given specific knowledge concerning the identity of the traitor. I tend to believe him."

Müller and Bormann exchanged looks, and Bormann said, "Captain, will you excuse us for a moment?" They regarded Schedle's three enlisted men and the hovering clerks and withdrew to a quiet area near the row of filing cabinets.

For a moment, Schedle watched them whisper back and forth; then he cast his attention toward the clerks and typists, not wanting to seem overly curious. Most of the clerks had settled nervously back to their desks, but they seemed to be paralyzed, a kind of tableau, poised over their adding machines and typewriters, but afraid to operate them for fear of disturbing the Reichsleiter.

Schedle's eyes fell on one nervous-looking individual in particular, an SS officer who didn't really belong here in the first place. Gruppenführer Fegelein's adjutant. The man had come to the hallway early this morning during the first interrogation session and had remained. He claimed he had been sent down by the Gruppenführer to check some SS expenditures and had asked one of the clerks to bring him a hefty file. He'd been sitting beside the clerk's desk ever since, carefully poring over the file's contents. It seemed sadistic to Schedle. The file could easily have been taken elsewhere for study. But the man had stayed. Perhaps he was just one of those people who take pleasure in another man's pain.

Reichsleiter Bormann and the Gestapo chief were still

whispering by the filing cabinets. They seemed to be arguing about something. Müller's hands chopped the air as he
spoke, and he shook his head violently. Whether he won or
lost his point, Schedle couldn't tell, but the discussion was
apparently over, for Bormann turned abruptly and motioned for Schedle to join them. Schedle hurried to obey.

Bormann glanced at the others in the corridor, then
whispered, "Captain, we must know more about this possible traitor." He measured his next words carefully, as
though trying not to say too much. "The Russians have
broken through our defenses on the Oder. At this very
moment, the Führer is meeting again with our generals,
trying to devise a stratagem to save the city. There are important developments on the verge of realization. State
events about which we cannot speak at the moment. It is
conceivable that the traitor, if indeed there is a traitor and
he is in a position of trust, may have some incomplete
knowledge of these events. It is also conceivable that he
may have leaked word of them to the Anglo-Americans.
That could explain this foolhardy attempt to raid the Chancellery. Do you follow me?"

"Yes, sir," Schedle said. Then, thinking better of it, he
said, "No, sir. Not exactly."

"Never mind," Bormann said. "I wish you to question
the prisoner more intensely." He glanced beyond Schedle's
shoulder at the others in the corridor. "These people are
to be removed. Also, dismiss your three assistants. You
alone are to hear what is said. You are to ask him intensive
questions about an operation known as *Schachmatt.*"

"An operation, sir?" Schedle said, seeking clarification.
"We have already succeeded in learning the name they gave
their operation. It's Export. *Ausfuhr.* As one of my assistants suggested it may be a grisly pun: *aus,* to take away;
fuhr, pertaining to our Führer."

Bormann waved a pudgy hand, as if brushing away a
fly. "No, my interest is only in *Schachmatt.* I want to know
if he's heard anything, anything at all, about it. Question
him thoroughly. Use whatever pressure is necessary."

Schedle hesitated. "Sir," he said, "if this is important,

I suggest the prisoner first be treated by the Chancellery surgeon. His condition is none too good."

Gestapo chief Müller looked at Schedle disapprovingly. "Your concern is misplaced," he interjected. "The man is an enemy soldier. He was sent here to do harm to the Führer."

Schedle quickly said, "Sir, I do not suggest medical attention as a matter of concern for the man. It is merely that a prisoner under interrogation is of value only so long as he is capable of providing answers. This man, unless treated, will die."

"He will die in any event," Müller said. "I frankly do not believe it possible that he or any of the other prisoners could have the slightest knowledge of this subject, but if Reichsleiter Bormann wishes to make certain, very well, I accept his decision in the name of caution. But once you have spoken to this man of the matter mentioned by the Reichsleiter, he must be executed. There is no alternative."

Schedle swallowed. "Yes, sir. I understand, sir."

"Good. Now clear these halls. We will expect a detailed report as soon as you have finished with the prisoner. It is to be delivered to Reichsleiter Bormann by you personally. No one else is to hear of this."

Schedle bowed and watched the two men depart, then called one of his enlisted men over and instructed him to clear the corridor. As the clerks grumbled and gathered their belongings, Schedle leaned against one of the desks and frowned to himself. *Schachmatt?* What could it be? A new military operation? One of the long-promised miracle weapons? An espionage thrust from the Abwehr? Why was it so important to the head of the Gestapo and the deputy Party leader? They should have told him more. He would never be able to ask the proper questions with so little working information.

As it turned out, he was able to ask only a few questions anyway. Bormann and Müller should have listened to him. If they expected to learn anything from the American, they were to be disappointed. The man died within ten minutes, without even seeming to understand.

5

Sunday—April 22, 1945

Kameraden, Soldaten—die Zeit ist gekommen!

"Comrades, soldiers—the time has come!"

—line of dialogue from early
German propaganda film

1

Adrian Courtney was so distracted by the Export exercise
and the baffling silence from its participants that he scarcely
minded his wife's anger when he absent-mindedly left her
at their front door. He went straight back to his car, where
Sergeant Ann Christy stood waiting. It had been a dismal
Sunday morning anyway. His mind, all through the sermon,
kept drifting back to Export, and he hadn't absorbed a
tenth of what the righteous Reverend Mr. Compton had
to say on the endless subject of St. Augustine's injunction
to let the beauty of nature elevate one to refreshment and
peace unfailing. His wife had commented bitingly about
his inattention all the way home.

Almost forty-eight hours, and there had been absolutely
no word yet. The planes had returned from the rendezvous
point yesterday as empty as when they left, to report that
there had been no radio linkup, no sign of the Export people in the airlift sector, no contact of any kind. Holley and
Courtney had stayed together in Courtney's office most of
the day, hoping that something might occur to explain the
silence, perhaps radio contact with the Elbe forces, or a
visual sighting by Mosquitos ranging the area. But the wait
had been fruitless.

Courtney settled himself in the back seat and massaged
the bridge of his nose. He'd had a sleepless night worrying
about what might have gone wrong, and his wife, who
thought he gave too much of himself to the office and the

government in the best of times, had been complaining of his preoccupation even before he told her he'd be skipping the Sunday meal to return to the vigil. That he was being driven away by a tall brunette with midnight-blue eyes no doubt put the cap on her temper. His wife had never liked for him to have pretty women on his staff. Pure and pious, Courtney always took care in choosing only the attractive ones, then enjoyed a silent revenge for his wife's chronic acidity.

Once under way, Sergeant Christy said, "I checked with Colonel Norman, sir, as you instructed me. He's just spoken again with Colonel Holley."

"And?"

"Nothing, sir. Operations sent a pair of recon planes to sweep the area once again, but still no sign. It looks as if we've come a cropper."

Christy's voice was quiet, but there was a breathy note, as though she was involuntarily gulping air. It would be enough to worry any girl, to have two beaux vanish simultaneously, but she seemed to be handling it well. Courtney was pleased. Self-control was expected of his staff. He murmured, "Well, of course, it's too early to tell yet. We shall just have to keep our fingers crossed."

"Of course, sir," Christy said. She seemed to seize on his note of mild enthusiasm. "Colonel Norman reports Colonel Holley still sounds optimistic about it. He apparently feels it's only a matter of time. He told Colonel Norman that perhaps they've just bagged so many, ah, big shots, that they couldn't get them all on the pickup planes. He thinks they may have headed straight across country, to bring them out overland."

How eagerly she communicated everything she knew. Courtney said, "An interesting theory." Then, thinking of the future, he made his voice crisp. "Meanwhile, a small reminder: Even theories must be kept to just ourselves. As you know, you have been made privy to information that must, from this moment on, remain absolutely confidential." He closed his eyes to indicate he didn't wish to talk any more, and they made the rest of the journey to St.

James's Park in silence. But the moment Courtney reached his own office, he waved off Colonel Norman's inquiry as to whether he'd like tea, and dialed Holley's home telephone number.

Holley's voice came on after only the first ring, sounding expectant. "Hello?"

"Mumford here," Courtney said. "Anything?"

"Oh, it's you." Holley sounded disappointed. "No, not a damned thing. But listen, I've got a new idea. If something had gone wrong, the Germans would be bragging about it on Radio Berlin, wouldn't they? But there hasn't been a peep out of them so far. Maybe our boys got the old bastard, but they're having trouble getting past the Germans. Maybe the Germans are keeping it quiet in hopes they can rescue him. You think so? You think that's what might be happening?"

Courtney examined the notion. "It's conceivable," he said.

Holley said, "Well, if it's true, we've got to get some help in to them. And fast."

"In where?" Courtney said, beginning to lose patience. "We don't know where our people are."

"We could drop another agent or two and let them poke around. Couldn't we?"

"I doubt the committee would give us clearance," Courtney said. "There have been rumblings already. They apparently expected tidier results."

"Hell, so did we," Holley said. "Who did the complaining?"

"It came down from Whittingdon," Courtney said. "They've asked for a review of the plans and specifications. I had Colonel Norman send a packet over this morning."

"Oh shit," Holley said.

Courtney massaged his nose again, thinking. "Still, I expect your thought that we send someone in for a look is a good one," he said. "Why don't we cable Stockholm and have one of your people get in touch with that Swedish journalist, the one who set up the initial meeting with General Fegelein."

"What good would that do?"

"None, perhaps. It depends on whether Fegelein's cover was blown during the course of the raid. If the Germans have already picked him up, then I fear we've had it. But if not, I'd like very much for the Swede to fly in and ask him some questions. At least we might get an inkling as to what took place."

"Suppose the Swede doesn't want to play? The Russians are getting pretty close."

"He's been co-operative so far. Perhaps he'll do this one last thing, if approached properly. Have your people offer him a bonus. Offer him a medal. Good Lord, offer him anything. It isn't as if we have many options at this point."

"It might work," Holley said. "Okay, I'll get right on it." He cleared his throat. "By the way, Mumford, I'm going to ask the Swede to report directly to you. If the committee is planning an investigation, there's something we should make clear, just for the record."

"Oh?"

"Well, this Berlin raid was *your* idea, you know. You set it up, and you sent them in. I was only trying to give you a little friendly assistance. I just want to make sure you remember that, if anyone from the committee starts breathing down your neck."

Courtney was silent for several moments, trying to decide whether to be angry. In the end, he found he hadn't the emotion to spare. "Your reminder is accepted and noted," he said. "I'll let you know when I get a response from Stockholm."

He hung up the phone, taking care not to bang it. No point in being as loutish as Holley. How quiet everything was. Sunday quiet. He could hear only his own breathing and, no doubt aided by imagination, a rustle from the spider web in his window, as though a fly had been caught and now strained to get away. For the first time, Courtney's sympathies were for the flies, the moths, the occasional prey that might blunder into the web. Then, from the outer office, came a consoling sound—the clink of teacups. Courtney didn't know how Colonel Norman could manage, what with his two sticks, but he laid silent odds that his aide's sensitive feelings had picked up his distress, and Colonel Norman would be bringing tea after all. The old man probably didn't dream that his courage was more heartening to Courtney than any cup of tepid tea.

Courtney leaned back, waiting. After all, he'd seen many a stubborn creature batter its way from a spider's web.

2

In Berlin, sooty raindrops smacked the pavement explosively, creating a film of grime that made walking treacherous. It was the second day of rain. Bascom, out of his cellar hideaway for the first time, stood nervously at the corner of Unter den Linden and Markgrafen Strasse, shoulders hunched and hands in pockets, and stared through the wet, gray distance toward the center of the city.

He hadn't really intended to come this far from Formoy and the cellar. He'd told himself at first that he was only going to make a quick sally to scout up food, but the closer he got to the inner city, the more he thought about Fegelein. The Adlon Hotel was down there, just a jog from the Brandenburg Gate with its twelve massive columns. And at the Adlon would be the assistant hotel manager who could put him in touch with Fegelein—if Bascom had the nerve to go there.

Bascom had worried about coming out at all, about walking openly on the streets. If someone spotted him for a foreigner, maybe his phony identity card would work, maybe not. But the busier streets had turned out to be so clogged with refugees pouring into the city from villages to the east that so far no one had spared him a second glance.

If. The ifs maddened him. *If* the idiots back in London had used their brains and know-how, they might have thought to provide an adequate survival kit. They'd given him plenty of money, and with it one could theoretically buy food. But they had provided only the tools to get away from danger, not exist in the middle of it. They hadn't bothered to include food ration cards.

If he had the nerve, he might try stealing food. Though it was Sunday, most of the stores were open, particularly the food stores, and many storekeepers seemed eager to clear out their bins, as though hoping to sell their goods before the Russians came and took everything without payment. He'd seen no policemen, except for an unshaven pair helping to burn documents in front of a municipal building. Most of the police had apparently been assigned to fighting units by now. But *if* he were caught lifting a can of sardines or a loaf of bread, an outraged storekeeper might find some way to get him tossed in a German pokey, and the game would be up. Formoy would be left helpless and alone.

The biggest if was Fegelein. Of the thousands of things that could have gone wrong that night at the Chancellery, could it have been Fegelein who set them up? If not, if Fegelein had nothing to do with the fiasco, he would be ripe for approach. In fact, he'd be scared to death by now, worried that someone like Bascom might link him to treasonous acts for which there could be no explanation. He might be willing to do anything. Get a doctor for Formoy. Arrange an escape, anything to keep himself clear. Or he might do his damnedest to kill them, to keep them quiet. On the other hand, if the nervous German had been the one who betrayed them, there was no doubt about what he would do to someone like Bascom. Walking down the street to the Adlon Hotel would be tantamount to laying one's head on a waiting chopping block.

Bascom's indecisiveness bothered him almost as much as his hunger. He shouldn't be so hungry, anyway. When was the last time he had eaten? Noon, Friday? Only a couple of days? Big deal. Surely the body could go for far longer without food. Formoy hadn't eaten either. Probably couldn't, even if the food were placed before him. Or could he? Formoy had been comatose last night when Bascom had found a tattered quilt for him in the upper level and came down to cover him, but this morning Bascom had seen Formoy's eyes move, following him around the cellar for a while as he paced, before the wounded man rolled his head back on the dirty floor and resumed staring at the ceiling.

But it was a sign of life, and Bascom, feeling as though his belly button had taken up permanent residence next to his backbone, told himself grimly that life demanded food. He had to find something to eat for both of them, even if it meant grubbing through refuse cans. Nobody seemed to be collecting garbage any more. Maybe he could find a restaurant that was still operating, check the alleyway in back, pick out morsels that weren't too old or disgusting.

Wondering with genuine curiosity if he were really that hungry, Bascom walked only a block before he encountered a throng of people lining up in front of a large building that looked like a warehouse. He might have passed on, but he heard a magic word: meat. A woman coming out of the building stopped with friends toward the head of the line and tore open a bag to show them. They oohed over a half kilo of pork and a quarter kilo each of what the woman said were rice and pulse.

They were "crisis" rations, Bascom gathered quickly from eavesdropping on the woman and her friends. The bags were being handed out free at several points in the city, she said. The largess was due to the Russian breakthrough. Bascom had inferred that the Russians were getting closer, because their guns were a hell of a lot closer. Even as he stood in the rain and stared hungrily at what looked like a can of vegetables and even one of fruit in the woman's bag, he could hear the muffled boom of artillery shells exploding in the eastern suburbs, and, sporadically, he could hear the occasional bigger shell scream overhead toward the center of Berlin. But, like him, the Germans in the line seemed more interested in food. There was enough in the bag to last eight days, the woman told her friends, until the Russians were repelled and General Steiner came down from the North, or General Wenck's relief army arrived from the West.

Bascom ignored the rumormongering but thought hard about crisis rations. If they were free, maybe ration cards weren't required, either. He was tempted to ask the woman, but she clutched her bag to her breast and moved on. Could it be possible? Hell, he could feed both Formoy and himself for a week if he had a pound of meat and some rice. And pulse, whatever that was, was bound to be edible. He might be able to hold out for days, maybe even until the Russians arrived and rescued them.

Preoccupied, Bascom was slow in noticing the approach of an automobile, even though it was the first automobile he had heard since coming out of hiding. So he was shocked to see, coming straight up the street, a heavy, open-air six-wheeler, with an SS officer and a driver in the front and six SS men three abreast in each of the two rear seats. They wore the markings of the elite Hitler Guard, the same people who had come pouring out of the Chancellery that terrible, chilling night of the raid.

His throat instantly clogged with fear. He wanted to bolt, but his intellect shook its head. They were going elsewhere. They would quickly pass. Bascom ducked his chin and moved to the end of the line, stepping in behind two older women talking to a young girl. He slouched, trying to look casual, as though he belonged. He found himself staring into the face of the girl.

When panicked, hold still. The age-old animal instinct told Bascom not to move. The girl was no more than fifteen or sixteen, still in braids. But she was dressed in the uniform of the Bund deutscher Mädchen, the young woman's equivalent of the Hitler Youth movement, and she peered at him with obvious suspicion on her face. Had she seen him turn away from the carload of SS men?

The SS car was closer now. It was slowing down. It was . . . oh good God, pulling over in front of a small stationer's shop by a bombed-out building, just down the street.

Bascom looked away, to find himself staring into another pair of hostile eyes. This was an old man, in his seventies, who had joined the line in back of him, and Bascom was relieved to see the same suspicious look on the girl's face when she shifted her attention to the newcomer. Perhaps it was just her standard expression. It didn't change when the old man, speaking to himself, to Bascom, or to the world at large, began complaining about the Russian shells.

"Have you timed them?" the old man demanded. "Every thirty seconds or so. The Ivans are deliberately torturing us. It's their way of telling us they're coming. Well, I'll tell you, I've been ducking for cover all morning. A man feels a fool when he ducks and the explosion lands eight or ten blocks away. We just get accustomed to judging the fall of bombs by their sound, and the Russians throw a whole new set of sounds at us."

No one replied to the old man. Ahead in the line, the women were discussing sorrel and how to make it palatable, and the old-timer appeared put out. He muttered, "Fool women. You steam sorrel and douse it with vinegar. Everybody knows that. But who can cook, anyway? The radio says anyone who uses electricity for cooking will be shot. I suppose they expect us to eat everything raw."

The BdM girl looked at him coldly. "You can always cook over a fire, Grandfather."

"I'm not your grandfather, and I don't have a fire," he said. "I have a hot plate, and the government won't let me use it. What do you expect me to do? Chop up my furniture to cook a meal?"

To Bascom, their bickering voices were like the buzzing of flies around the face of a dying man. His concentration was solely on the SS officer who stepped into the stationer's shop, then emerged a moment later with the shopkeeper. The shopkeeper pointed at the bombed-out building. Another of the artillery shells chose that moment to flutter overhead, a rasping sound that streaked across the sky like a locomotive doing two hundred miles an hour. Bascom saw the shopkeeper flinch, but the SS man didn't move a muscle.

The old man jerked Bascom's sleeve. "Listen to that," he said. "I hear the Russians are already approaching the suburbs around Müggelsee. Isn't that wonderful? Soon we'll be able to visit the front by streetcar. Or we can wait a few days, and they'll be right here, right in the center of the city. Damned if I won't be glad to see them come.

Maybe we'll be allowed to use the electricity again."

The BdM girl's chin jerked. "That's defeatist talk, old man," she said. "Take care, or you won't live to see any of it."

The old man blandly ignored her. He jerked Bascom's sleeve again, as the SS officer beckoned the men from the rear of the heavy automobile. Full-force, they moved cautiously toward the burned-out building. The storekeeper ducked back into his doorway to watch.

"Now, if we'd built some proper defenses, we might not have the Ivans in our laps," the old man said. He nudged Bascom harder. "Have you seen the pitiful thing they're doing to stop the Russians? Digging little ditches and stacking a few old cars and trucks in the road?"

Scarcely hearing, Bascom shook his head.

"Don't look," the old man said. "It will break your heart. They say it will take the Russians an hour and five minutes to break through. An hour to stop laughing and five minutes to push the barricades aside."

There was a shout down the street, and one of the SS men pointed up at a glassless, gaping window on the second floor of the building. All along the food line, heads belatedly turned to see what the commotion was about. A figure wriggled through the window and dropped to the ground, slipping and sliding across a mound of loose bricks. He was wearing a soiled uniform, German in cut, but British khaki in color and with British markings. One of the assault team people. Bascom froze.

The SS troopers let him get about twenty feet before they opened up with Schmeissers. The man pitched face down in front of an abandoned shop, coming to rest on a pile of shattered glass from the smashed shop window. Two of the SS men ran forward to make certain he was dead. One nodded to the officer. The people surrounding Bascom in the food line watched while the SS men shouldered their weapons and began to drag the body by the feet back toward the waiting vehicle.

One of the women found her voice. "What do you suppose that was all about?" she asked.

"Probably some poor deserter from the front," the old man said. "Those idiot SS people are shooting them up all over the place. If the Russians don't get you nowadays, our own ghouls will."

The BdM girl glared at him. "Would you like me to summon those officers and report your words?"

The old man shrugged. "They're too busy," he said. "Besides, what do I care?"

The SS men dumped the body in the rear of the big car and clambered in after it. The officer stopped briefly to thank the man at the stationery store, then they drove off. Bascom watched them go with nerves screaming, conscience aching. There was nothing he could have done. It had happened too fast. But he felt less of a man for not having at least tried.

The line inched forward again. "I wouldn't mind so much if my son would come home," the old man said to Bascom. He chattered on, but the BdM girl was staring at Bascom again. What was it? Was she wondering why a young man with no apparent debilitating injuries was dressed in civilian clothing? Or had he stared too openly, and with much too obvious distress, at the shooting scene? He smiled at her wanly, but it didn't help.

"I saw a bunch of old Volkssturm geezers digging in a tank on my street this morning," the old man said. "They just dug a big hole in the pavement, then soldiers drove the tank down in it, and they covered it over with rocks and bricks until only the turret showed. You know why? Because we haven't got enough gasoline to run tanks, that's why. All our glorious Party chiefs have been stealing the gas to drive to safety. Do you see any of us driving to safety? They got us into this, now they're running out and leaving us to hold the bag."

At least it got the BdM girl's attention. "You have a big mouth, Grandfather," she said. "It's going to get you in a lot of trouble."

"I'm only speaking the truth," the man said. He looked at Bascom. "Isn't that right, young man? Tell her."

The girl's eyes turned back to Bascom, daring him to

agree. He cleared his throat, then said only, "I'm late," and quickly withdrew from the line. Those behind seemed happy to see him go, but the old man was annoyed. He muttered "rudeness" . . . "young people," and turned away.

The only one who seemed unwilling to let it drop was the BdM girl. As Bascom hurried away from the food dispersal center, he glanced over his shoulder to see her following uncertainly in the rain, trailing him down the street, just a few tentative steps, as though wondering if her suspicions were important enough to cause her to give up her place in line. If Bascom had been able to contain the urge to run, she might have given up on him, but his nerves, already frayed, snapped and twanged like a faulty rubber band, and he took off, heading on the fly for the far corner. The girl shouted and ran after him.

He felt ridiculous, running from a girl, and only a young girl at that, but he didn't slow down. He worried that others might join the chase, and he swiveled his head to check as he ran. The girl alone followed behind him.

Because his legs were longer and anxiety was his fuel, he quickly put distance between them. She was a good fifty yards behind when he reached the corner. He skidded around it, then yanked to a halt. Down the street, huddled over a small bonfire beneath a rain-soaked tarpaulin, a group of gray-clad Wehrmacht soldiers squatted near a battered Tiger tank, stirring milled wheat and butter into a smoke-blackened pot.

The sound of running feet said the girl was nearing his corner. His eyes darted quickly for a place to hide. Between buildings to his left, a narrow opening led to a small allotment garden filled with young cabbages. None of the soldiers were watching. Bascom ducked through the opening and circled to the rear. A small shed leaned against a fence on the back edge of the garden, and he hurried to it and tried the door. Locked. There was a rusting wheelbarrow beside the shed, and he clambered up on it and boosted himself to the roof. He sprawled flat in the rain, hugging the tin roof, breathing hard.

The sound of the running footsteps drifted around the

corner and slowed, then moved down the street toward the soldiers. He heard the girl's voice calling to them, asking if they had seen a man running this way, and he heard them answer cheerfully, making rough jokes about how desperate the man shortage must be if she had to chase one. One of the soldiers suggested that he would be easy to catch, and she told the soldier without hesitation what he could do with himself, a biological impossibility that set the other soldiers to laughing.

Eventually it grew quiet, and Bascom thought the girl had given up, but when he raised his head for a look over the edge of the shed roof, he saw her creeping silently along the narrow walkway from the street to the garden. He pressed his face to the tin roof. God, God, he told himself. Let me get out of this and I'll never leave the ruin again. I'll stay in the cellar quietly and wait for the Russians, I swear, and take care of Formoy, and go hungry if necessary, and never complain. Just let that stupid little girl give up and stop looking for me.

And she did. She checked the garden and poked in the corners and rattled the door of the shed and convinced herself that he wasn't hiding anywhere back here, then headed for the street. The soldiers cat-called her again and she cursed them vividly, and the street finally got quiet.

He waited fifteen minutes, though it seemed longer, then lowered himself to the fence behind the shed and dropped into another lot filled with the remains of a collapsed building. He worked his way slowly through the debris until he reached a street a block over from the one where the soldiers were resting, then began the long walk back to his own Kreuzberg ruin.

3

Erika Bollenen's worldly goods consisted of a bottle of '37 Vouvray her fiancé had brought her after the fall of Paris, four tallow candles, an ancient alarm clock, some blankets, miscellaneous children's garments and old clothing of her own, a navy-blue Mainbocher coat that still looked so nice she hated to wear it in the rain, a sack of dried peas, a half kilo of rotting apples, four kilos of carrots, several yeast cakes but no flour, assorted bowls and kitchen utensils, a cooking pot that was always too large for the amounts of food she was able to scrounge, and her dead sister's teddy bear. The bear's yellow plush was largely worn off. One ear was gone and one blue-button eye was missing, leaving only a black thread dangling where the eye had been. Erika had buried her own teddy bear in a mock funeral at age eight, but she'd not been able to throw away her sister's bear. With the other possessions, it was stacked in a wobbly baby carriage that she pushed before her. Since the rain seemed to make the mud stickier and the pram heavier at every step, she found herself almost wishing she'd been left with nothing at all.

The two children who trudged beside her, tired from the ten-mile cross-country walk they'd had to make to reach the outskirts of Berlin, were not possessions, but, rather, obligations. At least, Erika had thought of them as obligations until the Russians had swarmed into Petershagen the day before. To her amazement, all those scary headlines people had been whispering about from the *Völkischer Beobachter* may have been right: The victorious Ivans had clearly demonstrated they had little but rape and robbery on their minds. For robbery, they seemed to prefer bicycles and wrist watches. For rape, they preferred fat women, regardless of age.

Erika was slim. Cadaverous, she thought, thanks to her war-induced diet. But she was pretty, if no one objected to tawny curls and tawny, almost golden eyes that would not have looked inappropriate on a young lioness. She was also incredibly dirty, according to her prewar standards. When the two drunken Russians burst into the barn last night, she'd thought for one wild instant that her gamy odor was the reason they had shoved Frau Zarn back into the shadows instead of herself. But the one with the revolver had made the matter clear. Seven-year-old Anne-Lise and five-year-old Friedrich were cowering in the hay

next to Erika. "Lee-tle children," he'd crooned in halting
German, gesturing at them. Waiting for his turn for Frau
Zarn, the Russian had then pointed to himself and counted
on his fingers. "Me lee-tle children. One—two—three."

Even this morning, with the road jammed with liberated
war prisoners and fleeing civilians trying to keep ahead of
the Russians, the two orphaned neighbor children Erika
had taken under her wing now seemed to serve as her protection. No one had even robbed her of the carrots that
she herself had stolen by the midnight moon from an untended root cellar.

But to the hard-boiled Berliners, now that they'd reached
their destination, Anne-Lise and Freddy were less appealing. They only took up room and brought appetites.
Erika understood. She was a native Berliner herself, and
she knew what the Berliners had been through. So she
moved on with no rancor when the inhabitants turned her
away at the first two intact houses she tried, insisting their
cellar shelters were already too crowded. A pity that the
Kukenbachers' house had been hit. They were friends, and
they surely would have taken her in, but their whole block
was so badly damaged that Erika couldn't even be sure
she had the right crater where a house had once been. One
more thing to try not to think about.

Partially to escape the dreadful thought of what might
have happened to the Kukenbachers, and partially in fear
that the Ivans would follow all too rapidly into the city's
outskirts, Erika picked up the weary children and added
them to the load in the pram. She plodded deeper into the
city. At unpredictable intervals, the distant wail of Russian
artillery shells turned to high-pitched shrieks, and only the
heavy pram kept Erika from darting about like a crazed
insect. The shelling sounded worse in the city than it had in
the countryside, but Erika's fear of the Russian soldiers
was greater than her terror of their shells. She went on,
pushing the pram before her, across the Warschauer Bridge
and into the Kreuzberg district, where she tried another
house, but the cellar committee, as represented by a tall

old woman cradling a temperish-looking fox terrier, turned her down again.

"We have no room," the woman said shortly. "Besides, you wouldn't be safe here. Haven't you heard? The Tartars entered Petershagen and Rudersdorf yesterday and burned out every cellar with flame throwers. Everyone was burned alive."

In revenge, Erika didn't tell the woman she had just come from Petershagen, and no such thing had happened. But Freddy started to cry when they got back to the street, and when Erika lifted him back on the pram, its left front wheel fell off. Both Freddy and the alarm clock tumbled out. Erika replaced them, biting her pale lips, and her lion-colored eyes turned dangerous. Three doors down was a bomb-damaged building too shaky to appeal to regular Berliners, yet perhaps solid enough to offer temporary shelter. Neither the children nor the pram were in any shape to go farther. She would try the building with the missing front wall, but if it wouldn't do, the woman and the bad-tempered fox terrier had better prepare for a different kind of invasion.

Erika had to take the children out of the pram to haul it over the pile of debris that led up to the gaping front hall. There, the missing wall no longer gave protection for the building's once-elegant parquet flooring, and rain poured in. But the stairs to the cellar, several meters beyond a ruined kitchen, were undamaged. She stood in the gray light with the children at her side, staring down the stairs, wrestling with a private demon.

When her parents, thinking to escape the bombs falling daily on Berlin, had evacuated to Petershagen, they'd only stepped forward to meet their fate. Less than three weeks after moving to the "safety" of the small village, while Erika stood in a baker's line only a block away, a stray bomb had tumbled their rented house on top of them, burying them. Mother, father, sister. They were dead, of course, by the time the neighbors dug them out. But Erika kept wondering how long they had fought for breath in that suffocating darkness before the ultimate darkness took them. It was hard now for Erika to go into any cellar.

The children clattered down the stairs before she could force herself to breathe calmly. She followed, leaving the pram behind. The cellar seemed extensive. A large outer room with smaller rooms leading off it. A trunk room here. She'd look through those locked trunks later. Racks, empty, for wine in a room beyond. Another large room, a furnace room, with more doorways. There appeared to be servants' quarters toward one side, but the rooms were completely empty, not a stick of furniture left in them. Long before Erika was through tapping the stone walls and inspecting beams for sturdiness, the children had sneaked back to the pram and were crunching raw carrots from it and, with children's abnormal resilience, clamoring to go out and play.

"No," Erika said firmly. She had learned early on that she had to be immensely firm with Anne-Lise, who had a rebel's temperament. "The shelling is too dangerous."

"That's silly, Aunt Erika," Anne-Lise told her just as firmly. "The bombs of the Amis were lots more dangerous."

"And what about the rain?" Erika demanded. Above them, on the parquet flooring, they could hear rain still pattering hard against their "roof." "You're already soaking. Do you want to catch pneumonia? Get out of those wet clothes, and stay off the street."

Anne-Lise pouted. She wandered away to explore, and Freddy, naturally, went with her. Since his parents' death —bombing, again—he never let Anne-Lise out of his sight. Erika was left alone to wrestle the pram down the stairs and search for dry clothing.

But the children were back almost instantly. "Aunt Erika," Anne-Lise panted, "there's a room for coal, and—"

"Coal!" Erika exulted. "We can build a real fire."

"No, there's no coal. But there's a man asleep. He looks hurt."

Erika followed them, more curious than alarmed. A deserter, possibly. Deserters from the German armies, exhausted, disheartened, had been skulking through Peters-

hagen for days. But they were too apathetic to be dangerous. They begged the first woman they saw for a bit of
food, a change of clothing so they could hide their uniforms, and passed on.

But the shaggy, bearded man lying in the stillness of the
small coal room didn't look like the other deserters Erika
had seen. The air was close here, almost warm, and he
appeared to have thrown off a threadbare quilt that was his
only cover. She studied the dim form and suddenly realized
what was wrong. He was well fleshed. Not puffy. Not skel-
etal. Although the Army got first choice on food, and
civilians got only the scraps that were left over, few German soldiers were in the pink of condition these days. And
how soundly the man was sleeping. Erika sent Anne-Lise
for a candle, and when it came, she bent over the man.
She drew back instantly. Brown eyes stared back at her,
wide open and unmoving. But the man was breathing.
Erika firmed her chin and looked closer, discovering the
first of many bloody bandages, some black with old blood,
one on his shoulder black and red, with new blood seeping
through.

"God in heaven!" Erika whispered. An artillery shell?
Shrapnel? Even in Petershagen they'd heard how the knife-
edged shrapnel from the Russian shells ripped through
stone several meters away from an explosion. But how had
the man gotten here? Who had tended him, then left him
here all alone?

Erika was so tired that each step was an act of will, and
she had little energy left over for wondering. Two streets
away she had seen one of the outdoor water taps that now
served as the city's water system. The children were still in
their wet clothes. She swallowed her misgivings and allowed Anne-Lise and Freddy to scamper out with the big
cookpot to bring back water, and while they were gone
she ripped out enough of the parquet flooring from the
upper floor to start a gypsy's cook fire toward the front
of the cellar, where the shock from some Allied bomb had
conveniently carved a smoke vent.

While she waited for the children, she went through the

man's pockets, searching for identification. She found a small oilskin packet. She opened it and was startled to find money, both notes and gold coins, and a worker's identity card made out to Maurice Lavaud. Was he not a soldier after all, not a deserter? But how could that explain his well-fed appearance? Foreign workers were given even less to eat than German civilians.

She was tempted by the money. She had none, not any more. But as she heard the children returning with the water, she put the money back in the packet with the man's identity card and a little cellophane envelope containing some kind of pill, and replaced everything in his pocket. By the time the children reached her, she was back tending the fire.

Soon both she and the children were in dry clothes, a scanty stew of carrots and peas was simmering, and she had a pot of warm water beside her as she knelt to see if water alone would help the injured man's wounds.

He made no protest. He made no sound. She had no bandages, but she cut the blood-soaked one from the man's shoulder with her kitchen knife and carefully washed the wound. She regarded his quilt. It looked clean. Perhaps she could cut strips from it for new bandages.

But even as she reached for the quilt, a heavy thud overhead turned her eyes to the ceiling. She inhaled deeply as the fear of being buried alive swept over her again. But Anne-Lise moved to the door of the coal bin and peeked through, then came back to her side. "A man is coming down the cellar stairs," the little girl whispered.

Erika's eyes riveted on the door. A man dressed in a black sweater and a cap started to step through, then stopped, frozen, staring at her. Erika stood and swept the children behind her. But the man just stayed there, so she said sharply, "This is your friend? You are an oaf as a nurse. But I suppose I'm not much better. Have you brought him a doctor?"

"No," the man said haltingly. "I couldn't find one."

The stranger's German was heavily accented. Erika was instantly suspicious. Another foreigner? Perhaps even a

Russian? Even in Petershagen, Russian war prisoners had been assigned to work some of the farms as forced labor. "Is this your cellar?" she asked. "No, I think not. Who are you? What are you doing here?"

"Don't cry out, please," the man said. His greenish eyes looked frightened. "I'm French. I work in a tank factory."

Erika switched easily to French in an accent well polished by childhood summers spent in the gentle decay of Deauville. "Which factory?" she demanded. "Where?"

His French was worse than his German. "Uh, it's been moved from the city," he stammered. "There was a mixup. I was left behind."

He was obviously a Russian. Perhaps even a spy. She stooped for the kitchen knife she had left lying beside the unconscious man. She didn't brandish it at the man in the doorway, but she held it so he could see it. "No, I think not," she said again. "You had better leave. I won't tell the authorities. But that is all I will do for you. Now, move away from that door."

"Please," he said, switching back to his clumsy German. "I won't hurt you."

"Indeed you will not," Erika assured him. This time she did brandish the knife.

He stepped back from the doorway. Cautiously, keeping the children behind her, Erika edged forward to make sure he went all the way, and she felt a thrill of fear to see that the Russian had stopped after only ten or so feet. He was standing hesitantly in the big room where she had made the cook fire. He looked indecisive. But, of course. He didn't want to leave without his injured companion.

She gestured again with the knife. "Very well," she said, "you may take him with you. Go now. Go far away. The SS was here not thirty minutes ago, searching for deserters. They will be back. I don't want to have to tell them about you, but—"

The man grimaced and said something in yet another language. English? Then in German, he said, "Please, just let me talk to you a moment."

"What was that word you just spoke?" she asked. "Was

it English? Russian? You aren't French. What are you?"

"No, no," the man said hastily. "I'm French, just as I told you. I'm part of a battalion of foreign labor conscripts." He glanced uncomfortably at the silently staring children. "Please, if we could just have one private word. I promise, I won't try to hurt you."

Erika considered her position quickly. The stranger looked able-bodied, but she had the knife. And even if Russians seemed to like children, they were to be protected, not to give protection. Perhaps it would be better to do as he asked. She said, "Anne-Lise, Freddy, you may go upstairs and play on the first floor. But you are not to go out into the rain. Do you understand? If you get wet again, you'll have to go to bed."

Anne-Lise made a face. She'd probably made it many times, sent away when adults wished to talk, and Erika thought for the hundredth time how badly her parents had spoiled her. Yet the child went, taking Freddy with her. The man moved a step toward Erika, but she waved the knife at him.

"Not too closely," she warned. "And now you will tell me the truth. You *are* Russian, aren't you? Are the Russians already here?"

"No," the man said quietly. He sighed, a gusty outpouring of despair. "I'm an American."

4

The time to kill her had passed. If he had done it right away, during those first moments of shock at seeing her, it might have been all right. But he had been too dumfounded to move. Now it was too late. Those skinny kids, big eyes staring, watching the whole thing. The woman, dirty, frightened. Amber-colored hair, curling up in wet ringlets. That ridiculous knife, weaving nervous circles in the air. He couldn't possibly do it now.

He wanted to. God, how he wanted to. She was an iron

door, clanging shut just as he was ready to step through it. So much for happy endings.

He was sunk. He couldn't sling Formoy over his shoulder and run, not in daylight. And he couldn't stay. She'd made that plain. So what was left? Nothing. Damn the woman. He stood there, his words ringing in his ears: "I'm an American."

Her reaction was unexpected. "An American?" She lowered the knife and closed her eyes for a moment. He made a move, automatic, to catch her, thinking stupidly she might faint. But she only rocked gently, as though feeling waves of the relief that appeared on her face. "Thank God," she murmured. "Americans in Berlin. If we must surrender, better anything than the Russians." Then, abruptly, she said, "But where are your troops? Why are you hiding?"

"There are no troops," he said. "We're alone."

"No troops? My God, you don't mean to tell me the Americans are going to let the Russians take the city? I've *seen* the Russians."

Bascom tried to read her face and her hopes. Perhaps there was a way out, after all. Could he lie convincingly? He'd have to try. "No, our troops are on the way," he said. "Just a day or two to the west. I was part of a team. To reconnoiter, you understand. Then we got cut off. My friend was badly hurt, and well, someone had to stay behind to look after him."

"To stay with an injured companion," she said. "That was brave."

She regarded him with obvious respect, and he blinked. He hadn't thought of it as brave. Only inescapable. Oddly embarrassed, he said, "Well, someone had to do it."

But her mind had apparently moved on to other things. "A real live American," she said, as if unable to control her excitement. The Amis will be here soon? When?"

She plied him with dozens of optimistic questions, one tumbling after the other almost as fast as he could manufacture answers. Were the British coming as well? Would they come in force? Bringing food? Medicine? Would they help the Germans turn the Russians back from the city? His answers were vague by necessity, but she seemed eager to believe everything he told her.

And she seemed just as eager to answer his questions when she settled down enough for him to ask a few. She chattered as though he were an old friend, reunited after years of separation. Her name was Erika, and she had just returned to Berlin from one of the little towns to the east, only a step or two ahead of the Russians. Everyone she knew was living on borrowed time and borrowed hopes. The most important hope of them all was for relief by the Americans. She's heard it a hundred times in the last week or so. When would the Americans arrive? Everything would be all right when the Americans came. The Americans will soon be here, you know. Hold out, hold on. Help is on its way. It didn't matter that the Americans had dropped bombs all over the city. The important thing was that the American foot soldier carried chocolate in his shirt pocket and would smile. And he was not Russian.

Finally, as though the time had come to discuss business, she paused and her face grew serious. "I would like to strike a bargain with you," she said.

"What kind?"

She sniffed in the direction of some marvelous-smelling concoction cooking on the small wood fire and went to stir it. She seemed hesitant, as though afraid he wouldn't agree to whatever it was that she wanted.

"I will help you," she said at last, staring into her pot, "if you in turn will help me. I will say nothing about you to anyone, and I will help to hide you and your friend. In return, you will protect me if the Russians should arrive first, and keep me safe until the Amis get here."

"Certainly," Bascom agreed. "It's only fair." He wasn't as confident as he tried to sound. It occurred to him briefly to wonder: Could he even protect himself and Formoy from the Russians? They were likely to come in shooting and ask questions later, if they bothered to ask questions at all.

"And you will tell the American authorities that I have helped you, and assure good treatment for me?" she asked, making sure he understood the terms of the agreement.

"Certainly."

"And good treatment for the children? They're not really mine, but, well, they have no one else."

"Oh Lord, yes," Bascom said. He smiled for the first time. "Even the Reds wouldn't do anything to hurt the children. And Americans are crazy about kids."

Erika smiled back. "What an unexpected turn to a terrible day," she said. "Now I have my own private Ami."

"Sure, an insurance policy, that's me," he said. "I come to maturity on the day the war ends. Now, about the premiums—" He looked longingly at the pot. Peas? Carrots? He'd never liked vegetables, but they had an ambrosial smell now. "I know you probably don't have much food and children are always pretty hungry, but—"

Her smile faded. "You have no provisions?" she said. "Your leaders sent you on a sortie with no supplies?"

"Well, yes. But in the fighting, well, I'm afraid I had to jettison everything but my friend. I've got some money, though. If you've got a ration card, I've got plenty of Reichsmarks."

"A ration card does little good when there is no food to be had," she said. "Cigarettes? Have you any cigarettes?"

"I don't smoke. Sorry."

"Ah well," she said. "Perhaps I can find food tomorrow. This evening we at least have carrots. Would you like a raw carrot?"

"God, yes."

She turned to the pram, then hesitated and asked him one last question. "In the fighting that injured your friend —did the German troops fight well? I mean—"

He thought he understood. "Like lions," he assured her. "We never expected to meet such heated resistance. I've never seen anything like it."

She sighed. She took three carrots from the sack in the pram, then, seeing how hungrily Bascom eyed them, she took three more. He decided instantly to fill up on raw carrots and leave the pea-and-carrot concoction for her and the kids. No need to be greedy. But then his eyes fell on a bottle of wine in the pram, and greed surged upward. It appeared to be French. Vouvray or something.

"I don't suppose . . ." he said, pointing at the wine bottle. "Could I have a sip of that?"

She hesitated, then said, "No." She quickly covered the neck of the bottle with an old sweater. She stood up and handed him the carrots. Her eyes softened. "I don't mean to be rude," she said. "The bottle is special. My fiancé presented it to me before he went to the front. We are to open it to celebrate the end of the war when he returns."

"Oh. Sorry."

"He's a lieutenant. In the Army."

"I understand. Well, he should be home soon."

"I only hope so," she said. She looked down at the sweater, at the wine-bottle shape showing through it. "He was with Field Marshal Paulus and the Sixth Army at Stalingrad. I've had no word from him since the surrender. More than two years now."

Bascom opened his mouth, but he couldn't think of appropriate words of comfort. Lamely, he settled for, "Maybe he's a prisoner. Maybe he's all right."

"Perhaps," she said. She smiled and gestured at the carrots. "Eat. They're stolen. I took them from a farmhouse. One can try to live on hope, but it is never enough. I find the body is often happier with a few stolen carrots."

He nodded gratefully and shoved one in his mouth. She started for the cellar stairs, as if to call the children, but again she hesitated.

"I'm sorry our troops fought so hard," she said shyly. "If the Amis are coming, the sooner they arrive, the better. It would be easier if our soldiers didn't resist so hard. And yet . . ."

He looked at her with sudden compassion. "I know," he said. "It's hell to lose, but at least they're going down fighting."

Guarded optimism had been the watchword in each evening's Führerbunker conference for the first few days of the Russian assault, but now optimism gave way to gloom. Bad report followed bad report, hammer blows driving nails into the coffin of the German Third Reich. The front had collapsed. Heinrich's Army Group Vistula and Busse's Ninth Army had been split apart by a Russian wedge almost twenty miles wide. Soviet tanks were grinding toward Bernau in the North. Zossen, temporary headquarters of the German High Command, had fallen this morning to Russians in the South. Russian troops were within sight of the city. It would take at least two hundred thousand men to defend Berlin properly, and one had only to look around to see that there were no such men. At most the city could depend on some eighty-odd under-strength battalions of creaking, age-bent Volkssturm, weary, weak-eyed old men of the home militia; a few thousand children of the Hitler Youth; two battalions or so of Guard troops, and a ragtag collection of clerks, subway attendants, and firemen banded together in something called the "Alarm" brigade. Scarcely sixty thousand men, if you could call them men, poorly trained, poorly equipped, poorly motivated, and yet they would have to hold off two million Russians. Unless relief arrived soon, Berlin was doomed.

Hitler studied the faces in the cramped underground conference room and bent over a broad map table for a closer look. "Where is Steiner?" he demanded. "How far has his attack progressed?"

Only silence answered him from the circle of faces around the table. Generals Krebs and Jodl looked away. Field Marshal Keitel, standing between a Luftwaffe general and Vice Admiral Voss, pointedly studied the maps. White-faced adjutants rifled busily through briefcases. Even Martin Bormann, standing near the door, refused to meet his eyes.

"I will ask again," Hitler said. "Where is Steiner? I ordered him to bring the III SS Panzer Corps to Berlin two days ago. He should be here by now. General Krebs?"

Krebs, whose face was pitted with two-year-old scars from his time in Russia, whose head was swathed in bandages from a month-old air raid in Zossen, and whose psyche cringed in day-to-day terror at the thought of bearing yet another disappointing piece of news to his reproachful leader, blanched and said, "Nothing to report, my Führer."

"Nothing to report?" Hitler's cheeks flamed. "Can no one tell me the truth for a change? How can there be nothing to report? We need Steiner's men. I demand to know how far they have come!"

General Jodl chewed at his lower lip for a moment, then reluctantly said, "General Steiner's Panzer Corps is operating at only partial strength, my Führer. He has barely ten thousand men, and they are mainly new recruits."

"He can't be at partial strength!" Hitler snapped. "I ordered all available replacements to him several days ago. Are you trying to tell me that my orders have been ignored?"

Jodl's face drained of animation. "No, my Führer. We tried. Steiner has every man we could find. But he is still badly under strength. You are asking him to drive through a hundred thousand Russians with only ten thousand men."

"The German soldier has always been equal to ten Russians," Hitler insisted. "Now tell me. How far has Steiner's attack progressed?"

Jodl looked at Krebs. Krebs swallowed. "The attack hasn't yet started," Krebs admitted. "Steiner refuses to move until his Corps is brought to full strength."

Hitler's mouth opened. He stared at them, and his breath turned ragged. He stumbled back a foot and sank into his chair. For a moment he was silent, then he said tightly, "Please clear the room. Deputy Party Leader Bormann will stay. Field Marshall Keitel and Generals Jodl and Krebs will also remain. The rest of you, out."

He stayed on the edge of his chair, staring at the clutter of maps on the table, while the room quietly emptied. Krebs and Jodl stood across from him, pale and worried. Keitel edged back, as though wishing he could become a piece of furniture.

When only Bormann, the field marshal, and the two generals were left, Hitler struggled to his feet and faced them. His face purpled, and he raised his right arm, fingers curled in a fist. Spittle glistened at the corners of his down-turned mouth. Then in a rage, he thundered, "I am surrounded by liars and traitors! Traitors, do you hear me?" The four men flinched as he slammed his fist to the table, and listened in shock as he screamed at them, raving uncontrollably of betrayal, deceit, and cowardice. He shouted nonstop for almost three minutes, face livid, saliva spraying the air, eyes demented. Then, his passion vented, he collapsed back into the chair.

They stood at rigid attention until he regained control; then his face came up to stare across the room at them. His chin trembled, and he gazed at each of them in turn, bestowing sad, regretful smiles like medals for heroism. "I am sorry, my friends," he murmured in a weak, hopeless voice. "You look to me for miracles, and I give you only defeat. The war is lost. We are finished."

"No, my Führer," Keitel said. "We can still—"

But Hitler waved him silent with a look of contempt. "No more lies," he said. "It's done. Steiner was our last hope. Nothing remains now but to die."

The three military men exchanged looks. Krebs touched his heels together and said, "You must keep faith, my Führer. Wenck is on his way. We may still turn the tide."

Hitler shook his head.

"Then leave Berlin now," Krebs implored. "Fly today, this instant, to Berchtesgaden. There you will be safe."

"Yes," Jodl chimed in. "Berchtesgaden. It is no longer possible to command here. In Berchtesgaden, you could continue to guide us. Berlin is a death trap. You must leave today."

Hitler's head drooped. "Useless," he said. "No, we're

finished. I shall never leave the bunker. You may go if you wish, but I shall stay here to the end."

"No, no," they said, almost in unison.

"I will not leave," he insisted. "I will carry on the fight from here, alone if I must. And when it is no longer possible to fight, when the Russians are upon us, I will take my own life. I will die here, in Berlin."

He looked at them, his eyes reddening. Tear tracks marked his cheeks. Then he put his face in his hands and sobbed, his shoulders quaking.

The sobbing frightened them more than the earlier shouting. Each of them had seen the Führer lose control on occasion. Each had heard the Führer condemn inefficiency and incompetence at the top of his voice, sometimes with an almost hysterical frenzy. But none had seen him break down when it was done. None had seen him so discouraged, so completely beaten as to permit tears. It shook them deeply and they looked away, standing in awkward silence.

6

Drapes separated the narrow underground reception lounge from the conference corridor in the lower level of the Führerbunker. Captain Franz Schedle approached the drapes with some misgivings, sidling past the generals and aides who still lingered in the lounge after Hitler's evening military conference. They seemed to be agitated, whispering in small groups, faces almost bloodless in the artificial light of the bunker. Things had apparently not gone well in tonight's session.

Schedle wasn't in the lower bunker because of the conference, of course. There was no room for lowly captains when the mighty met. Quite frankly, he wasn't sure why he was here. He had been summoned only minutes earlier from his post on the upper floors of the Chancellery, supposedly by Reichsleiter Bormann, though Schedle couldn't imagine why Bormann should want to see him. Schedle had made it clear in his report yesterday that the prisoner had said nothing of importance before he died.

Schedle nervously pushed the drapes aside. Bormann and the Führerbunker surgeon, a doctor named Stumpfegger, were sitting on a bench on the far side of the map table, flanking General Krebs. Domed lights beamed down starkly from the thick concrete ceiling, casting a yellowish tinge on the three men. An outsized oriental rug covered the floor, tucked under at the edges to make it fit. Schedle knew it to be from one of the Führer's private rooms on the upper floors, but it didn't make the gray walls look any homier.

Schedle removed his visored cap and tucked it under his arm, waiting to be noticed. Bormann's mouth was close to Krebs's ear. Bormann talked quietly and earnestly. Krebs looked sick; his face was pale, and the skin sagged beneath his eyes. The door to Hitler's suite was closed. The Führer had apparently retired after the end of the session.

Dr. Stumpfegger noticed Schedle standing by the drapes and murmured. Bormann looked up. Schedle said, "You wanted to see me, Herr Reichsleiter?"

Bormann rose and smiled, though the smile seemed uneasy. "Yes, Captain. It was good of you to come." He walked around the map table to offer his hand.

Schedle took it, surprised. Reichsleiter Bormann had never even shown any signs of noticing him before yesterday. Now handshakes and smiles? It didn't make sense.

"Was there anything wrong with my report?" Schedle asked. "I included every word that was said."

"No, not at all," Bormann said. "Your report was very thorough." He glanced at Krebs and Stumpfegger and said, "Gentlemen, could you excuse us for a moment? I'll get back to you both later."

Stumpfegger, a small man with dark eyebrows and a perpetually impish expression, stood and nodded slyly. "I quite understand," he said. Krebs also stood, but he seemed distracted and headed for the door without a word.

When they were gone, Bormann clapped Schedle on the shoulder and smiled again, more confidently this time. "I sent for you, Captain, because I may have some duties for you."

"Of course, Herr Reichsleiter. Anything at all."

"I was sure you would say that, Captain. I've made inquiries about you. You are regarded as a totally loyal officer. Both to the Führer and to our cause."

"Most assuredly, Reichsleiter. I would give my life for the Führer."

"So would we all," Bormann said smoothly. "Captain, I spoke to you of something yesterday, an action called *Schachmatt*—an action, I must hastily add, that is quite sensitive, known only to a small number of people for the moment."

"You need say no more, sir. The incident is already forgotten. I will repeat it to no one."

"That isn't precisely why I sent for you," Bormann said. "True, the existence of the operation must remain secret for the present, but my purpose in summoning you goes deeper."

"Sir?"

"It appears the military situation is far more serious than we expected, and the time for the implementation of the action may be near at hand, even though all the details have not yet been worked out. I find I must broaden the circle of responsible people involved in it. I am not prepared just yet to acquaint you with all its facets, but let me say that the events of the next few days are vitally important to the survival of our beliefs. You are to become a part of these events."

Schedle blinked, his cheeks flaming warmly. "I am honored, Herr Reichsleiter."

"Others are being brought into the activity as well," Bormann said. He glanced at the bench where General Krebs had been sitting. "You have seen one of them, an accident of timing for which I am at fault. I will not, for the moment, divulge any other names, except to say they are men of honor and loyalty, such as yourself. As the time draws nearer, you will learn who they are."

"Yes, sir. I understand, sir."

Bormann hesitated, framing his words. "If the operation is to succeed, certain . . . logistical decisions . . . must be implemented in the next two or three days. You may need help. I want you to pick six men, trustworthy men like yourself, from the ranks of the Führer Guard. Relieve them of all other duties and have them stand by. Tell them nothing, of course. Anything they do will be authorized by an order bearing my signature and seal. They may see the orders, but you will return all documents to me for destruction after each activity is completed. Is that agreeable?"

"Anything you desire, Herr Reichsleiter."

"Excellent. The first order of business must take place tonight. You needn't involve anyone else in this one. It can be done by you alone. A message must be transmitted shortly after midnight to a U-boat currently patrolling in the Kattegat Strait. The captain is under special instructions to surface each evening at ten minutes past twelve for radio contact. You will bear the message to the military communications center in the Zoo Bunker and see that it goes out precisely at that time. If the message is received, the U-boat will respond so, *Turmbereit*. If the response does not come, the message must be transmitted again tomorrow night at ten minutes past twelve. It is vital that the message be received either tonight or tomorrow night at the latest, in order that the U-boat have sufficient time to reach Sassnitz for special outfitting."

"Yes, sir. What is the message?"

Bormann shook his head. "You will not understand it. It will be a series of coded co-ordinates. I will deliver it into your hands later tonight, just prior to your departure for the Zoo Bunker."

"Yes, sir. Is that all, sir?"

"For the moment, yes. There will be additional duties soon for you and the men you select. I'll call you to my quarters as they arise. Thank you, Captain, for coming, and thank you for not asking any questions. When the time comes for *Schachmatt* to burst on the world, you will

realize how extremely valuable your contribution has been
to the fate of the Fatherland."

It seemed to be a dismissal, so Schedle clicked his heels,
did an about-face, and stepped smartly through the drapes,
so smartly in fact that he almost collided with Gruppenführer Fegelein, standing just on the other side. Schedle
bowed in apology, and Fegelein moved hastily away.

Schedle slipped his cap on, and his eyebrows dipped in
a slight frown. Was Gruppenführer Fegelein also one of
the people whose names Deputy Party Leader Bormann
preferred not to mention just yet? Fegelein's adjutant had
been present during the interrogation yesterday, just before
the Reichsleiter and Gestapo chief Müller appeared, and
now here he was himself, standing within easy hearing
distance of the conference room. It was possible, of course,
that Fegelein had only been waiting to see the Führer, but
it was also possible that he was waiting to be called into the
map room by Reichsleiter Bormann, just as Schedle had
been.

Perhaps it would be better to take no notice. If the
Reichsleiter had wanted him to know which people were
a part of the select circle, he would have told him. He
would eventually, anyway. He had promised as much.
When and if Gruppenführer Fegelein's name came up,
Schedle would pretend not to have already guessed. Nothing would be gained by allowing the Reichsleiter to think
he had been snooping.

He paused in the lounge, immensely pleased with himself. Much of what Reichsleiter Bormann had said was
only flattery, no doubt, but the fact that he had been
chosen from among all the others was extremely satisfying.
He must be careful not to let it go to his head.

Generals Krebs and Jodl were still standing in the
crowded lounge, as though uncertain where to go next.
Schedle bowed deeply to them and received an instant
reminder of his lowly position when neither man deigned
to take notice. Chastened, Schedle moved quickly through
the room toward the circular steel staircase that led to the
upper level.

TWO

The City

6

Front und Heimat kennen nur ein Ziel,
Kampf bis zum Sieg!

*"Front and Home know only one goal,
the struggle for Victory!"*

—slogan on Berlin poster

1

All flights to Berlin had been canceled, a tearful Lufthansa girl informed Nils Frychius when he called the German flight desk at Stockholm airport the next morning. The city itself had come under attack, she said, and for the first time since the beginning of the war, Tempelhof authorities deemed the situation too perilous even to continue a restricted schedule of commercial flights. The last passenger plane out of Berlin was slated to leave for Stockholm that very afternoon. Only nine people had been permitted to book passage on it.

Frychius hung up his telephone and let his breath hiss through flaccid lips. He should have expected the bad news. Wire reports at his newspaper office indicated that Russian tank armies and infantry divisions were now trying to encircle the city. Koniev's forces had swept within range of Potsdam in the South. Zhukov's armor had raced north of the city and had reached the upper arm of the Havel. If those two Army groups pinched toward each other and closed the twenty-mile gap between them, the city would be locked in a ring of steel. Already the big guns were reported close enough to shell the city. Tempelhof runways would probably be targeted by artillery fire in the next day or so.

He swiveled his chair to the office window and looked out at the Stockholm skyline, at the tops of buildings, gray

and sooty, stretching off to the eastern shores of Lake
Malaren. What could he do? With the planes shut down,
how could he go? Did he dare go? Suppose he got in somehow and the city were shut off? The OSS certainly didn't
ask easy favors.

He still wasn't too sure what the Allies wanted of him,
anyway. The OSS man from the American embassy had
been vague, as though perhaps he didn't know himself.
Something to do with the Fegelein contact. Apparently
there had been another meeting in Berlin on Friday, and
something had gone wrong. Now they wanted Frychius to
go in and see what had happened, and report to some
Britisher in London.

Still, Frychius felt a responsibility, in a way. A commit-
ment. It was by his own initiative that the original Fegelein
feeler had been forwarded to the Allies in the first place.
He couldn't let it drop now, just because of a little squeam-
ishness over his own safety. If there was a chance that one
more trip might help the cause of peace, he had to make it,
regardless of the danger.

Perhaps it would be possible to reach the city by some
overland route. He could hire that fishing boat in Malmö
again, and have the captain take him across to Lübeck.
There was a Swedish legation in Lübeck, and he could
check in for last-minute situation reports before committing
himself to the 150-mile road trip to Berlin. If things looked
bleak, he could always change his mind and come back.

But it bothered him. The vagueness of the request left
a bitter taste in his mouth. It didn't feel right. It was almost as though they were holding something back from
him, perhaps even something that would affect his personal
safety.

2

Alexei Volkov climbed to the top of an abandoned, bullet-
pocked control tower for his first look at the distant German capital. Russian tanks had overrun the airstrip at

dawn, a small fighter field called Schönefeld, and had swept on to storm the streets and buildings of the small municipalities that snuggled up to the main city.

Powder smoke drifted in leaden puffs from the nearby suburbs, and he could hear the rhythmic exchange of rifle and mortar fire only a mile or so away, yet here it was almost peaceful. Russian supply detachments had already clip-clopped across the cratered runways with their canvas-covered supply wagons and set up shop near two burned-out wooden hangars. While a drayer unhitched horses and mules and tied them off where he could water and feed them, a team of sweating cooks in stained aprons poked through the hangar debris looking for wood to start a cook fire.

Volkov slipped his glasses over his nose, then turned his attention with almost lustful pleasure to the gray, cloudy distance. Beyond the hulks of riddled German aircraft below, beyond the wrecked runways stretching north, beyond the explosions and rattle of small-arms fire marking the slow advance of tanks and infantrymen into the outlying suburbs, lay the shimmering, rain-soaked outline of southern Berlin. Black wisps of smoke hung like grimy cobwebs across the intervening miles, but he could see the occasional glint of rail lines and the spires of church steeples. Streets and avenues, now battered and broken, crisscrossed into infinity through the ugly shells of bombed-out factories and apartment buildings and homes. The silvery flash of the Spree River, the only clean-looking thing in sight, wound up through the eastern thigh of the city and disappeared in the haze. Far to the north, perhaps ten miles or more from his vantage point in the Schönefeld control tower, he could almost make out the southern rim of the elevated S-Bahn, and beyond it the wide, flat emptiness that marked the cramped runways of Tempelhof, the inner-city airport. Had the day been clearer, had the smoke been slightly less thick, he felt he might have seen all the way to the heart of the city, to the Brandenburg Gate and the government buildings that clustered around it, to the cellars and basements in which besieged German leaders now crouched, surely aware that it was only a matter of time until they were surrounded and their hideous ambitions forever thwarted.

He drank deeply of the sight—a heady brew, long in the fermentation. Many miles and many dead comrades had gone into the mixture, and it was stronger than any mere alcohol. He sampled it again and again, with revenge as a chaser. He drew pictures in his mind, savoring the momentary intoxication, pictures of Nazi flags trampled underfoot, of stone façades and carved German eagles crumbling to the ground, of German hands trembling and held high in capitulation. And the headiest vision of them all, the monster cornered in his last refuge. Hitler, cowering on his knees, staring up into a revolver held by Volkov himself.

"Comrade Volkov? Are you up there?"

The voice drifted into his thoughts from below, and he leaned through a paneless window to look down. It was Vasili Ivanov, a handsome, blue-eyed lieutenant from Leningrad who had been assigned to his search team. Volkov removed his glasses and waved acknowledgment.

Ivanov cupped his hands and called, "I've been looking for you. You have visitors." He gestured at a pair of weary, dirty Russian infantrymen near the closest hangar. They were holding on to an even wearier, dirtier-looking man, a German prisoner in shabby civilian clothing.

"I'll be right down," Volkov said. He took a last look at the gray, inviting horizon, then lowered himself through the trap door and descended a wooden ladder.

The two infantrymen, summoned by Ivanov, trudged across the runway, dragging their prize. He was a gray-haired man, with wide ears and rheumy eyes, and he kept stumbling as they yanked him along. When they reached the base of the control tower, they shoved him down on his face at Volkov's feet. The German tried to rise, but one of the infantrymen kicked him flat again. The German covered his head and began to shiver.

"What's this?" Volkov said.

The senior infantryman, a sergeant major with oil and mud stains on his tunic, looked puzzled. "We were told to bring you prisoners, Comrade Captain. We took this one in Falkenberg about an hour ago. He threw away his weapon and tried to hide in a cellar, but we dug him out."

"He must have put up a furious struggle," Volkov said. "He looks to be at least sixty years old."

The sergeant major frowned. "They all look the same age when you put them behind a rifle, Comrade Captain. The trigger pulls easily. Perhaps you wouldn't know that back here."

Volkov decided to ignore the impertinence. He regarded the trembling man at his feet and said in German, "You. Sit up. I wish to ask you some questions."

The German flinched, surprised at hearing his own tongue. He raised a grimy, bewhiskered face. Gaunt eyes stared from puffy, gray skin. "Yes, Excellency," he quavered. "Anything you wish."

"What division are you attached to?" Volkov asked.

"None, Excellency. Not exactly. The LVI Panzer Corps has authority in our sector, but most of us are either in the people's militia, the Volkssturm, like myself, or attached from the Hitlerjugend. We are not real soldiers, I swear."

"How long has your outfit been in the city?"

"The city is my home, Excellency. I've never been away from it."

"If that's true, then you must know a great deal about the city. Where is Hitler? Where is he hiding?"

"I . . . I beg your pardon, Excellency?"

"Hitler. Your leader. You must know where the government has taken shelter. Are they in the Reichstag? In one of the larger bunkers, like the flak towers at the zoo, or the Friedrichshain? Where have you seen the most troops? What do your friends say?"

"My apologies, Excellency. We don't talk much about the government. Most of us just talk about surviving."

In Russian, Ivanov said, "You don't expect to learn anything from an old fart like this, do you?"

Volkov shook his head. "Probably not. But it's always well to ask." He glanced at the two infantrymen. "You may as well take him away. He's useless to us. Bring us real soldiers, someone who knows what is going on. Bring us officers."

The infantrymen exchanged glances. The sergeant major said, "Begging your pardon, Comrade Captain, but take him away where? We were told to leave him here."

"We have no provisions for prisoners yet," Volkov said. "We'll be moving up in an hour or so. Take him wherever prisoners are being assembled."

The sergeant major looked at his companion again, then slung his rifle across his shoulder and yanked the prisoner to his feet. The three of them, frightened German and two Russian escorts, set off across the runway without another word, heading back toward Falkenberg. Lieutenant Ivanov watched until they disappeared behind one of the gutted hangars, then said, "What can we expect to find out even from officers, should they bring us some?"

"I don't know yet. A word, a hint. Someone must know where the leaders are hiding. Hitler has a tendency to send personal directives even to the smallest of units. There must be some chain of communication. I'll even accept rumors. We'll have to know where to look if we hope to cut off Hitler's line of retreat."

"You still expect to find him in Berlin?"

"Our information tells us he is there."

"Yes, but for how long? Hitler is no fool, Comrade Volkov. He'll surely flee the city in the next day or two, if he hasn't done so already."

"He will stay," Volkov said confidently. "He's a stubborn man. He has proved it time and again with his no-retreat policies. To withdraw himself at this point would destroy the faith of his followers. He must stay."

The sound of a rifle shot, one sharp, clear report, echoed loudly across the abandoned airstrip, and both men looked quickly in the direction from which it had come. After a pause, the two Russian infantrymen appeared from behind their hangar. They were alone.

"Those bastards," Volkov muttered.

"What did you expect?" Ivanov said. "They can't waste time tracking down a prisoner-collection point. They've got to get back to the fighting."

"They could have let him go. He was nothing but a frightened old man. Why make war on old men?"

"He was a German soldier," Ivanov said. "With or without a uniform, no matter how old, he was still a German soldier."

Volkov eyed the handsome young lieutenant coldly. "Your disregard for Germans is commendable, Lieutenant. I, too, have a great loathing for them. But not for old men and children. You'll find that hatred is more effective if you channel it into a single, white-hot beam. Diffuse it, waste it on small people, and those who deserve it most will never feel its heat."

3

For a city under siege, Berlin behaved oddly. Some of the more vital services either ceased or functioned so erratically as to become useless. Gas mains shut down. Water taps dried up. Electricity sputtered and died. Streetcars and subways stopped running. Bakeries stopped baking.

Yet newspapers continued to publish. The *Völkischer Beobachter* appeared on the streets every morning and would continue to do so for another three days until it was replaced by a four-page propaganda sheet called *Der Panzerbär*. Breweries kept producing, even through the worst crises, so that it wasn't unusual to see a Schultheiss brewery wagon jostling through the streets with a load of beer kegs behind a team of oxen, fighting for the right-of-way with ammunition trucks from the factories in Spandau. Telephones worked with precision throughout the emergency, as well, even after the Russians entered the city and began to fight their way through the streets. Dog-tired Red soldiers laughed as the report went around of one Russian officer with a quixotic sense of humor who telephoned the

Chancellery during the height of the battle, asking to speak to Dr. Joseph Goebbels. He got him, too, though the conversation was said to have been rather brief.

For Bascom and Erika, the discovery that the telephones were working came as a shock. Bascom had spent the morning clearing debris from the upper stairwell of the derelict house he now shared with the German girl and her young wards, and she insisted on spending the afternoon rummaging through the upper rooms in hopes of finding food, usable mattresses, or even furniture that could be broken up and burned. When a sudden ringing startled them both, Bascom's stomach turned over, and he felt absurdly like a burglar.

Apparently the children heard it, too. Before Bascom and Erika could locate the phone, both children came running up the stairs from the lower floor, where they had presumably been playing. Anne-Lise found the shrilly insistent phone beneath a heap of chair cushions. She grabbed the receiver. Then she just sat there listening, while a tinny voice repeated, "Fräulein Wendt? Fräulein Wendt?"

Freddy tugged at Erika's skirt. He whispered, "Auntie, we saw a woman at the corner with food. Can we go, too?"

But Erika shook him off and took the phone from Anne-Lise to apologize to the caller for the little girl's bad manners. Then she began calmly explaining that if this was the residence of Fräulein Wendt, it was no longer habitable or inhabited. There was a pause. She said, "Yes, I can't believe it. The telephone is actually working!" She paused again. "You did? Who did you reach? You *did?* Where are you? What's it like there?"

Wondering at the ways of women with telephones, Bascom left Erika listening with a rapt expression. There was still a lot of work to do. And, after all, if she wanted to talk to a complete stranger, what harm? Freddy followed him a few steps. "We really did see a woman," the little boy said. "She told us there was food for the taking. Shouldn't we go?"

Bascom scolded absent-mindedly. "Freddy, what has your Aunt Erika told you about wanting to go out on the street by yourselves? Now go wait for her, and if you want to go somewhere, ask her." He started down the hall. Off an empty bedroom, he found a locked door, but when he broke through it, that room was empty, too. He shook his head, wondering what kind of person would carefully lock an empty room. Erika's voice still murmured. He looked further, and on the east side of the building he had better luck: two beds and two mattresses, though they were the kind that only a German could invent, made of three sections so you could be certain of spending your nights sleeping on a slowly widening crack. Down in the cellar, Formoy was already lying on the first mattress that Bascom had scavenged, but Erika had seemed determined to find bedding for everyone, even if it meant poking around on shaky upper floors. She'd be pleased when she saw these extra mattresses.

He paused and looked out the paneless east windows. A lot of smoke on the horizon, apparently where Russian shells were landing. In their own area, they'd been luckier. He'd been jolted awake a few times by German flak, but the only other sound he'd heard through a long, calm night was an occasional moan from Formoy, still holding on somehow with all that lead in him, still breathing. Now, by late afternoon, the periodic roar of German flak had been joined by increasingly persistent howls of Red artillery. Most of it was still falling to the east, but it was getting closer. And the sky, black with smoke at the lower edges, was still gray overhead with rainclouds that threatened, but unlike the artillery, did not release their burden.

Erika was excitedly dialing the phone when Bascom passed her, lugging the first bulky mattress. On his way down the stairs, he heard her murmur, then shriek, "Gerta! My God, I've got Dresden! I can't believe it!" On his way back up, she was still talking. She was dialing again when he awkwardly carried the second mattress past her line of vision. Her eyes widened, and she seemed to realize what he was doing.

She caught up with him on the stairs. "What a beautiful mattress," she exclaimed. "And can you believe it? In spite of all the damage, telephone calls are still going through. Or some of them." Her golden eyes darkened. "One of my best friends lives on the Alexanderplatz. I got no ring there."

She seemed to need consolation, so Bascom cast about for words. "Probably the wires are just down," he said.

"Probably." She seized one of the mattress segments, nearly causing him to drop the others, and clattered down the stairs behind him. "But I talked to Gerda Eber, who lives in a village near Dresden. That's almost a hundred miles from here. And do you know what? Her baker still has rolls every day. And another store was giving away free butter. Of course, it was rancid, but think of it! A pound to everybody! Free! Is that good, or is it bad?"

Bascom found it easy to identify Erika's ambivalent concern. Free butter could mean German officialdom was on the verge of giving up. Erika would obviously welcome the end of a losing battle, but losing always meant pain.

But before he had a chance to speak, a new thought struck her. She stopped near the bottom of the cellar stairs and said, "Where are the children?"

"I thought they stayed upstairs with you," Bascom said.

"I thought they had gone on with you," she answered.

With wordless simultaneity, they dumped the mattresses and rushed back up the cellar stairs to head for the street. The danger of spent flak fragments and Russian shelling seemed to mean nothing to Anne-Lise. She had remained stubbornly unconvinced that she shouldn't go outside and play.

The kids were nowhere in sight. The first clue Bascom and Erika got to their whereabouts was the sight of three women with empty boxes and shopping baskets hurrying toward Linden Strasse, while coming from the other direction was an elderly man who frowned with antlike determination as he half carried, half dragged a vast slab of bacon. The three women cast envious looks at it and hurried their pace. Two more women dashed out of a basement, almost colliding with the old man's bacon. "It's true,"

cried one. "Hurry, before it's all gone," cried the other.
They turned toward Linden Strasse.

"What in the world?" Bascom said.

"Good God, that must be what Freddy meant," Erika
said. "Something about food. Didn't he say something
about food?" She pushed Bascom so hard he almost stumbled. And she took off after the other women.

Bascom literally followed his nose to a small, once-
elegant hotel, in front of which an eager crowd milled. He
picked up snatches of information. The hotel's inhabitants,
largely wealthy widows, had long since been evicted. The
Oberkommando der Wehrmacht, the Armed Forces High
Command, had requisitioned the building for visiting staff
officers, and provisioned it accordingly. Two days ago, before the Russians moved in, the OKW had fled its Zossen
headquarters, ten miles to the south. Officers and staff cars
were hopscotching rapidly toward the Danish border, trying to stay ahead of the Russians—and, not inconsequen-
tially, said officers had abandoned their supplies in Berlin,
leaving the hotel's cellars stuffed with food and firewater.

It was the sharp smell of spilled wine that guided Bascom
through the crowd, then the sight of sacks of oats, sugar,
and soap powder being hauled away by the first arrivals.
Some lucky few had found great legs of beef, and in the
hotel foyer two women stabbed viciously with umbrellas
over an almost equally prized comestible, a disputed bag
of potatoes. Bascom spotted Erika gazing at some sight
behind the registration desk, and when he shoved his way
to her he discovered she had found the children. Anne-Lise
and Freddy crouched in a corner over a collection of con-
densed-milk cans, three cans with no labels, sundry turnips,
a miniature postal scale the desk clerk must once have
used, and two empty marmalade jars. Anne-Lise clutched
a third jar, and she and Freddy were swallowing marmalade
as fast as their fingers could scoop it out. They grinned
stickily and hilariously at Bascom.

"They'll be sick tonight," Erika said, but she sounded
hilarious herself. "Come. Let's see if we're too late for one
of those legs of beef."

The mob making for the cellars was not so good-natured. The Germans' ingrained habit of lining up in orderly fashion seemed to have vanished. Men snarled over barrels of jam, and a young boy, no more than twelve, sat tight on a huge barrel of sauerkraut, cursing at everyone who came close, perhaps left there as a guard by his parents. A trio of men with bottles cradled in their arms paused in the hall long enough for one to crack the neck off a brandy bottle and take a deep pull, while an elderly woman marched past them with a sniff of disapproval. She had opted for chocolates and soap. "There was even coffee, but I got none," she told Erika in passing. "Our heroic officers. They lived well while we starved, didn't they?"

Erika hurried on, sniffing like an intelligent bird dog. She found the meat locker, but it was already empty. In another dark storage room filled with shoving people, she managed to grab six packets of noodles from a high, overlooked shelf and handed them to Bascom. She added canned plums and peaches and jars of honey; then, with an eager cry, she fell upon a large untended box half full of miscellaneous cans and, under them, potatoes and sausages. Quickly, she unloaded Bascom's burden into the box and whispered, "Into another room. And don't let go of that box."

They found bread dropped on a floor where soap had been spilled earlier. Erika didn't let the powdering of soap disturb her. She jammed loaves into the box, then brushed off a loaf and stuffed part in her mouth. She didn't forget Bascom. She fed him like a baby bird, offering chunks of bread to his willing teeth while he clung to the box. They found more turnips and carrots, but she passed them by. Then they found the wine cellar, a swamp of spilled spirits and splintered glass, and she topped Bascom's box with randomly seized bottles, tucking several more under her arm.

That was all. Suddenly, she was afraid to stay in the cellars. "My God, what if the OKW hasn't really left?" she whispered to Bascom. "What if they come back? They'll line us all against a wall and shoot us. Worse, they might take the food away from us. Hurry, we must find the children and get out of here, before we lose everything."

The little cache of goods that Anne-Lise and Freddy had collected was almost Bascom's undoing. As Erika filled his pockets with the children's finds, he could feel his knees buckling.

"For God's sake, leave those empty marmalade jars," he said. "I can't carry another gram."

Like a spendthrift paterfamilias with his family in tow, Bascom puffed out of the hotel clutching the heavy box to his chest. A hand reached out of the crowd for one of the teetering wine bottles on top of the box, but Erika charged with a lionlike snarl, and they reached the street with their loot intact. Freddy carried the postal scale as though it were the most precious booty of all.

Once they got clear of the swarm of other looters, Bascom leaned against a wall and tried to get a better grip on the box.

"Put it down for a moment," Erika said. She helped him lower it, and as another bottle teetered, she took it with a glance at a group of young boys who were thirstily gulping wine from the same cellar. Fate had not provided corkscrews. Like the boys, Erika smashed the top off the bottle, drank carefully, then offered it to Bascom, as if to give him strength. He shook his head.

"Drink," she said. "You must be as thirsty as I."

The wine was cool. Bascom had always wanted to crack open a wine bottle with a pirate's ferocity, and he was only sorry he hadn't thought of it first. He paused to breathe, then gulped again, but sharp pain forced him to lower the bottle abruptly. "Damn," he gasped. "I think I cut my lip."

He felt it gingerly. Blood dampened his upper lip, but he couldn't tell if it was just a nick or a deeper cut. Erika gasped, too. She quickly handed him a piece of linen tablecloth she had taken as a handkerchief after using the rest to change Formoy's bandages.

"Sorry," Bascom said, thinking the sight of blood had bothered her, but she was staring at the label on the wine bottle.

"The OKW did itself well," she said in a small voice. "It's a vintage Vouvray."

"Sorry," Bascom said again, though he didn't know what he was apologizing for.

She shook her tawny curls. "It doesn't matter. It's a different year, anyway. Anne-Lise, give me one of your marmalade jars. We'll finish it like civilized people."

So they had brought the empty jars after all. Bascom sighed in wonder. He tried to stanch the bleeding from his lip before taking the jarful of wine she held out to him.

"Me, too, Aunt Erika," said Anne-Lise.

"No," Erika said, "this is only for grown-up people." She gave Bascom a level look, and he suddenly remembered—a '37 Vouvray. That's what she'd been guarding all these months to celebrate the end of the war with her fiancé. Now she stood formally holding out to him their stolen wine in a sticky white jar, an obvious prewar import labeled "James Keiller & Son, Ltd., Dundee Orange Marmalade, Made in Great Britain." He raised it in a brief, wordless toast to the gods of war and drank it down to the bottom. It tasted of wine, of the orangy dregs of the marmalade, of a faint dilute of blood. She refilled for herself and did the same, then dropped the empty wine bottle in the curbing. They started home.

The wine on a near-empty stomach bubbled quickly to Bascom's head. He felt good. The children obviously didn't, not after gorging themselves, and as soon as they reached their cellar, Erika scrubbed their hands and down-turned mouths and put them to bed in the trunk room on one of the new mattresses Bascom had found that afternoon. He looked in on Formoy. As always, there seemed to be little change, either for the worse or better. The Britisher had taken some carrot broth this morning, but he continued to gaze blankly at the ceiling between sips, noting nothing. How hard that burly body held to life, Bascom thought, looking down at him. But, then, life was all anyone had.

In the large second room, only dimly lit by dusky twilight pouring in through the crack in the front wall, Bascom found Erika inventorying the liquid portion of their spoils. The food was already hidden away somewhere.

"God in heaven, they drank only the best," she said, glancing up at him. "Romanée Conti '21. Meursault '33. An old armagnac that would bring the dead back to life. We shall see tomorrow if your friend can swallow a few sips. And the champagnes. Look, there are two magnificent Louis Roederers and a Moët et Chandon. Unbelievable."

Bascom felt the soft lift of the earlier wine expanding in his blood vessels, swirling in his brain. "Let's drink two or three of them," he said. "Which is the best?"

She rose, looking scarcely steadier. "Well, the Louis Roederer. But we should eat something."

"We did. Bread. And I doubt the kids would feel up to eating anything after all that marmalade."

"No, they're already asleep," she said. "Full stomachs, the poor little things. I wouldn't have dreamed they could keep it all down. Let's fix up one of the mattresses and have a picnic."

She'd started for the front room when a shell hit not two blocks down the street. First there was only a low, whizzing sound, but it rose to an eerier howl, ending in a tremendous roar. The wine bottle at Bascom's feet clinked gently as the earth beneath them shook. Erika sank to the floor as if hit by an ax, and Bascom lost two seconds trying to convince himself the world had stopped rocking before he could leap to help her. She clutched at his hands, a strong grip demonstrating she was neither dead nor unconscious, and he quickly helped her rise. They stood, waiting. There was only a distant rumble of guns.

"Just a stray shot," Bascom said, reassuring himself as much as her. "It's going to be another fairly quiet night."

"The mattress . . ."

"To hell with it," Bascom said. "You can't get comfortable on those things anyway. Let's just stay in here."

Her voice steadied. "Perhaps you can't, but I can. Besides, I . . . I'd rather be in the outer room, near the stairs. There's more air. You go make us a corner. I'll just check the children."

"All right," he said, "but bring the wine."

Her face swung toward him quickly, dim in the twilight. He couldn't see her expression. Maybe she wanted to save the wines, he thought as he moved to the outer room. Barter. Champagne for sauerkraut. That was okay, he guessed. As he had had recent occasion to learn, food was more important anyway. He dragged the remaining mattress sections to a corner and tried to arrange them comfortably next to the wall. A picnic? His mind roamed to more of the good bread and perhaps even a touch of the kid's marmalade.

But when Erika joined him, she had a bottle with her, neatly opened. The efficient girl had found a corkscrew among her belongings. "Drink," she said. "Here. Turn and turn about on the bottle."

Bascom took it gratefully and sank down on the mattresses. He tilted the bottle and swallowed. One of the champagnes. On his tongue, bubbles burst, giving out a faint flavor that was almost like drinking the fragrance of summer roses, and he involuntarily opened his eyes wide in pleasure and surprise. "That's marvelous," he said. "Which one is it?"

"Do you mind that it's champagne?" she said hesitantly. There was a grave, expectant look in her tawny eyes. "At least it's the best. For us."

A faint rush that wasn't the wine suddenly tingled in Bascom's veins as she sank down beside him, her thigh touching his. Silently, he handed the bottle back to her. She swallowed deeply.

"It would be better if we were in a park somewhere," she said. "In the open. We could drink and watch the night fall, then sit and stare at the stars."

"We could always pretend," Bascom said.

"No. To be alive in a dirty cellar is better than to be half dead and pretend. Drink again. We'll drink it all. And when it's done, we'll drink another. For one night, at least, let us forget the war."

And they did. Later, Bascom hardly noticed the inevitably widening cracks in the segmented mattress. He was

conscious only of welcome pain, her wholehearted kisses
on his cut lip, and of the warmth of a body that worked
with his toward a temporary surcease, a time of forgetting,
out of time, out of chaos, the final simplicity.

4

Hermann Göring's Luftwaffe chief of staff, General Koller,
was aflame with emotion when he reached Göring's home
in southern Germany. Acting on permission of General
Jodl, he flew out of Berlin in a Heinkel 111 to bring Göring the news of Hitler's breakdown in the previous day's
Führerbunker conference.

The Führer had collapsed, Koller reported. The Führer
had threatened to take his own life, might well already
have done so. Everyone was fleeing. Even Keitel and Jodl
would attend their last Führerbunker session today, then
would head north, following the OKW caravan to safer
ground.

Ambitious to the end, Göring envisioned being propelled
to the headship of the Party. With Hitler dead or in-
capacitated, he was next in line. He gathered his Luftwaffe
advisers quickly. Should he fly the next day to meet with
Eisenhower for "man to man" discussions in hopes of
negotiating peace? Or should he call upon the German
people to stand by their guns? At least one of his advisers
suggested it would be well if first he cleared the change of
command with Hitler. To assume control without authorization could be misconstrued.

The other advisers agreed. To give Göring's intentions
a semblance of legality, they resurrected an official document drafted by Hitler himself in 1941, a few days after
the beginning of the Russian campaign, naming Göring
as the legal successor, should Hitler be prevented from
carrying out his duties by illness or death. Using the document as a base, they carefully drafted a message to be sent
to Berlin. It read:

My Führer, in view of your decision to remain in Fortress Berlin, is it your wish that I immediately assume total control of the Reich with full freedom of action at home and abroad as your deputy, in accordance with your decree of June 29, 1941? If no reply is received by ten o'clock tonight, I shall have to assume that you have lost your freedom of action, and I shall therefore take control in the best interests of the Fatherland and our people. God bless you and protect you.

> Your loyal servant,
> Hermann Göring, Reichsmarschall

But Hitler was more resilient than Göring or his newsbearing chief of staff might have believed. In the twenty-four hours since his collapse in the Führerbunker, Hitler had not only regained his strength of will, he had also regained his temper. A response to Göring's message came quickly, an hour ahead of Göring's ten-o'clock deadline. It began:

YOUR ACTION REPRESENTS HIGH TREASON. . . .

5

The dentist flicked off the high-intensity lamp and beamed down at the man they called Rösselsprung. "That's it," he said proudly. "You may inform Reichsleiter Bormann that my part in this exercise is fulfilled. And a beautiful job, if I do say so myself."

Gestapo chief Heinrich Müller raised an eyebrow. "You are completely finished?"

"Yes, and most successfully—assuming, of course, that you follow through on the other suggestions I submitted, the X rays, the charts, the duplicate bridges. No amount of artistry on my part will succeed unless you take care of all the loose ends."

"I intend to do that, doctor. All the loose ends. Can he be returned to his cell?"

"By all means."

Müller nodded to the two young Gestapo guards, who boosted Rösselsprung from the dental chair and ushered him through the door. The dentist peeled off his white smock. "I wouldn't make use of him right away," he said. "Not if it can be avoided. A few more days to allow additional tartar buildup would be most advantageous."

"Another loose end?"

"Oh, he's ready. If circumstances dictate, you could use him immediately. But it would be better if you could hold off for a time." He hung his smock on a coat hook and reached for his jacket. "I hope the Reichsleiter will remember my part in this when it is all done."

"The Reichsleiter has already asked me to express his gratitude," Müller said.

The dentist smiled. "That is most kind. Not that I expect any reward, of course. As a loyal Party member, I feel I have done no more than my duty. But I would welcome any help in securing an exit permit from the city. The Reichsleiter and I have been friends for some years. Do you suppose he would be willing to assist me?"

"You still intend to leave Berlin?"

"Yes, and not a moment too soon. The corridor to the west is in danger of closing, they say."

"Where will you go?"

"To join my family. My wife took the children to Bernberg a month ago."

"Bernberg may fall to the Americans in the next day or so," Müller said. "Perhaps it has already."

The dentist sighed. "Yes, I know. Actually, we anticipated that, my wife and I. Anything is better than sitting in the path of the Russians. I'm hoping the situation will still be confusing enough for me to slip through."

"I imagine it will be," Müller said. "Is there anything I can do personally to speed you on your way?"

The dentist, arm extended as he pulled on his jacket, paused and said appreciatively, "Why, thank you. Yes, please. Anything you can do will earn my undying gratitude."

"Very well," Müller said. He undid his holster flap and pulled out a Walther P-38 automatic. "Have a pleasant journey, doctor." He fired twice.

The dentist, arm tangled in the half-donned jacket, stumbled backward and fell against the high-intensity lamp. His eyes glazed in surprise, and he slipped to the floor.

Müller gazed down at him, watching for signs of life, then stepped forward and touched the gun barrel to the man's temple. He fired twice more.

When it was done, he crossed to a row of file drawers and stripped out armload after armload of dental files, dropping them in a heap on the floor. He found a bottle of medicinal alcohol in a glass-fronted cabinet and sprinkled it over the files for good measure, then touched a match to the pile. Blue flames licked out and spread.

Once the fire was going, Müller nursed it, feeding it with magazines, wooden chairs, everything he could find to build up its intensity. The flames responded eagerly. Higher and higher they rose, until they assumed a greedy life of their own, consuming, growing. The wall paint nearest the fire began to blister. Protecting his face from the heat, Müller dragged the body across the floor and heaved it into the blaze. The dentist's clothing smoldered and began to burn. Müller watched for a moment, then let himself out and jogged down the stairs toward the darkened street.

It was a black night outside, no stars, no moon. But the eastern horizon was ablaze, a long curtain of flaming red sky stretching from north to south, marking the advance of the Russians. He glanced back up at the dental office, at the glow of flames surging toward the window. One more fire in a city filled with fires. It was doubtful that anyone would even notice.

7

Tuesday—April 24, 1945

Meine Ehre heisst Treue.

"My honor is loyalty."

—motto engraved on all SS daggers

1

Before daybreak, one of the SOE scouts crawled wearily back to Sidney Longland to report he had found a rowboat enmeshed in reeds near the riverbank. It was large enough for six people, he said, providing at least a pair of them kept busy with bailing buckets. Perhaps they could take turns crossing.

"Is the river definitely the Elbe?" Longland asked.

The scout, a man named Butrick, was silent for a moment, then shrugged. "I hope so," he said. "At least it should be. Unless every compass in the outfit is broken and we've somehow doubled back on ourselves, it has to be."

"Did you see any signs of the Americans on the far side?" Longland asked.

This time Butrick didn't hesitate. "No. I saw nothing. Neither Americans *nor* Germans."

Longland closed his eyes and tried to decide. They had crept westward for three nights since escaping the city, moving only by moonlight, crowding under dubious shelter by day, constantly in danger. They had seen many Germans. Patrols and scouting parties from Wenck's understrength Twelfth Army, eyes alert for the occasional downed Allied airman. Trucks, tanks, and horse-drawn supply wagons waiting for the order to march east to join the battle against the Russians. Ragged strings of frightened civilian refugees stumbling toward the west, hoping to surrender to the Americans. And above it all, British

and American planes ranged at will, shooting at anything
that moved.

Longland's small band had made excruciatingly slow
progress. Not only were they hobbled by their wounded
and short on food and medical supplies, they had also been
forced out of their meticulously planned escape route almost from the beginning. After leaving the Havel, they
had tried to circle to the southwest, as mandated, but a
German relief column from Belzig came slogging through
the rain, aiming toward Potsdam, and frightened them
back. They headed northwest to bypass it and took shelter
the next day in a German barn, where at least it was dry,
but an American P-51 had dropped from gray clouds to
riddle the place with machine-gun fire. The casualties
were a cow and two horses; a fire started in the hayloft;
and one of Longland's men, who had taken a .50-caliber
slug in the chest before they could all scatter to safety.
After that they kept to the fields and pine woods, wandering in a generally westerly direction by night, crouching
in gullies by day, avoiding the roads and villages and farmhouses.

They had reached a river yesterday, the Elbe, they assumed; near Magdeburg, they suspected. But they spotted a
German rear guard dug in along the riverbank and had to
pull back and divert once more, this time south. Now they
were on the river again, the same river, they hoped, in an
area that seemed reasonably clear of German troops.

"Well, what do we do?" Butrick asked.

"We go," Longland said. "Now. Five men, all armed,
for the first trip. I'll take the lead. The rest will stay here
with the wounded until we're certain of our ground."

He chose the men who would accompany him and included the scout. Then he stared at the river. It would take
at least four crossings to get everyone across, and it would
all have to be done in the open, there on the exposed surface of the river. With luck, before sunrise. "Someone
will have to make the round trip, if we're to get the boat
back," he said. "Any volunteers?"

Butrick sighed. "I don't like it, but I'll do it."

Longland nodded gratefully. At the riverbank, they waded out to pull the boat loose from the reeds. There were no oars, but by removing the seats and using the planks to paddle while kneeling in the bottom of the hull, they managed to wallow silently across the wide river in less than fifteen minutes.

As they approached the dark western bank, Butrick whispered, "What shall I do after I put you ashore? Shall I wait, or start back immediately?"

Longland shifted his plank to his knees. "You might as well wait until we check it out. If it isn't the Elbe, the others won't be needing the boat."

One of the men up front, a buck-toothed Britisher named Fridd, turned to whisper, "What if it's the Elbe, but the Yanks have pulled back? What do we do then?"

Longland was unable to answer. He resumed stroking. It was a distinct possibility. God only knew what might have happened over the past few days. The Germans could have counterattacked. Eisenhower could have ordered the troops to withdraw. Anything.

The boat nosed into the reeds at the river's edge. Longland exchanged his plank for his Sten and gestured for the others to follow him. They hurried up the muddy bank at a crouch while the scout stayed below and watched.

At first they could see little. Cloud cover had dissipated, and the sky was filled with early-morning stars. Still, except for a faint graying of the eastern sky behind them, the landscape seemed as dark and barren as a desert.

But after a few moments, shapes began to take form. A hillock there. A tree beyond. A stone fence, shell-pocked and broken, probably by tanks roaming the bank. Longland winced. Daylight was creeping up on them. Too fast, too fast.

And suddenly, no more than fifty yards ahead of them, someone stirred. They heard the clink of metal on metal, like dogtags or German identification disks, rubbing against each other at the end of a chain. A figure rose from a shallow foxhole, stretching sleepily in the darkness. They hugged the ground and watched anxiously as the figure wandered to the side and undid his fly. They could see him more clearly every second as the eastern sky lightened, a young man in battle fatigues, clutching a carbine in one hand and directing a stream of urine with the other.

It was an American infantryman, relieving himself on the sacred soil of Germany. It was the most beautiful sight Longland had ever seen.

Overcome with relief, he jumped to his feet and waved his arms. "Hallo, hallo," he called.

The American jerked and whirled around. The stream pinched off as though a spigot had been turned. He stared at Longland for the space of three heartbeats, then whipped his carbine to his shoulder and opened fire.

Longland hit the dirt. "Good God!" the buck-toothed Fridd gasped. "What's gotten into him?"

More Americans poured out of their foxholes to open fire. Slugs whined wildly overhead.

"Bloody hell!" Longland shouted. "Off it, you Yanks!"

But his voice only served as a locater for the Americans, and the wild shooting became a concentrated fire, kicking up teacup-sized chunks of mud around them.

Longland took a deep breath and changed his approach. He shouted, "Lucky Strikes! Chevrolet! Goddamn! Fuck the Germans!"

Fridd looked at him in surprise, but the shooting quickly tailed off. The Britisher turned round eyes from Longland to the wary figures in the distance. "I say," he whispered, "how did you manage that?"

"By speaking American," Longland whispered back. "Not too articulate, but they're about the only words they seem to know."

"Who are you?" a voice yelled.

"We're a British unit," Longland called back.

"Prove it."

"How the bloody hell can I do that?" Longland called.

"For one thing," the voice yelled, "you can explain why you're wearing those fucking German uniforms."

Longland's eyes dropped to his specially tailored uniform

tunic and he muttered, "Damn, I'd forgotten about these things."

Fridd raised his head a few inches and called in an outraged voice, "You, there. You might have been decent enough to allow us to identify ourselves before you started shooting."

"You still haven't identified yourselves," the voice yelled back. "And you better do it pretty quick, Mac."

"Our officer just told you," Fridd shouted. "We're English, and we're tired. We don't need harassment from a bunch of bloody fools. You let us come forward, or we'll have you on report."

"Ah, go shit in your helmet," the voice said.

The buck-toothed Britisher blinked. "Why did he say that?" he asked Longland. "I'm not even wearing a helmet."

It took the better part of fifteen minutes for Longland and his small beachhead party to talk their way into the American lines, but by the time they did, American officers had appeared. To a bird colonel and two lieutenants, Longland identified himself and explained their plight—the exhausted men on the far bank waiting for the return of the rowboat.

The colonel obviously wanted to ask Longland about the strange uniforms and what they were doing coming from the German side of the river, but Longland summoned up the efficiency to cut him off. "My group is made up of British agents and OSS men. They've all had a hard time, Colonel, and some are badly wounded," he said. "I'd appreciate your help in getting them across."

The single mention of "OSS" did it. The colonel instantly turned to one of his officers and ordered, "Lieutenant Spade, you will dispatch a crew with rubber boats. Uh . . . and Major Longland, I wonder . . . are any of your party up to going back with my people? We wouldn't want any repetition of this, uh, regrettable shooting incident."

"Good thought," Longland said. "Cox, Fridd? Think you

can accompany the boats? And fill in Butrick. He'll go back with you, too. Acceptable, Colonel?"

The officer nodded. He was obviously still curious, but he stifled the impulse to ask questions, and substituted orders to the remaining lieutenant arranging food and medical treatment.

Longland fought to keep his eyes open. The relief of having it all over. That's what it was. "And transportation, please," he said. "It's essential that we get these man back instanter."

"I'll do what I can to get them priority transport to a rear-echelon airstrip on the next round-trip Red Ball Express convoy," the colonel promised. "Satisfactory?"

"Most," Longland said. He couldn't help it. He yawned.

The colonel paused. Curiosity still peeped from his eyes, but he tried to be discreet. "And, uh, just in case you need to notify anyone that you and your men have made it from, er, wherever you've been, can I give you a lift to the nearest communications center? My Jeep is parked up by the road." Longland hesitated, too. Another yawn split his face. He didn't really want to leave until all the men were across, but, thanks to the colonel's reminder, a little eddy from a forgotten world tugged at him, then tugged harder. The real world contained a superior named Mr. Mumford. The other world, filled with field gray German uniforms and .50-caliber machine-gun fire from American P-51s, began subtly to fade.

Longland left the buck-toothed Britisher in charge and climbed into the colonel's Jeep, eager to feast his eyes on miles and miles of friendly Americans and American tanks and guns and American safety.

But he didn't see much of it. He fell asleep within moments, a deep, restful sleep, with his head lolling on the startled colonel's shoulder.

A shell slammed into the street outside and jarred Bascom awake. The cellar walls shook, and dust sifted from the ceiling in thick clouds. He jerked upright, blinking, forgetting for the moment where he was. Then the low, permanent rumble of Russian artillery and the jumble of empty wine bottles teetering against the wall brought memory flooding back. He looked at his clothing, scattered on the floor at the foot of the mattress. Idiot, he told himself. Life was a matter of surviving from minute to minute, and he had to get fancy with a German *Fräulein*.

Another explosion thundered, even closer than the last, and the whole cellar floor seemed to shift. Particles of plaster and cement rained down on him. Christ, close! Voices murmured somewhere above, nervous, pleading. Bascom struggled into his shirt and trousers, worrying quietly about his changed situation. Erika. The kids. The kids were okay, but they talked too much. They couldn't help it. One of them was bound to mention him and Formoy to the neighbors sooner or later. He could hear them now, voices rising on the landing above the . . .

Voices? He stiffened. It wasn't the children he heard. Those were adult voices, women's voices, a man's voice.

Quickly, he pulled on his sweater and reached for his shoes. Erika was up there. He could make out her voice. Arguing? With strangers? Who the hell? Should he hide? What about Formoy? Barefoot, he hurried to the coal room. The stocky Britisher was resting quietly, from the look of him. Would it hurt to move him? Maybe just slide his mattress to some other room and poke him out of sight? Erika would get rid of the people, most likely. But what if she couldn't? What if it was the Gestapo? In that case, they would surely search the whole building, including the cellar, and not even the darkest corner would escape their notice.

He paused with one shoe on and the other poised over

his toes. Come on, he told himself, think straight. Go find
out. Tiptoe out close to the stairs. There, see? That couldn't
be the Gestapo up there. Those were definitely women's
voices, at least a couple. And the man's voice sounded old,
shaky, even frightened.

Before he could fully convince himself, another shell
tore into a building across the way, and the cellar danced
beneath him. One of the female voices shrieked, and he
heard footsteps hurry toward the stairs. Erika called out,
"Henri, Henri, are you all right?"

He froze, his second shoe still in his hand. She was
trying to warn him. Hide. But then her face appeared on
the landing, and a man's head, grizzled and shaking with
fear, leaned over her shoulder. They stared straight at him.

"Uh, yes," he said.

Erika turned and gestured at the man and some people
behind him and said, "Come quickly. We'll be safe down
here."

Bascom stood in immobilized silence, shoe still clutched
in his hand, and watched in stunned disbelief as they scurried down the stairs. Erika led the way, arms covering her
head. The man came next, an emaciated beanpole with silver hair and withered skin and a nervous grin that showed
ill-fitting false teeth. He was wearing baggy trousers and a
rumpled coat, and his arms were loaded with bedding and
packages. On his heels came an equally emaciated woman,
arms equally loaded with bundles and a covered bird cage.
They seemed to belong to each other. Bringing up the rear
was another woman, younger, perhaps in her thirties, with
a priggish, suspicious face and a nose like a butcher knife.

Another shell whined in, but this one hit at least a hundred yards down the street. Erika and the old couple
flinched, as did Bascom, but not the knife-nosed woman.
She made a quick circuit of the room, nose twitching as
though her investigation were conducted by scent. She
peered through the inner-room door, then checked the
coal room and apparently saw Formoy, resting quietly in
the corner. "What's the matter with him?" she asked.

Erika stood near the stairs taking long, shuddering breaths. "Oh, Maurice," she said. "Poor Maurice. He was badly wounded two days ago when Russian planes strafed Moritz Platz. We've done what we can for him, but doctors are in such short supply."

"Does he groan much at night?" the knife-nosed woman asked. "It's difficult enough to get any sleep with Russian guns shooting all the time."

Erika's eyes narrowed. "He has been a considerate patient so far," she said coldly. "But if you think it would bother you, perhaps another cellar somewhere will take you in."

"No, this will do," the woman said. She glanced toward the coal room again. "I suppose I can get used to him."

The old man looked embarrassed. As the shelling receded farther, he smiled at Erika and crowded closer to the woman with the bird cage to show that neither had anything but gratitude to offer. "We are most thankful for your kindness," he said. "We tried many places as we walked in from Köpenick, but most of them were filled to capacity already. Then that terrible artillery. Will it stop, do you think?"

"We must all hope so," Erika said. "Please, put down your things. Make yourselves at home."

"Uh," Bascom said.

"Oh, I'm sorry," Erika said. "Herr Fiebeck, Frau Fiebeck, this is Henri Cadiot, a childhood friend from France. It is he whom you should thank. He found the cellar for the children and me when we first arrived. In a way, it belongs to him."

"Ah, a Frenchman," the old man said, his Adam's apple bobbing nervously. "I fought the French in the first war. Verdun. Good soldiers. Very brave. I admire the French. We all admire the French." He set his bundles on the floor in order to shake Bascom's hand. "I am Otto Fiebeck, of Köpenick. My wife, Klara. And this is our neighbor, Frau Schiller. We thank you, Herr Cadiot, all of us, most sincerely, for your generosity."

"Uh, Erika," Bascom said.

"French?" the knife-nosed Frau Schiller said. "What is he doing in Berlin?"

"Henri is a foreign labor conscript," Erika said smoothly, "though he wasn't actually conscripted. He was a volunteer. But his factory was burned out a few weeks ago, so he has no place to go."

"He's very young," Frau Schiller said. "He should be in uniform."

"Erika," Bascom said, "could I speak to you?"

She shot him a nervous look. "Of course," she said. To the others, "Please, look around. The wine room is sturdy. Put your things there and make yourselves comfortable. I must look in on the children."

Bascom pulled on his shoe and led her to one of the small dark rooms in the rear of the cellar. "What the hell is going on?" he whispered. "Who are these people?"

"Please, don't be angry," she said. "I felt so sorry for them. The Russians blew up their house. They've been walking all night. They looked so tired. And then the shelling—"

"You invited them to move in with us?"

"I didn't exactly invite them. The shells falling so near drove them in. I couldn't very well turn them away. Besides, it will be safer in a way. The more people we have, the less notice for you if the authorities should chance to come. None of them speaks French. I checked."

Feet shuffled to the doorway behind them, and the frail figure of Herr Fiebeck leaned in. He coughed to get their attention and dropped his eyes. "My wife and I have been talking," he said. "We're truly sorry, we should not have imposed. If Herr Cadiot wishes us to go, we will move on."

"No, you can't," Erika said firmly. "It's much too dangerous on the streets. Henri was merely concerned that our hospitality may fall short. We haven't much food, you see. Nor water. He worries that we wouldn't have enough to share."

"Oh, if that's all," the man said. Behind rimless glasses, his eyes shone with hope. "You won't have to trouble about us. I'll fetch the water for everyone. Twice a day, if you wish. As for food, we don't eat much these days anyway."

"There, you see?" Erika said to Bascom. "Please, Henri. As a favor to me."

Bascom mumbled noncommittally, but the man chose to regard it as an affirmative response. His thin face beamed, and he hurried back into the main cellar. "We can stay," Bascom heard him tell the two women. "Herr Cadiot says we can stay."

"They won't be any trouble," Erika whispered. "And they'll be so grateful.'

Her eyes also seemed to speak, telling of a gratitude of her own that she would be willing to demonstrate. Was that all it had been last night? Bascom turned away. He didn't want a woman on those terms. Nor did he need another obligation like Formoy—three more, with Anne-Lise and Freddy included in the package—to look after. But, terms aside, it looked as though he'd firmly saddled himself with them all.

Two new explosions rocked the street, and the walls swayed. Close! Bascom inhaled deeply. So much for his idea of waiting underground until the Russians arrived. If the intensified shelling was any sample of what was to come, they'd be lucky to live through another day or two. And now with strangers moving in to take up residence in the cellar . . . No, it was too much. "I'm going out," he said abruptly.

"Out? You're mad. The Russians are bombarding the city."

"So I noticed. That's why I'm going. There's a man I must see. I should have gone sooner. He might be able to help us.'

Erika looked at him suspiciously. "What man? How can anyone help us?"

"He's an important man," Bascom said. "Maybe I can persuade him to help us leave the city. We can't just sit here. It's too dangerous."

"You are making this up," she said. "There is no such man. You intend to leave and never come back, don't you?"

"No, of course not. Use your head, Erika. My friend is stuck here. How could I leave him?"

She wasn't convinced. "Do you promise? You swear that you will come back?"

"I'll be back," he said. But he wasn't all that certain, not really. If he followed the course of action that was forming in his mind, a course that seemed to become more inevitable with each passing moment, he might not be alive an hour from now.

The copper roofing had been removed from the top of the huge Brandenburg Gate months ago, probably for melting and use as war materiel, but the four massive stone horses still pranced at its peak, hitched to the battle-scarred chariot of the goddess of victory. The goddess, her great sculptured visage chipped and shrapnel-marred, stared down sadly from her perch on a scene of smoking defeat.

The Pariser Platz had been hit from the air repeatedly over the months, and even now, as the focal point of the inner city, seemed to attract the special attention of long-range Russian gunners. The I. G. Farben building, across the way, all but wiped out in earlier air raids, was burning after taking three artillery shells. The French embassy was a shambles. The beautiful corner houses built by Karl Schinkel in the early nineteenth century to complement the victory gate had been heavily damaged. The Hotel Adlon, though it had taken no direct hits as yet, had lost all the glass from its upper-floor windows due to the blast waves.

Bascom sheltered in a boarded-up doorway across the street from the Adlon and called himself a dithering fool. The booms of exploding shells thudded all around him. The hotel had been turned into a field hospital for troops from the outer edges of the city, and the place was crawling with German uniforms. A long line of creaking horse carts, just about the only transportation left, inched toward the entrance, each with its dismal load of wounded soldiers, blank eyes staring, faces streaked with smoke and pain, cringing at the sounds of Russian artillery shells, waiting interminably for their turns at unloading. Uniformed medics and grim-faced enlisted men with rifles slung over their shoulders shuffled back and forth between carts and the hotel entrance, carrying bloody stretchers. A weary doctor in a red-spattered smock stood at the door, passing medical judgment on each patient with a quick glance. Some he sent inside. Others, already too close to death, merited only a shake of the head and were abandoned on the sidewalk, to be moved later.

Bascom assured himself that his choice was even more clear-cut. But it was like facing a first attempt at a double somersault from a ten-meter diving platform. You can step to the edge. You can tell your muscles, "Now!" But the muscles make their own decision when to act.

That he had to do something, he was convinced. The Russians, on whom he had vaguely pinned his earlier hopes, would be no help. They were, in fact, the enemy, just as were the hundreds of thousands of German soldiers and civilians who surrounded him, just as had been his own bombers ranging overhead on that first morning in Berlin. Odd that he hadn't thought it through. He'd envisioned Russians rolling triumphantly into the city in truck convoys, like peaceful liberators, enabling him to approach quietly with white flag in hand and carefully prepared explanations of who he was and what he was doing here. But the Russians were already at the edge of the city, bringing up their big guns to pulverize whatever the British and American bombers had left. And long-range guns, like bombs from the air, were damned indiscriminate about who they blew to bits.

Would Fegelein be any better? If he crossed this street and put himself in Fegelein's hands, which way would the German send him? To safety or to hell? One thing was certain: If he didn't cross, it would only be a matter of time until the Russians homed in on his cellar shelter, or until some German civilian—three more candidates now, thanks to Erika's softheartedness—blew his cover. Either way, he would be a long time dead.

"Now!" he said to himself. His feet didn't seem to want to move. Come on, he told himself, cross the street. All it

took was a short walk, across the cobbles and up the hotel
steps, through the door. Find the Herr Robeus his Swedish
newsman friend had mentioned, and ask to speak to Fegelein. An hour, probably less. Then Fegelein would come
or not, with an SS escort or not, and it would be over,
one way or the other. "Now!"

"You are looking for me?" the man said. He had a
pinched, harried look. On his nose perched thick-lensed
spectacles. His hands were greasy, and he wiped them on
a kitchen towel.

"Are you Herr Robeus?" Bascom asked. He kept his
tone servile, obsequious, just as he had through the three
clerks he approached upstairs, a nervous laborer, uncomfortable in the grandiose surroundings of a luxury hotel,
out of his element.

"I am," the man said. He was behind a stainless steel
counter, helping an engrossed chef check beef sides as they
were carried into a walk-in cooler. "What can I do for
you?"

Bascom watched the beef disappear on the backs of
white-coated chef's assistants. Would it end up on the table
of a government official or one of the high-ranking SS officers who still frequented the Adlon restaurant? Or would
it be saved for the wounded on the floors above?

"Well?" the man said.

The chef went into the cooler. Bascom unclamped his
teeth. "I've come to see Herr Fegelein," he said.

The man's eyes shifted slightly, glancing beyond Bascom
toward the meat carriers. He said quietly, "Fegelein? There
is no Fegelein working in this hotel. Are you sure you've
come to the right place?"

"I speak of Gruppenführer Fegelein," Bascom said.

The man looked at him blankly. "I have heard of Gruppenführer Fegelein," he said. "In better days, he used to
visit the hotel for cocktails. But what has that to do with
me?"

There was something else. A code phrase or a counter-
sign. Theater tickets? Anchovy paste? What was it Fry-

chius had told him about the exchange of code signs? Bascom couldn't remember. He cleared his throat and said, "I come as an emissary from a mutual friend. A Swedish neutral. Nils Frychius. The Gruppenführer knows him. The Gruppenführer has also met me. I believe he will be willing to see me again."

The man cocked his head and appeared to consider Bascom's words, then said, "Wait here. I will return in a moment." He waved his hands at the chef's assistants, shooing them like chickens toward a row of bushel baskets filled with early lettuces and beans. He looked at Bascom once more, then headed across the cavernous kitchen toward a wall telephone.

Bascom waited. His eyes fell on a rack of meat forks, attached to the side of the steel counter. He checked quickly to make sure no one was watching, then slid one of the forks, a long-tined, sharp instrument with a wooden handle, out of the rack and stuffed it under his sweater. His conviction that he was a damned fool deepened, but he kept the fork. If all hell broke loose, perhaps he could brandish it as a weapon. Fight his way out. Or at least skewer a couple of SS apes before they finished him off.

Robeus came back moments later. "Follow me," he said. He marched through the kitchen with Bascom on his heels and stopped at a freight elevator. Apparently the hotel was on its own generator, for the elevator worked. They rose three or four floors, Bascom wasn't sure how many, then entered a musty hall. Artillery shells still boomed outside. The hallway was dark and quiet. There were apparently no paying guests in the hotel, or if there were, they stayed strictly to their rooms. Or perhaps down in the Adlon's underground shelter, rumored to be among the sturdiest in the city.

Robeus unlocked a door and led Bascom into a darkened suite. Slits of light came through loosely nailed boards at the windows. Sheets covered unused furniture. Robeus stripped a dust cover from a couch and gestured for Bascom to sit, but Bascom's fork held him stiffly upright, and he declined.

Quietly, Robeus asked, "Who are you?"

"No one," Bascom said. "Just an emissary from Nils Frychius."

Robeus poked his glasses farther up on his nose. "I think you are more than that," he said. "The Gruppenführer sounded very strange when I told him there was a man here to see him."

"Strange?" Bascom said.

"Yes. Nervous. Startled. He thought you might be Herr Frychius, but when I told him you were not, his voice became strained, far away. He wanted me to describe you."

"And did you?"

Robeus shrugged. "What is there to describe? A workingman; obviously a foreigner. Your accent is atrocious."

"Did that help him?"

"It didn't seem to. Are you from the Allies?"

An artillery shell ripped into buildings nearby, and the shock wave rattled the window frames. Bascom's hand, hanging limply at his side, edged to the hem of his sweater, nearer the meat fork. "Would it make a difference?" he asked Robeus.

"To me, yes," Robeus said. He waved a hand quickly. "Not in the way you think. You needn't reach for your gun. You see, my friend, I am not a brave man. I can see the writing upon the wall. It spells *finis*. If you are from the Allies, I offer my service. I have done what I could to help, already. If you know Herr Frychius, you know that."

"Perhaps I know Herr Frychius only as a newsman," Bascom said.

"Perhaps," Robeus said. He folded his arms in a wait-and-see pose and waited to see.

Bascom might as well have accepted the invitation to sit. They had to wait for almost half an hour, Bascom pacing, Robeus watching his every step. Finally, Bascom heard a soft footfall on the carpet outside the door. He touched the fork handle. Now the lady or the tiger. Either Fegelein would come alone through that door, or a rush of bodies would swarm in.

The door opened slowly. One face, the large-nosed

countenance of Gruppenführer Hermann Fegelein, leaned around the edge. Gone was the haughty expression. Gone was the self-important veneer of confidence. He looked smaller, more nervous. His breath came in quick gulps, but that could have been from climbing the stairs instead of using the elevator. He was alone. He peered through the dimness, then his small eyes widened with the shock of recognition. "Major Broome!" he blurted. "What . . . what are you doing here?"

It was a mistake. Robeus, standing in the shadows to the side of the door, drew a sharp breath. Fegelein, only now aware that Robeus was in the room, tried to regain his air of hauteur. He stepped inside and peeled off his gloves. "Thank you, Max," he said lazily. "You may go."

Robeus shook his head. "I think not," he said. "Major Broome, is it? American or British?"

Fegelein's eyes darted nervously. "It would be safer for us all were you to forget that," he said. "Now please leave us."

Robeus pushed the door shut and planted his back firmly against it. He said, "With all respect, Herr Gruppenführer, I must decline. If the ship is sinking, I claim my place in the lifeboat. You owe me that."

Fegelein looked at Bascom, asking for a decision. He obviously considered Bascom the master of the situation. Bascom felt such relief that his legs almost gave way. Say something, quick. Don't let him see your own fear. Hide it.

"Do you trust him?" Bascom asked.

Fegelein nodded.

"Then he has my permission to stay. Sit down, Gruppenführer. I want to talk to you."

Bascom watched with growing satisfaction as Fegelein meekly obeyed, hurrying to perch on the edge of the couch. To test his man a degree further, Bascom said coldly, "You took your time getting here."

Fegelein wet his lips. "It is forbidden to leave the Chancellery without cause. I had to fabricate an excuse. I apologize, Herr Major Broome. Had I realized it was you, I would have come more quickly."

Bascom relaxed his grip on the fork handle, but he kept his hand beneath his sweater. Let them think he had a gun, if they wished. "We are very disappointed in you," he told Fegelein. "You didn't show up Friday night as promised."

"I . . . I would have," Fegelein said. "You didn't give me sufficient time." He hesitated. "You . . . you lied to me. You said I was to be met by a negotiator."

Bascom shrugged. "There was a last-minute change of plan."

"But to attack the Chancellery . . . How could you expect me to take part in such a despicable venture? I am not a traitor."

"That remains to be seen," Bascom said. "Because of you, the mission was a failure. That's why my government has sent me. To find out what went wrong. Did you betray us?"

"No!" Fegelein said. He looked shocked. "I had nothing to do with it. Your people brought failure on themselves. They attacked the wrong bunker."

"Wrong bunker? Is there more than one?"

"There are four," Fegelein said. "More, if you consider the underground garages and workshops. The Führerbunker is under the garden, but your people never even came close to it. They were foolhardy."

"We were working with incomplete information," Bascom said. "It would not have happened if you had come to meet us as promised. I fear you have made some very powerful enemies."

"Even if I'd been willing to help you, I couldn't have made it to the rendezvous on time. There was an air raid."

"Of course there was an air raid. It was designed as cover. You should have known that."

"No one told me."

Bascom sighed. So that's what had happened. A tiny slip like that, and the whole thing collapsed. It was only of personal advantage to know that Fegelein hadn't set them up. Don't think of the men who died unnecessarily. Think of how to make use of him. Careful. Lead up to it carefully.

"This matter will be hard to resolve with my superiors," Bascom said.

"Surely they will understand it wasn't my fault," Fegelein said plaintively. "I can't be held responsible for something that no one bothered to explain to me. Perhaps you could intercede on my behalf. Perhaps you could convince them of my partisanship."

"It may be too late," Bascom said. "My superiors would need some new show of faith on your part. Some direct evidence of your willingness to co-operate."

Fegelein bit his lip. "I can provide information," he said. "I could bring the latest accounting of the military disposition in Berlin. It should prove useful in overthrowing the city."

Bascom shook his head. "That would be of more value to the Russians than to us."

"Then help me give it to the Russians. Surely you have lines of communication? Perhaps the Russians will offer me their protection." Robcus made a sound of disgust in his throat. Fegelein whirled on him. "The city will be overthrown in any event," he said. "You don't know what it's like. The Chancellery is a disorganized shambles. Even the Führer has lost hope. People are deserting him on all sides. We will lose everything. Perhaps horribly."

The hotel man asked, "Then why do we not surrender?"

Fegelein shook his head helplessly. "The Führer refuses. He has sworn to stay and die. Berlin will die with him. And Germany will die as well."

"Madness," Robeus muttered.

The individual organism's desire to survive spoke loudly to Bascom. He intervened doggedly, still trying for a way to get Fegelein to offer his help in escaping the city. "It's a waste of time to talk to the Russians," he said. "Unless you can think of some effective way to display to my superiors your willingness to co-operate, your personal lack of future is assured."

Bitterly, Fegelein broke out, "Your government should have listened to Reichsführer Himmler's proposal. This could have been avoided. There might already have been peace."

Bascom shook his head. "Surrender is one thing, but your Reichsführer was trying to buy his way into the post-war German leadership. He asked too much."

"He is on the verge of asking it again," Fegelein said. "Perhaps this time your government will respond in good faith."

"What do you mean?"

"He's to meet with a representative of the Swedish Red Cross this afternoon. In Lübeck. He will offer once more to capitulate. At least in the West."

Bascom arranged a pessimistic expression on his face. It wasn't difficult. "He's wasting his time. Even if he gives up his claim to leadership, my government will never permit a piecemeal surrender."

"You can't be certain. The situation may have changed. God in heaven, man, give us at least some hope." When Bascom didn't respond, Fegelein grated, "Then you bring the consequences on yourself. There will be more bloodshed. Even now, in the face of imminent defeat, there will be one last terror weapon thrown at you."

"Terror weapon?" Bascom was suddenly alert. This might give him the opening he sought. "What kind?"

"I don't know. Apparently it is a high-level enterprise. Very few people, even at the Chancellery, seem to know about it. I only overheard Reichsleiter Bormann speaking of it two days ago. He was closeted with General Krebs for a while, then with one of the SS officers from the bunker guard. I couldn't get close enough for details. He called it by a chess term. *Schachbrett,* or *Schachfigur.* I forget which."

"When is it to be used?" Sound interested. Make him think it's urgent.

"Soon, I would imagine. The Reichsleiter told the SS man that the time of implementation was near at hand.

Apparently there are mechanisms that must still be worked out. The SS man was assigned to help."

"An SS man? Not a scientist or a military expert? Are you sure it's a weapon?"

"Well, I . . . I assumed it to be."

"Did they say it was a weapon?"

"No. Not that I recall. But what else could it be at this late stage?"

Now. Make your move. Keep it subtle. "Perhaps a political maneuver of some kind. Or even a withdrawal to the National Redoubt. We've heard consistent rumors that the German leaders will eventually go into hiding in the Alpenfestung. My government is extremely eager to learn more about the possibility. Could that be what the Reichsleiter is planning?"

"I don't think so. I told you, the Führer refuses to leave Berlin. Without him, the Alpenfestung is a dead issue. Besides, there was mention of a U-boat. The SS officer was to send a coded message to a U-boat in the Kattegat Strait, ordering it to report to Sassnitz for special equipment. I assumed it to be an underwater weapon of some sort."

Fegelein had missed the cue. It didn't matter. Even without the Alpenfestung Bascom could make it work. "Could you find out more about it?" he asked.

Fegelein swallowed. "It would not be easy. One would have to approach the Reichsleiter, or go through his personal files. It would be very dangerous."

"I'm sure my government would be grateful. You *must* co-operate if you wish to return to their good graces."

Fegelein swallowed again. "Could you guarantee their gratitude?"

"Unquestionably. Particularly if you could arrange for me to leave the city with the information."

"But surely . . . I don't understand. You are here. Surely if you arranged to enter the city so easily, you've made your own arrangements for exiting."

"It is best if you don't inquire too closely into such matters," Bascom assured him with complete sincerity.

Then, less sincerely, he continued, "As it happens, my present duties were to require me to stay for a certain length of time. In a place of safety, as you can imagine. But if I am to aid you by delivering the information you provide on this *Schachbrett* or *Schachfigur* matter, I must depart as soon as possible. You must get me a car. The proper exit papers."

"But the risk—"

"What risk? Who would question papers signed by an SS Gruppenführer? The simplest method is often the best. I'm sure I would be safe."

"I meant the risk to myself," Fegelein said.

Bascom raised his eyebrows. "Your safety is directly intertwined with mine, Herr Gruppenführer. If, to consider an example, I were to be caught here in Berlin, your people might force me to tell of your part in the action at the Chancellery the other night. Unless you agree to help me, all manner of things could happen."

The dog still had teeth. He showed them. "You need not threaten me so blatantly," Fegelein said. "I'm quite aware of the peril you represent. I'm not a fool."

Bascom nodded. "I'm sorry. But, considering this new information you've given me, I do need your help."

"It . . . it would be very difficult," Fegelein said. "The car in particular. The few that are available are locked in the underground garage behind the Chancellery. One has to have a permission. Also gasoline. They are very cautious of gasoline these days." He regarded Bascom's wool trousers and worn sweater. "You would also have to have better clothing, perhaps a uniform. There are roadblocks. They would wonder instantly what a workingman was doing in an official car. Then the exit papers—"

"Papers for two," Bascom said. "I have an associate."

"You are making it more difficult. One person is hard enough."

Bascom hesitated. "Make it five," he said. "There's a girl with two children. She has been helpful. I promised to protect her."

"Five? But what excuse could I possibly give? How could I explain five people on the exit papers?"

"My associate is injured," Bascom said. "Let the papers say I'm taking him out of the city for medical attention. The girl can be listed as his nurse. The children as his family."

Robeus cleared his throat. "Major Broome, if you will permit a suggestion? As long as the number is growing, perhaps one more? A driver? You need help. Your German, forgive my saying so, is somewhat hesitant. You would fare better with someone to speak for you. If the Gruppenführer can add me to the list and provide another uniform, I will accompany you."

"It might be hazardous," Bascom said.

Robeus shrugged. "So is staying in Berlin."

Bascom cocked his head at Fegelein. "Well?"

Fegelein's tongue brushed his lips. "I . . . I will try," he said. "I only wish I could think of some way to include myself. Do you think your superiors would welcome me if I accompanied you?"

"I'm certain of it," Bascom lied enthusiastically. Fegelein's presence would be the ultimate safety valve. No one would dare interfere with a German general, no matter how suspect the other car occupants might seem.

Fegelein thought about it a moment, then nodded. "Very well. I will return to the Chancellery and see what I can do. I suggest we meet tomorrow for final arrangements. I will know by then whether I can arrange the car and the gasoline."

"Here?" Bascom said.

Fegelein shook his head. "No, I would feel better if we could meet away from the center of the city. I have a house in Charlottenburg. Do you know the area?"

"I used to."

"Good. I live near Wilmersdorfer." He pulled a leather notebook from his left breast pocket as though the act gave him some assurance, and jotted the address. "Come at noon. If the car is available, we will drive back together to pick up your associates." He tucked the notebook back in his tunic and rose. "I hope this is not a mistake," he said. "I trusted you once, and you put my life in great jeopardy."

"This time my life is in your hands," Bascom said.

Fegelein agreed thoughtfully. "Very well. Tomorrow. My house. At noon." He strode to the door and eased it open; then, with a last glance at Bascom and Robeus, Fegelein slipped into the hallway.

When he was gone, Robeus studied Bascom's face and said, "How serious are you about this information the Gruppenführer has promised to provide?"

"Very. Why?"

Robeus shrugged. "I thought I detected a greater interest in, shall we say, the simple prospect of survival."

Bascom looked away uncomfortably. "The information could be vital," he said. "My life is unimportant, but I must do what I can to make sure word gets back to my government."

"Perhaps I was mistaken," Robeus said. "Shall I go with you tomorrow to meet the Gruppenführer? I know the way."

"Thanks, but I can find it."

"Then tell me where you and your friends are staying. I can wait with them and save you a trip."

"I'd rather not," Bascom said. "You wait here. If the car is available, we'll call you and tell you where to meet us."

"How do I know you'll come for me?"

"We'll come."

Robeus sighed. "As you wish."

Bascom stared at him. "Make damned sure you are alone when you show up," he said. "I won't hesitate to shoot you if you try to pull anything."

"With a fork?" Robeus said. He smiled weakly and opened the door. "That, my friend, sounds extremely painful."

The harried Wehrmacht lieutenant said, "I cannot allow it. Only official traffic is supposed to be permitted through here. My God, don't you realize what is happening?" He gestured. "The Russians are somewhere there in the east, and the British are driving on us from the south. We don't even know how long we can keep the road open."

"But I'm a neutral," Nils Frychius told him. "I would be in no danger. I must get through to Berlin."

"I have my orders," the lieutenant said. He was standing beside Frychius's hired car, a small Opel with a cracked windshield. Behind him, three stubble-cheeked enlisted men fingered their weapons nervously. The road, just twenty kilometers out of Lübeck, was blocked on both sides with coils of barbed wire, leaving a center channel large enough for one car at a time. The channel itself was guarded by a slender green-and-brown pole on a counterweight. It wouldn't have stopped a speeding bicycle, and the soldiers obviously knew they were the only deterrents.

"At least let me drive on to Schwerin," Frychius argued. "Perhaps I can join a military convoy there."

"There are no military convoys," the lieutenant said. "Not to Berlin." His chin trembled. "I would advise you to return to Lübeck."

"My business is in the capital." Frychius said.

The officer shook his head. "I'm trying to save you grief. Even if I let you through, they would only stop you at the next roadblock."

"I'll take that chance," Frychius said.

"Herr Leutnant?" It was one of the enlisted men. He gestured south at a big Mercedes limousine coming up the road. Bright red pennants flapped from each of the front fenders.

The lieutenant watched until he could make out the jagged lightning symbols of the Schutzstaffel on the pennants, then said, "Shit, one of them." He frowned at Fry-

chius and said, "You'll have to back up and make room.
If you're smart, you'll keep backing up all the way to
Lübeck. Even better, keep going north. Try for Denmark."
He ducked under the pole to intercept the limousine.

Frychius backed the Opel out of the channel, then eased
to the side of the road. He waited. The Swedish consul in
Lübeck had warned him that even if he talked his way
through the roadblocks, the situation was highly uncertain.
And eventually, if he managed to keep going far enough,
the men at the roadblocks were likely to be speaking Russian.

The lieutenant leaned through the window of the limousine, but his head jerked back out almost instantly, and
his spine stiffened. He turned to the enlisted men, his face
ashen, and ordered them to raise the barrier. Fast. Must
be a big one, Frychius decided.

Frychius did not consider himself a particularly brave
man. He would have been perfectly willing to conduct his
Berlin business by telephone if possible. He'd even tried.
But the lines were apparently down somewhere between
Lübeck and Berlin. They'd tried to reroute his call through
Wismar or Schwerin, both of which supposedly still had
intermittent service with the capital, but the link was never
joined. It was beginning to look as though he would have
to go all the way, and Russians be damned—assuming, of
course, that he could get through these blasted German
roadblocks.

The sleek limousine, side curtains fastened across the
windows, roared past Frychius's parked Opel. He watched
it through his rearview mirror, keeping it in sight as it
accelerated down the road toward Lübeck. In a damned
hurry, whoever it was.

He started his engine and pulled into the channel again.
The lieutenant, cheeks still pale, only glanced at him. The
disappearing limousine seemed to command his full attention.

"Well?" Frychius said. "Will you let me through? Or do
I have to double back and find another route?"

"What?" the lieutenant said. He seemed distracted.

"Will you let me through?" Frychius repeated.

"Oh. Yes. I suppose so." He gestured at the enlisted men to keep the barrier up. As Frychius put the car in gear, the German said, "Are you sure I can't persuade you to turn back?"

Frychius shook his head. "I can't. I must go on."

The officer shrugged. "Good luck," he said. "I fear you'll need it."

4

Fegelein lurked miserably in a darkened alcove beneath the Chancellery gallery, less than fifty feet from the cramped underground office of Reichsleiter Martin Bormann. He waited for Bormann's deputy assistant to leave. As Fegelein knew, Bormann was at this moment even deeper underground, down in the lower level, attending a meeting with Generals Krebs and Burgdorf. If the meeting ran true to form, the deputy assistant would eventually be summoned to deliver reports and carbons to the meeting room. Fegelein had gathered up every key he could find, just in case. With luck, he could take advantage of the empty office for a few uninterrupted minutes with Bormann's private files.

Luck. What a rotten joke. Very little of that elusive substance was left in Fegelein's crumbling purlieus. Bad enough to be here, trapped in the center of a maelstrom. But for the Allied High Command to send a spy all the way to Berlin, just to tell him that he was in serious trouble over a failed mission that had been none of his doing? And on top of that, to expect him to turn traitor, risk his life, and even help the spy pass through German barricades?

Russian shells thundered to ground somewhere in the city above, some hitting so close that the thick concrete walls of the bunker corridors quaked and groaned. Fegelein hunched his shoulders, feeling sorry for himself. How long had he been waiting now? Twenty minutes? Thirty

minutes? It seemed more like a lifetime. Surely Bormann's
deputy would get the call soon. Bormann never carried his
own papers. He always waited until he knew what was
needed, then sent a runner.

Standing here was the difficult part. What if one of the
bunker guards came along and saw him? How could he
explain? Perhaps he should give up, go back to his own
quarters. What could the Allies do to him if he refused to
co-operate, anyway?

Try him as a war criminal, that's what they could do.

Shoot him.

Or hang him.

An incoming round crumped into the garden somewhere
overhead, and the hanging light fixtures swung back and
forth. Someone in an office down the corridor laughed
nervously. Those damned guns. It was all Reichsführer
Himmler's fault. Fegelein knew himself to be an unimportant man. He need never have been involved in anything
so complex. But the Reichsführer had insisted, dragged him
into it. Now Fegelein was here, in mortal jeopardy, and the
Reichsführer was safe, somewhere in the North. It wasn't
fair.

Wait. There it was. One of the radio clerks from the
Führerbunker monitoring room, hustling up the corridor
from the direction of the old Chancellery building. Coming to fetch Bormann's deputy with the position papers?
Yes, he was angling toward Bormann's office. Fegelein drew
back into the alcove and held his breath, listening. He
could hear the deputy's deep voice, then a murmured
jawohl from the radio clerk, followed by the rumble of
sliding file drawers. Moments later, the two men hurried
out of the office and headed back toward the old Chancellery basement.

Fegelein counted off exactly ten seconds, then swallowed
and scurried toward the office. He looked both ways before
opening the door. The deputy would come straight back,
most likely. But it should take him at least five minutes to
make the round trip, passing through the bulkheads and

checkpoints, up and down the stairs. Fegelein let himself in and closed the door quickly.

Five minutes. Should he waste time on the regular files? Probably not. Bormann never kept anything important where his deputy or his secretary might run across it. Still, it wouldn't take a moment to check. Look under "S" for *Schachbrett*. No, not *Schachbrett*. *Schachmatt*. That's what it was. "Checkmate." It had such an ominous sound.

He breathed deeply. Hurry. Don't dawdle. Bormann's deputy might have forgotten something, might come back. He moved quickly to a row of black filing cabinets and tested them. Unlocked. Good. Slide the "S" drawer open. Flip through. No? Flip again. Not there. No *Schachmatt, Schachbrett,* or anything remotely similar.

Soft clicking sounds. Boot heels in the hallway? The deputy coming back already? He glanced at the corridor door and froze. No. No, not boot heels. Something else. A clock. It was a clock on the wall. Right above his head. He let his breath gush out.

Bormann's special drawer. In his private desk. Once, back in calmer days when the desk was still above ground in the spacious office overlooking the Chancellery garden, he had seen Bormann slip a beribboned packet of letters and a framed portrait of Manya Behrens, the actress, into his lower left drawer and lock it when he thought the Führer was about to pay him a visit. Bormann hadn't known he had been seen. His door had been only partially closed, and Fegelein, who had come ahead to tell him the Führer would be detained, had paused in the outer office, watching through a two-inch gap. He'd glanced with interest at the drawer in later weeks, always from a distance, fascinated by the thought of what it might contain, Martin Bormann's inner soul, but it was double-locked, probably reinforced, and Bormann was always hovering above it, so he pushed it from his mind.

It was the most logical place. No *Unternehmung* could be launched without paperwork, and if *Unternehmung Schachmatt* was as secret as Bormann had led Krebs and

Schedle to believe, then the papers were undoubtedly kept under Reichsleiter Bormann's special lock and key. Undoubtedly? Well, possibly.

This was the tricky part. While he might be able to explain if caught in the deputy's office, what could he possibly say if someone chanced in and found him in the Reichsleiter's cubicle? But there was no option. He tiptoed to Bormann's inner office and slipped inside. Terrible clutter. And Bormann had always seemed so beautifully organized. Stacks of papers and reports on his desk. A half-empty coffee mug. Cigarette butts. The Führer would be furious if he knew Bormann had been smoking underground. Smoking was strictly banned. The ventilating system was inefficient, and the Führer was always convinced someone else's smoke would end up circulating through his own quarters.

Fegelein sat in Bormann's chair and tried the drawer. Locked, of course. Did he dare try to open it? What would they do if they caught him? Bormann would howl for his blood, particularly if he realized what Fegelein was up to. He would deny it. He would deny everything. The Führer was reasonably fond of him, and unlikely to believe ill reports unless Bormann could produce proof. Very well, look only. Take nothing. If they caught him, he would tell them the story about the love letters and claim he was only consumed with curiosity.

He took out his assortment of loose keys and tried them one by one, hoping against hope that one might accidentally fit. Most wouldn't even go into the keyhole. One almost did, but jammed about halfway in and for a panicky moment he was afraid he wouldn't be able to get it back out. He was greatly relieved when it came loose.

So much for the keys. How else could he get the drawer open? Pry it loose? But how? Perhaps his SS service dagger. He unsheathed it with trembling fingers and inserted the tip in the crack. He applied pressure. Difficult. Stop shaking. Try again. Oh God. The tip of the knife. Broken. Stuck there in the crack. A dead giveaway. Retrieve it, quickly. But how? It was jammed in solid, much worse than the key. Try again. Force the blunted dagger back in the crack. Pressure. There. There, it seemed to be coming. Wood splintering. Open. Snatch the loose fragment and put it in pocket. Sheath the blunted dagger. Get out? No, not yet. The drawer, open. Do what you came to do. Look.

Papers. Personal belongings. More clutter. Nothing labeled *Schachmatt*. The love letters, still there, after all this time. Nude photographs. Was that Manya? Hard to tell. The face was hidden behind long hair. Amateurish. Bad lighting. Grotesque poses. Perhaps the Reichsleiter took them himself.

Bankbooks. A stack of bankbooks, wrapped in a rubber band. Foreign banks. Switzerland. Sweden. Turkey. Spain. Saudi Arabia. Venezuela. Argentina. Even the United States. Look inside. God above! So much money! We've all squirreled a bit away, just in case things went bad. But so much? It was a national treasury. Bormann could be shot out of hand for something like this.

He wrapped the rubber band back around the bankbooks and laid them in the drawer quickly, as though their touch could burn. Leave the man's private life alone. Look for *Schachmatt* material. There, a map. Maybe that would help. He lifted it and unfolded it. It was a portion of the Greenland coast, a small German weather station. Perhaps the weapon was to be launched from there? That could explain the submarine. But there were no markings on the map. No code words, no routes marked from the Baltic or the coast of Norway, nothing to link it to any secret military operation. Besides, there couldn't be more than ten or twelve men at the weather station, assuming it was still functioning. They would need more to set the weapon up, wouldn't they?

His eye fell on a file folder at the bottom of the drawer. A hospital report? Was Bormann ailing? He pulled it out and looked it over. No, it was a report on someone else. An inmate from one of the concentration camps. There was his picture, complete with prison number. What on earth? Why should Bormann be interested in a concentration camp inmate? He flipped the file cover over and looked at the tab. One word: Rösselsprung.

Rösselsprung? That was a chess term, too, wasn't it? Yes, the knight's move. The jump of the horse, two squares one way, and another to the side. What could it signify? An erratic move. Through the air. It could jump other pieces. Did that mean anything? Or was it the horse? Trojan horse?

The clock continued to tick noisily in the outer office, growing louder and . . . God in heaven, it wasn't the clock this time. Footsteps, echoing clearly, coming this way. He fumbled the medical folder back into the drawer and stuffed the map on top of it. Drawer shut. Quick, quick. Splintered wood. Bormann was bound to notice. Can't be helped. Out, quick. Close his door, quick. Across the outer office to the corridor, quick. No, too late! The footsteps had stopped. The corridor door was opening.

Bormann's deputy flinched. "Herr Gruppenführer," he said. "Forgive me. I didn't know you were here. Did I hit you with the door?"

"It doesn't matter," Fegelein said.

"You startled me. I've been down in the . . . What are you doing in here, anyway? Looking for the Reichsleiter? I'm afraid he's in a meeting."

"No, not the Reichsleiter. I was searching for a duty roster. I seem to have misplaced it."

"A duty roster? Here? It wouldn't be here, would it?"

"No, perhaps not. My adjutant said he stopped in earlier, and I thought he might have left it."

"Your adjutant? I haven't seen your adjutant all day."

"Perhaps I misunderstood. I'll try elsewhere."

The deputy held the door for him, a puzzled look on his face. Fegelein hurried through.

God above, he was in for it now. Bormann would surely notice the broken drawer sooner or later—if not this afternoon, then certainly first thing in the morning, when he started his day's business. Would the deputy remember seeing Fegelein in the office this afternoon? Would he mention it? Would Bormann put the two incidents together? God, God. He had to get out. He had to leave the Chancellery immediately. Now. This minute. Hide.

5

Erika met Bascom at the stairway to warn him as soon as she heard him enter the ruin overhead. There were two more new faces in their basement shelter, a young girl from Lichtenberg, forced inward by the artillery bombardment, and her seven-year-old brother. They were only children, she told him when his mouth tightened and his face clouded over. She used the pronoun of intimacy, the *Du*, but risked frowning back at him. She couldn't help herself, she explained. The girl looked so lost. Like the others, they had no place to go. And the little boy had already become fast friends with Freddy. She'd instructed them to put their things in the empty servants' quarters, and they seemed so grateful. He would meet them shortly. Everyone had gathered for a modest meal.

Erika must have seen the quick resignation in his eyes, for she kissed him then, a quick, happy kiss, and skipped down the stairs. But as a form of retaliation, he decided not to tell her until later about his meeting with Fegelein and the possibility that he might be able to take her and the children out of Berlin. Besides, she would be seething with questions, and he could explain nothing with people crowding all around. It would be easier when he was alone with her, and the others were asleep. Alive with hope, he also felt alive with tenderness. Being alone might be more rewarding, as well.

He followed her to the room with the chimney fissure. Frau Schiller was poking a spoon in the cookpot, and something tasty was in the air, an aroma that maybe even hinted of sausage. Herr and Frau Fiebeck were sitting on a gunny sack in the corner, sniffing in hungry anticipation. They both stood and bowed respectfully when Bascom entered the room. Fiebeck was still wearing the tightly belted baggy trousers and rumpled coat, but he had donned a sparkling celluloid collar for the occasion.

The newcomers, an alarmingly thin girl with dark hair and haunted eyes and a small boy with a wide forehead and trembling mouth, also rose, very uncertainly, and waited for Bascom to notice them. Apparently they had been told that Bascom was the "landlord" of the cellar establishment, for they stood still, as though in terror of displeasing him, while Erika performed the introductory rites. Their names were Hanna and Peter, it turned out, and they didn't relax until Bascom found a smile and took their hands, one by one, in welcome. The welcome was sincere, and he discovered that his smile was, too. After tomorrow, he'd have no further use for the cellar. These pathetic waifs were more than welcome to it.

Frau Schiller wasted no more time. She began ladling the contents of the cookpot into mismatched bowls. She set the first aside with only broth for the sick man, and measured out the rest of the food with severe equality. Everyone's eyes watched the bowls and throats swallowed, but Fiebeck tried to make polite conversation.

"Well, Monsieur Cadiot," he said, "you've had a very productive day. Fräulein Bollenen told us what you were up to."

Bascom glanced uneasily at Erika. "You did?"

She smiled quickly and said, "Yes, I explained that you were going out to search for extra food, and, with luck, a doctor for poor Maurice. I found the noodles and sausage you brought back and left upstairs. That's what we're eating tonight. And the peaches. What a wonderful surprise! We'll share them for dessert. Wherever did you find a can of peaches?"

So that's what was going into the bowls. Part of their secret cache from the OKW stores. "I found what I could," he said.

"And the doctor?" Frau Fiebeck asked. "I hope you had as much good fortune finding a doctor?"

Bascom shook his head. "Not yet. I tried at the Adlon,

but they've too many wounded soldiers to look after. I'll go out tomorrow and try again."

Frau Schiller scraped the last drops from the pot. Then the bowls were passed around, and silence fell, broken only by the clink of spoons and the wet, chewing noises that are so repugnant unless one is busily chewing oneself. The children finished first, but the adults weren't far behind, and everyone settled down to watching Frau Schiller again as she picked up a can opener and began opening the peaches.

Lips slightly greasy, eyes blissful, Frau Fiebeck returned to the conversation. "A pity about the doctor," she said. "It's so difficult nowadays to find a doctor when you need one."

Herr Fiebeck licked the last trace of sausage from his mouth and nodded agreement. "Of course it is," he said. "And you know why? It's because so many of them were in the Party, and now they've fled or gone into hiding. Damn them. Damn all Party members. The Ivans will take retribution for their crimes out of our innocent hides."

Frau Schiller stopped cranking the can opener. "That is a most ungracious comment, and unlike you, Herr Fiebeck. Doctors are hard to find because they are all in uniform." She glanced at Bascom. "As should be others, if you want my opinion. It's shameful to see a healthy young man not in uniform."

Bascom thought of ignoring her, but she was staring straight at him. "I'm not a German national," he said mildly.

"I don't know what difference that makes," she humphed. "There are plenty of foreigners in the Wehrmacht, helping to fight off the Russians. I've seen them. Norwegians, Danes, Spaniards. French, too."

Erika slipped her arm around Bascom's neck. "Really, Frau Schiller, we need Henri here. You might have eaten water soup for your dinner, with only salt for flavoring, if it weren't for him."

"Better than borscht," Frau Schiller said. "How can we

win the war when there are so many slackers about?" She helped herself first to the peaches, taking a segment with a fork and savoring it, peach juice running down her chin, before passing the can along to Fiebeck. Bascom watched her with a faint smile and decided to make no rejoinder. How admirably consistent the woman was. Once fed, she obviously had no compunction about attacking a mere foreigner.

But Bascom had an advocate in Herr Fiebeck, who looked unbelievingly at the sharp-tongued woman in the blue kitchen apron and might have forgotten the peaches if his wife hadn't nudged him. He gulped his share hastily and passed the can along. "Did my hearing suddenly fail?" he said. "You still expect to win, Frau Schiller? Can you be serious?"

"We'll win," she said stubbornly. "Our cause is just."

"Win? But Frau Schiller, we saw together, you and my wife and I, a dying city only yesterday. How can you forget such sights?"

"The Führer has promised more *Vergeltungswaffen*, vengeance weapons, to fling at the enemy. As soon as they are put to use, Berlin will be saved and the Russians driven back. You'll see."

"Ah, the promises of the Führer," Fiebeck said innocently. "He promised us a greater Germany. And we walked through much of what is left of it on our way inward from Köpenick."

Frau Schiller stiffened. "Are you deriding the Führer? Herr Fiebeck, you and I have been neighbors and friends for many years, but I am deeply disappointed in you."

"Yes, disappointment. The Führer gave us that, too."

Frau Schiller's knife-sharp nose rose angrily. "Shame!" she said. She turned to Erika. "This arguing will spoil our feast. Are you going to sit there and allow Herr Fiebeck to speak so disrespectfully?"

Erika stiffened, too. "This discussion of the Führer is ill-timed," she said. "Here we are, living like rats, thankful for a few morsels of food, and you ask me to enforce respect for the man responsible for it?" She made a gesture that encompassed the dingy cellar, the bomb-cracked wall, the ravaged city that lay around them. " 'Yes, all this we owe to the Führer.' "

It was a slogan they'd all heard a thousand times, Bascom knew. Throughout the years of German victory, it had been printed on posters, painted on walls, uttered in praise and thanksgiving in speech after speech. He patted Erika's knee, in sympathy for the bitter mockery with which she had spoken the words, and he was surprised a moment later to see her looking apologetic when Frau Schiller cried again, "Shame!"

"I'm sorry," Erika murmured. She gestured again, this time to the children, whose frightened eyes reflected the growing intensity of this dispute. "Let us enjoy these wonderful peaches."

Frau Fiebeck, apparently upset that her husband had offended her friend and neighbor, said, "I suppose we ought to remember the good the Führer has done." She smiled shyly at Frau Schiller. "I'm sure we are in his thoughts every day, and he will do everything humanly possible to save us."

Herr Fiebeck nodded. "I meant no disrespect," he said. "The Führer has done many wonderful things. I fear I allowed my own discomforts to color my thinking. God knows, the man has many burdens on his shoulders."

"Yes, of course," Erika said. "Freddy, look, here is all this juice still in the can. Get a spoon, and you children must share it. No cheating, mind you. Henri, you watch them. I must take the broth while it is still warm to poor Maurice and see if he can eat it."

She slipped from the room, leaving Bascom blinking after her with troubled eyes. Had her apology been offered as oil for ruffled waters, or had she really meant it? Had any of them meant it? He knew he couldn't trust them, but he'd thought it was because they were frightened of the regime. It hadn't occurred to him that anyone but a diehard like Frau Schiller might still believe in Hitler.

Consistent to the end, Frau Schiller interrupted his thoughts. She cleared her throat sharply, and he glanced around to see her frowning at him once more.

"Well, Monsieur Cadiot," she complained, "I do think the rest of us might have been consulted."

She nodded at the new little boy, the one with the trembling mouth, which trembled harder at her stare. His hand trembled, too, as he lowered the spoon he had been raising to his mouth.

"A child's sweet tooth is all very well," she concluded, "but some of the rest of us might have enjoyed a taste of the extra peach juice."

Before the encouraging interview with Fegelein, Bascom wouldn't have dared, but now he frowned back at her. Hard. Might as well make things a little easier for those who would be left behind. "Woman," he said sternly, "the food that I have provided will be divided as I say by any who wish ever to eat more of it. Know that Fraülein Bollenen speaks for me. And if both she and I ever chance to be absent, know that authority passes directly to Herr Fiebeck. The Party rightly glorifies the man, and I will hear no more from a mere woman. You children—eat!"

The knife-nose twitched, but the mere woman subsided.

Bascom leaned back to enjoy the sight of the children eagerly obeying his order. He also thoroughly enjoyed the satisfying feeling that he had annoyed Frau Schiller by turning the words of her own beliefs against her. If the annoyance went deep enough, maybe she'd have a second thought or two about the glories of her Führer and his Party. Especially now that Bascom was leaving it, he didn't object to doing his small part in creating a better Germany.

6

Max Robeus stood in the shadows across from the Kreuzberg ruin. So this was the "place of safety" where the American spy was hiding. Following him had been easier than Robeus expected. Small wonder. A very attractive woman, the one who met the spy at the head of the stairs shortly after he hurried inside. Probably thinking of her all the way home. Was she the one he mentioned to Gruppenführer Fegelein? And there were others in there as well. He had seen a wisp of smoke coming through the crack in the cellar wall, and had crept closer for a few moments. Voices down there; several, it sounded like. On its façade, an every-day shelter, but perhaps containing a full detachment of spies.

Very well, Herr Major Broome, if that was really the spy's name. Tomorrow would see whether or not he was acting in good faith. If the American brought the car to the hotel for Robeus, well and good. But if he tried to slip away, tried to cheat Robeus of his right to escape, one could always take revenge on his spy apparatus. And Robeus now knew where the spies had their headquarters.

He marked the spot in his memory and headed down the street, back toward the Adlon.

7

The limousine with the bright red pennants on its fenders and the tightly drawn side curtains pulled up in front of a modest two-story house in Hohen-Lüchen, near Lübeck. From the rear of the sleek car stepped Reichsführer Heinrich Himmler and SS Brigadeführer Walter Schellenberg.

The house, a red-tiled masonry structure set back from the road and guarded by a wrought-iron fence, had recently been established as a branch of the Royal Swedish legation to Germany. Standing in an arched portal, waiting to greet the two high-ranking SS officers, was a small party of Swedish diplomatic personnel, headed by Count Folke Bernadotte of the Swedish Red Cross.

Himmler bowed stiffly, then offered his hand to Bernadotte. Bernadotte took it, and noted that it was cold. He welcomed them both formally and led them inside.

A room had been prepared for the meeting, a small

dining room that flickered with the light of twenty candles. Himmler, his face abnormally pale, looked at the room solemnly, then shrugged out of his leather greatcoat and took a seat. He was wearing a gray uniform with no decorations for the occasion, and Bernadotte noted that, too.

A member of the Swedish diplomatic party offered coffee to Himmler and Schellenberg, but Himmler refused. He seemed eager to get on with the discussion. Bernadotte waved the coffee away and excused the diplomats.

When they were alone, Himmler raised his hand in a resigned gesture and dropped it. "I admit that Germany is beaten," he said. His voice shook.

Bernadotte nodded in silence.

"The Russians are at the gates of Berlin," Himmler said. "The Führer may well be dead by now. I feel I am no longer bound by my personal oath to him."

"What do you wish of me?" Bernadotte asked.

Himmler adjusted his glasses. The words came hard. "Under the circumstances," he said, "I consider my hands free. In order to save as much of Germany as possible from the Russians, I am prepared to capitulate unconditionally on the Western front so that the Western Allies might advance as rapidly as possible toward the East. Are you willing to forward my decision to the Swedish Minister for Foreign Affairs, so that he might inform General Eisenhower?"

"Yes, I am willing."

Himmler nodded. "Please advise him that I will not capitulate on the Eastern front. I am, and always have been, a sworn enemy of Bolshevism. I must try to save the millions of my countrymen who would otherwise fall under Russian occupation. We will continue to fight in the East until Eisenhower reaches Berlin."

Bernadotte hesitated. "Reichsführer, in my view it will not be possible to capitulate on the Western front while hostilities continue in the East. I believe the British and Americans will refuse to accept such a provisional truce with Germany."

"I realize it will be difficult," Himmler said, "but I must try. The fate of millions is at stake."

"I will transmit your plea," Bernadotte said. He paused. "May I ask what you will do if they reject your proposal?"

Himmler drew himself up stiffly. "If that is their response, I shall do the only thing possible for a soldier: I shall take command of a German battalion on the Eastern front and fight until I die."

Bernadotte acknowledged the Reichsführer's ringing declaration by another grave, silent nod, but he had the distinct impression it would never come to pass, no matter how the Western Allies reacted.

8

"Our greetings to the brave troops
of the First Amerikan Army."

—banner posted by Russians
at Torgau on the Elbe, April 25

1

Sir Adrian Courtney's cheeks blazed with unaccustomed
color as he stepped into the sunlight and walked briskly
to his car. The committee had abandoned him completely.
Not one of the SFHQ people had spoken in his behalf
during the forty-minute session. Whittingdon had been particularly nasty, filling the air with cutting remarks in that
quiet, understated manner of his. Never mind that Whittingdon himself had unofficially approved the mission. To
listen to him, you'd think Courtney had acted strictly on
his own. And Holley, the bastard, hadn't even appeared.
A British matter, he had called it. Glad to do anything he
could to help, but not really his concern. Courtney had the
carpet all to himself.

Sergeant Christy saluted and opened the rear door. His
face must have given him away, for she said, "Rough go,
sir?"

"Not the most enjoyable morning I've ever spent," he
said.

He'd come to the session with slightly raised spirits. After
all, having just received word that some of the assault team
had reached American lines meant that it hadn't been a
total disaster. At least they'd be able to figure out what
went wrong, perhaps even gear up for another try. But the
committee had dashed his hopes the moment he walked
in the room. The PM was fuming, they told him. A political disaster of the first water. What in the world had he

been thinking, sending an armed party into the heart of Berlin after the Russians had been assured that no such thing was to happen? Was he deliberately trying to sabotage relations between the Eastern and Western Allies?

Their reaction wasn't unexpected, of course, to an experienced strategist like Courtney, but how remarkably unpleasant it had been to have such an expectation confirmed. This, from men who had sat in on the earlier planning sessions and given him tacit approval. Next time, by God, he'd use one of those clever little recording devices the war had helped develop. If there was to be a next time. After that sound chewing, it was possible that he'd be shipped off to Somaliland or the Seychelles or some other hellhole.

"Where to, sir?"

He glanced at Christy's face in the rear-view mirror. "God, I don't know. The office, I suppose. There's little we can do about any of this until our assault-team survivors arrive."

Her blue eyes flickered in the mirror. Bit of red around the irises? Possibly. He had said nothing to her about the coded list of survivors, not the fact that Longland was among them, nor the fact that her young American was not. But Colonel Norman, incurable romantic that he was, had probably sneaked a look for her, or at the minimum made a few broad hints. The devil with her. His world was shaking, and he had no time for inconsequential romances.

The worst of it was, how the bloody hell could he face Longland and the others when they returned? If Courtney himself ended up in the Seychelles, he knew it wouldn't be forever. It was just part of the great game that he had played since being recruited by a Magdalen Fellow at Oxford. There were other gamesters. Courtney supposed they all fancied themselves as rather like David Hogarth, molding, preparing that other promising young Oxford student who eventually became known as Lawrence of Arabia. The game board was the world, and play designed to shape its affairs, a practice that ever appealed to the grand-scale adventurer.

But Longland and his men were pawns, not players. It was bad enough sending them into that wretched situation, but now to face them and tell them that their sacrifice had been for nothing at all, that they could never speak of it, that their comrades had died for nothing, and they could never speak of them either?

He'd have to get to Holley sometime today and make sure he was present when the handful of raiders climbed off the plane. Someone had to tell the OSS chaps as well. Sorry, men. You're all under house arrest until you've been debriefed. Those who died, did so in traffic accidents in unspecified rear areas. Those who survived are forever to hold their tongues or face prison sentences for breach of the National Secrets Act. A remarkably uncivil way to greet men who had risked their lives for King and country. Not with awards and decorations, but with threats.

For that was what the committee had decided. Officially, the raid had never happened.

2

"Where is Gruppenführer Fegelein? Reichsleiter Bormann is asking for him."

The adjutant jumped to his feet, stomach in, chin out. "I don't know, Herr General. He left for a brief time yesterday, then returned. After an hour or so, he left again. He has not come back."

"Not come back? What do you mean?"

"Just that, sir. His quarters are empty. His bed was not slept in."

"What? Everyone on the Führer's staff is required to stay in the Chancellery at all times! Those are the Führer's direct orders! He knows that, does he not?"

"Yes, sir. I'm sure he does, sir."

"Then where is he?"

The adjutant swallowed. "I'm sure I don't know, sir. I know only that I have not seen him. Not since late yesterday afternoon."

The general fumed silently for a moment, then said, "How did he appear to you before he left? Sick, perhaps?"

"No, sir." The adjutant hesitated. "Well, yes, sir. In a way, sir. He seemed agitated. Worried. I thought nothing of it at the time. We've all been . . . I mean the war news isn't very . . ." He trailed off miserably.

"Do you think he has deliberately deserted his post?"

"Oh, no, sir," the adjutant said, shocked. "The Gruppenführer would never knowingly desert his duty."

"It would seem otherwise," the general said. He picked up a desk telephone and handed it to the adjutant. "Get me the guard room. I want him found and brought back. Immediately."

3

Bascom ducked behind an overturned car as a Russian Yak skimmed across the rooftops and circled toward the zoo. He could see the pilot clearly, goggles and fur-lined helmet, face straining toward the gunsight. Moments after the plane disappeared beyond a line of buildings, he heard the wing guns open up.

Fegelein's house lay just ahead. It hadn't been easy, getting here. Not only were the big guns getting closer, but now the Soviets controlled the skies. Great swarms of Yaks and Sturmoviks shrieked overhead at treetop level, shooting and bombing everything in sight.

The attacks were heaviest in the inner citadel, along Unter den Linden and Charlottenburger Chaussee. Bascom had been driven to cover time and again, plunging into crowded subway staircases, vaulting wrecked fences. He had found himself shoulder to shoulder with Germans also seeking shelter. Women who had come out to forage for food with scarves and wet rags tied over their noses in an attempt to filter the smoke. Gray-whiskered Volkssturmers in grubby work clothing, with armbands for uniforms. Children with pinched faces, cursing the planes at the top of their high-pitched voices.

Most of his temporary companions, like himself, had nothing to say, just hugged the ground and sweated it out. Some, perhaps to ease their nerves, gabbled at great length, sharing rumors, describing escapes. Bascom spoke to none of them, but he listened. No one seemed certain just how deeply the Russians had penetrated the city, but penetrate they had. The Pankow and Weisensee districts had fallen to the north. Russian infantrymen had crossed the Teltow Canal to the south and were closing in on Tempelhof. Tanks had been seen at the foot of the Avus Speedway, approaching the forests of Grunewald. Even the corridor to the west, through Spandau, was on the verge of closing, they said. It was only a matter of time until the Russians had the city locked in a vise of steel.

The last worried Bascom most. How long would the corridor stay firm? Even if Fegelein had the car ready, it would be better to wait until nightfall, to keep from getting shot up by the roving Russian planes. But if they waited, the Soviets might link up beyond Spandau and shut off the escape route. It would be tough enough driving through German checkpoints. They sure as hell couldn't drive through the Russians.

Three more planes zipped across the sky at the southern end of Wilmersdorfer, curving toward the flak towers. Not that it would do them much good. Concrete walls nine feet thick. The towers were practically impregnable. If Flying Forts hadn't been able to level them in two years of concentrated bombing, no amount of last minute harassment from a few lightweight fighters was going to make much difference.

But at least the flak towers gave the fighters a target and kept them from buzzing around up here in the residential district. Fegelein's house and those surrounding it had taken a few hits, but the scars appeared to be old ones. No new fires burned. No bomb craters smoldered. The injuries had been done weeks ago, perhaps months ago, most likely by the British and Americans.

He ran the last few yards to the house and raised his fist to pound on the door, then stopped. An old fear crossed his mind: It wasn't too late for Fegelein to have screwed up his courage and decided to turn Bascom in. What if an SS detachment was waiting inside? But he quickly shook it off. No sense in being paranoid. Fegelein was his last chance. Bascom rapped his knuckles on the door, loudly enough to be heard over the distant, nonstop thunder of guns.

Fegelein was slow to appear, and when he did, he opened the door almost casually. He looked odd, like someone who has finally burned out. He wasn't in uniform anymore. He was wearing brown slacks and a white shirt, open at the collar. He hadn't shaved, and his eyes were dull.

"What's wrong?" Bascom asked.

"Nothing. Everything is fine." Voice weary, emotionless.

The Gruppenführer led Bascom into the living room. Two suitcases, packed and waiting by the sofa. A topcoat slung carelessly across them. A bottle of brandy, uncorked and half empty on the floor.

"Did you get the car?" Bascom asked him.

"I was unable to arrange an official car, but I have my own parked behind the house."

"Can we get it through the barricades?"

Fegelein shrugged. "Perhaps."

Bascom was puzzled by the man's lack of enthusiasm. "What's wrong with you? Has something happened?"

"Nothing is wrong," Fegelein insisted. He looked at Bascom guiltily. "Well, there is one small matter: I was unable to discover anything of importance about the *Schachmatt* project."

Thank God. Bascom had been afraid it might be something important. But to keep his bluff going, he frowned and said, "Did you try?"

"Of course I did," Fegelein said quickly. "You must believe that. You must persuade your superiors that I gave it my best effort. I even broke into Reichsleiter Bormann's desk. But found only a few love letters and certificates of deposit on foreign banks. We all have those." He hesitated. "There was a medical file on a political prisoner from one of the concentration camps, but I was unable to fathom its meaning."

Bascom nodded. "It doesn't matter. The important thing now is to get out of here with what we have. I'm sure my superiors will recognize your effort in helping me and my associate. You will be rewarded."

"Yes," Fegelein said.

Spiritless again. He was beginning to make Bascom restive. "What about exit documents? Did you arrange them?"

Fegelein looked away. "Not exactly. I . . . I didn't have time."

"No time? You had almost twenty-four—"

Bascom broke off. With the feeling of reliving a nightmare, he listened. Engine sounds approached from the near intersection, and Fegelein's chin jerked up. Some kind of heavy-duty vehicles. They rumbled to a stop. Feet hit the pavement, and a voice called out sharp commands. Bascom prodded himself. Move! The window! He jerked the curtains back an inch, and a sense of *déjà vu* overwhelmed him. But this was no might-have-been. This was real. Two armored cars were angled in at the curb, and a dozen SS men were fanning out around the house.

Bascom let the curtains fall and whirled on Fegelein. "You bastard!" he hissed. "You set me up!"

Fegelein shook his head. "They're after me," he said. He sounded miserable, but not particularly surprised. "I left the Chancellery yesterday. It is forbidden to do so. Someone must have missed me and reported my absence."

"Good God, why did you leave so soon?"

"I couldn't stay. I was frightened. Someone . . . saw me leaving the Reichsleiter's office."

One of the SS men pounded on the door and called Fegelein's name.

"We've got to get out of here," Bascom said.

"It's too late," Fegelein said. "You must hide. If they find you here, I'm doubly doomed. Quick, upstairs. There is an attic chamber above the bathroom."

"What about you?"

"Perhaps I can talk my way out of it. I'm not without influence. Quickly, go. Your presence places me in extreme jeopardy."

Bascom didn't like it, putting himself under the Gruppenführer's control, but there seemed little choice. Rifle butts pounded at the door. He took the stairs three at a time.

He barely made it to the top of the landing before the SS troopers burst into the living room. He jerked around the corner and froze, afraid they might hear his footsteps if he went any farther, and overheard a young SS officer say, "Gruppenführer Fegelein, you are under arrest. You have been accused of disloyalty to the Führer and desertion of your post in the face of the enemy."

Fegelein almost regained a touch of his old hauteur. "This is preposterous," he snapped. "Who is responsible for this outrage?"

"Do you deny that you abandoned your duties without permission?"

"I left my post, certainly," Fegelein said. "But not my duties. Duty compelled me to return to my home to claim important papers. I was pinned down by the Russian shelling and forced to stay the night. That can hardly be called desertion."

"What about those suitcases?" the officer said. He sounded less confident. After all, Fegelein was a high-level officer, and, it was said, a personal acquaintance of the Führer himself.

"Items that I wish to have with me at the Chancellery," Fegelein said. "Do you suggest that I am not allowed to bring personal belongings to the Chancellery?"

"Open them," the officer told one of his men.

"How dare you!" Fegelein said. "I do not take this lightly, sir. I suggest you reconsider your position before you presume to such liberties."

"Open them," the officer repeated.

Bascom clung to the wall and listened to the sound of leather buckles being undone, then clasps snapping open. Clothing rustled. A voice murmured indistinctly.

"So," said the officer. "Currency and jewelry? These are the items one needs at the Chancellery?"

"For safety only," Fegelein said, but his voice was weaker. "I can explain this. Please allow me to telephone the Führer or some member of his staff. I can explain it all."

'You will have that opportunity," the officer said. "I am instructed to bring you back to the Chancellery without delay. I'm certain someone will be available to hear your explanations."

"Very well," Fegelein said. "I will return in my own car."

"No, sir. You must come with us. Now."

"But I certainly can be trusted to return on my own. I came here only to retrieve some papers, as I told you."

There was a moment of silence, during which the officer must have gone to the suitcases and poked through them on his own, for his voice finally said, "I see no papers among your possessions, Gruppenführer. Can you explain that as well?"

Fegelein tried again for authoritative arrogance, but he was beaten and he knew it. It showed in his voice. "The Führer shall hear of this," he explained in a half whine.

"I'm sure he will," the officer said. "Take him outside."

There were sounds of movement toward the door. Quiet at first, then a brief shuffle, as though Fegelein were resisting pressure, possibly a hand to his elbow or shoulder. The officer spoke sharply to his men, and the flurry subsided.

Bascom was afraid to look, but he had to know. He slipped into a bedroom at the front of the house. The curtains here were lace, and through a spray of graceful, lacy flowers Bascom saw Fegelein assisted into one of the two armored cars. Though he tried not to, Fegelein couldn't resist one last look at his house, and Bascom shied back from the window, lest one of the SS men glance this way as well.

Engines turned over. Gears clashed as the armored cars pulled away. Bascom shuddered with the hurt anger of the betrayed. Life wasn't supposed to be this way. He'd tried, hard. It wasn't fair for him to be left with no hope, no way out. Even if Fegelein persuaded his bunker superiors he was on a legitimate errand, he would be too scared to try again. And without Fegelein's authority, or a convincing set of exit papers to take his place, Fegelein's car was useless. Bascom was trapped. There would be no escape from Berlin. Ever.

He chided himself for being childish. Real life didn't play by the rules. Although he had to force himself, he started for the stairs. Might as well get out of here. Back across the city to the cellar. Something would turn up. There was bound to be a way out of this.

But as he reached the ground floor, he thought of another jeopardy: What if Fegelein couldn't wriggle off the hook? What if he broke under questioning and told the Germans everything? Even about Bascom? Of course, the Gruppenführer had no idea where Bascom and Formoy were hiding, but he could describe him, describe his clothing. If they wanted him badly enough, they might institute a house-to-house search. No, check that. No sweat. The Russians were too close for them to waste time hunting through houses in a city the size of Berlin. The only other link was the Adlon Hotel, and Bascom had no intention of returning there.

The Adlon. Robeus, the assistant manager. If Fegelein broke, Robeus would go down. Bascom hesitated. Even if life didn't play fair, he had his own standards, and here was a duty to do a decent thing. Bascom detoured to a telephone on a cherry-red secretary. He picked it up and listened for a dial tone. It hummed serenely in his ear. Typical.

He looked up the number and dialed the Adlon. It took time to get through to the Adlon switchboard, and even longer for them to locate and summon Robeus. Bascom sweated it out, although self-interest whispered to him to flee, to leave Fegelein's house and lose himself in the streets before the SS men decided to come back for some reason or other. He began to hear things. More brakes squealing outside. Feet tramping to the door. Each time it turned out to be only whistling artillery shells or the *takatakataka* of Sturmovik wing guns.

"Hello?" At last. Thank God.

"Herr Robeus, this is the man who came to see you yesterday. We had some unfinished business about a car."

"Oh. Yes. I recall. Is it ready?"

"No. The man who promised to sell it to us has just been picked up at his house by his friends. I'm afraid we're out of luck."

"I see." Guarded, hesitant. "Were his friends angry?"

"Extremely. They might apply pressure and find out about our efforts to buy the car. If so, they may come to see you about it."

Silence. Then, sadly, "I understand. Perhaps I should take a few days off."

"That would be wise."

"Thank you for your courtesy in calling," Robeus said. "I wish there were some way I could repay you, but I think it best that we not meet again. I shall leave immediately."

"As shall I," Bascom said. "Good luck." He hung up.

4

Robeus sat over the telephone and watched it like a ticking time bomb, waiting for the minutes to pass. Had the American lied to him? There seemed to be no logical reason for it. If they had intended to drive away from the city and leave him behind, surely they would simply have departed with no word. Why bother to call at all, unless it were true? And yet if it were true, if Fegelein *had* been arrested, why would an American whom he had met only once, to whom he meant nothing, risk his own safety to warn Robeus?

He stretched his hand to the phone, hesitated, then withdrew it. Not yet. Make sure enough time has elapsed for the arresting party to return their prisoner to the Chancellery. He could only call once. Too many calls might arouse suspicion. Call too early, and it would be wasted. On the other hand, each moment he spent in his office, waiting, could be a moment closer to his own arrest if the American had told the truth. Or, if the American had lied, each moment allowed the Gruppenführer's car to get farther from the center of the city, through the roadblocks.

He checked his watch. Surely that was enough time. It was only some ten kilometers from the Gruppenführer's house back to the government district. Even with Russian planes overhead, it couldn't take them all day to cover so little ground. They had to be there, if they were to be there at all.

He picked up the phone and told the hotel switchboard to put him through to Gruppenführer Fegelein at the Chancellery. His palms grew moist while he waited. An operator's voice answered. There was hesitation, some confusion. Then the call was switched. A man's voice. More confusion. Finally Fegelein's adjutant came on the line.

"Who is calling?" he wanted to know.

"Herr Robeus from the Adlon," the hotel switchboard informed the man.

"Very well, put him on," the adjutant said.

"This is Robeus," Robeus said. "May I speak to the Gruppenführer, if he isn't too busy?"

"He is, ah, indisposed at the moment," the adjutant said. "An important meeting. May I ask the nature of the call?" A subtle click in the background. Someone monitoring the call.

Robeus's mouth went dry. "Perhaps I should call back later," he said. "It isn't terribly important."

Someone whispered to the adjutant. The adjutant cleared his throat and said, "Ah, the Gruppenführer may be in conference for some time. If you will please tell me what you wish with him, I'll see that a note is passed."

Jesus God, it was true! And here he was on the phone, already identified, with someone in the background listening to every word! Why hadn't he believed the American? Why had he taken such a terrible chance? He swallowed a mouthful of cotton and said, "It is really an unimportant matter. I came across a case of Norwegian sardines this morning, and I remembered the Gruppenführer's fondness for them, so I thought I would offer to bring a few cans over."

Whispering behind a shielded mouthpiece again. "Thank you," the adjutant said. "I'm sure the Gruppenführer will be delighted. If you will be in your office for another ten minutes or so, we'll send someone over for them."

"Yes, I'll be here," Robeus said. He hung up quickly.

Ten minutes? More like six or seven, if they hurried. Damn fool. Why hadn't he left quickly, while he still could? He snatched up his briefcase and began to pile things into it from his desk drawers.

The phone rang at his elbow and almost scared him out of his skin. It rang again. Should he answer it? It could be the Chancellery, calling back to keep him occupied until arresting officers arrived. Or it might be the American major again.

He picked it up cautiously and said, "Hello?"

"Herr Robeus, thank God I caught you. I've been trying to get a line to Berlin for the past two hours." Static on the wires. Accented German. A foreigner, but more fluent than the American. Familiar, somehow. Of course. It was the Swedish newsman. Herr Frychius.

"It is not necessary to speak your name," Robeus said quickly. "I recognize your voice. Where are you?"

A surprised silence, then, "I'm in Rheinsberg, waiting for a written road clearance. I, um, thought you might be willing to set up opera tickets for this evening. I should reach the city in a few hours." He paused. "Why should I not speak my name?"

"Trunk calls are often checked by the Gestapo," Robeus said. "For my part that no longer matters, but you will want no obstructions when you leave the country."

"I see. Are you suggesting I leave the country?"

"As soon as possible," Robeus said. "Your opera contact has been arrested. Your intermediary called earlier to tell me. I just finished verifying it."

"My . . . what?"

"Your intermediary. The man named Broome."

"Broome? I know no one by that—" There was a sudden intake of breath. "Good God! The American? Tall, young man, dark hair, greenish eyes? He's in Berlin?"

"Yes. The opera contact tried to arrange transport out of the city for him, but there is little hope of that now. I fear he is lost."

"Is there anything I can do to help?"

"No, nothing," Robeus said. "All that is left for him, for either of us, is to get out of sight and hope for the best. I was about to leave when you called."

A burst of static obscured the Swede's next words, then, "—to help him if I can. I could be there by nightfall. Do you know where he's hiding?"

"I think so."

"Good. Then I'll leave immediately, as soon as my papers have cleared. Perhaps I can use my neutrality to get him through the roadblocks."

"No, wait," Robeus said. "If you really want to help him, you will finish his work. He was trying to reach his lines to transfer some information. He had planned to stay on here, otherwise, apparently in safety, but he seemed to think the information important. Something to do with a U-boat called the *Schachbrett*. I believe they said it was stationed somewhere off Sassnitz. He told me only yesterday that it must take precedence over everything else. I'm sure he would rather you pass the information to his superiors than to waste your time worrying about his personal safety."

There was a harsh click on the line, unlike the sputter of static. Robeus pulled the phone from his ear and stared at it.

"A U-boat?" the Swede said. "Is that all? Didn't he say more than that?"

The line clicked again, a series of metallic hiccups. Someone trying to trace the call.

"I'm sorry," Robeus said. "I must go. I suggest you do the same. At once."

"No, don't hang up," the Swede said. "I have questions. There are things I must know if I'm to—"

Robeus broke the connection. He sat immobile for a few seconds, staring at the flotsam of his private life lying in the open desk drawers, then stood and snapped his brief-case shut. Leave the rest. Go now. Through the kitchens and out the back way. Quickly. Or there might never be time for more flotsam to accumulate.

5

Bascom climbed up the brick pile in front of the Kreuz-berg ruin to the shattered first floor. He stood still a mo-ment, breathing hard, listening for sounds from the cellar. He didn't want to go down yet and face Erika, but he knew he couldn't wait long. She would be worried. Given the shelling, given planes, given German tanks clanking out to meet Russian armored thrusts, it had taken him more than three hours to get back from Charlottenburg. Smoke now hovered to the east, north, and south, almost ringing the city. Between booms of the big guns, one could hear the far-off rattle of small-arms fire and antitank weapons. No more than three or four miles away. They were coming fast. Once they reached the elevated S-Bahn circling the inner city, the battle would begin in earnest.

He shook his head, trying to shake off futile thoughts. He had played it over and over in his mind. If he had reached Fegelein's house fifteen minutes earlier . . . per-haps if he had started earlier, or taken a different route. Or if he hadn't paused to listen to useless scuttlebutt in that last subway shelter. If he had arrived earlier, perhaps they could have been gone before the SS troops came. As always, if. If.

His hand throbbed. He tightened the bloody handker-chief he had wrapped around the palm. He'd cut it skid-ding on his stomach in front of a collapsed apartment building near the Anhalter Railroad Station. A fluke. He wouldn't even have come that way, except that he had

almost stumbled into one of the SS flying courts-martial.
He had rounded a corner just in time to see them drag an
Army deserter out of a foyer. Six hideous, now-familiar
figures, clean black uniforms and bright red armbands,
cuffing and dragging the poor rattled Wehrmacht soldier
down the street to a garden wall. They shoved him against
it and shot him, while Bascom watched, then strung him
to a lamppost with a placard hanging around his neck: "I
betrayed my Führer."

Bascom doubled back and changed directions, of course.
But it had only put him in another wrong place at another
wrong time. He was working past Anhalter Station when
a Red fighter pilot homed in on him and sent him diving
into broken glass. The damned plane had looked like one
of the Lend-Lease Bell Airacobras. If so, he resented it
doubly. It was a sobering experience to be singled out as
a specific target by any pilot, but particularly maddening
when the pilot was sitting in a good old made-in-the-U.S.A.
cockpit.

Yet, it could have been worse. He could still move his
fingers easily enough. The main problem was the filth. He
hadn't realized he was cut until after several more blocks
of alternately stumbling and hitting the ground, and by then
the damned hand was coated with dirt. Wouldn't that be
just his luck? Formoy was down there in the cellar with
holes all through him, but he even seemed to be gaining
a little. Bascom, the way things had been going, would
probably come down with blood poisoning in the little
finger and die in twenty-four hours.

He wearily faced the cellar stairs. Might as well go down
and tell Erika the bad news. There would be no ticket to
safety this day. And from the sounds of approaching small-
arms fire, their chances were growing slimmer.

She was sitting on a wooden box at the foot of the
cellar stairs, almost as though waiting for him, peeling a
pile of scroungy potatoes and turnips with a paring knife.
The potatoes went into a large pot, the turnips and peelings
into a smaller pan, presumably to be used for soup. The
kids, including the newcomer, young Peter, were sitting

tailor-fashion in front of her, watching the peeling process. He could hear voices murmuring in one of the other rooms.

She smiled in welcome and relief as he started down the stairs; then her eye fell on the handkerchief around his hand. The smile faltered. At once she was on her feet. "You've been gone so long. What happened to your hand?"

"Erika, I've got—"

"Let me see," she interrupted. She pulled him toward the light of a paraffin lamp hanging from one of the rafters. That was new. She must have been digging through the upper floors again.

"Really, it's nothing," he said. He tugged his wrist away. "Erika," he said, "I've got to tell you something."

She looked up at him under tawny eyebrows, and she knew even before he said it. "It didn't work out?" she whispered.

"I'm afraid not. Looks like we'll be staying here."

She glanced away. Disappointment? No, there was more to it than that. She said haltingly, "Then I fear I have disturbing news for you as well."

He stared at her. Formoy. The bastard had waited until now to die. "My friend?" he said.

"Oh, no. Your friend is better. That's part of it. The good part."

"Then what?" He looked beyond her, scanning the cellar, wondering. The kerosene lamp. New. The potatoes and turnips. They had used the last of the turnips last night. "Oh God," he said with sudden understanding. "You haven't taken in more people?"

"I thought we would be leaving," she said.

"How many?"

"Only four," she said. "Two spinster sisters and a woman with a child from the Neukölln district. The Russians are advancing from Treptow, and they barely got out in time."

His hands curled automatically into fists, and he barely noticed when the cut palm protested. "Erika, what are you doing to us? That's nine people in all. Nine strangers."

"They are not strangers," she said. "They are people in need."

"They're Germans," he said. "They'd turn me in for a song."

"As I am German," she whispered tightly.

"You know what I mean. You heard that talk last night. They're the enemy. One word from any of them, and I'm a dead man."

"Your enemy? For your information, one of the spinster sisters is a nurse. She was tired and frightened when she arrived, but she spent the entire afternoon tending the wounds of your friend. She was also afraid to probe for the bullets but even more afraid to leave them in. When she was done, she was so exhausted that she fell asleep while eating. We had to carry her to a pallet. Despicable of her, wouldn't you say? Obviously the unreasonable conduct of an enemy."

He winced. "All right. But that doesn't change things. What happens if one of them catches on? Erika, it's dangerous to have so many people hanging around."

Anne-Lise came toward them, wondering why they were whispering so loudly. "What's wrong, Aunt Erika?" she piped in her clear, bell-like voice. "Is Henri angry with us?"

Erika gave Bascom a warning look and said, "No, dear. His hand is hurt, that's all. He's angry with himself for being so incredibly foolish."

Apparently the child's voice caught the attention of others. The old fellow, Herr Fiebeck, leaned around the corner and said, "Ah, Monsieur Cadiot, back from the wars." He grinned nervously. "We have more tenants, you know."

"So Fräulein Bollenen tells me," Bascom responded coldly.

"All women," the man said. "We're surrounded by women. Freddy and Peter and I have been sorely outnumbered today. We're glad you're back, to take up for us. What's wrong with your hand?"

"He's hurt it," Erika said. "Is Elfriede awake yet? Perhaps she would be willing to look at it."

"I think she is," Fiebeck said. "Maurice was asking for her, so my wife went to fetch her. Those Woelki sisters, they're remarkable women. We're lucky to have them with us."

"Yes, lucky," Bascom said. It almost slipped past him, but then, with a jolt, it sank in. "Asking for her? My friend spoke?"

"Oh yes," Fiebeck said. "He's been chattering away all afternoon, off and on. He isn't making much sense yet, but he's obviously feeling better."

Alarmed, Bascom brushed past the old man. He heard voices as he approached the coal room, a man's murmuring haltingly, a woman's responding. In German. Thank God, in German.

Formoy was on his mattress, propped on an elbow, while Frau Fiebeck spooned broth into his mouth. A short, lumpy woman with gray hair kneeled on the other side of him, rinsing a washcloth in a pan of water. In spite of her age, gaudy patches of rouge dotted her cheeks. She looked tired and barely awake.

Bascom slipped inside, heart pounding. "Is he all right?" he asked.

Formoy's head wobbled upward and he said, "Who's that?" Again, in German.

"It's me," Bascom said, leaning closer. *"Henri Cadiot, your old friend from Paris."* He put particular stress on the name and location, trying to clue Formoy in.

Formoy focused dazed eyes on Bascom's face. "Oh," he said. "So it is."

The woman with the rouged cheeks said, "Monsieur Cadiot?" She dried her hands. "I am Elfriede Woelki. I wish to thank you for accepting us into your small community. My sister and I are in your debt."

"How is he?" Bascom asked.

"He seems much better," the woman said. Her voice was husky. "The fever is down and he's fairly alert, as you can see. But I fear infection. It would be better if we could get him to a hospital."

"There's no room," Bascom said quickly. "They're full of soldiers."

"I know," the woman said. "How long has he been like this?"

Erika and Herr Fiebeck were at the door now, peering into the gloom. Bascom said, "I wonder if you would all give me a moment with my friend. I'd like to talk to him."

Erika understood instantly. She said, "Of course. It's been so long and you've been so worried. You must have a great deal to say to each other." She shooed Herr Fiebeck out and gestured for Frau Fiebeck and the other woman to join her.

The woman with the rouged cheeks rose and said, "I wouldn't tire him, if I were you. He's still quite weak."

When they were gone, Bascom whispered in English, "How do you feel?"

"All right, I think. A little bewildered."

"You didn't say anything, did you? About us, I mean."

"I don't think so. Bit of a shock, though, coming out of it in a coal room with women all about. Where are we? In Germany, I gather."

"We're still in Berlin. A cellar in Kreuzberg. It was the only thing I could find."

"What are our chances?"

"Not too good. The Russians have all but surrounded the city. Another day or so and they'll reach the inner circle. There's going to be a hell of a fight."

"Our mission?"

"A flop. You were hit the night it happened."

"How long?"

"Close to a week now. I thought you were a goner."

Formoy rested his head on the mattress. He was silent a moment, then said, "The others?"

"I don't know. I lost sight of them in the flurry. Some of them got away, I think."

"Sounds like we made a pig's breakfast of it. Have to try again. Duty. When I'm better, we'll take another crack."

"Sure, sure," Bascom said.

Formoy nodded and closed his eyes. For a moment, Bascom thought Formoy was drifting off, but then Formoy said, "Why did you stay?"

Bascom couldn't help grinning. "Damned if I know. I've asked myself that same question a hundred times."

" 'Preciate it," Formoy murmured. His chest rose and fell, a deep breath that hinted sleep was on its way.

"Hold on, don't conk out on me," Bascom said. "There are things you've got to know. These people, they're Germans. You've got to watch yourself."

"Hmmm?" Formoy said.

Bascom didn't shake him. Instead, he put urgency in his voice. "Formoy, listen to me. We're in a cellar with a bunch of Germans. If they catch on to who we are, we're finished. You've got to stay on your toes. Do you understand?"

"Good people," Formoy murmured. His breathing became deeper. "Nice people."

Bascom leaned back. "They'd damned well better be," he muttered. But Formoy didn't hear.

Bascom sat over the shaggy man for a full minute, watching his lungs swell and empty, then went back to the outer room, where Erika was finishing the potatoes and turnips. The children were still there and the woman with rouged cheeks, holding a paper bag.

"He's asleep," Bascom said.

"Good," the older woman said. "That's the proper medicine."

Bascom nodded. To Erika, he said, "I'm sorry. You know, about what I said earlier. I know you were only doing what you thought best." Then to the older woman, "I want to thank you for helping my friend, Frau Woelki. I'm sure he'll thank you himself, when he's better."

"Fräulein Woelki," she corrected. "My sister also. Something was said about a hand. Yours?"

"It's nothing to worry about," he said. "Just a few glass splinters."

"I'll look at it," she insisted. "Come to the light." She limped to the kerosene lamp and opened her paper bag.

"My medical kit," she said. "Not as handsome as a doctor's valise, but just as serviceable. Show me your hand."

He held it out, and she unwrapped the handkerchief. The cuts appeared, ringed with angry red streaks, and she clucked her tongue. "That is a proper mess," she said. "Sit here, under the light." She took a flask of alcohol and a wad of cotton from her sack. "How did you do this, breaking into a store window?" She smiled to show she was joking.

"I got it sliding on the ground," he said.

"We can fix it. First we'll clean it." She glanced at the children and said, "Fräulein Bollenen, why don't you and Anne-Lise take Freddy and Peter into one of the other rooms?"

Erika looked up alertly. "Why?"

"I can work better without distractions," the woman said. She soaked a cotton ball with alcohol and began to swab Bascom's hand, working smoothly and effortlessly. It stung like hell.

Erika hesitated, then led the children from the room. The woman said, "That wasn't entirely true, what I told her. There are things I wish to discuss with you."

"Oh?"

She kept swabbing. "We walked a long way today. We saw many things. The Russians reached Tempelhof this morning. You may have heard the sounds of battle coming from the south. Our soldiers are trying desperately to hold on to it. Once the aerodrome falls, there will be few supplies reaching the city."

"And?"

"We saw some of it from a distance. Terrible. Clouds of chlorine. Explosions. The screams of wounded. My sister cried. Then came German reinforcements. Four hundred schoolboys. Perhaps five hundred. We could see them in their black academy uniforms, marching toward Tempelhof with *Panzerfäuste* on their shoulders. The Russians saw them, too. They tried to warn the boys away with yellow flares. But the boys kept coming. So the Russians

opened fire. Boys, no more than fourteen or fifteen years
old. They all went down."

"I'm sorry to hear it," Bascom said. "But I'm not sure
I understand the point you're trying to make."

She set the cotton aside and took a small set of surgical
pincers from her bag and deftly began removing bits of
glass from the fleshy part of his palm. "My point is that
many things have gone tragically wrong in our country.
Most of us believed in the honor of the German people.
We might still believe, if our leaders hadn't cheated us. We
have gambled and lost, yet they will not admit it. They
force us to endure the consequences of their mistakes.
When boys die for nothing, honor is dead."

"What are you trying to say?"

"I'm trying to say that you need not fear us. We will
not betray you. We want only for the war to end, so we
may reassemble the fragments of our lives."

"Betray me? What the hell are you talking about?"

She traded the pincers for a roll of gauze. "Your friend
was incoherent when he first spoke this afternoon. His
mind was fevered, and he made no sense. But his first
words were English. My sister lived in Gibraltar for four
years before the war. She recognized it."

Bascom snatched his hand away. "Your sister is mistaken. My comrade is French."

"Please," she said. She reached for his hand. "I told
you. We will say nothing. None of us. You are our friend."

"French!" Bascom thundered. "He's French! We're both
French!"

The woman nodded gravely. "Very well, if you prefer.
But still, you have my assurance that we will not—"

Erika, apparently alarmed by Bascom's bluster, reappeared at the doorway, accompanied by Herr Fiebeck.
Bascom turned and stalked up the stairs to the first floor.

He didn't go far. He wanted to. He stared at the breached
front wall and the waning, smoky sunlight, and his brain
bucked and stammered, telling him this time he had no
choice but to flee. One man alone might still somehow find
an escape route from the city. But he wasn't one man

alone. There was still Formoy, his bleeding, bearded anchor. And now his betrayer, through some carelessly uttered words.

He hated Formoy at that moment, and hated himself for hating him. He groaned and turned to the rear of the house, poking under a slanting, sagging segment of plasterboard which blocked the way, seeking a quiet place where he could think. He found it in what had been a pantry, now only a small, square room lined with empty shelves. He leaned against the wall and tried to gauge clearly what possibilities he might have left. Fegelein's car? Maybe the SS hadn't confiscated it yet. Three minutes before, it would have still seemed too dangerous to attempt, with no papers, no Fegelein, probably too little gasoline, but Formoy's hapless return to consciousness had changed all that. Perhaps Bascom could get the car back across the city, yes, load Formoy in the back, and then simply see how far they could get. If they had to die, better to die trying. Anything would beat seeing those clean black uniforms and bright red armbands come through the door for them.

The plasterboard shook, and Erika crawled through, hugging the roll of gauze and a pair of scissors. She rose and reached for his hand. She worked in silence for a few seconds, then looked into his eyes and said, "Fräulein Woelki told me what happened. She thought her words would reassure you."

"Just the opposite," he murmured. "Did you know?"

"Yes. I was present at the meeting this afternoon. I didn't want to say anything, for fear of worrying you. That's why I was so irritable when you spoke unkindly of them."

"Meeting? God, how many of them are in on it?"

"All of them. Except the children. We had to make certain we were all in agreement."

"The Fiebecks?"

"Yes, they were there."

"Frau Schiller, too?"

Erika smiled. "It was she who insisted on the pact of silence. She says you are *our* Ami, to be shared with no one. She was determined to evict anyone who didn't agree."

"Jee-sus."

She tied off the bandage. "There. That's much better. Won't you come down now? They're all trying to be your friends."

"For how long? Until the pressure builds? What happens when they remember the penalty for harboring an enemy soldier?"

"You're incorrigible."

"No, just scared. I've never had so many hands resting on my throat."

Grit crunched under feet in the hallway, and the plasterboard stirred as someone else crawled under it, then stirred again, and again. They came in a troupe, Herr and Frau Fiebeck, a birdlike woman he had never seen before, Elfriede Woelki and another dumpy, oldish woman wearing bright red lipstick whom he assumed to be Elfriede's English-speaking sister, and Frau Schiller, bringing up the rear. They hovered in the darkened doorway outside the pantry, and Herr Fiebeck cleared his throat. "Monsieur Cadiot?" He glanced at the women standing behind him. Frau Schiller nodded, prompting him to go on. Fiebeck cleared his throat again. "Monsieur Cadiot, we owe you an apology. We realize you are, after all, a Frenchman. We meant no disrespect to the country of your birth. We will not speak of it again."

"The French are a wonderful people," Frau Schiller said, her knife-nose twitching. "Hooray for the French."

"Merci," Bascom said.

The group looked at each other and laughed nervously. Fiebeck said, "You will come down now? We're going to have a real dinner. The Woelki sisters have added to our larder."

"Soon," Bascom said. "I thank you all for your understanding."

They shuffled uncertainly, then followed Herr Fiebeck back along the corridor. The plasterboard creaked again as back after back scraped under it.

"You see?" Erika said. "You now have six new friends,

more counting the children and myself, and I count myself as more than just a friend. You are no longer alone. Does that not mean something?"

He sighed. "Yes, it does."

She snuggled under his arm, content to share the darkness with him. But as he leaned in silence, thinking of the cellarful of people waiting down below, contemplating the dangers, he realized he had never felt more alone in his life.

9

Thursday—April 26, 1945

Berlin ist eingekesselt!

"Berlin is surrounded!"

—pronouncement on Soviet
pamphlet dropped from the air

1

He was sipping a cup of malt coffee with Herr Fiebeck the next morning when the German soldiers came. There were three of them, a captain and two *Unteroffiziere,* and they burst into the cellar without warning.

It was an evil moment. Elfriede Woelki had just handed Bascom the white mug of steaming ersatz coffee, his first hot drink in days. At the second sip, vile-tasting but heavenly, the sound of boots hit the stairs, and the three soldiers dropped into sight. One of the women cried out. Bascom's hand jerked, splashing hot coffee on his knee.

The officer held a Luger in his hand, and he swept it around the room. The two sergeants took immediate defensive positions, one bracing himself on the stairway, the other rushing to the inner doorway a few feet beyond Fiebeck. They both had machine pistols.

For a moment, no one spoke. Then Erika, drawing the children to her side, said, "What's the meaning of this?"

The officer regarded her briefly, then motioned for the man at the door to check the rest of the cellar. The sergeant hurried to obey, his gun swinging ahead of him.

"There are no deserters here," Erika said stoutly.

"We aren't looking for deserters," the officer said. His eyes never stopped moving, scanning the faces, probing the corners, resting briefly on Bascom and Fiebeck, then moving on.

Fiebeck's wife and the other Woelki sister couldn't help glancing at Bascom. He tried to act normal, tried to raise the mug to his lips for another sip, but his hands shook and he lowered it. Betrayed? Had one of them slipped out during the night and passed the word? Or a neighbor perhaps, someone who had seen his comings and goings from the bomb-shattered building. The officer had looked at him with more than passing interest.

"Then what do you want?" Erika demanded.

Bascom shook his head at her. Don't push it, he told her with his eyes. Let the man be. Don't get him mad.

The sergeant came back. "A wounded man," he said. "Otherwise, there are only these people here."

"Collect their papers," the officer said. Then, to the room at large, "Who is in charge of this shelter?"

"No one is in charge," Erika said. "We live as equals."

The officer seemed unsurprised that a woman was speaking for the group. "My apologies for our abrupt entrance," he said. "We have little time for niceties, and we have found that a slower, more formal approach sometimes gives the women of a shelter time to hide their menfolk."

"What do you want with our men?" It was Frau Fiebeck, a note of panic in her voice.

The captain spoke patiently: "Gnädige Frau, we are fighting for our lives. The enemy is no longer at our gate. He is in our living room. We need every man we can get, to bear arms against him."

"An impressment gang," Erika murmured in disgust.

"We are a recruitment team," the officer said stiffly. "All men are expected to do their duty and volunteer."

The blood drained from Frau Fiebeck's face. "My husband? You would take my husband?"

"The Russians outnumber us five to one," the officer said. "There will be no relief from outside. We are cut off. If we do not stop them here, all Germany will die."

"But my husband is sixty-three years old. He has a heart condition."

The sergeant had collected all the identity cards and he

carried them to the officer, who holstered his handgun and went quickly through them. He stopped at one, and without looking up, said casually, "Which is Henri Cadiot?"

"I am," Bascom said.

"You are a French national?"

"Yes, Herr Hauptmann."

"It says here you worked in the Krupp und Druckenmüller tank factory. Is that correct?"

"Yes, Herr Hauptmann."

"You are lucky to be alive," the captain said. "Tempelhof fell yesterday. The factory was destroyed." Just as casually, he asked, "Who is the wounded man in the other room?"

"Also a foreign laborer," Erika said quickly. "He worked on my family's farm in Petershagen before we were driven out by the Russians."

"How was he wounded?"

"During an aerial attack. He was carrying my belongings and couldn't take shelter quickly enough."

"Is he fit?" the officer asked his *Unteroffizier*.

"No, Herr Hauptmann," the sergeant said. "The wounds are severe."

"Very well. Then we shall have to settle for these two." He tucked Fiebeck's and Bascom's identity papers in his tunic and handed the others back to the underofficer for return to the women.

"You can't take them," Erika said. "Herr Fiebeck is an ill man, and Monsieur Cadiot is not a German national."

"That won't matter a great deal to the Russians," the captain said. He hooked a thumb at the sergeant. "Bring them."

"No!" Frau Fiebeck wailed. She rushed to Fiebeck's side and threw both arms around his neck, almost a stranglehold. Fiebeck tutted consolingly and pried her arms loose.

"Don't worry," he said gently, "I'll be all right, *Liebchen*. I'm a veteran. They need men like me."

Bascom rose even before the sergeant on the stairs gestured with his machine pistol, and dithered briefly, but only about what to do with his coffee mug. For the rest, he had no options. Elfriede Woelki took the mug from him. She patted him on the arm. "Don't worry about your friend," she whispered. "We will take care of him." It was her gift to him, the only words of comfort she could offer.

Erika and Frau Fiebeck offered arguments, following the three soldiers all the way to the breached wall that was their front door, but the captain pointedly ignored them. There were more soldiers on the sidewalk, standing guard over a group of impressed "volunteers," mainly older men like Fiebeck, though there was at least one obese fellow in his middle forties, face yellow and sweating profusely in the early-morning sunlight. There were a few children in the group, as well. The oldest, a gangly kid with pimples, appeared to be about fifteen. The others were younger, smaller, and fidgeting with excitement.

Bascom helped Fiebeck down the spill of bricks. They could see scouts coming from other buildings on the block, some bringing more fodder to the growing fold, some returning empty-handed. It was strangely quiet, with only a low rumble of artillery underscoring the shouts and commands of the impressment squad. The thought struck Bascom that the night had also been oddly peaceful. Like the eye of a hurricane. As though the Russians had decided to take a rest break before launching the final attack on the inner citadel. Even the skies were clear. In spite of a dazzling early-morning sun, not a single Soviet fighter seemed to be in the air.

Frau Fiebeck sobbed from the landing above them, and her husband murmured up at her, "Don't worry, don't worry, don't worry," over and over, but so softly that she couldn't possibly have heard. Erika stayed, too, her arm around Frau Fiebeck, but there was nothing to say. Or do. Bascom mustered one smile for good-by, then looked away.

The captain seemed to be counting. Aloud, he finally said to one of the sergeants, "Let's move."

Fiebeck watched over his shoulder until they turned the corner up Oranienstrasse, then he looked at Bascom and smiled with genuine pleasure. "Imagine," he said. "Me.

Back in uniform after all these years. By God, it's enough
to make a man feel young again."

2

Fegelein paced from wall to wall in his cramped underground quarters. No one had come. No one had questioned
him. True, they had confined him to his bunker bedroom
and stationed an SS guard outside his door, but no one had
shown any further interest in him. Perhaps there was hope
after all.

The touchiest part for him had been entering the Chancellery underground complex. As they passed Bormann's
fateful office, who, by ill luck, should step out but Bormann
himself? Fegelein had expected an explosion of denunci-
ations, but the Reichsleiter was preoccupied and had said
not a word, hadn't even seemed to notice him. That was a
good sign. If Bormann was unaware that Fegelein had been
in his office and gone through his things, then the only
reason for his arrest might well be his unauthorized absence. He could find ways to explain that away, given a
chance.

The room was so small. He'd never noticed that before.
One grew accustomed to cramped spaces as long as one
could leave them at will. But now, with the door locked
and egress blocked, the room seemed smaller, the walls
grayer, the recessed light dimmer, the whine of the venti-
lator more irritating.

He'd sent word that he wanted an audience with the
Führer, to explain, but the Führer had neither come to his
quarters nor sent for him. That wasn't necessarily bad.
The Führer would be incredibly busy at the moment, directing the defense of the city. Besides, the longer it took,
the more likely his anger, if indeed the Führer was angry,
would dissipate. Fegelein would wait. Cheerfully.

Perhaps he should send word to his sister-in-law. She
might be willing to intercede on his behalf. On the other
hand, she was such a brainless, immature young woman.

And selfish. She would probably turn him down, or, worse, speak against him if she thought it might jeopardize her own position in the inner court. No, best save her as a last resort.

But it wouldn't come to that. The Führer admired him. Didn't he?

Fegelein would stick to his story about the missing papers. That would explain his absence from the Chancellery. He would just say he thought they were at his home, and that he was appalled when he discovered they were not. They couldn't disprove it.

Could they?

Oh Lord, what if the American were caught? Perhaps Fegelein should devise a credible explanation and present it first, just in case. Something that would keep him in the clear. He could say the American contacted him, sent by Reichsführer Himmler. That he met with the American only to discover to his horror that the Reichsführer was about to betray the Führer. He could tell them the whole story, as he knew it, the attempt to meet with Eisenhower, the determination to capitulate to the Western Powers, everything, and say that he had learned of it all for the first time from the American.

They would want to know why he hadn't reported it immediately. Very well. He would say that he was trying to trap the American. The real reason he left the Chancellery and went to his home was that the American promised to meet him there and bring documents to prove that the Reichsführer was working with the Allies, but the SS guards came and arrested him before the American could arrive.

Bringing the American into it would raise eyebrows, however, particularly since he could produce no evidence that Reichsführer Himmler was set on a course of treachery. The Führer was inclined to trust Himmler, often referred to him as *"Der treue* Heinrich," and might refuse to believe ill of him without absolute proof.

Maybe he could tell the Führer about Bormann's hidden assets. Millions, perhaps hundreds of millions, tucked away in foreign banks. But then wouldn't he have to explain how he knew? Besides, the Führer trusted Bormann the same way he trusted Himmler. Bormann could hide the bank certificates and deny everything, and it would be only Fegelein's word against the word of the Reichsleiter himself.

If only Fegelein could think of some way to help them catch the American. That might go a long way toward confirming his own loyalty.

Or would it be better to stick with his story about the missing papers?

It was all so confusing.

3

By noon, Bascom's group of civilian "volunteers," nearly forty strong, had been herded to the eastern end of the East-West Axis and ordered to stand by for unloading duties. The Russians had increased the tempo of action with the strengthening sun, and incoming shells plowed into the wrecked trees of the Tiergarten below them, throwing up geysers of dirt and splintered wood.

Boys and old men for the most part, they were uniformed with painful simplicity. They had each been issued a canvas bread bag, empty, and a round water canteen, full, to be hooked to their belts, and a dark strip of felt material bearing the words "Deutscher Volkssturm—Wehrmacht," to be worn on their coat sleeves. They had no weapons yet, but their identity papers had been confiscated and replaced with regulation military paybooks. Fiebeck, disappointed at the unmilitary outfittings, muttered, "That's a well-organized Germany for you. No uniforms, no pay, no food, but the paperwork is always properly done. Bureaucracy *über alles.*"

Bascom smiled a frozen smile, but he knew better. The paybooks weren't just a quirk of habitually red-tape-minded officials. With their original identity papers still in hand, it would be possible to ditch the armbands, slip away from their units, and go home. With paybooks, desertion became more difficult.

Like an animal that seeks instinctively to camouflage itself when in the path of a predator, Bascom concentrated fiercely on doing precisely as the others did. His fellow conscripts slumped, waiting? He slumped, waiting. They muttered among themselves? He tried to think of something to mutter. His body took over, rabbit, hop when the other rabbits hopped, and his thoughts focused on a single goal: Attract no attention.

The East-West Axis, where they now waited, was the broad triumphal avenue that ran from the Brandenburg Gate on the east all the way to the Grosser Stern, along the northern edge of the Tiergarten. A handsome, spacious thoroughfare, it had been completed in 1939 by Hitler's favorite architect and soon-to-be Minister of Armaments, Albert Speer, just in time to be used as a parade ground following each of Germany's early World War II victories. Later, when the American and British bombers began to come with regularity, an enormous camouflage curtain had been erected to cover it, stretching more than a mile long and 150 feet wide. It was only in the latter months of the war, when Russian and American troops began to close in, that the curtain came down and engineers cleared the street to provide an emergency airstrip in the heart of the government district. Labor squads swarmed out daily to fill in bomb and shell holes. The black lamp standards so admired by Hitler were removed to make room for larger planes. Luftwaffe officials also wanted to clear away twenty to thirty yards of trees along the Tiergarten side, but Hitler rejected the plan. The avenue was broad enough for most planes, he insisted. And trees, once felled, would take years to replace.

Because the Soviets had left the skies relatively clear this day, a few German transports had been ordered to slip into the city with supplies and attempt to land. The first two to appear were cumbersome tri-motored Ju52s, winging in low over the buildings with puffs of flak following in their wake. They circled awkwardly above Bascom and his fellow conscripts and dropped to street level, touching down about a hundred yards west of the Brandenburg Gate. By the time they rolled to a stop, they were halfway down the avenue. Slowly, ponderously, they turned and began to taxi back to the east.

Most of the Wehrmacht recruitment team had moved on to hunt new bodies, leaving Bascom and the others under the temporary supervision of an *Unteroffizier* until they could be turned over to a permanent leader, and the *Unteroffizier* now directed them to the first of the planes. Willy-nilly, Bascom helped unload it quickly, crate after crate of *Panzerfäuste*—long, one-shot steel tubes bearing anti-tank projectiles. As quickly as the conscripts stacked the crates, ordnance men broke them open and passed them out, two at a time, to a horde of young BdM girls, who lashed them to the handlebars of bicycles and pedaled off to deliver them to the front.

Even before they finished unloading the first plane, carts and ambulances packed with wounded began to roll in from the Adlon. Both planes kept their engines idling, and the pilot of the first hung his head out the window, yelling at Bascom's crew to work even more quickly.

Within moments, his reason for haste became obvious. Alerted by Russian observers who had seen the two transports circle in, a flight of Yaks roared in from the east and dived on the street for a strafing run. Bascom spotted them first. He yanked Fiebeck under the left wing of the big Ju52. Bullets furrowed the cobblestones, and the fighters whipped past and started to climb. Only then did Bascom realize that he had pulled Fiebeck to shelter under the transport's fuel tanks. Bascom shivered and hustled Fiebeck back into the open.

While the Yaks climbed and circled, and the German pilot cursed and yelled encouragement, they hurriedly snatched the wounded from the carts and wagons and ambulances and shoved them none too gently into the plane. Men in casts and head bandages, some on foot, some strapped to stretchers, went tumbling through the door, grimacing, crying out in pain, yet deliriously happy to have come so close to escape. Then, in the midst of the loading process, the Yaks came again, and everyone scattered.

That was it, as far as the pilot of the first plane was concerned. Already fidgety, he released his brakes and throttled up, in spite of the fact that he could have taken several more wounded. He began to roll. He picked up speed as the Yaks peppered him. Bascom saw somone lean out and reach for the flopping hatch and wrestle it closed; then the plane was off the ground and gaining altitude. The Yaks zoomed past.

Bascom's group shifted to the second plane and began to unload it, but it was difficult to avoid peering skyward. Swinging crates from man to man, they kept watching the first ungainly German transport maneuver in an attempt to evade the faster Yaks. No matter how it climbed and banked, the Yaks stayed right on it.

Then a surprising thing happened. A lone Me109, the first German fighter any of them had seen in days, swooped down from a cloudbank and dived right through the flight of Yaks, scattering them like a hawk pouncing on chickens. The Russian fighter pilots were apparently as startled as anyone on the ground to encounter a German warplane in the skies above Berlin, and two of them took hits before they could get over the shock. One of them nosed down and sailed into the ground. The other, smoking badly, turned and limped back to the east.

The German pilot, completely outnumbered, wheeled and made another pass at the remaining Russians, trying to give the cumbersome trimotor time to reach the clouds. It was awesome to watch. The boys and men surrounding the supply plane on the ground stood rooted, crates straining their arms, all eyes fixed upward. Another Yak spiraled off in flames, and the unloading crew shouted in triumph. It was infectious. Even Bascom found himself close to cheering.

The fight lasted only moments. As soon as the big

transport dipped into the clouds, the lone Me109 turned
tightly and followed. Yaks swarmed after him, like hunting hounds after a fox. In seconds they had all vanished.

The diversion gave the ground crew time enough to
finish unloading the sister Ju52. Crates came out on the
double, and wounded went in. This time they packed a full
complement of stretchers and walking injured into the
plane before they slammed the door. The plane eased
around and revved up. Those for whom there had not
been enough room, another twenty to thirty wounded
soldiers, watched from the carts and wagons with desperate eyes.

As the plane began to roll, Bascom turned to look for
Fiebeck and almost didn't see the Yaks coming back. They
had given up on their cloud search and were bearing down
on the avenue from the west, coming head-on toward the
loaded transport. They opened fire just as the big plane
reached takeoff speed, and strings of powdered pavement
ripped up in long trails. As far as Bascom could tell, none
of the Russian guns hit the German plane, but they might
as well have. The German transport pilot, overreacting to
the planes' bearing down on him, wrenched to the right,
and a wingtip brushed the front of a house just as he became airborne. The big plane shivered and stalled, then
cartwheeled along the street and slammed into the buildings on the north side of the street. The fuel tanks exploded. Burning gasoline surged ahead in a flaming wave.
The plane blew apart and scattered wreckage for sixty
yards. Black smoke mushroomed. The Yaks thundered
past and zoomed over the Brandenburg Gate, disappearing
to the east. They didn't come back. They didn't have to.

For a long time, the ground crew stood and watched
the wreckage burn. Then, one by one, prodded by their
officers, they gave up and resumed their activities. Bascom's team finished breaking open the crates. The ordnance
men passed out the *Panzerfäuste*. The BdM girls tied them
to their bikes and pedaled away. The cart drivers clucked
up their horses and carried the leftover wounded back toward the Adlon. The cheering was done for the day.

❋ ❋ ❋

The group leader for Bascom's band of demoralized conscripts, when he arrived, turned out to be an SS lieutenant with feminine features and icy blue eyes, accompanied by a Waffen-SS corporal. They came from the direction of Bendlerstrasse, and they handed the Wehrmacht *Unteroffizier* a set of heavily stamped documents. The *Unteroffizier* studied the papers carefully before calling the group to attention. He seemed embarrassed. Apparently he had expected a regular Army officer.

While the SS man and his corporal looked on, the *Unteroffizier* shuffled his feet. "This is your new leader, Oberstürmführer Hans Rantzau," he said. "From now on, you will take your orders from him."

The SS lieutenant looked them over silently. There were forty-two of them by now, each shouldering two of the *Panzerfäuste*, standing in clumsy ranks. The SS officer was not impressed. "Are these the best you could do?" he asked the Wehrmacht man.

"Yes, sir," the underofficer said. "I'm afraid so, sir."

"Have they been instructed in the use of their weapons?"

"No, sir. I was just about to begin."

"My corporal will see to it," the lieutenant said. "I would prefer a word with you before we release you to other duties." He looked coldly at the ragged group of boys and old men, and his eyes fell briefly on Bascom. Then he said, "Corporal, instruct them. There in the trees will do. I will join you shortly."

The Waffen-SS corporal, a thirty-year-old with dark circles under his eyes and a worn spring camouflage smock over his uniform, slung his Schmeisser over his shoulder and took the recruits to the side. He borrowed a *Panzerfaust* from a boy in the front row to demonstrate the weapon's handling. It consisted of a steel tube about two inches thick, with a hollow-charge bomb sticking out of the front. The tube went under the right arm for firing, with the projectile aimed forward. A sighting mechanism was raised to arm it, and a spring lever in the sighting mechanism was depressed to fire it. It was a one-shot, disposable weapon, so one threw away the tube after firing and reached for another. The effective range was about sixty meters, the corporal told them, and it could knock out even the heavily armored Russian T-34s, if one hit them in a vulnerable spot. He spent a few moments explaining the vulnerable spots.

Their basic training lasted between ten and fifteen minutes. Then the Waffen-SS corporal put them through dry runs, sighting in on a German Tiger tank parked at the edge of the Tiergarten. It was a simple weapon, and most caught on quickly, though a few, like Fiebeck, had trouble getting the hang of it. Fiebeck had seen newsreels of German troops handling the *Panzerschreck*, an earlier imitation of the American bazooka, and it was always fired from the shoulder, rather than clamped under the arm. He couldn't understand why the corporal kept snarling at him for shouldering the *Panzerfaust* the same way.

Then the SS lieutenant sent the Wehrmacht *Unteroffizier* on his way and came to join them under the trees. "That's enough," he told the corporal. "We have battles to fight. Line them up for inspection."

Bascom, prey facing predator, hopped hastily with the others. He tried to wipe all thought from his mind. Not knowing from what atavistic source the instruction came, he even breathed shallowly. Thoughts might leak. Breath might whisper of something alien to the icy-eyed SS lieutenant, who slowly, silently, walked down the line, considering each man in turn with the ice-blue eyes.

Inspection finished, the lieutenant clasped his hands behind his back. "You are a feeble lot," he informed them, "not worthy of the honor being entrusted to you. My orders are to march you immediately to Bendlerstrasse Bridge on the Landwehr Canal, where you will join other units to repel the Russian advance in that area. It is to the degradation of Germany that we must fight the Russians with such as you, but fight them we will. Any man or boy among you who shows cowardice in battle, anyone who attempts to run, will be shot. You have my promise on that."

Fiebeck held up his hand. The SS officer raised disapproving, delicately arched brows, then gestured with a flick of the chin that he might speak.

"Don't we get guns?" Fiebeck asked meekly. "I'm a good shot. I can do better with a gun, if you'll give me one."

"You'll fight with what is provided," the officer said. He regarded Fiebeck's scrawny body and shook his head in disgust. "You will not fight well, but you will fight. All of you." He ran his eyes across them once more, then singled out Bascom. "You," he said. "Step forward."

Bascom hopped slowly, teeth clamped.

"You are a foreign worker, I am told. Do you speak sufficient German?"

"I speak it," Bascom said.

"Good. Then listen well. I do not like foreigners, and I do not like your sullen expression. You will obey my orders instantly, and you will show respect. I will be watching you with a special eye. Now get back in ranks."

Good God, had his face given him away? Bascom stepped back, but he couldn't will his expression to change.

The SS officer frowned at the group once more and said, "Very well, Corporal. Form them up. Let's go kill some Russians before half our enfeebled forces died of old age."

4

Alexei Volkov hurried through the darkness along the railroad tracks south of the Landwehr Canal, carrying his mess kit back to the field kitchens. Lieutenant Ivanov, damn his eyes, had gone back for supper with one of the sergeants earlier, but he had brought only enough for himself and the enlisted men. He claimed it was because Volkov had been at corps headquarters and he hadn't known when he would return, but Volkov suspected it was an act of petty revenge, Ivanov's way of getting back at him for his insistence that they all work round-the-clock shifts. Ivanov and the rest of the crew would have preferred a more relaxed nine-to-five existence.

His men weren't the only ones. He heard laughter off behind a garden wall to the right of the tracks. Russian voices bantering drunkenly. Female voices shrilling back at them. Three field guns parked near the wall, caissons unguarded. Draft horses munching short grass on the railroad embankment. Malingerers.

He'd noticed this new tendency for the first time last night. Soldiers, good soldiers, who nevertheless drew up at sunset and thought only of making themselves comfortable in the shadows. Some, like these, had found female companionship. Not only artillery, but infantrymen as well. Such a lackadaisical approach to battle might have been controlled in the field, under the watchful eyes of officers, but deep in a city like this, with battered buildings and broken walls offering safe havens, it was impossible to keep them all moving. Oh, they fought hard enough during the day, but droves of them simply dropped out of sight once night fell. He couldn't blame them. Most of them seemed to feel the war was finished. All of them wanted to live through it to see home again. But that was a dangerous attitude. Unless someone came up with a way to halt these post-sunset lulls, they were apt to get their noses bloodied. The Germans didn't stop fighting at night.

He was twenty meters past the wall when the mixture of male and female voices and rough laughter were joined by a new sound—a high-pitched voice pleading in German, "Don't. Please don't." Another woman, from the sound of it, but younger. He stopped and listened more carefully. Yes, a German girl.

He retraced his steps in the darkness and clambered down the railroad embankment. The light of a small cook fire flickered beyond the wall, exposing a wide split where stones had collapsed. The girl's voice became more urgent. He hurried past the abandoned artillery pieces and looked over the wall.

There were five of them, artillery men all, lounging around the fire in the courtyard. Three German women, buxom, perhaps in their late thirties and early forties, clung to them, lured from cellar shelters by the smell of food. The women laughed breathlessly at every comment from the men, not understanding any of it, but eager to please. Even as they laughed, their eyes glittered nervously in the firelight.

Beyond the cook fire, a young Russian corporal stood at the doorway of a two-story house, trying to drag a blond girl outside. She was eighteen or nineteen years old, probably, and she had smudged her face and arms with coal dust to make herself look dirty and unattractive. Even so, she was uncommonly handsome: long, slim legs and pert breasts under a shapeless dress, disheveled golden hair that had fallen to her shoulders.

The five men around the fire hugged their female companions and urged the corporal on. The youngster needed encouragement. The girl was like a spitting cat, hands and arms flailing, nails digging in. The corporal tugged her through the door and pulled her to the middle of the dirt yard. Two older women watched from a window in silent horror.

"Throw her to the ground," a sergeant yelled. "Take some of the fight out of her." He laughed raucously and pinched a breast that leaned over his shoulder. The woman behind the breast giggled hysterically.

The corporal took the sergeant at his word. He pushed the girl down and flung himself on her, fighting her blows with one hand and trying to yank up her dress with the other.

The men at the fire hooted. "Stick it to her," one of them yelled. They hadn't yet seen Volkov approaching from the broken wall.

The corporal pinned the girl's throat with his elbow and groped for her skirt. Her legs continued to thrash, but he got his fingers on the material and snatched it up, exposing white, fleshy thighs and loose panties. He bore down harder on her throat until she began to choke, then slipped his hand to the crotch, grasping the cloth like a handle, and tried to tug the panties off. He got them only as far as the

knees before he ran out of armspan. Afraid to let loose of
her throat for fear she might get away, he wrenched the
panties back and forth, trying to rip them loose.

"That's enough," Volkov said.

The corporal didn't hear him and kept tearing at the
panties, but the men at the fire did. The sergeant turned
angrily, only to see Volkov's collar tabs and rank insignia.
He rose to his feet, too slowly, swaying unsteadily, but he
saluted. When one of the women reached for his sleeve, he
pushed her away. "Just having a little fun, Captain," he
said.

"Not for the girl," Volkov said.

The corporal loosed a cry of triumph. The panties, hanging in shreds, waved from his hand like a victory flag. He
flung them away and tried to get his pants down.

"I said enough!" Volkov snapped. He pulled his pistol
from his holster and leveled it.

"Wait, don't shoot him, Captain," the sergeant cried
urgently. "It's his first piece. He's just a kid."

"You have five seconds to pull him away," Volkov said.

The sergeant looked sullenly at Volkov for two seconds,
then spoke gruffly to his fireside companions. Two grunted
and rose. They strode across the garden and grabbed the
corporal by the shoulders and dragged him away.

"Get him out of here," Volkov said. "Take him and
report back to your outfit."

"We didn't mean anything," the sergeant muttered. "We
were just trying to have a little pleasure. Everybody's doing
it."

"Win the war first," Volkov snapped. "Then enjoy your
pleasure. Now get him out of here."

The artillery men grumbled, but not loudly. They gathered their belongings, including the food, and the three
German women, seeing even the smallest scraps go into kit
bags, glared at Volkov with loathing. The sergeant added
his own share of loathing in a quick sidelong glance, then
waved his men toward the break in the wall. The women
hesitated, then slunk off after them. The soldiers wouldn't

go far, Volkov was certain, but at least they might restrict their impromptu celebration to willing parties.

The two older women who had been peeping from the window now came rushing from the house to the young girl. One of them turned on Volkov. "Barbarian!" she panted. "You are all barbarians!"

"What would you know of barbarism?" Volkov said.

The woman seemed surprised that he could speak German. She left the sobbing girl to the other woman and drew herself up. "I know that pig soldier came into the house and dragged out my niece and tried to violate her. What more do I need to know?"

"A good deal more," Volkov said. "And you could learn it from your own soldiers."

"They never did anything like this!" the woman hissed.

"No? I wish you could tell that to a girl I once knew. She was twelve years old. Her name was Klarsetta Sokolov. She was from my village. It would please her to know no such thing ever happened."

"A Russian girl," the woman said. "We've heard how your Russian girls acted. If a German soldier stepped out of line with her, she probably asked for it."

"Not one soldier," Volkov said. "Nine. They tied her mother and father to a wagon wheel and forced them to watch. They took turns with the girl. When they were finished, they nailed her to a barn door and left her to die."

"That's a lie. That's a filthy, dirty lie!"

"Believe what you like," he said. "There were tens of thousands like her."

The woman looked away in disgust. "Why do you tell us such a wretched thing?"

Volkov shrugged. "I don't believe in taking a woman by force," he said. "But there will be others behind me who do. I just want you to understand their reasons. They learned the hard way, from finding what was left of their women after the Germans withdrew. It was not a pretty sight."

"Lies," the woman said. "I don't believe you."

"As you wish," Volkov said. "At any rate, it would be wise for you to leave here and take shelter elsewhere. Those men may come back before the night is over. I won't be here to stop them next time."

The women exchanged shocked looks and quickly helped the young girl to her feet. "You'll stay here and protect us until we gather our possessions?"

He considered it briefly. The girl was badly shaken. Pretty, too. But he was tired of their arrogance, tired of their willingness to believe ill of any save their own. Besides, he was hungry. He stook his head and said, "Forget your possessions. Go while you can."

The woman scowled at him. "Pig," she said. Then she wrapped her arms around the girl and hurried toward the house.

Volkov started to turn away, then his anger boiled up. He called after them, "Ask your own soldiers, if there are any still alive when we finish. Watch their faces. If you see any shame, it will be the miracle of the ages. Then you'll know who the pigs are."

5

The Fiesler Stork, a lightweight, high-wing German observation plane with a gawky, stiltlike undercarriage that gave it its nickname, skimmed over the Havel lakes and entered the air above Berlin shortly before midnight. At the controls of the unarmed two-seater was General Robert Ritter von Greim, commander of a Luftwaffe wing in Munich. With him, huddled against the cold in the rear seat, was Hanna Reitsch, the popular aviatrix and test pilot.

The city was a sea of flames. Blazing wreckage littered the outlying streets. Strings of tanks crawled toward the inner city, silhouetted against burning buildings. Machine guns spat white streaks of fire through the darkness. Exploding shells flickered both beyond and behind the line of advance as German and Russian artillery traded blows.

Walls tumbled. Gas mains erupted in towering torches. Block after block being slowly pulverized.

Greim had been summoned to Berlin by telegram. He had no idea why. Bormann had sent the wire the day before, telling him only that he was to report to the Führerbunker as soon as he could arrange air transportation. He wondered if it might have anything to do with the rumors about Reichsmarschall Hermann Göring. Göring, who had abandoned the city before the Russians closed in, was now in the South, in the relative safety of Berchtesgaden. Those who were close to him said he sent a message to besieged Berlin, suggesting that he take over the reins of government from Hitler. If true, it was damned tactless and poorly timed. Hitler would be furious.

Greim's companion, Hanna Reitsch, had not been mentioned in the wire from Borman, but she was a strong-willed woman and had insisted on making the trip with him. Would that irritate Bormann? He hoped not. No one welcomed Bormann's anger. Still, she was a friend to the Führer, and the Führer would no doubt consider it an act of the highest loyalty that she insisted on flying in with Greim to pay her respects. Let Bormann become angry if he wanted. The Führer would cool him down.

Whatever the reason for the summons, Greim hoped it was important. It hadn't been an easy flight. From Munich to Mecklenburg, accompanied by an escort of fighters, then on toward Berlin. Tempelhof had fallen, so he had landed at Gatow airfield under Russian fire and had transferred to the Stork for the last leg. Now he had to come in on the East-West Axis, no doubt again under fire. He was beginning to wish Hanna had stayed behind.

A bright burst of orange opened up ahead of them. New trouble. Russian flak. They'd been spotted. The little Stork trembled in the blast wave. Lower, lower. Get under their range. Another. Closer. Drop to the trees. Another. And another. The plane shaking. Damned foolish, insisting we come in person . . .

The plane rose as though a giant fist had struck upward. Hanna cried out in wordless alarm. Damn. White-hot pain.

He tried to move his right foot. Hurt. What happened? A hole, tattered metal in the floor of the cockpit, near the rudder pedals. Must have been hit. Blood. Foot shattered. Growing numb. Hold on, for God's sake. Don't pass out. Still a good ten miles to go. Vision dimming . . .

He was only vaguely aware of her voice. Arms, her arms, coming past him, wrestling for the controls. Everything going dark, as though the miles of leaping flames below had suddenly been snuffed out. He slumped to the side, head resting against the cool cockpit window. Pain abated as consciousness left him. Was this the way it ended? The pain gone? Peace and darkness? It wasn't so bad. He may have smiled. . . .

When he came to, a young SS captain was bending over him. The Brandenburg Gate, dark arch pitted against the glowing sky, loomed overhead. The Stork, floorboards ripped away, was parked twenty meters to the west, at the edge of the broad street. They'd made it? They'd stayed in the air even after he passed out? But how?

"Are you badly hurt?" Hanna asked. She was kneeling beside the SS captain.

"I think not," Greim said. He tried to raise his head. In the background, several soldiers hurried down the East-West Axis, extinguishing the soft red lanterns that had guided them to a landing. "Did you fly us in?"

She nodded. "We have a stretcher coming now," she said. "This is Captain Schedle of the bunker guards. Reichsleiter Bormann sent him to fetch us to the Chancellery."

"I'm sorry about your foot," the SS man said. "I'm sure the Führer will have his personal surgeon look at it as soon as we arrive."

"Yes, rotten luck," Greim said. "I didn't expect their guns to be that accurate. Particularly at night."

The stretcher came within minutes, borne by four strapping young SS men from the Führer's personal bodyguard. Greim winced as they lifted him onto it, and winced again as they set off at a jog, carrying him down Hermann Göring Strasse toward the Chancellery with Hanna and the young SS officer following.

Greim gripped the sides of the stretcher. Shattered walls rose above him, standing like bleak ghosts against the most depressing sky he had ever imagined. Cherry-red embers sifting on the wind. Ash falling like gray snow. Stars blotted out by rosy clouds, reflecting the scattered fires of a burning city.

The streets were utterly deserted here in the inner citadel. Even the Chancellery, when they reached it, looked forsaken and empty. No guards at the outer portals. That was strange. It was as though discipline had broken down completely. In earlier times, one might go through six different checkpoints before reaching the inner sanctum, but tonight they were all the way down to the first of the bunker tunnels before they encountered a soul. Even then it was only a solitary gun-bearing guard who passed them on with hardly a murmur.

Bormann must have been waiting for them. He was sitting on a bench in the corridor lounge of the Führerbunker with two uniformed adjutants when Greim's four SS escorts wound carefully down the spiral staircase to the lower level, struggling to keep the stretcher on an even keel. Bormann jumped up instantly, his face stricken. "What happened?" he demanded.

The young SS captain, Schedle, said, "They were hit by Russian anti-aircraft guns. His foot needs attention."

"Yes, immediately," Bormann said. He sent one of the adjutants quickly to fetch the bunker surgeon, then leaned over Greim. "Can you still fly?" he asked.

It seemed an odd question. "Not unless you can put wings on a wheelchair," Greim said. He meant it as a brave joke, a way of showing his ability to smile through pain, but Bormann's tortured expression never wavered. Could the man really be that concerned about his welfare? Greim was touched.

"Where did it happen?" Bormann asked.

"Coming over Schmargendorf, just past the Grunewald," Greim said. "The Russians are thick in there."

"Could you have avoided them by coming in another way?"

"Possibly," Greim said, puzzled. "It's hard to say. Maybe if I'd come north from the Grunewald to Spandau. There seemed to be less activity along the corridor. Why do you ask?"

Bormann's eyes flicked away. "Just worrying," he said. "We must still fly you out of here in a day or two, after your foot has been tended. The Führer wants you to take over the Luftwaffe."

So it was the Göring thing, after all. But why summon him to Berlin to tell him? They could have handled that by telegram.

There was a commotion at the end of the lounge. Bormann stiffened and backed away from the stretcher. Greim raised his head, wondering who it was.

It was the Führer himself, coming through the curtains from the map room, accompanied by the bunker surgeon, Dr. Ludwig Stumpfegger. Greim's stunned eyes told him what his heart had feared. The Führer looked dreadful. Pale. Tired. Thinner. His once strong face had developed a tic under the left eye, and his left arm, still ailing from the June 20 bomb conspiracy, hung limply at his side.

The Führer shuffled to Greim's stretcher and stared sadly at the shattered foot. Greim's chin trembled. His eyes turned moist. "My Führer," he said, "forgive me for being unable to rise—"

10

Berlin: Massengrab für Sowjeipanzer!

"Berlin: Mass Grave for Soviet Tanks!"

—headline in *Panzerbär*, newspaper
for the defenders of Greater
Berlin, April 27

1

The chittering sounds of tank treads grinding on cobble-stones echoed through the early-morning mist, and Bascom strained to catch sight of them. It had been quiet for almost an hour, if you could call concentrated mortar and artillery fire quiet, while the tankers regrouped beyond the buildings to the south and tried to figure a better way to hit the bridge. Three times during the night the Russians had tried to break through to the canal, and three times they had been repulsed, leaving burning tank hulks in their wake. From the smoke and sounds of artillery fire to the east and west, they'd had no better luck with any of the other bridges.

Bascom was no military expert, but his one long night in the field convinced him the Russians were using the wrong strategy with their tank armies. Tanks were deadly in the open, where they could use their armor and speed, but in a cramped city like this, where every collapsed building offered a natural bunker and cover for defenders, the tanks were working blind. They came up the empty streets, often in single file, looking for trouble, and so far they had found it, but not in the way they were expect-ing. The Germans were dug in on both sides, behind the rubble, in basements, in attics, in corner rooms, waiting for them. The tankers never saw them until it was too late;

then one or two of the *Panzerfäuste* would whoosh, and the lead tank would go up in a fireball. With luck, the Germans often got one of the rear tanks as well, pinning the others in between where they could be picked off one by one. It might not have been so easy had there been more co-ordination between Russian ground troops and the tanks. Infantrymen could have worked ahead of the armor to locate the danger spots, then the tanks might have been used more like rolling artillery, to knock them out. But for some reason, Russian infantrymen had seemed in short supply during the night. A few had come along in what the Germans called *Trauben,* the bunch of grapes that trail a moving tank, but not nearly as many as Bascom had expected. It was as though most of the foot soldiers had taken the night off. Now, with daylight breaking through the gloom, things might get a little hotter.

The chittering was louder now, a high, squeaky, metallic sound, and the mortars were slacking off. Bascom nudged Fiebeck, who came awake with a start. Fiebeck's false teeth slipped and he said, "What ith it?" He clamped his plates together to reposition them against his palate, but Bascom had understood.

"They're coming again," Bascom whispered.

"Damn them, how do they expect a man to get any sleep?" Fiebeck complained. He grasped his *Panzerfaust* and crawled to a gap in the rubble that had once been a stylish three-story house. The house was no longer stylish. It was no longer even recognizable as a house. Scrabbling sounds told Bascom that other men in his group were rousing themselves, slipping into firing positions among the piles of rubble. There were fewer than thirty of them left, not counting the cold-eyed SS officer and his overworked corporal. Several had been killed during the night when a Russian T-34 had put two 85mm shells through the front wall. A few others had disappeared later, including the fat forty-year-old, but Bascom had no idea what had happened to them. Killed, maybe. Run away, possibly. No one else seemed to know, either.

Conscious of the SS man somewhere behind him, Bascom squirmed after Fiebeck and positioned himself at the gap. Other German units along the approach to the canal bridge had heard the tanks as well. Bascom could see dim movement across the street and in the ruin next door. He laid his *Panzerfaust* on the bricks in front of him and armed it, but he was determined not to fire again. He'd faced the same dilemma before each of the assaults. The first time was the worst. He knew the tanks were coming, and he knew the SS lieutenant was watching him. If he didn't open fire with the rest of the group, he was likely to catch a bullet in the back of the head. But at the same time, he wasn't sure he could bring himself to open fire on friendly forces. He struggled with the problem, agonizing silently, and finally settled on what he thought was the only solution. He would fake it, going for near misses with the little one-shot bazooka tubes. That would keep the SS man off his back, and at the same time salve his conscience about taking potshots at allies.

But with the drop of darkness and the coming of the first Russian thrust, he'd found himself looking into the awesome throat of a T-34 turret gun. The tank rounded the near corner at the head of a column, jerking over the rough street, with its armored turret swinging like some long-nosed creature from Mars, firing blindly into the walls. Flames burst, and the roar was ear-splitting. The friendly tanks of Bascom's thoughts and this terrifying tank in its reality were such far different creatures that his brain froze and his moral dilemma was instantly reduced to a simpler gut-level dichotomy: Kill or be killed. The choice had proved to be incredibly easy.

But he wouldn't fire again, and to the devil with the SS man. There had been too much time between attacks to think. Now, with the sounds of a fourth attack on the way, his moral dissemblings were done, and nothing was left but fear; fear and the nagging realization that his first shot fired in anger had been fired on behalf of the enemy, an enemy he had been trained to hate. It might have been nice, he told himself quietly, if he'd been able to take up arms at least once for the Americans before going into battle as a Nazi.

The tanks rumbled into view at the far corner this time, growling around a scorched Russian tank hulk. A German antitank gun manned by regular troops opened fire from the foot of the bridge, sending a shell careening past the lead tank and into one of the corner buildings. The tanks, great rounded turrets sweeping simultaneously as though they were wired in sequence, homed in quickly on the antitank crew and blew them to bits with a salvo of shots.

They came on slowly, great greasy monsters, smoke pouring from their exhausts, engines whining, dreadful squeak of tread on road surfaces. Bascom felt his neck skin crawl. They were anonymous; that was perhaps the most chilling aspect. No humans in sight, just the inexorable approach of those big, noisy giants with their long, ominous, damned gun barrels.

There seemed to be more Russian infantrymen this time, dark brown and gray-green uniforms crouching behind the trailing tanks, but they still weren't co-ordinated. They followed the tanks no more than fifty feet before German snipers opened up from the upper floors of buildings and began picking them off.

With the infantrymen falling back, and the long tank guns wigwagging around, trying to spot the snipers, the *Panzerfäuste* opened up from basements and doorways, long tails like Roman candles flaring out of the demolished buildings, *whoo-o-o-o-sh, CRUMP!* the third tank in line blew up with a spectacular roar, but the two lead tanks kept rolling in spite of what had seemed to be direct hits. The turrets wheeled right and left, taking quick shots at the openings from which the fiery *Panzerfäuste* streaks had come. Another projectile whistled out of an overhead window, point blank. Again the blast hit dead center, and again the tank kept moving. Bascom, farther down the street and still out of range, raised his head cautiously, wondering what had gone wrong. The tough little hollow-charge missiles had worked like a charm in earlier attacks, but they seemed suddenly to have lost their potency.

The tank rolled through the smoke and flame and came into the clear, still firing, and he saw. The Russians, burned more than once by the efficient little tank-destroyers, had used the lull between attacks to strip nearby German buildings of bedsprings, mattresses, anything with sufficient thickness, and had lashed them with wire to the fronts and sides and around the turrets. The blunt-nosed rocket projectiles were striking the coils and mattresses and exploding without their customary penetration.

Two more tanks from the rear of the column got past the burning third tank and joined the leaders, shooting up the neighborhood. As fast as the German Volkssturmers fired, giving away their positions, the tanks shot back, finishing them off. Nothing seemed to stop the great, rolling monsters. They kept grinding on, heading for the bridge, getting closer to Bascom's building.

Then, squealing like a bunch of schoolkids heading for a frolic in the old swimming hole, a handful of Hitler Youth piled out of one of the ruins. They attacked the lead tank with their bare hands, swarming up on the sides and clinging to the turret, trying to untie the springs and mattresses. The trailing tanks swung their turret guns to bear, but didn't dare fire with the heavy stuff for fear of penetrating the armor. The second in line, however, had a clear field with its hull machine gun and fired a long burst, raking the tank deck. Two of the youngsters fell off. The others clambered quickly to the front, out of the line of fire, and went on working.

The tankers inside the besieged tank grew frantic when they realized what was happening. The turret gun began to swivel back and forth like a battering ram, trying to knock the kids off the hull. One fell at first swipe, and more went flying at the second and third. As quickly as the lead tank's turret gun knocked them to the ground, the second tank in line shot them down. The last two kids ducked and tried to run back to cover, and the lead tank spun to chase them.

More *Panzerfäuste* whistled out of the buildings, but the tank kept coming, following the kids as though it had a personal grudge against them.

"The treads!" Bascom yelled. "Go for the treads!" But no one could hear.

Unaccountably, he found himself through the wall of his ruin and out in the street, running with a *Panzerfaust* under his arm, cursing in both English and German. Someone must have spotted him through the periscope slit and informed the turret gunner, for the tank abruptly gave up on the kids and started to swing toward him. He dropped to his knees and fired his projectile without aiming, *tum-shoosh,* but he was close enough that it didn't matter—so close, in fact, that the blast of the impact knocked him flat. He rolled across the pavement and watched in a daze as a tread unwound and the tank wobbled to one side and stopped. An oil line caught fire. Tank hatches started popping open.

He wasn't quite sure how he got back to his ruin. He remembered seeing the Russian tankers piling out of the burning tank, and it seemed someone took a shot at him with a handgun; then a pair of strong hands grabbed him by the shoulders and dragged him away. There were more explosions, possibly other missiles following his lead and aiming at the treads, and all the engine sounds finally stopped or withdrew. And then he was in the ruin, shaking, trying to catch his breath, and the Waffen-SS corporal was grinning at him like an idiot, and Fiebeck was leaning against the wall, chest heaving like a busted bellows.

It was suddenly deathly quiet. Bascom could hear a baby crying somewhere. A baby? Was it conceivable that people still lived, cringing, terrified, among these ruins? He blotted out the thought. "What happened to the tanks?" he asked.

"They pulled back," the Waffen-SS man said. We've held them again. By God, we've held them."

Bascom discovered that his knee was numb, but he could see no blood. He shifted his leg tentatively, to see if it still worked, and was gratified to find that it did. "Thanks for pulling me back," he told the corporal.

"I didn't do it," the corporal said. He slapped Fiebeck on the shoulder. "This little bag of bones did it. By God, he flew out of here like an Olympic sprinter. I've never seen such strength."

Bascom blinked at Fiebeck. "You?"

Fiebeck nodded. "I lost my head," he puffed.

"You two have really put the Oberstürmführer's nose out of joint," the corporal said. "He was convinced we'd have to shoot you both before the day was out."

Someone rushed into the wrecked house from the street, and the corporal spun around, machine pistol up. But it was only a nervous man in a fireman's uniform, followed by a dirty young girl from the Labor Service Corps. The girl was lugging a cardboard carton.

"God in heaven, tourists," the corporal muttered. He lowered his gun and turned back to Bascom. "Can you believe a girl would actually come here? Even we will surely pull out before long. The lieutenant has started worrying about flame throwers. Spineless bastard. If they'd send him home to his mommy and give me a hundred men like you two, I'd win this stupid war for them."

The fireman and the girl whispered to one of the elderly recruits near what had once been the door, and were pointed in Bascom's direction. They hurried over the piles of rubble. "Are you the man who shot the tank?" the fireman asked.

"He's the one," the corporal said proudly. "Wasn't it magnificent?"

"We didn't see it," the fireman said. "An officer in the adjacent building told us about it." He reached in the cardboard carton and pulled out a black cross rimmed in silver, attached to a red, white, and black ribbon. "Here," he said, thrusting it at Bascom.

"What's this?"

"A medal," the man said. He looked again at the corporal. "Who is the one who rescued him?"

"This little bag of bones right here," the corporal said.

The hand went into the carton again. "Here's one for you, too." Fiebeck took it with eyes filled with awe.

The corporal pounded Bascom and Fiebeck on the shoulders. "The Iron Cross, second class," he said. "By God, isn't that something? You're heroes, now."

The fireman anxiously glanced around the ruin. "Have you anyone else here who might deserve one? We have to hand out sixty second class and twenty first class before we can go back."

"What about me?" the corporal said slyly. "At least I didn't run away."

The fireman seemed willing, but the Labor Service girl vigorously shook her head. "Sorry," the fireman said. "No one else in here? We'd better keep looking then."

As they hurried out, the corporal squatted and said, "You know, I think he was really about to give me one. What's happening to us, anyway?"

Fiebeck turned his Iron Cross in the dim light, admiring it. "It feels so strange. I fought my way through the whole first war, and I never got anything like this. Now in one day—"

"Don't get too carried away," Bascom said. "You saw the box."

"I don't care if they hand them out like Christmas cookies," Fieback said. "I'm still proud of it."

The silence was suddenly shattered by a horrible sound rising up a few blocks away, back behind the Russian lines. A series of howling shrieks, like a herd of primeval dinosaurs stuck in a bog and screaming for help. *O-o-o-o-w-o-h, o-o-o-o-w-o-h, o-o-o-o-w-o-h,* it went. On and on.

Bascom jerked upright. "What the hell is that?" he said.

The corporal wet his lips. *"Katyushi,"* he said. "Russian rocket launchers. We call them Stalin organs. They've probably brought them up to reinforce the tanks."

The first scattered booms shook the street as the rockets fell to earth, and Bascom flinched. "Shouldn't we get to cover?"

The corporal grinned. "Don't worry, hero. They aren't very accurate. They sound a lot worse than they bite."

The howls went on, and so did the booms. The rockets were far more accurate than the corporal had let on, although a number slithered off to plunge into the canal, and still others whirled and swirled to impact blocks away.

Rantzau, the cold-eyed SS officer, came out of his shelter in the rear of the house and cocked his ear at the wailing rocket launchers, looking worried and indecisive. His glance fell on the Iron Crosses dangling from the hands of Bascom and Fiebeck. He curled his lip and said, *"Iss ja zum kotzen,"* a Berliner expression that translated roughly as, "That's enough to make a strong man puke."

Bascom shoved the Iron Cross in his pocket. For once, he was in agreement with the SS officer.

2

Colonel Norman hobbled as rapidly as his two sticks would allow him past Somerset House, seeking the American intelligence man. On the Victoria Embankment, Mr. Holley had whispered before abruptly hanging up. Could the man really not know just how long the embankment stretched?

When Colonel Norman reached the corner, he gave up and hailed a cab. He was accustomed to his own snail's pace and no longer really minded it, but he had to worry that Mr. Mumford and Major Longland might reach Mr. Holley first. Happy things like this happened so seldom in intelligence work. Although Colonel Norman knew it was selfish of him, he was eager to share in the event, and he feared they might even conclude their business before he could join them. Besides, they would need the precise wording of the cable from Stockholm. He'd only hinted at the contents. Over telephones, one had to speak much too carefully for complete clarity.

A tweed back idly overlooking the Thames almost fooled him, but then farther up, on the Thames side of the labyrinth of courts and halls that joined Inner Temple and Middle Temple, Colonel Norman spotted his man. Alone. Splendid luck. He dismissed his cab and greeted Holley with great courtesy but without calling him by rank, since a man who had earned his own colonelcy by a lifetime's

devotion to the interests of the empire couldn't adjust all
that easily to the war's lavish conferral of titles. Then he
urged Mr. Holley nearer the street, where the eyes of Mr.
Mumford and Major Longland, although younger but perhaps not as sharp as the colonel's own, could spot them
more easily.

Colonel Norman was amused by the way Mr. Holley's
eyes kept darting about. How odd of the man to refuse
to meet them in Mr. Mumford's office. But since Mr. Mumford had been standing young Major Longland to luncheon
nearby at the old Cheshire Cheese, the meeting place
wasn't entirely inconvenient.

Colonel Norman set about easing Mr. Holley's mind by
telling the nervous fellow of his wife's early-budding roses.
He was delighted to see the approach of Mr. Mumford and
the major before he had to think of another topic. Major
Longland's eyes looked dazzled. Colonel Norman had seen
the expression before on the occasional underling Mr.
Mumford decided to woo. Partially thick-sliced roast beef,
no doubt, but probably plan-spinning, too. With this war
so nearly over, Mr. Mumford was doubtlessly already contemplating the empire's role in the next. There was always
a next, for which quick-witted men would be needed.

Mr. Holley immediately broke into complaint. "I hope
to hell this is important, Mumford," the American said.
"And if it's about that Export business, I've told you before, no one with a grain of discernment can hold me
responsible."

Mr. Mumford's face hardened. "I don't make a practice
of shunting blame off on others," he said.

"I should hope not," Mr. Holley said. "The whole
damned business was your idea. It's not fair for me to get
hit with any more of this Export shit."

Colonel Norman's bushy white eyebrows drew together.
So, he saw, did Major Longland's foxy red ones. Mr. Mumford's expression didn't change, but Colonel Norman
cheered inwardly at the faint but detectable sarcasm in his
superior's reply: "Then I'm sorry to be the one to tell you
this, Holley, but another of your men from the Export

mission seems, somewhat inconveniently for you, to have survived. Colonel Norman, would you repeat the message received from Mr. Frychius?"

It was brief. Even for a memory not quite as reliable as in earlier years, it was easy to recite: "Just returned from Berlin. Fegelein arrested. Captain Henry Bascom, alias Major Broome, alive at time of contact. At risk of life, relayed word of submarine *Schachbrett* near Sassnitz. Presumably highly important. No other information. Frychius."

Major Longland listened so eagerly that Colonel Norman had to assume Mr. Mumford had not confided even the little the colonel had been able to relay through the extremely public telephone at the Cheshire Cheese. "Alive?" the major said. "By God!"

"Jesus Christ!" Holley muttered, although in an entirely different tone.

"What about old Formoy?" Major Longland asked. "They were together when we had to hop it. Didn't the Swede say anything about him?"

Colonel Norman shook his head. "I'm terribly sorry," he said. "There was no mention of anyone but Captain Bascom."

A tall man in a silk hat walked briskly by, and they all fell silent. A banker. He and his associates wearing the inevitable bowler and carrying the inevitable umbrella were commonplace here in the City, or Square Mile, where most of the important business of the empire was transacted, but Colonel Norman noted with fresh wonderment that the American turned his back, as though suspecting the banker were an OSS spy trying to catch him in the company of Mr. Mumford.

The banker passed. Mr. Mumford said, "Well, Holley?"

"Well, what?" the American said.

"He's your man," Mr. Mumford said quietly. "How do we treat this news?"

"We don't treat it at all," the American said. "As far as I'm concerned, the message never arrived."

Major Longland's eyes clouded with sudden suspicion.

"Hold on here," he said. "You *are* going in for Bascom, aren't you? Hell's bells, I'll volunteer, if I have to."

The American looked outraged. "By God, no one's going in," he said. "You've got your orders. None of our people has ever been to Berlin. That includes Bascom. What are you trying to do, get my ass in another sling?"

"But he's your own man!" Major Longland said.

"You bet he is. And he knew his chances when he joined up. All my men do. Even if we knew where to look for him, I wouldn't lift a finger. He can take care of himself."

Major Longland looked to Mr. Mumford, but all he got from him was a shaking head. "I'm afraid Holley is right," Mr. Mumford said. "Perhaps I don't like it, but the orders are very clear. There's nothing either you or I can do to help Captain Bascom. He'll have to manage on his own. We'll make every effort to scoop him up when the battle is done."

"If he's still alive," Longland said harshly.

Colonel Norman's ancient head thrust forward like a vulture's, and he turned his best ear, the right one, toward the men. He couldn't have heard correctly. They weren't going to do anything? Why, here they stood in the City itself. It was the one part of London that had endured the most terrible agony from the bombs of the enemy, incendiary bombs that had blasted but blessedly could not burn the great hall of Middle Temple, just across the way. The City was as well the one part of London that most sternly followed the rule that a man's finest treasure was integrity. To let another chap down was to blot one's copybook. And for Mr. Mumford and Mr. Holley to refuse to hold out a hand to one of their very own chaps was sacrilege.

Major Longland may have thought so, too. He said hotly, "Then what about this business of the submarine? If you refuse to admit that Bascom is in Berlin, just how do you plan to explain where you got the information?"

Colonel Norman's white eyebrows flew up. Good point. But Holley said, "What's so important about one submarine? The damned Swede probably got everything mixed up, anyway. No, I say we mark off this message entirely. That includes Bascom and his stupid submarine."

"But he risked his *life* to get word to us."

The American looked aggrieved. "See here, Mumford, I came here at great personal peril to hear what you had to say, and I've given you my decision. I don't give a damn about this submarine business, and I don't have time to stand here listening to a lot of yap from your subordinates."

That ended it. Mr. Mumford quickly and coldly broke up the meeting. Colonel Norman approved of the coldness, but of nothing else, and it was with coldness that he declined Mr. Mumford's offer of a lift back to the office.

For the first time in his decades of service, he had to wonder about the men with whom he had been serving, and the thought came to him that he might not much longer be interested in reporting daily to the quiet old building in Whitehall. A proper soldier would wait until the war's end, but after that a proper soldier might find more honor in helping Emily with the roses.

Feeling tired, Colonel Norman started to hobble away, but then another thought struck him, and he stopped to peer after Mr. Mumford and Major Longland. Major Longland seemed to be quite upset. He was still arguing with Mr. Mumford. One could easily predict the outcome of that.

Yet, yet. Through serving in the quiet Whitehall building, Colonel Norman had come to know a great many people. Including a certain Navy man who controlled submarine patrols over the Baltic. Sassnitz, the town poor Captain Bascom had mentioned, was on the Baltic.

Colonel Norman hobbled faster. Major Longland obviously would be a willing ally. And Colonel Norman had just bethought himself of a tall brunette with midnight-blue eyes who not only had an extreme interest in Captain Bascom but who also might prove better than he in cajoling co-operation from the Navy man, were someone to arrange for them to meet.

Proper soldiers whose finest treasure was their own integrity could find more than one way to accomplish a goal for which a chap had risked his life.

3

The battle reached the Kreuzberg ruin in midafternoon. While German defenders held firm on the Landwehr Canal southwest of Kreuzberg, Russian troops of the IX Rifle Corps and the XI Tank Corps came up from the southeast, following the Spree River. Elfriede Woelki was the first to recognize the signs. Because they were low on water, Elfriede volunteered to slip out through the intermittent shelling with a bucket and the big cookpot to make the afternoon water run. But when she returned, she reported seeing a number of exhausted German troops and ragged Volkssturmers falling back from the direction of Görlitzer Railroad Station. Three gun crews stopped and dug in at the south end of the street, and some of the soldiers set up machine-gun posts in overhead windows. Elfriede detoured briefly to ask one of the gun crews for news. They had little to say, except that the Russians were right behind them, and she would do well to scurry to shelter and stay there.

The intensity of the Russian barrage varied. The opening salvos were mainly concentrated howitzer fire. Bad, but endurable. Then, late in the afternoon, the Russians brought up *Katyushi* and added to the din. One of the German field guns was wiped out in the first rocket barrage. By sunset, it seemed the world would end. *Katyushi* and howitzers combined in furious concert. Fires raged throughout the district. The barrages seemed to come closer and closer together. Then, shortly after the coming of darkness, a subtle shift took place. There were moments of awesome quiet, during which they could hear the lonely sound of the two remaining German guns, firing from the near corner. Sometimes the quiet would last ten or fifteen minutes, as though the Russians were toying with them, but then the eerie shrieks of the *Katyushi* would signal a new tempest, and a blooming of Russian shell bursts would ripple violently through the streets and buildings above them, shaking the cellar. The artillery and rocket bombardments, when they came, seemed just as severe as ever, just as earth-shattering. But the quiet calms in between stretched longer and longer.

It was between barrages that Erika finally said, "We must move from here. We must gather what we can and try to make our way to better shelter."

"No, please," Frau Fiebeck begged. "My husband. How could he find us?"

The women of the cellar, none too eager to brave the streets no matter how shaky their ruin might seem, offered a variety of counterproposals, but Erika said firmly, "We have no choice. If we—" But the wail of *Katyushi* rose from the distance and cut her off. Seconds later, the rocket projectiles impacted, and the storm began anew. Erika huddled on the floor of the coal room with Formoy and the other women, hugging the children, waiting fearfully for it to end. Hundreds of Russian rockets and artillery shells rained down outside with thunderous clamor, like another in a series of worsening cloudbursts.

It went on forever. Ear-splitting roar of explosions. Creaking timbers and groaning walls. Bricks falling on the parquet flooring above their heads. The children moaning in terror. Great rumbling booms as another building front collapsed somewhere beyond them.

When at last the howitzer explosions petered out and the *Katyushi* fell silent, Erika waited on the floor to see if it were only a momentary pause, or a full-blown lull. The silence lengthened. She got to her knees cautiously. One German gun boomed back. Only one. Someone called repeatedly for help somewhere on the street, a low, dazed voice, moaning over and over in the darkness.

"We can't wait any longer," Erika said. "This old building is apt to collapse at any moment. We must move closer to the center of the city."

This time the murmurs of dissent turned to murmurs of

agreement. Elfriede's bloodless face bobbed up and down. "Fräulein Bollenen is absolutely right," she said. "To stay here any longer would be suicide."

"What about him?" Frau Schiller said. She gestured at Formoy.

Formoy, a sheen of perspiration on his face, shook his head weakly. "Don't worry about me, ladies. I'll be all right. You go on, while it's still quiet."

"We'll rig a stretcher," Erika said. "Elfriede and I will see to that. The rest of you will select the most useful of our food items. We can't take it all, I fear." She glanced regretfully at her baby carriage sitting in the corner, with its cargo of clothing, teddy bear, and the bottle of Vouvray. "Nor can we take our personal belongings," she said.

One of the other women glanced just as regretfully at Formoy and said, "He looks awfully heavy."

"There are six of us, not counting the children," Erika said patiently. "Surely we can manage one man."

Frau Fiebeck's mouth trembled. "Five," she corrected. "I have to stay. My poor husband is bound to come back, looking for me. How could he ever find me if I went away with you?"

"Berlin is not so large a city," Elfriede said. "Besides, better a live wife to hunt, than a dead wife waiting. What would Herr Fiebeck think of us if we left you to die in a broken-down cellar?"

"But he's so helpless," Frau Fiebeck said. "He can't find anything. He can't even find his collar buttons unless I'm there to help him." She was close to tears.

Erika patted the older woman's shoulder. "Don't worry," she said. "Just as soon as we find a new place, I'll come back and mark the address on the wall with a piece of chalk. He'll find us. You'll see."

Frau Fiebeck's eyes widened hopefully. "Do you think that would work?"

"I'm sure of it," Erika said. Her mouth firmed. "Now let's get ready quickly and leave here before the guns begin again."

Like muted thunder, the guns also echoed and re-echoed against the cement walls of the underground shelter in which an insignificant little man was now forced to spend each hour of his endless days. He often wished, wistfully, that he were back in his third-floor cell, but he was so surprised when the doctor with the perpetually impish expression actually spoke to him directly that he almost missed his chance to stammer out the request.

"You're not eating enough," the doctor said sternly. "What is it? Is something troubling you?"

The little man's first impulse was to deny what sounded like an indictment. "No, Herr Doctor," he mumbled.

"The truth," the doctor demanded, and the little man realized that the doctor looked genuinely concerned. "The shelling?" the doctor guessed. "That's nothing for you to worry about. You're as safe here as any man in Berlin."

"Well, yes, the guns—a bit," the little man admitted. Then, gaining courage, "If I could just see the sun. In the mornings, at about ten o'clock, it always came into my cell."

That was as close as he could come to asking that he be taken from these suffocating gray walls where the thunder rumbled. But, to his amazement, the doctor seemed to understand.

"A touch of claustrophobia, is it?" the doctor said. "Why didn't you speak up? A light sedative will help. Then I might increase it later on. But see that you eat. No eating, no sedative." To the Gestapo guard who always hovered at his shoulder during his visits, the doctor said, "Roll up his sleeve. The left one." He reached into his medical kit, and the little man realized dismally that the interview was over. Yet, as he winced and the doctor plunged a hypodermic needle into the crook of his arm, the doctor said with satisfaction, "A nice touch. I should have thought of it before."

But he addressed the words to the guard, not to the man they called Rösselsprung.

5

SS Captain Franz Schedle felt distinctly uneasy about his duty assignment for the night. With the Russians pressing in on the citadel from all sides and every man needed to protect the Chancellery in the event of a sudden Russian breakthrough, Reichsleiter Bormann had sent him and six of his most trustworthy men out on a paper chase.

Schedle was beginning to fear treachery. The Führer was in an extremely vulnerable position. The Russians had battered through the inner defenses until nothing remained but a cramped belt running across the center of the city, some three miles deep from top to bottom and only ten to twelve miles wide. Koniev and Zhukov had finally closed the gap to the west. While there were still soft spots in the Russian ring, the city could be considered surrounded.

The situation was ominous. General Weidling, the new military commandant of Berlin, had estimated they would be able to hold out no more than three or four days. It was no longer possible to get supplies from the air in any appreciable amounts, and the Berlin garrison was shrinking daily in size, partly due to casualties and partly to desertions. According to bunker rumors, Weidling had proposed this very evening a daring breakout maneuver involving three echelons. He had sworn in conference that he could get the Führer safely through the Russian circle by marshaling all his forces and driving a wedge through the weaker links to the west.

It was common knowledge that the Führer had rejected Weidling's proposal. He was determined to hold out until Wenck's Twelfth Army arrived from the west. If Wenck couldn't make it, and there were few who believed he could, the Führer had sworn to die defending the city. A touching display of courage and loyalty to the German people, Schedle felt, but it had caused profound discomfort

to many of the Führer's closest associates, Bormann among
them. They had been trying for weeks to get the Führer
to leave Berlin. Not so much for his safety, Schedle suspected, as for fear of their own. If the Führer insisted on
staying, they would also be forced to stay. He'd heard
stories that Bormann had pled with one visitor after another to urge the Führer to leave Berlin while there was
still time. Lately, with the Russian circle closing, Bormann's usual aplomb had deteriorated. He was growing
more nervous, more irritable by the day.

Now this. Tonight's clandestine assignment. Once again
Bormann had summoned Schedle from the guards' bunker
for whispered instructions that would take him away from
his primary duty, protecting the person of the Führer.
This time he had been ordered to select enough men to
act as an escort for Gestapo chief Heinrich Müller and
two of his Gestapo officers, and see them safely through
the streets on an itinerary of quick, secret visits to offices
situated throughout the inner city.

As it turned out, Müller's two men were burdened with
piles of paper—memos, letters, files, charts. The offices
they chose to visit were in both state and private buildings.
In each case the buildings were dark and unoccupied, and
Müller entered alone with his two Gestapo men, leaving
Schedle and the bunker guards standing watch in the street.
In each case Müller and his men came out with burdens
as heavy as those they had carried in. Schedle found himself growing increasingly suspicious.

He glanced at a semi-open basement door of an office
building on the Kurfürstendamm, through which Müller
and his minions had disappeared only moments before, and
saw, reflected against the polished basement floor, the
muted gleam of a flashlight. He knew the building to be
one in which were kept the personal records of many of
the more important Party members. What could they be
doing? Destroying files? Perhaps their own? Replacing
medical charts and identifying characteristics to mislead
the Allies when the war was done?

If so, it was an outright act of defeatism. Something

should be done about it. Should he attempt to gain an audience with the Führer and tell him what was happening? It would be dangerous. One did not easily accuse a Bormann or a Müller of cowardice and defeatism without proof. And he certainly had no proof—not yet, anyway.

A thought teased its way into his mind. Suppose they were planning an escape? Suppose, with the Russians prowling nearer all the time, they had it in mind, both Bormann and Müller, to flee the city and take refuge in some obscure outpost until the war ended and the temper of the victors calmed down. It would not be incompatible with what he had seen this night. Falsified records to cover their trails. Fingerprint files exchanged. Dental X rays replaced.

Then another thought nudged the first. Perhaps if he said nothing, held his tongue, they would be willing to take him along. Perhaps they would offer him escape as well.

He felt instant shame at the flicker of hope. That he, a loyal servant to the Führer and to Greater Germany, could even consider his own personal safety at a time like this was deeply humiliating. And yet there it was. If they offered him a chance to flee the final bloodbath, would he turn it down?

To his own mortal embarrassment, he realized that he probably would not.

11

Wo ist Frau Brylla?

"Where is Mrs. Brylla?"

—inquiry chalked on wall
of Berlin ruin

1

By dawn the next morning, the Russians had thrown several pontoon bridges across the Landwehr Canal in the region of the Halle Gate, breaching the southern line of defense. Tanks and infantrymen poured across under cover of smoke screens and began a deadly fight for every demolished building, every house, every ditch, every bomb and shell crater. The northern defenses fared little better. The Soviet Third Shock Army was grinding inch by inch through Moabit, closing in on the north bank of the Spree River and Königs-Platz, within sight of Gestapo headquarters and the burned shell of the Reichstag building. The narrow belt along the inner city was steadily shrinking.

Bascom's small group, exhausted, down to their last few *Panzerfäuste,* pulled away from the canal shortly after word of the Russian pontoon crossing reached them. A general retreat had not yet sounded, but their SS lieutenant, Hans Rantzau, had called them together and told them with white face and a tic under the left eye that he had no intention of being cut off from the rear by advancing Soviet troops. They would fall back to the Tiergarten, he said, and from there march west toward the zoo. There were rumors that the Russians would assault the flak towers, and he wanted to be in on the battle. The fact that the flak towers had been judged almost impregnable and offered haven for anyone near enough to gain entrance was not lost on the listening Volkssturmers and the few remaining boys. If the lieutenant wanted to be close to safety, they would willingly go along.

The Tiergarten, under heavy bombardment for the past twenty-four hours, had utterly ceased to be a park. The few remaining groves had fallen. Trees lay like scattered bodies. Charred stumps and gnarled roots reared from torn earth at eerie angles. Once pleasant ponds and lagoons had turned into muddy quagmires. Gray figures, more retreating soldiers like themselves, worked feverishly throughout the blighted landscape, digging foxholes and slit trenches. Artillery rounds landed every few seconds, ripping up great gouts of mud and splintered wood. Smoke and morning mist merged and drifted.

"Verdun," Fiebeck whispered hoarsely.

Bascom looked around at him. "What?"

"Verdun," the old man said again. "It looks like Verdun. From the last war." He sighed wearily. "I don't think I can go much farther. I'm pretty tired."

"Hold on to my belt," Bascom said. "Let me pull you."

"You there!" The SS officer, six or seven paces behind them, had recovered his nerve now that they were safely away from the canal. "No talking! Keep quiet!"

They trudged another three hundred feet westward, Fiebeck holding weakly to Bascom, stumbling, detouring around deep, water-filled craters. Finally Fiebeck spoke again, whispering this time.

"Ami," he said, "I'm worried about my wife. If the Russians have broken through, our cellar in Kreuzberg is no longer safe."

"They won't hurt civilians," Bascom whispered back.

"I wish I could be sure. I should be there, to protect her. Do you think Lieutenant Rantzau would let me go? I can be of little more use to him."

"Not a chance. He's a pretty hard case."

Fiebeck nodded miserably. He was silent for several yards, then, "I don't care. My wife is my life. Let him do what he will. I've got to slip away and go back to her."

"Not now," Bascom said. He glanced back at the SS

officer. "That sonofabitch is watching every step we take. You make one move and he'll shoot you down."

"I must try."

"Hold on awhile," Bascom said. "When we get to the zoo, I'll find some way to distract him. Then you can make a break while his back is turned."

The SS officer strode up beside them. "I told you to keep quiet!" he snapped. "What are you whispering about?"

"He's tired," Bascom said. "The others, too. We haven't had any rest since day before yesterday. Can't you give them a few minutes?"

"You'll rest when you are dead," the SS officer said. "In the meantime, keep moving. We're almost there." He turned and waved the others on. "Hurry, all of you. The zoo lies just ahead."

Like the park, the rambling Tiergarten zoo was a shambles. The aquarium had been blasted to rubble. Most of the animal houses had been heavily damaged. Dead kangaroos, two elephants, slaughtered animals lay everywhere amid the destruction, and a lone baboon that had survived ran to and fro in its dangerously weakened cage, screeching in mindless terror at each nearby explosion. All the lions were dead, shot by their keepers as a safety precaution to keep them from roaming free in the event the lion house collapsed. The bird sanctuary was a snarl of wire mesh, filled with lifeless, feathered bodies. Even Rosa, Bascom's favorite hippo, was dead, floating belly up in her pond, an unexploded mortar shell half buried in her side.

To the west, overlooking the zoo through the morning mist, rose the flak towers, with their hundred-foot-high gun platforms. The main tower, a squat, bombproof concrete blockhouse thirteen stories high, contained its own power plant and water supply. Streaks of green paint on pocked gray walls, coupled with black powder smears where shell bursts had exploded harmlessly, gave it an overall copper patina, like some medieval fortress. There were said to be thirty thousand frightened Berliners sheltering inside.

Oberstürmführer Rantzau, never quite taking his eyes off the inviting nearness of the twin towers, indicated a gap in the south zoo wall near the deserted wolf enclosure and said, "We'll dig in here."

"Shouldn't we check in with the sector commander first?" asked the Waffen-SS corporal.

"We'll dig in here!" Rantzau repeated. He gestured at Bascom. "You. Since you seem so concerned about the physical comfort of the others, you will do the digging. I want a slit trench here, six feet long, and another over there. Corporal, give him your entrenching tool."

The corporal looked doubtful. "That's a big undertaking for one man, Herr Oberstürmführer. I'm willing to give him a hand, if you want me to."

"Nothing is too difficult for a hero," the SS officer said. "Let him do it alone."

The corporal unstrapped a short spade from his back-pack and handed it to Bascom with a look of apology. Bascom dropped into a shell hole and started digging.

"The rest of you take cover and get a few minutes' rest," Rantzau said. He dusted a teetering stone bench with a handkerchief and sat down to watch Bascom dig, but his eyes kept sweeping upward, toward the towering presence of the flak platform.

They rested in informal heaps, men and boys sprawling around the shell hole while Bascom dug, for ten or twelve minutes. Then a familiar sound drifted up from the south, the squeaking cricket song of tanks. One by one, the figures stiffened and rose. The tic leaped to life under Rantzau's eye. He hesitated, then slipped his field glasses from his neck and climbed to the top of the wall for a look.

Bascom paused in his digging. Four or five blocks below the zoo, from the sound of them, but coming this way. From the corner of his eye he caught cautious movement to his right, and he turned slightly, quick fear whispering that one of the site's former inhabitants, a wolf, still lurked here. Instead, he saw Fiebeck, mouth hanging open, breath coming in nervous shudders, edging toward the wreckage of the wolves' shelter. Rantzau, clinging to the top of the

wall, had his back turned, but that wouldn't last. Some of
the others were watching too, waiting silently to see if one
of their number could make good an escape. Bascom shook
his head, trying to warn Fiebeck. Not yet. For God's sake,
not yet.

The sound of a boot sliding against stone. Rantzau,
lowering himself to the ground. Then his voice, startled,
angry, "You there! Where do you think you're going?"

Fiebeck faltered. His eyes flicked toward Bascom, then
toward the wolves' shelter, only a few meters away, and
he seemed to make up his mind. He turned and ran, thin
legs pumping awkwardly.

The pop of a holster flap. Slither of gun from leather.
Bascom whirled to see the SS officer calmly drawing a bead
with his Walther P-38. "Don't," Bascom cried. He clutched
the spade and scrambled out of the shell hole, but the gun
cracked twice, bucking in the officer's hand. Fiebeck folded
in midstride.

"You bastard!" Bascom growled in English. Enraged,
he flung himself at Rantzau, swinging the entrenching tool
in a short, swift arc, like a sharp-edged battle ax. The officer
gaped in surprise and tried to backpedal, but the blade
caught him edgewise, hacking into his neck below the left
ear.

Lieutenant Rantzau stumbled backward, his hand jerking
up to cover the deep cut on his neck. He took the hand
away from the wound and stared in astonishment at the
blood. He wavered for a moment and tried to raise the
gun; then his eyes rolled up under the lids, exposing the
whites, and he toppled.

Bascom dropped the entrenching tool and snatched
the gun from the officer's hand. He swung it to cover the
others. The corporal, face stiff with shock, stared at him as
though one of the zoo wolves had indeed survived and
suddenly appeared before him. One of the small boys
looked away and yawned with fear.

Bascom backed off toward the wolves' shelter, holding
the gun on them, until he reached Fiebeck. He squatted
for a quick look. But the old man was already dead. The

first shot had entered the back between the shoulder blades. The second, fired as he fell, had taken a portion of his skull away.

"Frenchman, beware."

It was one of the older men. Bascom looked up quickly. The man inclined his head toward the Waffen-SS corporal, whose hand had crept to the shoulder strap of his Schmeisser.

Bascom leveled the pistol at him. "I wouldn't," he said.

The corporal appeared to think it over for a moment, then shrugged. He slid his thumb under the gun strap and eased it from his shoulder, allowing it to slide to the ground.

Bascom looked from face to face. "I'm leaving," he said. "Don't try to stop me, any of you."

"Don't worry," the corporal said. "I've had enough of this damned mess. I'm leaving, too. Anyone else?"

Hope crossed the faces of the tired old men and the boys around him. "We could go home?" one said.

The corporal took off his field cap and tossed it aside, then peeled out of his backpack harness. "No reason to stay here," he said. "It's over. We've lost." He faced Bascom. "Is that all right with you, Frenchman?"

"Do whatever you want," Bascom said.

The corporal nodded. "I suggest we disperse. Every man for himself. Don't stop to talk to anyone. Get under cover as soon as you can, and don't come out until the shooting stops."

The others seemed reluctant to move, as though the corporal were only subjecting them to some kind of test, after which he would shoot them for cowardice. But the corporal bounded over the zoo wall and ran for a line of buildings across the street, staying low. One of the older men murmured, "He meant it. It's true." He edged away from the group. Two of the boys were next, exchanging quick looks, then flying off through the zoo grounds toward the front gate. Soon they were all running, scattering in different directions.

Bascom waited alone for a few moments, his hand on

Fiebeck's thin, lifeless arm, feeling weary, feeling sad, feeling something wolfish snarling low inside himself. Then the sound of tanks grew steadily louder and he, too, began to run.

2

The Chancellery now came under heavy Russian artillery fire, along with the rest of the government district. Bunker walls shivered and groaned with each explosive impact. Light fixtures swayed. Into the underground rooms, whining ventilators sucked hot air, heavy with brick dust and the acrid fumes of bursting Soviet shells.

Sweating in the heat, a man in shirt sleeves sat in a cubicle on the upper level of the Führerbunker, his ears clamped under oversized radio earphones, monitoring enemy broadcasts. His name was Gustav Jupe, and he was an assistant to the Chancellery representative of Deutsches Nachrichtenbüro, the official German news agency.

It was shortly past noon and Jupe was hungry, but his relief wasn't due for almost an hour. He was also frightened, thanks to the steady rumble of exploding shells overhead, but he preferred to concentrate on the hunger. Because he was preoccupied, he almost missed an important BBC announcement. He had just turned to the door of his cubicle to hail one of the passing telephone switchboard operators and ask if she would fetch him a bit of smoked salmon on buttered pumpernickel, a cold chicken wing, anything for a snack. A moderately excited British voice broke into normal programming to announce a special dispatch from America, something about a peace proposal extended by the Germans.

Jupe was startled. No one had mentioned any peace feelers to him. He allowed the switchboard operator to pass and turned back to his radio to transcribe what was being said. It seemed that a Reuters correspondent attending a conference in San Francisco designed to set up some kind of United Nations organization had just learned that

Reichsführer Heinrich Himmler, acting through a Swedish intermediary, had made an offer of unconditional surrender to the Western Allies. Himmler, according to the dispatch, had authoritatively stated that he was in a position to arrange such a surrender, and that he was in favor of the surrender. Official confirmation was expected at any moment.

Jupe ripped the sheet from his notepad and studied it. Could it be true? Would there be peace, after all? No one from the lower level had said anything about it, but Reichsführer Himmler would surely never have made such an offer without the knowledge and consent of the Führer. Perhaps the Führer had only kept it quiet for fear it would be rejected.

Jupe quickly typed the contents of the radio message on the special Führer typewriter, a machine that printed everything in extra-large letters for the benefit of their leader's weak eyes, and carried it along the corridor to the spiral staircase leading down to what Jupe and the other upper-level workers called the "Golden Cage," Hitler's personal underground quarters.

He found the Führer in the map room, discussing situation reports with Reichsleiter Bormann, General Krebs, General Burgdorf, and Propaganda Minister Goebbels, who had recently moved with his family into the Führerbunker. Maps lay in disarray on the map table, marked with red crayon arrows that extended toward the center of the city, pushing pell-mell against dotted blue lines which had been scribbled, then rubbed out and rescribbled in steadily shrinking circles.

Hitler, his haggard face pale, looked up without interest when Jupe was ushered into the room by an Army adjutant. Nor did Hitler's expression change when Jupe humbly handed him the transcript of the radio dispatch. But as soon as Hitler began reading, his jaw muscles clenched, and he skipped to the top of the sheet and started reading again, more slowly. His face flushed patchily and he handed the typescript to Bormann and Goebbels without a word. He waited until they had scanned it. Seating himself in an armchair, Hitler said feebly, "It would appear that treachery has replaced loyalty on all sides. I did not expect this from Himmler."

Jupe's heart sank. So it was not an authorized peace proposal after all.

Bormann crumpled the paper. "My Führer," he said, "this is despicable. You can rest assured that no one in this room would ever do such a thing. Only the SS—"

"Where is SS Gruppenführer Fegelein?" Hitler interrupted.

"In his quarters, as you ordered," Bormann said.

"Bring him here," Hitler said angrily. Then, after a second thought, "No, wait. I don't want to see him. Send someone to question him. Instruct them that they need not be gentle. I want to know how much he knows about this."

"Do you suspect him of complicity?"

"Why else would he try to slip away? Spare no energy. Drain him. Make him tell everything. If he was involved in this treason in any way, take him up to the garden and shoot him."

"It will be done, my Führer."

3

Bascom's stomach wrenched when he first caught sight of the Kreuzberg ruin. The top floor had caved in, and a side wall had disappeared. Several of the surrounding buildings had fallen into the street. Two twisted field guns lay half buried under debris, and the stench of death rose from sun-baked piles of broken brick.

He loped down the street, pistol hanging forgotten in his hand. He had to squirm over and around massive new mounds of rubble to climb up to his ruin. A jungle of beams and wall board had spilled from the floor above, blocking the cellar stairway. He shoved the gun in his waistband and tore at the clutter like a wild man until a four-foot gap opened to the darkness below. He felt his way down the steps, dreading what he would find.

No one in the outer room. "Erika?" he called. "Erika, where are you?" Nothing. Silence. He moved from room to room, searching. Empty. The cellar was empty. Erika. The kids. The other women. Even Formoy. Not a soul.

He braced himself against the cellar wall, trying to summon fresh energy from long-depleted reservoirs. He'd gone through the edges of hell to get here from the Tiergarten. Shells raining down like white-hot hail. Burned-out vehicles and dead bodies. Mortars whistling. Black smoke everywhere. Machine-gun shells streaming overhead. The last few German tanks clanking off toward the Landwehr to meet the Russian breakthrough. Exhausted soldiers and Volkssturmers falling back like zombies to take up new positions. Some fleeing the first time their officers looked away. Others too numb to do anything but follow orders. He'd holed up time and again to avoid being spotted. Then to reach here and discover they were gone? Bleak regret drained all thought from his brain.

After a time, his stomach reasoned for itself. What was that? There by the furnace? Food? Could it really be food? He stumbled over. Yes, on the floor. Some shriveled turnips. A can with no label. Some moldy bread. He hefted the can first, but couldn't spot a can opener. Frustrating. Forget the can. The turnips. He shoved one into his mouth. Pulpy, flabby. Sharp taste. He chewed and picked up the bread. Mold on the surface. He rubbed it against the rough cellar wall, scraping most of the mold away, then dug out the rest with his fingernails. Bread into mouth with turnip. Stale. Heavenly.

He stopped chewing and rested. Forearm to head to wipe sweat from his face. Rough cloth. Armband. The idiotic Volkssturm armband. He was still wearing it. He pulled it off and stuffed it in his pocket. Keep moving. Look for signs. Maybe they left word.

He prowled the cellar again, a second turnip in his hand, munching, his brain beginning to hum now. Could the authorities have come and taken them away? Not likely. There was no authority. Not any more. Just people, trying to stay alive.

Erika's baby carriage. Over in the darkness. All her things, just sitting there. Even the teddy bear. They'd taken the food, at least most of it, but left their belongings behind. Must have left in a hurry.

His foot scuffed against one of the mattresses, lying askew on the floor. Coated with dust. Fallen plaster. He raised his eyes. Ceiling sagging in several places. Daylight filtering through cracks. Deep fissure facing the street. Bulging brick walls. Must have taken a real pounding. No wonder they left.

He tilted the mattress and shook it clean, then sat down. So tired. So damned tired. He took another bite of the pulpy turnip. Difficult. Chewing took energy. At least he wouldn't have to face Frau Fiebeck and tell her about her husband. Poor, dumb, brave little man. If he'd only waited a few minutes until the tanks came and the SS officer dived for cover. A waste, dying like that.

His eyes closed, and his head slowly drooped. He jerked awake, mouth still full of half-chewed turnip. God, tired. How long without sleep? He leaned over and spat the turnip on the floor. Should he rest for a moment? No, he didn't dare. He had to get out of here, find Formoy somehow. But where to start? Not possible. Hard to think. So tired.

His head dropped again, and he rolled over on his shoulder. Let it go. Rest a moment. It couldn't hurt. Just a couple of minutes. He wouldn't sleep, just rest. Rest . . .

4

At seven minutes past four that Saturday afternoon, with Soviet shells falling all around them, three SS guards led a protesting Hermann Fegelein up the blockhouse steps and into the Chancellery garden.

His epaulettes had been removed, his collar flashes torn away. He struggled as they marched him beyond the emergency bunker exit and repeated over and over, "The Reichsführer made me do it. I didn't want to treat with the Allies. Reichsführer Himmler is the guilty one. He made me. I only followed orders."

The chief guard, who had seen active duty on the Russian front in earlier years, propped Fegelein against an abandoned cement mixer and produced a typewritten sheet of paper bearing the Führer's signature and seal. He hurriedly read aloud the findings of a summary court-martial, eager to carry out the sentence and return to the safety of the underground rooms.

"Please," Fegelein objected tearfully. "Let me see the Führer. Or my sister-in-law. At least let me speak to my sister-in-law. She can explain my position to him."

". . . found guilty of treason by your own admission," the chief guard finished, "and sentenced to die forthwith." He folded the paper, then primed his weapon and nodded to the other two guards.

Fegelein's voice rose like a siren. "He made me. I didn't want to. No-o-o-o-o—"

The three bursts of automatic Schmeisser fire sounded flat and toylike in the midst of the thundering artillery bombardment.

5

Someone was breathing in the other room. Erika paused near the doorway, listening to deep breathing, labored breathing. It was so dark down here. If only she had brought the paraffin lamp back with her. She picked up a loose brick and moved cautiously through the door, searching the shadows. There in the darkness someone lay on the mattress, asleep. It was a man who turned fitfully, groaning. He wore work clothes, she saw. Then her eyes, adjusting to the dimness, made out a cloth cap, and her breath caught in her throat. Henri? Could it be Henri?

She edged closer to make sure, then stifled an outcry of joy. Yes! She kneeled quickly and shook him. "Henri, wake up!"

His dreams must have been frightening, for his hands

rose instantly and defensively. He gasped something at her in a hoarse voice, foreign-sounding, English. He looked terribly confused.

"Henri, it's I. Erika." She grasped his hands, calming him. "What are you doing here? How did you get away?"

He blinked up at her, but the confusion only seemed to deepen. "Erika?" His voice cracked.

"Yes, I just got back." Her fingers touched his face. "I didn't expect to find you here."

"What time is it?"

"I don't know. Ten, perhaps. Or later."

"In the night?" He sounded more like himself now. Suddenly clear, alert.

"Yes, of course."

"My God, I really conked out." He propped himself on one elbow. "Where were you? I was worried sick. Where are the others?"

"We had to leave last night," she said. "The shelling was so heavy. I wasn't sure I would even find our building standing when I got back."

"Formoy? Is he all right?"

"Who?"

"I'm sorry. My friend. Maurice."

"Oh yes." She nodded eagerly. "Elfriede and her sister are taking care of him. We found a place in Mitte. A large church. I only came back to post the address for you and Herr Fiebeck."

His face seemed to change. "The children?"

"They're fine. Frau Schiller promised to look after them until I returned. Where is Herr Fiebeck? Didn't he come with you?"

He looked away. "Herr Fiebeck died for Greater Germany this morning." His voice was bitter.

Erika was silent for a moment, thinking how difficult it would be to tell Frau Fiebeck. "How did it happen? He was killed by the Russians?"

"No. A lousy Nazi officer did it. Shot the top of his head off because he wanted to come home."

There was deep anger in his words. Although it seemed

directed at the officer, not at her, Erika couldn't help feeling defensive. She withdrew her hands.

"It was just so damned senseless," he said unhappily.
"The poor old bastard only wanted to come back to look
after his wife. No one would have missed him. What kind
of people are they, anyway, to shoot a tired old man, just
because he'd had enough of fighting?"

Defensiveness turned to a dull anger of her own. "Why
do you always reproach only the Germans?" she said. "Do
you think there are no mean, spiteful people on your side
as well? No cruel Americans? No brutal British? No savage
Russians? People are people, no matter what skin they
wear. Some are good, and some are not."

He sighed and sat up. "Erika, I know that. Good Lord,
we don't have anything to argue about. I'm just tired, and
a little sickened by what I've seen. Sorry."

He didn't sound sorry. She tossed her tawny hair angrily
from her eyes. "So you're sickened by what you have seen!
What would you know about what we've been through?
You are an American, an outsider. Your countrymen sit
pleasantly behind their borders, eating ice cream and complaining about sacrifice. Not enough sugar for their six
daily cups of coffee. Only three or four pounds of meat a
week. Sacrifice! How would Americans behave if they lost
millions of their young men on battlefields? How gentle
would they be if their skies were filled night and day with
thousands of bombers, blowing up their cities and killing
everyone? It is so easy to be self-righteous when one is
safe."

His mouth tightened. "Correct me if I'm wrong," he
said coldly, "but I seem to recall that it was your glorious
Führer and his Nazi cronies who started all this. The millions who died in the early days were all Polish and French
and Russian and Norwegian and Belgian."

"I see. Then revenge is in order, is it not? Returning
cruelty for cruelty is acceptable, is that what you're saying? Does that not prove my point? That evil can march
under any flag? Does it not show—" She stopped and took
a deep breath.

"Doesn't it show what?"

"Nothing," she said. "I don't want to argue with you anymore. You have put me in a position of defending something I find indefensible. Herr Fiebeck was a very nice man. I liked him."

He nodded. "So did I."

She touched his hand tentatively. "Please, Henri, don't be angry with me. You mustn't hold a grudge against me for the way he died just because I'm German. After all, he was German, too."

"Erika, no, I'm not mad at you. *You* never dropped any bombs on anybody."

"No, of course not. I'm not angry either. I don't know what made me fly off that way. After all, we could never be enemies. I need you. And I think you need me if we are to live through the next few days. To die in any fashion is difficult. But to die alone is too horrible to contemplate."

He reached to comfort her. "We aren't going to die," he said lightly. "I've decided I'm against the idea."

"Perhaps," she said. "But if we do—" She rose to her feet. "Wait here."

She left him on the mattress and groped her way to the wall where she'd left the baby carriage the night before. She was aware of his eyes watching her through the door while she felt through her meager belongings, first for the bottle of Vouvray, then the corkscrew. She carried them back and sat on the mattress beside him. "Here," she said, "open this."

"But . . . this is your special bottle."

"I know it. Open it. We will drink it together."

He ran his fingers over the bottle, obviously tempted, but apparently unconvinced. "You told me you were going to save it and share it with your young man when he gets back."

"He isn't coming back," she said. "I know that. I suppose I always have. You're my young man now. We will drink it and get gloriously drunk, and then we will make love."

"Are you sure?"

"I'm sure."

They lay in silence, bathed in the aftersweat of love, clinging for the moment each to the other, and for the moment she had no thoughts of war or dying or being alone. Her head rested lightly on his chest, and his breathing was slow, near to sleep. She didn't know how long they had lain like this, only that she felt complete, warmly used, gently loved. She moved her hand upward, from his chest to his throat, then to his chin, tracing a fine line to his lips. He stirred beside her, rousing. His hand touched her. She felt his manhood rising again.

Then suddenly, like an orchestra of squeaking hinges, a strange sound filtered through the distance, chilling her blood, jolting her back to the present. "What's that?" she said.

He lifted his head sleepily and listened, then his face turned rigid. "Tanks!" he said. "Dammit, tanks! Coming this way." He snatched her dress from the floor and thrust it at her. "Get into this, quick."

She slid the dress over her head, forgetting modesty and undergarments, and watched him pull on his trousers and shirt. "Perhaps they are ours," she suggested.

He shook his head. "Not damned likely. You don't have that many left. Besides, they're coming from the south." He slipped into his shoes and grabbed her by the elbow. "To the stairs. We've got to get out of here."

But when they reached the blown-out front wall at the upper level, he jerked her back. Down below, faintly visible in the darkened rubble, a dozen furtive forms in leather caps skipped from shadow to shadow, leapfrogging up the street.

"Scouts," he whispered. "We're too late." He pointed to the southern end of the street. More soldiers, some in helmets, some in fur caps, all in floppy coats and padded winter jackets, scooted through the darkness. Rounding the corner behind them, squeaking and clanking ominously, came the first of a slow line of greasy, oil spattered tanks, hatches down, gun turrets swiveling from side to side.

"Perhaps they will pass on," she whispered.

"They'll pass," he agreed. "But others will take their place. Artillery teams, mortar units. This whole damned street will be swarming with Russians within the hour."

"What will we do?"

"Nothing. There's nothing we can do. We're trapped."

"Perhaps we could climb out a window on the back? They can't be on all the streets."

He shook his head. "We show ourselves now and some trigger-happy infantryman is likely to fill us full of holes." He looked beyond her to the stairway. "Let's get back to the cellar. We'll dig in and wait until things settle down. Maybe the rear units won't be quite so nervous."

"And then what?" she said incredulously. "You'll give us up to the Russians?"

His jaw muscles clamped. "I don't know yet. We'll have to wait and see."

THREE

The Fall

12

Berlin bleibt Deutsch!

"Berlin remains German!"

—slogan scrawled on Berlin wall

1

The fighting eased off again during the night. The Russians, secure in the knowledge that the battle was almost done, used the dark hours to strengthen their stranglehold on the inner city, bringing up fresh supplies of ammunition and resting their front-line troops. At early light there would be three new main thrusts, one from the south to complete and stabilize the penetration of the Landwehr Canal, another from the east in an attempt to shorten at least one end of the central corridor still held by the Germans, and a third from the north toward the Spree River and a possible breakthrough to the burned-out Reichstag building where, for some strange reason, the Russians still believed Hitler and his military staff to be headquartered.

Only the west end of the corridor remained soft enough to offer any hope to the besieged Berliners.

At one o'clock that Sunday morning, after languishing for forty-eight hours in the Führerbunker surgical rooms for treatment of his shattered foot, General Robert Ritter von Greim, now sporting a field marshal's baton handed him personally by Adolf Hitler, was deemed ready to fly out of Berlin and take command of the dying Luftwaffe in place of the recently dishonored Hermann Göring.

Greim's Fieseler Stork, after two days in the open on the bombarded East-West Axis, was only a shattered hulk when the time came for his departure. Another small plane, an Arado 96 trainer, was flown through the Russian ring of guns by a steel-nerved Luftwaffe sergeant to pick him up. Greim and Hanna Reitsch were delivered to the Brandenburg Gate by armored car shortly after midnight and loaded into the plane. Russian searchlights tried to pick them up as they cleared the rooftops, but they climbed rapidly and flew into the darkness.

The man seemingly most disturbed by their departure was Martin Bormann. He stood vaguely in the background while they said their good-bys to Hitler. He watched dismally from the foot of the bunker stairway as SS men carried Greim up to the waiting armored car. When word came back that the plane had lifted off safely, he sat by himself in a corner of the lower-level conference room and brooded.

It was a time for decision. General Weidling arrived at the bunker less than an hour after Greim's departure and hesitantly informed the Führer that there was grave danger of the German pocket being split in half. If the Russians pressed their attacks from the north and south in the region of the Tiergarten, by now the narrowest part of the eight-mile belt, it was possible that German forces would be cut into two parts and destroyed piecemeal. He unfolded his maps and offered a new plan for a massed military breakout, one which he was convinced would carry Hitler to safety. Hitler informed him once more that he had no intention of being spirited from the city only to wander aimlessly through the German countryside until Russian troops caught up with him and made him a prisoner.

Martin Bormann listened.

Hitler Youth leader Artur Axmann, unaware of Weidling's breakout proposal, appeared at two o'clock that morning and breathlessly pledged his young warriors as a guarantee for the life and safety of the Führer. They were prepared to die in an all-out assault on the weaker Russian concentrations at the western end of the corridor, in order to effect the Führer's escape. Hitler thanked him, but declined the offer and sent him on his way.

Martin Bormann winced.

At three that morning, while the atmosphere grew heavier in the bunker and frayed nerves led to arguments among the lower echelons, Adolf Hitler retired to his suite of rooms with a civil magistrate summoned from a nearby Volkssturm unit and married Eva Braun, his mistress and companion of thirteen years. He then invited Joseph and Frau Goebbels, Bormann, and two of his favorite secretaries into his private chambers for a short champagne celebration.

Martin Bormann hovered in the background and sipped.

Following the wedding celebration, Hitler dictated his political testament and his personal will. His testament expelled both Hermann Göring and Heinrich Himmler from the Party for attempting to seize control of the state and for negotiating with the enemy, and named Admiral Karl Dönitz and Joseph Goebbels as his successors. His personal will left his possessions to the Party, or, if it ceased to exist, to the State, and named Bormann as his executor.

Martin Bormann clenched his teeth and accepted.

Early in the morning, as the sun rose outside and Russian salvos intensified once more, Hitler met in the conference room with Bormann and three young military aides: Lieutenant Colonel Wilhelm Weiss, Major Bernd von Freytag-Loringhoven, and Captain Gerhard Boldt. The three adjutants had volunteered to make their own small-scale breakout attempt through the western end of the corridor in order to inform General Wenck and his Twelfth Army, rumored to be approaching Potsdam, that they must hasten onward or Berlin was lost.

Hitler listened with great interest as the three younger men described the route they would take, by daylight through the fighting in the Tiergarten, beyond the Kurfürstendamm, on to the Adolf Hitler Platz, then to the Olympic Stadium, and finally to the bridges at Pichelsdorf. By night-fall, they expected to reach the Havel River, where they would confiscate a boat and make their way between Russian troop concentrations by sailing south to the Wannsee.

Hitler seemed fascinated. He made a few suggestions, including showing them on a city map where they might find some quiet electric boats, then wished them good luck. They left immediately.

Martin Bormann watched them go without a word.

It was almost noon before Bormann finally found a chance to speak to Hitler alone. He took him aside into Dr. Stumpfegger's small surgery and said, "My Führer, time is growing short. The *Schachmatt* mechanism is ready. We cannot trigger it until you make a decision."

"You, too, Martin?" Hitler said. "Are you so eager to join the others in escape?"

"No, my Führer," Bormann said quickly. "It is your legacy of which I think. We must protect and preserve your life's work."

Hitler ran a trembling finger along a stainless steel examination table. "I had a private visitor yesterday," he said. "A young officer who fears there may be treason at my back."

"Treason?"

"Yes. Young Captain Schedle. He told me about a series of bewildering assignments he has drawn from your office in recent days. He fears you and Heinrich Müller may be planning your own flight from the city."

Bormann was startled. "He told you that?"

Hitler nodded. "He is a pious young man, but very loyal to me. Loyalty is an unusual commodity these days."

Bormann drew himself up. "My Führer, surely you know by now that I will share whatever end comes your way. If you should choose to leave Berlin, I would be close behind you. If you elect to stay and meet your fate, then I shall stay also. You have my oath on it."

Hitler seemed distracted. "Are the guns louder, do you think?"

"No, my Führer. Not yet. But they soon will be. Please, you must make a decision. Until your death is announced, nothing more can be done."

"I don't want to think of that now," Hitler said.

"But I must know," Bormann said. "I must put the final gears in motion."

Hitler waved his hand irritably. "Very well. Do what you must."

"Then you accept the inevitable? You are prepared to take the necessary steps?"

"I will allow you to conclude the arrangements," Hitler said. "As to the matter of my death, I am still undecided. I will make my final determination tomorrow. I am not prepared to say more."

"That will be adequate," Bormann said.

He tried to contain his relief, but as he turned to leave, he took a deep breath. For the first time in weeks, he thought he caught a whiff of fresh air. It was only his imagination, he knew, but it was rich and satisfying, like coming from a dark tunnel into the sunlight of a peaceful Alpine meadow.

2

Two Dutch RAF pilots barred Longland's way as he eased from the bar, refills of three glasses held high over his head. Behind the Dutchmen, a party of Aussie infantrymen loudly but futilely proclaimed their rights to a refill of lager, but the row of British uniforms lined up solidly in front of the bar failed to give way. The White Tower near Soho Square had earned fame early in the war by the quality of its black-market roast mutton, and Longland mentally made faces at the swarm of uniforms that still patronized the place. To the right, a table of Eighth Air Force staffers drank bitters with three Mayfair girls, whose idea of slumming was to sit sipping Pimm's. To the left, Canadians, Poles, Czechs, Frenchmen, Belgians, and Yanks, everywhere Yanks, milled to and from the bar, largely from, as Longland's fellow Englishmen stanchly held the position won minutes before by the classic Napoleonic variant.

As adept as they, Longland mounted a penetration of the center and succeeded in elbowing both the Dutch pilots and the Aussies out of his path. He returned a foxy smile for their belligerent looks when he actually made it back to the table without spilling more than a third of the Navy pilot's brandy. Of his own and Ann Christy's, he spilled not a drop. Sighing inwardly at the necessity, he switched his own full glass for the pilot's. Not that he liked the fellow. All pilots were sods. Seemed to think they shared some wonderful secret inaccessible to those who didn't soar about the skies. But, as Colonel Norman had gently pointed out, they wanted something of the man.

Their man was leaning across the table, talking rapidly to Ann. ". . . some night?" Longland heard him say.

Ann dropped her dark blue eyes. "Please, it's very important," she said.

The pilot saw Longland then. He leaned back. "Yes, but the Baltic is filled with subs," he said. "The problem is, it's hard to find a particular one, even when one knows where to look."

Longland slid into his chair and gave the man a smile that had more jackal than fox in it—determined jackal that sees a rival approach too closely to his dinner. "Ah, but this particular sub is at or near Sassnitz," he said. "That narrows it down, don't you see?"

The pilot reached for his brandy. "Well, yes, but it might be standing out from Sassnitz by now. They're not exactly immobile. And they don't exactly float up occasionally and confide, 'My name is *Schachbrett.*' "

Ann said softly, "But you could try. Honestly, if it weren't important, we wouldn't be asking. One of our, mm, associates risked absolutely everything to send out an alert on the sub, but there was, mm, the hush-hush problem with the high potentates."

The pilot leaned forward, ostensibly to catch her words over the steady roar of other voices, but, Longland suspected, really just to draw closer to Ann. Longland grunted, "Well, what do you say?"

"Please," Ann said, "it's very, very important. To me personally."

She sounded sincere, and Longland had to wonder suddenly if Bascom was really that special to her. More special than himself? She also sounded enchanting, and what man could resist the appeal in those midnight blue eyes?"

The pilot apparently couldn't. "Well, of course, we can try," he said. "My patrols sink every sub they can find anyway, but I'll pass the word that something unusual may be happening in the Baltic and get my boys to bear down. But my dear Sergeant Christy, don't get your hopes up too high. There's rather a lot of briny deep out there."

Ann thanked the sod too profusely, Longland thought. In fact, they were into their third brandy by the time she finished thanking him. The pilot went his own way with evident reluctance, and Longland was pleased to see that Ann missed his good-by wave at the door. She stared into her brandy glass instead. And kept staring.

"Penny?" he offered.

"Oh, it's nothing," she said.

"Is it Bascom?"

"No. Yes. Oh Sidney, what good would sinking some silly submarine really do? He's probably dead by now. Dead."

Good God, had she really loved the fellow? But posthumous jealousy was an unbecoming trait. Longland gave up his expectations for the evening which, with the setting sun, would soon be on them, and instead of envelopment of both flanks, applied an attack in oblique order to the task of worming his way to the bar to get the poor girl a solacing drink.

The fading light in the cellar told Bascom that the sun was setting even before the nearby Russian gun emplacements calmed down for the night. It had been a nerve-wracking day of waiting. The guns, mainly howitzers, had opened up at sunrise, banging away from the street outside Bascom's and Erika's building, empty shell casings clanging against the cobblestones as they were ejected from smoking breeches and the next rounds rammed home. All day the guns blustered, all day the empty shell casings clanged, until Bascom inhaled the noise of the guns with every breath. Then, at sunset, they ceased.

Bascom waited only a few more minutes before leaving Erika in the cellar and slipping to the head of the stairs to reconnoiter. His deafened ears hummed, and at first he had to rely on his eyes only. The gun crews, perhaps fifty or sixty men in all, lounged near a horse-drawn mess wagon, eating from tin plates. A handful of German children had crept from neighboring cellars to gape at the food. As hearing returned, he could tell that the battle still rumbled elsewhere in the city, but these particular artillerymen seemed to be putting in bankers' hours. It was puzzling. Up with the sun to send salvos to the center of the city, down with the darkness for rest and relaxation. Not one of them appeared to be worried about counterattack. There was even music farther up the street, someone with a concertina, squeezing off an incongruously gay tune.

He crawled back to the furnace room and Erika. "I don't know," he whispered. "It looks as though they're through for the night. They're sitting out there stuffing their faces like they were on a picnic."

"Perhaps we can leave soon?" she suggested. "There are smaller streets to the west. Surely we can find one that crosses the lines. Or we could go through the buildings."

"I've been thinking about it," he said. "If I could find someone who speaks English, I could try explaining who I am. We could surrender and get a free ticket out of here."

"I don't want to surrender to the Russians," she said.

"What difference does it make? Even if we work our way back to the German side, the Russians will finish it in a day or two. It's a case of surrendering now or two or three days from now."

"It's too dangerous."

"They seem quiet and calm. They're even trying to talk to some children out on the street, make friends with them. If we give up now, that would give us time to clear out any red tape and arrange medical attention for Formoy. Then you could lead us to him, just as soon as the shooting stops."

"That's all very well for you and your friend," she said. "Not for me. I'm German, remember?"

"Hell, Erika, they aren't going to hurt you. They're just a bunch of tired soldiers. Remember what you said about people being just the same, no matter what skin they wear?"

"That did not apply to Russians. You haven't seen the bestial way they act. I have." She hunched her shoulders as if she were cold. "I'm hungry. Is there anything left?"

"There's still that damned can, whatever the hell is in it. Maybe I could knock it open."

"I saw a loose board with nails in the outer room. I'll get it. Perhaps the nails will help. See if you can find the can."

As she went through the door, he poked through the debris on the floor. The can wasn't where he remembered tossing it. Maybe it had rolled. He got down on his hands and knees, scrounging in the darkness, and reached under a pile of loose wall slats and . . .

A noise from the front of the building. A brick dislodged, rattling down to the street. Bascom stiffened. Deep voices murmuring overhead. More bricks, then the thump of feet as someone clambered over the wall and dropped to the parquet flooring. Two of them, from the sound of it. Footsteps moved across the floor above him. Floorboards creaked as one of them turned toward the cellar stairs.

He crawled to the doorway and motioned Erika to him,

but he was too late. A pair of boots stepped down the stairs, and a face leaned over to peer into the cellar. A flashlight beam clicked on and swept the floor. It came to rest on her.

For a moment Erika and the Russian stared at each other, then he unslung his rifle and said gruffly in childish German, "You, voman. War *kaput*. Germans *kaput*. Any soldier you got? Volkssturm? Any gun?"

Erika shook her head numbly.

He came the rest of the way down the stairs and into Bascom's vision. An ugly man, squat torso, slightly bow-legged. *"Uri,"* he said, pointing to her arm. It may have been his version of the word *Uhr*, for wristwatch, or perhaps the plural, *Uhren*. When she didn't respond quickly enough, he grabbed her wrist, then the other, but her wrists were bare. The flashlight beam ranged farther and stopped on the baby carriage. The Russian grunted, gratified, and reached for the teddy bear, perhaps meaning to give it to the wistful street children to win them over.

"Don't," Erika said. She tried to grab it back, but the man shoved her to the floor.

Now the other soldier, alerted by the sounds of their voices, dropped quickly into sight—a taller young man, with clean features and quick eyes. He saw immediately what had happened and spoke harshly to his comrade. Bascom pressed back against the wall, out of sight, and slowly drew the pistol from his belt.

He could hear the two Russians arguing for a few moments, then the young one switched to a broken German of his own and said, "Sorry, voman. No mean frighten. You got mans here?" Apparently Erika shook her head again, for the young Russian said, "We go now. Not bother. You toy keep. Take."

"You're giving it back?" Erika said in a surprised tone.

"No steal from voman. Not good."

The two soldiers headed back up the stairs. Bascom peered cautiously through the door. Erika rose slowly to her feet in the shadows by the stairwell, clutching the teddy bear. She stood very still until their footsteps moved back across the ceiling and down the spill of bricks, then she began to tremble. Bascom slipped the gun back in his belt and hurried to her.

"You win," he whispered. "Let's get out of here. A bunch of clods from a gun crew aren't the kind of people we should surrender to."

She trembled even harder. "No, no, we might encounter more of them. We must wait until they go to sleep. They will post only a few guards, surely. When it's completely safe, we'll climb out the back."

He put his arms around her. Her trembling didn't come from cold, but his impulse was to keep her warm. "I'll go check the back windows," he said. "If only I could spot a Russian officer—"

"No, please, no surrender. We must leave the city. The priest at the church said the corridor to the west still offers a chance. The Russians are firing on the bridges, but hundreds of refugees, perhaps thousands, have made it through to the countryside. It would take us only a few days to reach the Americans."

"Honey, I can't leave Formoy," Bascom said. "Not now."

She hesitated. "He'd be safe in the church. Even Russians would honor the sanctuary of a church."

"You don't believe that any more than I do. Now, admit it."

The floorboards creaked again, stealthily. Bascom touched his finger to his lips and pulled her into the furnace room. The footsteps inched overhead toward the stairs. No flashlight beam this time. Just a slow, steady trail of creaks, which reached the top of the stairs, then stopped. A long silence. Dead quiet. Then a voice, calling softly, "Voman? You here?"

"It's the young one," Erika whispered. "The nice one. He knows I'm still here. I'd better go."

Bascom shook his head at her.

"I must," she whispered. "Otherwise he might come looking for me and find you." She pulled away before Bascom could object and stepped into the outer room. "Yes?" she said. "Did you forget something?"

The young soldier smiled shyly from the top of the stairs and said, "No forget something. Remember."

She moved a few more steps from the doorway. "What did you remember?"

He ducked his head and came slowly down to her. He put his hands behind his back and said shyly, "No nice, my friend scare you."

"That's all right," Erika said. "We're all a little shaky at the moment."

"You nice. Good voman." Head still down, too shy to look up.

"Thank you. You are nice, too. I want to thank you for saving the teddy bear. It's a memento, you see. It belonged to my little sister, who's dead."

He looked up and smiled at her, then cocked his fist and belted her under the eye.

Erika, caught off guard, bumped against the cellar wall and fell to the floor. The soldier was on her instantly, clawing at her skirt. She moaned and tried feebly to ward him off, but she was too dazed to be effective. Her moans seemed to excite him.

Bascom was stunned. For a moment he couldn't believe what his eyes were telling him. Then he wasted another moment trying to decide what to do. He almost pulled the P-38 from his belt, but he couldn't shoot, not with Russian soldiers on the street above. What then? Storm into the outer room and play hero? Or hide in a corner and let Erika take her lumps so that they both might live?

But Erika moaned again and the Russian laughed and ripped her dress open at the neck, popping buttons all over the floor, and Bascom's rational self plummeted behind a film of gray insanity. He lunged through the doorway, a low, animal growl rising involuntarily through clenched teeth.

The Russian heard him coming and tried to pull away from Erika, but Bascom was across the room in an instant, wrestling, pulling, driving him to the floor. They went down in a heap in the darkness, and Bascom's hand closed on a two-by-four. He swung it like a club, a glancing blow across the Russian's scalp, then swung it again, hearing the crunch, feeling the bone give way. A sigh, one last gasp of breath, slipped from the man's lungs and his body went limp, but still Bascom pounded. He pounded the face, he pounded the head, he pounded the shoulders. He pounded without awareness. Then, abruptly, his vision cleared. He stopped swinging the board and gazed in surprise at the battered mess on the floor. He turned to the side and thrust the board away. "Good God," he murmured.

Erika, hands clutching torn dress to throat, stared up at him with eyes still dazed, but wide with horror. Horror at what he had done? God knew, he was horrified himself.

Shakily, he dragged the Russian's body out of sight, rolling it under the stairwell.

"Do you know what you've done?" her voice whispered.

"I've got eyes."

"I don't mean to him. I mean to us. You've killed us."

He returned and lifted her. For a moment she let her body stay close to his, then she pulled away, an almost unconscious movement, but one she couldn't control.

"They'll come looking for him," she said. "When they see what you have done, they'll shoot us both."

Bascom backed away from her a few inches, backing away from her words. "He wouldn't have told anyone where he was going. Even if he did, they aren't going to barge in while they think he's still enjoying himself. We've got time."

"For what?"

"To try getting the hell out of here. If we stick to the side streets and shadows and keep our eyes open for sentries, we might make it."

"Back to the German zone?" she said hopefully.

He nodded slowly. "We no longer have a choice."

She looked toward the stairwell. "Why did you do it?"

"What did you want me to do? Let him knock you around?"

"You could have stopped him without killing him. Couldn't you? Especially the . . . the way you did. Why?"

He turned his face away. He couldn't explain it. There

was no sense in trying. For a few deranged moments, everything had seethed up in him, all the fears and frustrations,
all the terrors of the past few days. He had become, for a
brief eternity, an unwilling madman. How do you explain
a thing like that? Even to yourself?

And so they crept up the stairs in silence.

                              4

She was a Type XXI U-boat, out of the Norwegian bases.
Commissioned in June of 1944, she carried a crew of fifty-
six men, and she had sunk eight merchant ships and damaged two British frigates since going into action. Her captain, a lanky, one-eyed veteran from Kiel, known affec-
tionately to his crew as old *Scharfschütze*, or "Deadshot"
(they were careful never to refer to him as "Deadeye"),
was a patient, clever hunter, seldom confused by enemy
tactics.

But currently he was confused, and not by the enemy.
He knew the land war had been going poorly, and had
expected at any moment to receive the code word *Regen-
bogen*, or "Rainbow," which would call for scuttling his
craft to keep it from falling into enemy hands in case of an
Allied victory. But the code word, when it came, was
Schloss, a special directive that sent him to a small oilskin
packet of sealed orders delivered to him by a personal
representative of Reichsleiter Martin Bormann before his
last sailing.

The code word had come seven days ago, and each
night he had opened a new envelope from the oilskin
packet to see what his next move was to be. First it had
been a recall from his patrol area in the Kattegat Strait
with instructions to set a course for Sassnitz, a small port
on Rügen Island off the North coast of Germany. That
made sense to him. His boat had been out long enough
and was due for resupply anyway. But the second night,
well on the way to Sassnitz, he opened the second envelope

and found that he was to change his compass heading a few degrees and head for Stralsund, instead.

Thus began his confusion. The envelopes, each in its turn, gave him orders, then counterorders, like clues in a scavenger hunt, leading him in a zigzag course to yet another seaport on the coast of northern Germany for fuel and supplies. To heighten the mystery, some of the supplies came aboard in sealed cases, so large that he had to beach ten of the U-boat complement to make room for them.

He had put back to sea hurriedly, following envelope No. 4, changed course with envelope No. 5, and come to slow-ahead in the middle of the Baltic Sea with envelope No. 6. Now the boat was riding submerged with its *Schnorkel* breaking the surface so the diesels could recharge the batteries, and it was time for envelope No. 7. The last of them. Presumably the answer to the puzzle.

It was a cheerless hour. Even at slow-ahead, the rough Baltic waters often slopped over the *Schnorkel* breathing apparatus, forcing the float valve shut. When that happened, the diesels sucked their oxygen from the interior of the boat and blew their exhaust gases back into the air system. The air turned foul, and the sudden pressure changes often gave the captain headaches, though he never let on to his crew.

He had a headache now as he settled in his cabin to open the last envelope. The pain always centered behind his eyes, and oddly, was sharpest behind his dead eye, lost to him in October of '42 when a depth charge knocked him off balance and threw him against a valve handle in his first U-boat. He'd thought at the time that his military career was over, but the need of the Fatherland for experienced seamen had outweighed his disability, and he had been reassigned to sea duty in less than six months. His record, a phenomenal one in these last years of the war, had proved his value as a one-eyed captain—better, in fact, than that of a lot of two-eyed captains.

He unwrapped the oilskin packet slowly, allowing his

personal suspense to build. He still hadn't the faintest idea
what the assignment was to be, but it was obvious to him
from the special precautions that someone considered it
important and wanted to make damned sure it stayed secret.

The final envelope that emerged from the packet was
yellow, thick, and heavy like the others, with a waxed
seal covering a red tearaway ribbon. He blinked his good
eye and broke the seal.

One sheet of closely packed ciphers. He placed it under
his reading light next to his code book and began tran-
scribing, confidently expecting an explanation. But he was
quickly disappointed. The last set of instructions left him
as bewildered as before. Instead of sailing orders with a
final destination, as he had hoped, he was directed to hold
his present position for at least a week, riding submerged
by day and surfacing each night for a period of one hour
between 2400 and 0100 hours.

The captain rubbed his hand through close-cut graying
hair. Surface? But these waters were filled with submarine
hunters. What could be so important that he should jeopardize his entire crew nightly? The instructions didn't make
it clear. They stated only that there was to be a rendezvous
during one of those nights, but whether by boat or plane,
they didn't say. Simply that the rendezvous craft would
identify itself by an additional code word.

There would presumably be additional instructions at
that time. Would someone finally tell him what it was all
about? He hoped so. He was eager to stop this sailing in
circles and get back to the fighting line, where he could
do some damage before the war ended.

If it wasn't already lost.

13

Kapitulieren? Nein!

"Surrender? No!"

—slogan scrawled on Berlin wall

1

Fires flickered as Bascom and Erika darted from building to building in the center of Berlin. Though it was only an hour or so past midnight, the skies raged red and bright, almost like daylight.

"This way," Bascom said.

"I'm coming," Erika said.

They had skirted through the Russian lines with difficulty, barely escaping discovery before they found a small street between Oranienstrasse and Gitschiner that was so completely blockaded with rubble that the Russians had ignored it. Then it took the better part of an hour to worm through the obstructions, and when they emerged, they were behind the thin German lines and into a rainstorm of Russian artillery fire.

"Oh God," Erika said.

"No, don't look," Bascom said.

Death lay everywhere. German soldiers dangling from windows and crumpled in the streets where white-hot shell fragments had cut them down. Bloated horses lying dead, still hitched to shattered carts. The putrid smell of decomposing bodies from damp cellars where civilians had been trapped in collapsing buildings.

"Keep down," Bascom said.

"I'm trying," Erika said.

Signs of hurried desertion appeared more consistently. Armbands shucked in dark doorways. Weapons dropped in gutters. Uniform tunics discarded along the sidewalks. An occasional male figure ducked furtively through the firelit shadows, seeking shelter, avoiding Bascom and Erika as eagerly as they in turn avoided all comers.

"I think I'm lost," Bascom said.

"We're on Friedrichstrasse," Erika said. "Or perhaps it's Wilhelmstrasse."

They inched their way through the burning streets, trying to find their way to the church where Formoy had been taken. The Russian barrages had piled destruction on destruction until it was hard to determine exactly where they were. Streets which Bascom had traversed only days before had been rendered almost unrecognizable. And through it all, the *Katyushi* wailed and the artillery shells thundered about them.

"I see people," Erika said.

"Hide here," Bascom said.

Civilians, mostly women and children, hastened through the explosions, shielding their heads with packages and suitcases as they scurried across a fire-bright street and ducked out of sight, heading for the corridor to the west. More civilians appeared a few seconds later and darted across the intersection.

"We could follow them," Erika said.

"Not without Formoy," Bascom said.

They detoured away from the civilians and sought another street. As they crept around a corner, the Russian barrage stammered to a stop. Except for a few stray shells that fell irregularly in the Tiergarten area to the west of them, an uncommon quiet settled over the night. For the first time, they could hear the crackle of flames.

"Why have they stopped?" Erika asked.

"Maybe just to cool their gun barrels," Bascom said.

A chatter of small-arms fire drifted from the north, from the region of the Moltke Bridge. Machine guns opened up, followed by mortars and light field pieces. Bascom and Erika had no way of knowing it, but the Soviet barrage had lifted momentarily because the Russian Third Shock Army was about to storm across the Spree and assault the government buildings around the Königs-Platz.

The Russians were particularly obsessed with taking the old, burned-out Reichstag. Every Russian formation north of the Spree River wanted to be the first to reach the Reichstag and to plant the Red Army flag on its shattered cupola.

"Sounds like it may be heating up," Bascom said. "This way."

"Isn't this the wrong direction?" Erika said.

The battle for the Reichstag would be a long and bloody one. The building had been garrisoned by five thousand men, mostly ill-equipped and ill-trained Volkssturm battalions, along with some small units flown in from the Naval School in Rostock, but the walls along the lower floors had been strongly reinforced with concrete, steel, and earth, and all the windows had been bricked up. It would take hours for the Russians to break through the walls, and even then the battle would be fought floor by floor, staircase by staircase, and room by room. It would crash and thunder unceasingly for the next two days, a desperate little war carried on out of sight, attacks and counterattacks up and down the stairs. It would not end until half the Reichstag garrison, more than twenty-five hundred men, were dead.

"This looks familiar," Erika said. "Isn't that a street sign?"

"Keep moving," Bascom said. "We've got to get to the church before daylight."

They turned into a once-wide avenue, now narrowed by shattered buildings. Bascom took Erika's arm to help her over a towering pile of smoke-blackened stone. As they skidded down the far side, the Russian guns, silent for the past several minutes, opened up again. Shells crashed into the buildings around them. Geysers of mortar and brick blew into the air. Concussion knocked them to the ground. Pebbles and pulverized stone rained down on them. Dust rose like a heavy fog.

"We've got to hide," Erika said unnecessarily.

"That building over there," Bascom shouted over the noise of explosions. "Come on."

They scrambled to the side of a tall, four-story brick building with row upon row of broken windows and a great gaping hole torn above a double entrance. Bascom looked up at a chipped, scarred balcony hanging above them, then spotted a breach in the wall a few feet farther along. He dragged Erika to it and pulled her inside.

"Where are we?" she said.

"I don't know," he said.

A large room with ornate office furniture, sagging on a drunkenly tilted floor. Ceiling demolished and the legs of another desk poking through from the floor above. Filing cabinets overturned. Papers scattered. Another shell landed in the street outside, and Bascom kept moving, hauling Erika deeper into the building, through corridors and smashed offices. They came to a marbled hallway with a staircase leading upward, strong pillars supporting the ceiling. Dust hung in the air, and the walls shook. They stopped to catch their breath. Explosions rumbled all around them.

"Is this the way it ends?" she said.

"Don't think about it," he said.

They sat on the floor, cringing together, while shells hammered the area. An hour passed, perhaps more. They clung to each other, feeling the jolting shocks of each explosion, listening to the groaning marble walls, choking on plaster dust, expecting at any moment the direct hit that would bury them. But the death blow didn't come. Slowly, so slowly that they were almost unaware it was happening, the carpet barrage rolled away. Near misses became safer misses, then most distant misses. The sound of explosions never let up, but the building trembled less and less, and the groaning of the walls gradually died to a whimper. They were still alive.

"What was that?" she said. "Did you hear something?"

"Shh. Voices?" he said.

It was. Steel door clanging. Footsteps on a basement stairwell, coming up toward the marble hallway. Young voices. Male voices. That meant military voices. Bascom pulled Erika to her feet and hurried her upward to the next floor. They pressed back in the shadows and watched through the balustrade. Several black-uniformed SS men, shoulders powdered with cement dust, coming up from shelter. The SS men laughed. It sounded false. They traded insipid jokes about the artillery barrage, then began to spread out. More SS men came behind them.

"Oh my God!" Erika whispered. "We're in a death zone."

"Death zone?" Bascom said. "What's that?"

A group of the SS men started up the marble stairway toward them, and they retreated rapidly, fumbling in the darkness, climbing higher. The SS men climbed after them, boots echoing against the marble stairs.

"We must find a place to hide!" Erika whispered. "If they see us they will kill us."

"Why?" Bascom whispered back. "Where are we?"

Two of the SS men peeled off on the second floor and moved toward the front of the building to take up guard posts. The others kept climbing. Bascom and Erika retreated still higher, heading up a narrow wooden stairwell to the top floor. Holes gaped in the ceiling, and the red glow of distant flames washed over them. They hesitated briefly, then hurried toward the rear of the building. More of the SS men broke away on the third floor, but at least one was still climbing. They found a small office by the rear wall and cowered like hunted animals behind a dusty desk caked with ceiling plaster, only a few feet from a shattered window.

"What's a death zone?" Bascom whispered.

"A forbidden area," Erika said. "No one is allowed to enter without authorization."

The footsteps reached their floor and turned toward the front. Minutes trickled sluggishly. They waited, listening. The broken window became more distinct behind them. The red glow diffused with gradually strengthening white light. Was it nearly daylight already? Had it taken so long for them to come this far?

"We must leave," Erika whispered. "Before they find us."

"How?" Bascom said. "They're all over the place."

The light became stronger with each slow minute. A feeble sun struggled over the horizon, burning through the hanging smoke. They kept still, waiting, waiting. The window, no longer a hazy form, was complete now, and they could see jagged glass shards framing a streaky morning sky. Bascom watched it, curious to know what lay outside. When he could stand it no longer, he crawled cautiously to the window and raised his head to look.

Below, in a ruined garden filled with felled trees and shell craters, sat a thick concrete blockhouse next to an oddly shaped silo of some sort, a circular concrete structure with a conical roof. The building in which Bascom and Erika had taken shelter, smoke-blackened and pocked with shrapnel scars, bordered the garden on the east. Another building, newer in appearance but just as badly scarred, formed an L shape around the southern edge of the garden.

Bascom stared at the newer building, at the long, battered grace of its yellow-brick design, taking up the whole block from end to end, and gasped with the shock of recognition. He'd only ever seen it from the front, but he knew it at last. It was the building from which his compatriots had come pouring on that dark night eons ago, with the SS men following and their guns firing.

And that meant this building, the building in which he and Erika were hiding, was part of the most dangerous structure in the whole of Germany. Hitler himself, if he was still alive, was down there below the garden, fifty feet below that churned earth. And Bascom and Erika were trapped above him.

They had haplessly taken shelter in the old Reich Chancellery building.

2

Bormann hurried through the Führerbunker corridor to the bottom of the emergency exit tower. It had been a busy night and morning of preparation, and he felt both tired and testy. The Soviets, according to hazy field reports, had launched a ground attack on the southern fringes of the Tiergarten this morning, leaving very little time and very little space.

All the arrangements were now complete. The route was set. An armored escort team alerted. Radio confirmation to the Rostock Naval Air Station. Rendezvous site on Lake Havel fixed. He'd even arranged a scout car for himself, if everything went as planned.

The last roadblock was the Führer, now off having luncheon with some of his favorite female secretaries, probably chatting lightly as though everything were normal, while he, Bormann, had to run about and do all the work. The man had accepted everything in principle, but he hadn't yet agreed to the final step necessary for the implementation of the project. Would he withhold his sanction still? Or would he at last see that there was no other way? The Führer had responded so inconsistently to the pressures of these last few days. Well, no more. That would have to change. He would have to come to a final determination this morning. There was no more time for procrastination. It was now or never.

Bormann stared upward at the four flights of concrete steps leading to the Chancellery garden. He checked his watch. Nearly noon. What was keeping them? They should be here by now. Were they waiting for the garden guards to clear out? That was another problem. That damned Schedle. The man was only a captain, yet he had the gall to sneak behind Bormann's back and suggest to the Führer that there were improprieties afoot, perhaps even treasonous activities. This very morning, when Bormann summoned him and instructed him to dismiss all guards from the garden and order all the others to stay at their posts in the front of the buildings, the insubordinate little *Klugscheisser* had reacted with open suspicion. Well, his time was coming. Soon his usefulness would be at an end. Bormann believed in revenge.

A steel door clanked open far overhead, and a weak spray of daylight washed the upper walls of the tower. At last. Bormann clasped his hands behind his back, his impatience easing slightly.

Krebs, who had only an inkling of the dimensions of the scheme, would have to be told the rest, since he would have to keep the guns silent. Schedle, too, despite Bormann's new dislike for him. But Schedle would have to understand the full gravity of the situation if he was to be of use in selecting the first team. Should he tell others as well? He would have to check with the Führer. It would be much safer if the number could be kept down.

Two men—Heinrich Müller and Dr. Ludwig Stumpfegger—finally came into view. They supported a third man between them. The man in the middle was conscious, but only barely. His head lolled on his chest, and he murmured incoherently.

"What is wrong with him?" Bormann asked.

"Nothing," Dr. Stumpfegger said. "He's sedated. We thought it would be best to keep him that way until the final moment."

Bormann stepped forward and raised the man's chin, examining his face, his color, his general appearance. "Remarkable," he said.

"Is everything ready at this end?" Müller asked.

"Almost," Bormann said. "Let us take him to your surgery, Dr. Stumpfegger. No one will see him there."

They moved carefully into the cramped conference corridor of the Führerbunker, Bormann leading the way to make certain the corridor was empty, Müller and Stumpfegger following with the sedated man dragging between them, and slipped quickly into the doctor's small treatment room, just across the hall from the Führer's private quarters.

"Wait with him here," Bormann said. "I shall summon the Führer."

He hurried back through the conference corridor and up the circular stairway to the upper bunker. Yes, what an imprudent waste of time. Hitler was in the communal mess, lunching with Frau Junge, Frau Christian, and Fräulein

Manzialy. As he chatted with the women, his face, pasty white from too many sunless days in the underground bunker, was animated, almost cheerful, as in the old days. But his hands gave him away, trembling noticeably as he forked a bite of vegetable omelet, one of the soft foods which, given his vegetarian preferences and the bridgework that largely served him as teeth, he liked best to eat. The three women strained to match his attempts at buoyancy, but there was an unshakable aura of doom hanging over the room, spoiling their efforts. Bormann paused at the door until they looked up.

"Yes, what is it?" Hitler said irritably, obviously displeased at the interruption.

"A private word, if I may," Bormann said. "An important communiqué has arrived."

"Can't it wait?"

"No, my Führer. It's urgent."

Hitler grimaced and excused himself from the ladies, then limped wearily into the hallway. "What is it?" he said.

"He's here," Bormann whispered. "Müller and Dr. Stumpfegger just brought him."

"I don't want to think about that now," Hitler said.

"You must," Bormann insisted. "The resurrection of eternal Germany is at stake! But we can delay no longer. If it's to be done, it must be done this afternoon. You must prepare yourself."

"Eternal Germany!" Hitler snorted. "Do you think I care about Germany? Ingrates. The German people weren't worthy of me. We could have won, but for the cowardice of the German soul. I've been betrayed, Martin. At every step, I've been betrayed. Perhaps to die is the best thing after all."

Bormann hesitated, selecting his words carefully. "I understand the temptation, my Führer, experiencing it as I do myself. But there are larger commitments that must be honored. The world will recognize your greatness in time, but only if those of us who would otherwise die gladly at your side are permitted to preserve the broad spectrum of your thought and philosophy. We cannot allow your legacy to perish under Russian boot heels."

Hitler sighed. "Yes, all right. Take me to him."

Bormann breathed deeply in relief. As they started to the lower bunker, Bormann said, "You won't be sorry, my Führer. Everything is in readiness. It remains only for you to determine which of your successors is to be informed."

"I thought you preferred complete secrecy."

"I do, my Führer. But I would not presume to dictate to you. You might desire, for example, to enlighten Dr. Goebbels or Grand Admiral Dönitz. It is they who must deal with the Allies after your death. If you decide either is to know, I will make certain everything is explained later, after it is done."

They passed through the lower-lounge corridor, and Hitler said, "No, I'm sure you're right. If it is to be done, complete secrecy is always best."

"And Fräulein Braun?" Bormann inquired.

"Frau Hitler," Hitler corrected. "Have you made preparations for her?"

"No, my Führer."

"Then what is the point in telling her?"

"None, my Führer. Very well. Only those who must know to carry out the various stages of the program will be informed. And we have already arranged methods to protect the purity of each individual confidence."

They turned into the surgery. Gestapo chief Müller, seated on a straight-backed chair blocking Stumpfegger's inner room, rose quickly to bow. Bormann nodded at the door, and Müller opened it.

Hitler stepped inside, his blue-gray eyes sweeping from Dr. Stumpfegger to the man lying on the examination table. Hitler's hands shook, and he moved forward to look more closely at the semiconscious man. "Is this the one?" he asked.

"Yes, my Führer," Bormann said. "This is the man we call Rösselsprung."

Hitler's eyes burned brightly for an instant. Then he turned away. "Very well," he said. "I die this afternoon."

Erika's fingers dug into Bascom's shoulder. "This might be our chance," she whispered hoarsely, "while the guards are gone."

He marveled at the strength of her frantic grasp, but his eyes never left the concrete blockhouse below the window. "They aren't gone," he said. "They've pulled out of the garden for some reason, but I can still hear them in the building."

The spring sky was turning heavy, great gray clouds lumbering in from the north. The ground still sweated dampness from the rains of earlier days, and already it looked as though another storm was rolling in. A raw wind murmured through the shattered windows and the crevices of broken walls, chilling them both. Artillery shells drubbed the Tiergarten to the west, and the *plat-plat-plat* of small arms and the crumping sound of grenades continued to echo from the vicinity of the Reichstag, a half mile north.

Bascom's senses probed his window world with the alert patience of a timber wolf. The ears saw. The nostrils heard. Something was going on down there. A breath of hope had touched his mind when the guards withdrew from the garden shortly before noon, sent away by an SS captain who had come up from underground. But then, only a few minutes later, two men, one in a high-ranking Gestapo uniform and the other in Party black-and-brown, came into the garden from the new Chancellery building, supporting a semiconscious man between them. They had hurried across the wrecked garden, heads swinging warily as though to make sure they were alone, then had disappeared through the recessed doorway of the concrete blockhouse. They had not reappeared. Nor had the garden guards.

Foreboding stirred continuously in the pit of Bascom's stomach, going in waves, weaving around and through his nerve ends, like something alive. Why? What was all the stealthy activity about? Had the guards been dismissed

from the garden to keep them from seeing the three men?
If so, why hadn't the guards come back? He didn't know
what his senses were warning him about, but it reeked of
evil. Some new badness dwelled below, and all of Erika's
urging had been insufficient to make him withdraw from
this one lurking place until he could divine its meaning.

Erika's hand closed spastically on his shoulder again,
and he glanced at her pityingly. Her tawny hair hung in
stringy tangles. Her face, smudged with dirt, looked pale
with the strain of waiting through another endless day for
the nightfall which offered the preyed-upon their only hope
to escape a place so filled with predators. Yesterday, the
Russians. Today, the Germans. Yet the very strength of her
hand gave him comfort. Hungry, exhausted, the body could
somehow find stamina when it had to. She would need all
the stamina she could muster when darkness fell and the
time came to slip down the endless stairways.

"Don't worry," he told her. "I'll get us out of here.
We've made it this far, and we'll make it the rest of the
way."

He'd meant his words to be comforting, and he didn't
understand when she pulled away from him and hugged
her knees to her chest, her eyes as bleak as a rainy funeral.
"We could be gone already," she said. "There's no one in
the garden. Our way is clear."

He shook his head. "Even if we could make it to the
street, someone would spot us before we moved ten feet."

"You don't know that," she said. "You're making us
stay here." The tawny eyes studied him. "You've changed."

The animal senses that had augmented mere intellect in
Bascom's consciousness suddenly sharpened, focused, and
he examined the pale, troubled face before him with a
moment's suspicion. "Changed? In what way?"

"I don't know. You seem to be . . . relishing this. Ever
since last night . . . that Russian soldier—"

He felt his face empty of expression. Automatic response.
Hide the emotions that troubled him. He turned his eyes
back to the garden below, to the silent concrete blockhouse.
He became aware of a strange feeling of emptiness, vast

and total. The empty garden . . . ? No, it was personal, something to do with the Russian. Don't think about the Russian. Enjoying himself? How could she possibly understand?

A fresh gust of chill wind rippled through the ruined garden, and the timber wolf growing inside him roused again, repressing his demons, shushing his mind. At nightfall, the wolf whispered, he could quietly ambush and kill any SS guard who blocked their escape from the trap. Very quietly. He flexed his hands, feeling their own strength. If the time came to kill quietly this night, the wolf advised, he was well supplied with two natural weapons.

4

At three o'clock that afternoon, Adolf Hitler called his closest associates together in the lower level of the Führerbunker and solemnly bade them all farewell. The time had come, he told them, for him to end it. He shook hands with Dr. Goebbels, with Martin Bormann, with General Krebs. He spoke quietly to the three women who had shared his last luncheon only hours before. He embraced his personal servant, Major Heinz Linge, and told him to try to break out with the others after it was done. Then, as Eva cried and said good-by to the women, Hitler took his Waffen-SS adjutant, Colonel Otto Günsche, to one side and whispered urgently that he wanted his and Eva's bodies burned so the Russians wouldn't put them on exhibition in some wax museum. Bormann had arranged for the gasoline, Hitler said, and would supervise the burning, but Hitler wanted Günsche to help.

Then, with farewells completed, Hitler and Eva retired to his personal quarters in the bunker and closed the door. Silently, the assemblage broke up. Everyone left except Bormann, Günsche, and Linge. Bormann took a seat opposite the closed door and waited, fidgeting noticeably. Günsche and Linge waited in the anteroom.

Fifteen minutes passed before they heard the sound of

a shot. Bormann jerked off the bench with a start, then
rushed to the door, with Günsche and Linge right behind
him. Bormann threw the door open. The smell of gun
powder clung to the air, mixed with the sharp, bitter tang
of cyanide. On the far side of the cramped sitting room,
sprawled across a sofa, lay two bodies. Hitler's black
trousers and field-gray military jacket were flecked with
blood. A 7.65mm Walther pistol lay inches from out-
stretched fingers. Eva, her head back against the sofa
cushions, stared blankly at the ceiling, her nostrils oddly
discolored by cyanide poisoning. A flower vase, apparently
knocked over during the last convulsive moments of death,
had soaked her dress with water.

Bormann waited until he felt Linge and Günsche at his
shoulder, each straining to look into the room, then told
them to wait and hurried to the sofa to check for a pulse.
As Linge and Günsche lingered at the door, Bormann
looked up and said, "The chief is dead." He picked up a
gray Army blanket from the floor and somberly spread it
across the body.

Moments later, others appeared at the doorway. The
first was Lieutenant Colonel Erich Kempka, Hitler's private
chauffeur, who had just arrived from his command post at
the Brandenburg Gate with five cans of gasoline. "What's
happened?" he asked. Günsche answered him by pointing
his finger into his mouth like a pistol and cocking the
thumb. Then came Goebbels, shaken, and General Burgdorf. And finally, Dr. Stumpfegger.

Stumpfegger moved past Bormann and lifted the blanket
slightly to check for signs of life. Stumpfegger shook his
head. He dropped the blanket and stepped over to Eva.
Another shake of the head.

"Is the gasoline ready?" Bormann asked Kempka.

"Waiting in the garden," Kempka said in a choked voice.
"Two hundred liters. It was all I could scrape up."

Bormann glanced at Goebbels, leaning against the doorway, seemingly on the verge of collapse, and said, "His
orders were that his body be burned. Shall we proceed?"

Goebbels nodded assent, then bowed his head.

Bormann gestured to Linge and Dr. Stumpfegger, who gathered up the blanket-covered body and carried it gently toward the door. Bormann scooped up Eva and started to follow, but Kempka stood in his path and silently took her from him. Bormann gave her up without argument.

As the small funeral party headed for the emergency exit tower at the rear of the Führerbunker and the four-flight climb to the garden level, Bormann took a last look at the room in which the bodies had been found. He sighed, then closed the door and slouched after the others.

5

The Wolf's heightened senses knew before Bascom's eyes saw the people emerge. Down below. Coming into the wrecked garden. Bascom instantly drew back slightly into the shadows.

At his movement, Erika raised her head from the crook of her elbow. "I told you we should have left while the guards were away," she said in an accusatory tone. "They're back. Aren't they?"

"Shh," he said. He ignored the tone. In her fatigue, she probably didn't know she'd used it. "There are people coming out of the blockhouse."

She crawled to the windowsill, and he touched her shoulder to keep her from showing herself. Men in uniform struggled from the blockhouse exit, carrying bundles. Bursting shells rumbled in the background. Gray clouds skidded slowly overhead.

Two men laid one of the bundles in a shallow depression about fifteen feet from the blockhouse doorway. A blanket-covered body. A man. The face was covered, but Bascom and Erika could see black trouser legs and low-cut black shoes.

"What are they doing?" she whispered.

"I don't know yet."

Another man brought the body of a woman and laid her in the sandy depression next to the blanketed corpse. She was a pretty woman, blond, wearing a dark dress and cork-soled shoes. The wind blew up her skirt, exposing her garters.

Something about the woman was familiar, and Bascom probed futilely for understanding as the three men picked up heavy gasoline cans and drenched the two bodies, splashing hurriedly.

"They're going to burn them!" Erika said. "That's terrible!"

"Shh."

Three more men—a tall Waffen-SS officer, a chubby man in a brown uniform with gold trim, and a slight, dark man with a clubfoot—stepped into the open from the shelter of the blockhouse and drew near the shallow trench as the gasoline kept pouring.

"That's Hinkefuss!" Erika said, nodding at the man with the clubfoot.

"Who?"

"I'm sorry. Reichminister Goebbels. We call him Hinkefuss, the gimp."

"Do you recognize any of the others?"

She looked them over one by one, then shook her head. "The man in the brown uniform looks familiar. I think I've seen him at public functions, but always in the background."

A shell fluttered overhead and slammed into Hermann Göring Strasse, less than a hundred yards away. Startled, the men abandoned the gas cans, and all six quickly drew back to the safety of the blockhouse doorway. They stayed there a few moments, then two of the younger men darted back into the open and finished shaking the gasoline into the trench. By the time they finished, the two bodies were so thoroughly soaked that the woman's dress and the man's blanket hung heavily about them and not even the wind could stir them.

"A Viking funeral," Bascom murmured.

"What?" Erika whispered.

"It's like a Viking funeral. The man must be someone important. Hitler, even."

Erika inhaled sharply. "He can't die! His life is charmed. Besides, he promised to die at the front, leading troops."

The wolf peered at her curiously, but Bascom told the animal to mind its own business. "How else could you explain the presence of someone as important as Goebbels?" Bascom said.

One of the men stooped to soak a rag in the gasoline-filled pit and backed out of the wind to light it. As soon as the rag began to blaze, he tossed it toward the pit. An instant before it landed, recognition came to Bascom, and he strained forward. Then flames whooshed up in a sudden fireball, enveloping the two bodies.

While flames crackled and bodies burned, the six men by the blockhouse raised their arms in a solemn Nazi salute. They held it for several moments, then more shells screeched overhead, and one thundered to ground in the far corner of the garden. The men quickly dropped their arms and withdrew to the blockhouse, leaving only two of their party behind to keep watch.

The stench of burning bodies—an oily, bacon-sweet smell—rose on a dark column of smoke and blew past the window. Erika gagged and turned away. The corpses blackened and shriveled, visible only when the gusting wind parted the bright orange flames. Blowing strongly, the wind whipped the smoke back and forth, swirling it past the ventilation silo. It would be sucked into the bunker air system, Bascom knew, filling the underground ducts with the choking odors of burning flesh. No one below ground would be able to escape it.

The pit was not allowed to burn out. Eventually SS guards showed up with more gasoline, and the two men by the blockhouse kept feeding the flames. It became a *danse macabre.* They huddled in the recessed doorway while shells and shrapnel whistled overhead, then when the flames began to settle they would step quickly into the open and splash more gasoline into the ditch and leap back as the flames surged up again. They kept the fire going for almost

three hours. Twilight was creeping into the garden before
they finally let the fire die down and retreated to the
bunker.

The timber wolf inspected the gathering gray light with
approval, but the human cerebral processes in Bascom
knew more than the wolf did this time. That blackened
corpse that had once been a pretty blond woman was
known to him. Recognition had come like the rolling fireball that followed it. In the hours while he kept sentry
over the burning bodies, he had studied the blankly staring
face in his mind's eye, comparing it to a photograph he
had been shown so long ago—could it really be only a
couple of weeks?—when he was briefed for his one fling
at a field assignment, a meeting with SS Gruppenführer
Hermann Fegelein.

A gay photograph. A smiling Fegelein holding a champagne glass. Two figures in the nightmare SS uniforms, but
for the moment the photograph was taken wielding not
weapons but violins. A wedding cake on a table. And two
fair-haired, pretty women laughing beside Fegelein, because something about the violinists' tune must have been
funny. A candid shot, taken at the wedding reception for
Fegelein and one of the women, Gretl Braun, sister of the
other woman, Eva Braun, whose importance Hitler had
tried so hard to keep secret, but whom intelligence reports
identified as Hitler's longtime mistress.

That was the face he had seen below, in the twinkling
before it disappeared behind a sheet of flame. And beside
whom would Eva Braun's body have been burned? The
Chancellery janitor? Despite Erika's shocked, knee-jerk disbelief that Germany's mythical leader could have died, Bascom had the eerie feeling that he had been an unwilling
eyewitness to a long-anticipated historical event.

Hitler, dead? If Bascom was right, so much for the
wasteful night when he, Formoy, and all the others crept
toward this very building. Hitler would now never fall into
the hands of the Russians.

And if Bascom was right, the wolf's itch to slink toward
the gathering twilight was premature. Man's instincts, if

not the animal's inside him, told him something else was going to happen. The wolf would have to wait.

6

Bormann said, "Captain Schedle, you will dismiss all duty guards at ten o'clock and send them to the guard bunker, ostensibly to prepare their own breakout plans. Herr Müller will lead the escort patrol from the building ten minutes later." Bormann spoke swiftly, with an air of barely suppressed tension. "You have selected the men for the patrol, Captain?"

Schedle, his spirit burdened by secret knowledge, nodded. "Three men. Completely trustworthy. They will meet us here in an hour. I've told them nothing so far."

"Naturally," Bormann said. "Now, gentlemen, to coordinate our movements. Dr. Stumpfegger and I will remain here in the Führerbunker. It is our duty to keep the others occupied. We shall do that by organizing a second planning session this evening to consider a general breakout for, say, tomorrow night. I intend to propose Brigadeführer Möhnke as breakout leader and to invite all men who are able to walk, as well as any of the women who wish it, to make the attempt. I think I can guarantee a lively discussion which will last for some hours. Plenty of time for Herr Müller and his party to leave unnoticed."

Schedle glanced at Müller, sitting so emotionlessly on his left. He had to wonder when the Gestapo chief had stolen into the bunker. Schedle hadn't seen the man arrive, nor had any of Schedle's guards reported Müller's arrival. Perhaps that was the reason for Bormann's earlier order to clear the garden.

"To conclude," Bormann said, "General Krebs has sought a ceasefire in order to discuss armistice terms with the Soviet commander. Such an important discussion can be expected to be lengthy. He will closet himself with the Soviet commander for as long as he can stretch it out."

Müller spoke. "Where is Krebs?"

An impatient grimace from Bormann. "In a meeting with Dr. Goebbels and General Burgdorf. Always meetings, while the urgent things are left to dangle. He will be quit of them shortly. As for Dr. Goebbels, it is, of course, mandatory that none of you drops the slightest hint of our mission to anyone outside this room. Dr. Goebbels has been told of the request for a cease-fire, but he has not been acquainted with any other details. The Führer's orders quite naturally supersede any successor's. You will show the greatest respect to Dr. Goebbels, and treat him as Chancellor of the Reich, which by the terms of the Führer's last will and testament he now is. But you will tell him nothing of our obligations. Is that understood?"

The three men—Stumpfegger, Schedle, and Müller—nodded.

"Very well. Captain Schedle, you will please go now to the conference lounge to wait for General Krebs. Bring him to me the moment he is available. I suggest the rest of us make haste to prepare for the events of the evening. We may not all be together again in one room. Gentlemen, good luck."

Schedle hesitated. Stumpfegger pushed back his chair and went to his surgery. Bormann and Müller apparently had other things to discuss, for they waited silently until Schedle got up to leave, then put their heads together and began to whisper.

Schedle moved through the gloomy outer rooms of the Führerbunker, noting the despairing faces of people who had only recently heard about the deaths in the Führer's personal quarters and the makeshift funeral pyre in the garden above. It was as if their world had suddenly ended. Farther along, a few less respectful underlings sat drinking from a bottle of cognac. Two were smoking, something that had always been forbidden by Hitler. Schedle looked away.

Goebbels' meeting with General Burgdorf and General Krebs was just breaking up when Schedle reached the conference lounge. A handful of frightened adjutants shuffled papers while Goebbels limped into the hallway, his face gaunt, deep circles below his dark eyes. Burgdorf followed him. Then came Krebs, monocle screwed into his right eye, bearing stiff. Schedle raised a finger to catch Krebs' attention, then hung back until the three men parted.

"Yes, Captain?" Krebs said. He sounded dispirited.

"Reichsleiter Bormann would like to speak to you," Schedle said. "I am to take you to him."

"Probably wondering if the Soviets have agreed to the cease-fire," Krebs said wearily. He fell in beside Schedle, walking along the corridor. "On that point he can rest his mind. The Soviets seemed jubilant over the prospect of ending the battle quickly. The guns will fall silent in approximately one hour. But only in this sector, I fear. And I don't know for how long."

"You'll go alone?" Schedle asked.

"No. I will be accompanied by an interpreter and two guides. I understand I am to be taken to General Chuikov of the Eighth Guards Army."

"Will you be able to keep him busy long enough for safety?"

Krebs looked at Schedle silently, then said, "You are aware of the true purpose of this negotiating session, then?"

"Yes, my General. Reichsleiter Bormann explained it to me less than an hour ago."

"What do you think of it, Captain?"

Schedle shook his head sadly. "It wasn't what I expected."

"Nor I," Krebs said.

Schedle shrugged. "If you'll pardon my saying so, I feel . . . dishonored. Do you know what I mean?"

"I know, and I pardon it," Krebs said. "But I wouldn't repeat it to anyone else if I were you. We are soldiers and must do as bidden. Honor must come later."

"Yes, sir. I'll keep that in mind."

Jackboots slapped against the stairs. Shouted orders echoed through the empty Chancellery corridors. Fool, the wolf said, I told you not to wait. Now it's too late. They're going to search the building.

Bascom was baffled by the sounds drifting up from below. He had been so certain somehow that the garden was the center, the secret core, the omen that would lead them to their deliverance. Could the wolf be right? But the shouted orders became more distinct as the boots climbed higher in the building. Withdraw! They were being told to withdraw!

"What is it?" Erika whispered.

He put a forefinger to his lips, listening. The boots reached the landing below them, and the voice called again, summoning the guards. Voices responded from the front of the building and came back through the corridor. They reached the stairs and held a brief muffled conversation, then passed downward.

"They're pulling out," Bascom whispered in wonder. The window tugged irresistibly, and he peered warily down at the garden. Dark. Empty. Abandoned. He scanned the horizon. A red glow from the north, where fires burned around the Reichstag. More flames along the southern edge of Moabit and the buildings along the Spree. Small-arms fire still rattled sporadically, but the big guns were strangely subdued. A few rounds ripped at the western end of the Tiergarten, along the Tirpitz embankment and the Bendlerstrasse military compound. More guns pounded the Maikaefer Barracks north of the Stettiner Station. But quiet, ominous quiet, everywhere else.

"Maybe it's over," Erika said. "Maybe we've surrendered." Her voice sounded both melancholy and relieved.

"I don't think so," Bascom said. "They're still fighting up around the Reichstag. And I see gun flashes in the distance. Lots of them."

"But they aren't shooting here," she insisted. "And the guards seem to be leaving their posts. Surely that must mean something."

Bascom cast a last, reluctant look out the window. "It means now is probably our best chance to get out of the building." She rose eagerly, too eagerly, and he cautioned, "We can't be sure they're all gone, so watch your step. Take it slow. Don't make any noise."

Only a rustle, a scrape, ratlike sounds, accompanied their progress over dislodged beams and loose mortar as they made their way through the darkness, first to the stairwell, then down the stairs, a flight at a time, pausing frequently to listen. They heard nothing but the low rumble of distant guns. No voices, no movement. Apparently they were alone in the building. With each step they breathed easier.

But it was too good to last. With only one more flight of stairs and a short corridor standing between them and the refuge of the street, Bascom heard movement, a soft, scraping noise like their own, whispering through the silence. He gripped Erika's wrist. They stopped dead still, listening. A heavy door swung open somewhere in the garden, hinges grating.

Erika heard it, too. "They're coming back," she whispered urgently. "Hide!"

They retreated from the stairs and headed quickly to the rear of the building. The gray, red-tinged outline of a double window beckoned Bascom back to a view of his garden.

There. By the blockhouse, only a few feet below. Three SS men, standing outside the recessed entrance, scanning the area, machine pistols visible in the faint glow of firelight. One of the SS men turned to the blockhouse and waved an all-clear. Two figures in leather greatcoats stepped into the open.

Bascom studied the two men with frozen concentration as they followed their SS escorts quickly across the rough ground toward an entrance on the floor below. There was something familiar about them both. Though the greatcoats hid their clothing and disguised their builds, Bascom was certain they were two of the three men he had seen entering the blockhouse much earlier in the day. One was almost certainly the high-ranking Gestapo officer. Same high-peaked black cap. Same height. Same thin chest. Same nervous flick of the head, searching the shadows. The other man, wearing a slouch hat low over the forehead, was about the same size and weight of the semiconscious man who had entered with the Gestapo officer. He was conscious now, walking mainly under his own power, but he still wobbled a bit, as though none too steady on his feet.

The small party reached the Chancellery wall directly below his window. After a moment of silence, a latch loosened, and a door creaked open. The men slipped out of sight, and footsteps moved inward, clicking along the lower corridor.

At that moment, the way to escape came clear both to Bascom and the watchful, patient timber wolf that looked through his eyes. "Come on," Bascom whispered to Erika, "we're going to follow them."

She held back, uncertain, but he urged her silently on to the stairwell. Flashlight beams played along the floor below them, and they stood like statues behind the banister. The men below picked their way through the debris-filled corridor, not speaking, and headed purposefully toward the front of the building. At the last instant, they veered out of the corridor and entered one of the smaller rooms near the front wall.

In dead silence, Bascom prodded Erika halfway down the stairs. He could see the glow of flashlights through an open office door, and shadows on the wall. One of the shadows bent double and disappeared. Then another. The flashlights blinked off.

"They're going through the wall," Bascom whispered exultantly. "There must be a breach in there, like the one we used to get in. Come, hurry. They're going to lead us out of here."

Erika jerked her hand loose from his grasp. "But you

don't know where they're going," she objected. "What if they're on their way to a military command post?"

He shook his head. "No, love. Rats from a sinking ship, that's what we've got ahead of us. Some Nazi bigwigs scuttling for safety. You and I are going to slink and scuttle right behind them."

The moment the words were out he felt her stiffen. Not very tactful, that part about rats. She followed him wordlessly to the room where the five men had disappeared. Sure enough, a wide gap in the lower wall emptied out into the street. Through it Bascom espied their quarry picking a path across the Wilhelmplatz. The three SS escorts, machine pistols poised, formed an advance guard. They were making for the burned-out hulk of the Hotel Kaiserhof. Shell bursts flickered in the distance, freeze-framing them in awkward positions, like a malfunctioning strobe light.

"Let them go," Erika said. "We're on the street now. We can find our own way."

He hesitated, reluctant to lose sight of them. Besides, neither wolf nor man knew which way to go. South was out. The Russians had crossed the Landwehr Canal two days before. East was out, too. They'd come from the east last night, and the area was already thick with Russians. North? West? Sounds of battle raged in both directions. But the scurrying figures in the far darkness surely had a plan. "We're better off following them," he said. "You can bet they've figured out the best way to get clear of here."

"What if they see us?" Erika said.

"We'll keep our distance."

They broke into the open and ran softly, zigzagging through the darkness. Sliding and scrabbling over loose stones. Circling the larger obstructions. The five men from the Chancellery garden were a good fifty yards ahead, sometimes in view, sometimes hidden behind the massive clutter of collapsed walls. An overturned bus loomed up near the far curb. Bascom angled toward it, Erika on his heels. They ducked behind the bus, and Erika flattened herself against a bent drive shaft on the exposed underbelly.

"They didn't see us," she assured him giddily. "I watched. No one turned around."

But when they moved cautiously around the edge of the toppled bus, the men had disappeared. Bascom stopped, waiting for the wolf to take over. The great vacant ghost of the Kaiserhof towered above an empty street, and the wolf was silent.

"I thought they were headed for the hotel," he whispered.

"They wouldn't have gone inside. The walls are weak. It's too dangerous. Perhaps they went into the subway."

"There's an underground station near here?"

"Yes, near the hotel. It runs east and west, but the cars haven't worked for days."

"Good Lord," he said. "Of course. They can walk at will down there, without exposing themselves. Let's move it."

They hurried across the last remaining yards to the hotel, and Erika pointed out a bent U-bahn sign, standing a lonely guard above a flight of stairs that dipped below street level. Carefully, they started down.

The station was narrow and smelled of excrement. Some Berlin subway stations had been turned into shelters, though they were generally too close to the surface to offer much protection. This one, however, deep in the heart of the government district, was empty. A few soldiers and Volkssturm militiamen might have taken temporary shelter, which would explain the stench, but they were long since gone.

The edge of the platform was as black as the inside of a sealed metal box, a darkness so tangible that Bascom could almost feel it. His hand touched a supporting pillar, and he felt for the drop-off with his foot, then leaned out to peer both ways. The western end of the tunnel was even blacker than the station platform, if that was possible. But in the other direction, perhaps fifty or sixty yards along the tracks, faint flashlight beams wavered on the dark tunnel walls, silhouetting walking figures. They were headed east.

"What lies that way?" Bascom asked.

"The Friedrichstrasse line," she said. "There's another subway station about half a kilometer from here. They can go north or south along the Friedrichstrasse, or continue east to the Spittel Market."

He slid down to track level, half afraid she would refuse to follow, but she needed no urging. They trailed the flashlights eastward. The darkness was so incredibly intense that they had to pick their way by feel and sound. The flashlight beams were too far ahead to be of help, and they stumbled frequently until they began to catch on to the pattern of ties.

As they neared the Friedrichstrasse link, the flashlights veered off to the north-south line. Bascom forced himself to pick up the pace, trying not to lose too much ground. At the interlap, they climbed a set of stairs to get to the Friedrichstrasse tracks. The lights reappeared to the north. The distance had widened. Perhaps seventy or eighty yards now.

They hurried recklessly in an attempt to close the distance. In some places the tunnel was only nine or ten feet below ground, and direct artillery hits had smashed through the ceiling, leaving jagged holes through which faint surface firelight glowed. It illuminated the way, but at the same time worried Bascom, for fear the men ahead might look back. He found himself straining at each breach to regain the darkness. Slowly, the distance narrowed. To sixty-five yards. To sixty.

Then, quite suddenly, the gap closed. Bascom was trying to make out the ties beneath his feet, when Erika clawed at his arm. The men were standing absolutely still, checking their watches in the glow of the flashlights. They couldn't have been more than twenty yards ahead.

With one impulse, Bascom and Erika hugged the side of the tunnel. Bascom could hear voices, whispering. The voices were too low to catch in detail. Murmur, murmur. They, murmur, the time, one voice said. Murmur too early. Murmur, murmur had misjudged. The next murmur was set for 2400 hours, and they were several murmur short of that. Should they murmur here, underground, or go ahead and murmur, murmur?

A minute passed as Bascom and Erika breathed shallow-ly, watching the men take counsel. Another minute. Then, abruptly, the men started moving again along the tracks. As the distance widened, Bascom filled his lungs with air. "Close," he whispered. "Where are we?"

"I'm not sure," Erika whispered shakily. "Near the Unter den Linden station, I think."

The flashlights slowed again after a few hundred yards, and this time Bascom and Erika slowed with them. Long before a platform came into view, vaguely lit with kerosene light, the wolf's senses told Bascom that people were ahead. The wolf smelled fresh sweat and vomit, as well as urine and feces, and wrinkled its nose. As they neared the station, Bascom made out people on the platform, bundled together, crowding almost every inch of available space, some sleep-ing, some talking fitfully and fearfully, disturbing the slum-ber of their neighbors.

The five furtive men from the Chancellery put their heads together briefly, then the SS escorts boldly climbed up on the platform. They pushed people aside, breaking a path for the two greatcoated men. The German civilians moved out of the way without complaint. SS uniforms sig-naled authority to them, and authority was not to be de-nied. To Bascom's surprise, the men threaded their way up toward the street level.

Was this the end of their journey? Surely not. But why leave the safety of the subway? Bascom hurriedly assessed what he had been able to make out of the pattern of the battle. The German-held corridor still stretched from east to west, but the north-south limits had been squeezed se-verely inward. That must be the reason. The men were leaving the underground tunnels because if they went much farther, they might run into Russian soldiers instead of German civilians.

"End of the line," he told Erika. "If we go up here, will we be far from that church where you left the others?"

A weary shrug was his only answer.

"Well, we might as well find out," he said. They waited, counting off seconds to give the men time to ascend the subway stairs and go on to wherever they were headed. When he judged it safe, they approached the platform to pick their own way through the crowded jumble of people sheltering there.

Sleeping bodies also huddled on the lower stairs, and Bascom thought he'd never smelled anything as sweet as the smoky air when they finally reached ground level. The stairs brought them into the open several hundred yards east of the Brandenburg Gate. The area had taken severe punishment since the last time Bascom had seen it. The Gate itself, standing bleakly in the distance, looked badly mauled. Only a few hundred meters north of the Gate, barred from view by burning, barricaded buildings, the Reichstag reverberated with the muffled sounds of a pitched battle inside. Eerie, to think that the Russians had penetrated that close.

Bascom waited a moment to allow Erika to get her bearings, then said, "Where is the church from here?"

"I'm not sure," she said. "I think we—" Her eyes widened, and she tugged Bascom back down into the shadows of the subway stairs. "They're still here!" she whispered. "Look!"

The five men from the Chancellery stood in a cul-de-sac of sandbags, just a few yards from the subway entrance, fidgeting, as though marking time. One of the men seemed to check his watch. He spoke, then pointed to the north, in the direction of the Lehrter Station, across the Spree. Moments later, far in the distance, a rattle of rifle fire clattered in the night. No more than fifty or a hundred rifles, but it sounded like a small-scale counterattack directed at the Moltke Bridge. As though on cue, an air-cooled diesel engine cranked up somewhere to the west, and an eight-wheeled Puma armored car chugged and popped slowly up the street from the direction of the Brandenburg Gate, picking its way through the debris, jolting from side to side as it hit the larger stones.

The three SS men trotted out into the firelit street and

signaled to the Puma. It veered toward them and came on slowly. When it was within a block and a half of them, a star shell from a Russian Very pistol burst above the buildings to the north, bathing the area of the counterattack. The sky lit up like daylight. The armored car yanked to a stop, its green-and-yellow camouflage markings glistening in the cold, wavering light. The three SS men, unnerved, flattened themselves on the pavement.

Bascom was also startled by the light, but not nearly so startled as when he swung his gaze to the two men in great-coats, waiting among the sandbags. They had turned their faces upward to stare at the hissing Russian flare. Though the light was at least a quarter mile distant, their features stood out clearly. One, as Bascom had suspected, was the same high-ranking Gestapo officer he had seen enter the Chancellery garden at midday. The other, face frozen in icy calm, eyes vivid and alert beneath the downturned brim of the slouch hat, was as familiar to him as his own reflection in a shaving mirror.

Shaving mirror. Odd that Bascom's mind should settle on that. The man's mustache was gone, to be sure—shaved off, no doubt, before the small party left the Chancellery. But he was still recognizable, even without it. The eyes gave him away. Those obsessed, intense eyes, pinned on a sputtering star shell as it sank slowly behind the ridge of blasted buildings.

Bascom felt his blood turn hot—for there, standing not forty feet away, calmly gazing at the midnight sky in the middle of a burning, dying city, was Adolf Hitler.

14

Mit unserem Führer zum Sieg!

"With our Führer toward Victory!"

—slogan scrawled on Berlin wall

1

Bascom stood rooted to the subway steps as the small Chancellery party picked its way hurriedly down the broken street toward the waiting armored car. A hatch popped open forward of the Puma's camouflaged gun turret, and a smoke-grimed face called, "Hurry!" Bascom wavered for another second, then slipped the Walther P-38 from beneath his sweater and released the safety. He drew back the slide, cocking it.

"What are you doing?" Erika gasped.

"What I was sent here to do," Bascom said. "I've got to stop him."

She grabbed his arm. "You'll attack an armed party by yourself? You'll throw your life away? For what? They have nothing to do with you."

He shook free of her. "You saw his face. You know who it was."

"What about your friend? We have a chance now. We're close. So close."

Duty tugged against duty, but only momentarily. He knew deep in his bones what Formoy would have done, and he knew he would never have to ask Formoy for forgiveness. "This is more important."

The five men were halfway to the Puma, scrabbling across a rocky peninsula that had once been the front wall of a small neighborhood theater. Two of the SS escorts shouldered their Schmeissers to help the greatcoated men over the top.

Bascom slipped quickly after them, keeping to the shadows. Erika stumbled along beside him. "I know what you are thinking," she stammered. "But you are wrong. He wouldn't leave us. Not like this. He promised to stay with us to the end. It was only someone who looked like him."

Bascom put out an arm to stop her. She was talking too loudly. Her feet, carelessly placed, made too much noise. "You still don't know, do you? Erika, he's not the saint you think he is, not the great builder, not the tireless warrior. He's wrecked Germany, and now that there's nothing left, he's running out on you. Face it."

"I don't believe you."

"I don't care what you believe," he said. He pushed her, not gently, back toward the subway. "Just stay out of my hair and let me do what I have to."

She didn't go, but there was no time to worry about that. The way was clear now, and the five men dashed across the intervening yards separating them from the armored car. A panel clanged open on the side, and one of the Puma crewmen jumped out, beckoning them onward. Bascom leaned against a rubble heap and leveled the pistol. He gripped the butt in both hands and held his breath. The figure in the slouch hat was almost to the idling Puma. Bascom laid the front sight between the man's shoulder blades and waited for him to turn broadside.

"No," Erika said. "I care for you. I really do. But it's *my* country. You have to understand." She stooped and picked up a large paving stone. She held it high for a moment while he stared blankly at her, then let it drop harmlessly at her feet. She backed away.

The pistol sight wavered, but only for an instant. The man in the slouch hat was bending over, about to crawl through the open panel. It had to be now.

But, abruptly, Erika appeared in front of his rubble pile, running. Her arms waved wildly. "Look out!" she shouted. "He's after you! He's going to—"

The men by the Puma spun around. One of the SS men snapped up his Schmeisser and opened fire. The burst caught her across the waist, and she dropped like the paving stone. The man in the slouch hat looked at the crumpled body with complete lack of interest, then turned and climbed into the armored car.

Bascom, confounded with shock, squeezed off three quick shots. But he wasn't even close. One slug kicked up dust at their feet, the other two pinged noisily off the steel sides of the Puma. He cursed the hand that he now saw was trembling, and he tried to steady it.

The second greatcoated man, suddenly aware of his presence, scrambled for the open panel. The SS man who had opened fire on Erika dropped to his knee and sprayed the darkness. Bascom ducked involuntarily, flinching as slugs whistled all around his rubble pile, then leveled the pistol and fired again. The SS man whirled against the side of the armored car. A red spot, the size of a quarter and growing, spread above his right knee. He gripped the leg and hobbled to the open panel, through which the last of his companions had just vanished, and tried to pull himself inside. Bascom aimed carefully and fired again, catching him in the small of the back. The SS man jerked and slid to the ground. The panel swung free for an instant; then a hand reached out and clanged it shut.

Though it was useless, Bascom kept firing until his clip was empty. Bullets pinged and whined off the armored hide of the Puma as the driver rammed it in reverse and jockeyed to turn it around. One of the heavy tires lurched over the fallen SS man, and the big vehicle rumbled off to the west, weaving slowly through a maze of obstructions.

Bascom rushed to Erika. She was lying half doubled on her face beside a broken street sign, amid a widening pool of blood. He picked her up and rolled her back into his arms. Fires burned brightly to the north, and he could see a facial abrasion where her cheek had hit the stones, and a red drool from the corner of her mouth. She was still breathing. Her eyelids flickered open, and she gazed through him, not seeing.

"He . . . just . . . looked at me," she said. "I might as . . . well have been . . . a piece of . . . meat."

"Shh. Be still, darling."

"I can't breathe," she said. "Dig me . . . out. Please." She sighed. Her golden eyes glazed in the wavering fire-light and turned muddy, darker somehow, like wet beach sand.

"Erika?"

But she wasn't breathing anymore. He looked beyond her, at the armored car creeping slowly to the west. On these wrecked streets it couldn't be making more than three or four miles an hour, if that much. And there would be dead ends, streets jammed with collapsed buildings, back-ing up, looking for clearer routes.

A man could catch it if he tried.

He cradled Erika to his chest, rocking, "Don't worry," he said. "Don't worry."

Then he laid her back among the stones and started after the armored car.

2

Colonel General Vasili I. Chuikov, commander of the So-viet Eighth Guards Army, glanced at his watch when his men ushered the Germans before the broad desk he had chosen for himself in a building just north of the Landwehr Canal. There were three of them: a tall general with a monocle and deep scars on the side of the face, a young colonel with straight hair and shiny lips, and an interpreter. It was 0300 hours on the morning of May 1, 1945—per-haps a moment that would go down in history.

The German general greeted Chuikov with a Nazi salute. He introduced himself with stiff formality as General Hans Krebs, chief of general staff of the OKH, then handed over his service book to authenticate his identity. Chuikov, a good-natured officer who knew victory was at his finger-tips, decided to overlook the inappropriate Nazi greeting. He welcomed Krebs politely, if a bit coolly.

Chuikov took his time studying the service book. He knew the Germans had been shunted from one Soviet command post to another before being brought here, and that they were undoubtedly tired and frustrated. But he wanted them that way. So he allowed them to shift from foot to foot while he slowly read and reread every entry. When he felt they were nearing the end of their patience, he handed the book back to the general. "You may proceed," he said.

The general came right to the point. "I have come to speak of exceptionally secret matters," he said. "First, I wish to inform you that our Führer, Adolf Hitler, passed from this life yesterday afternoon at the Imperial Chancellery. He died by his own hand at 1500 hours. His body was burned in the Chancellery garden."

Chuikov was surprised at the news, but he kept his face bland. He had determined in advance that he would not allow himself to be taken off guard by anything this German officer might have to say, so he looked up calmly and said, "Yes, we know this."

The German general seemed disturbed by Chuikov's response, but he covered quickly by removing a sheet of paper from his breast pocket and saying, "I have a communication from our new Chancellor, Joseph Goebbels. Will you permit me to read it?"

Chuikov nodded.

The general adjusted his monocle. " 'To the commander of the Soviet Armies,' " he read. " 'We wish to inform you that today, 30 April, at three-thirty in the afternoon, the Führer voluntarily quitted this life. On the basis of his legal right as head of the German Government, the Führer in his testament has transmitted all powers to Admiral Dönitz, to myself, and to Martin Bormann. I am empowered by Bormann to establish contact with the leader of the Soviet forces. This contact is essential for peace talks between our two powers. Signed, Goebbels.' "

Chuikov listened closely to the translator's version, then said, "Does this refer only to Berlin, or to the whole of Germany?"

"I speak in the name of the entire German Army," the general said.

Chuikov nodded. "I see. And are we talking about surrender, or a negotiated peace?"

"If you will permit us to bring together our new government, appointed by the Führer in his will," the German general said, "then we can decide the question of peace to our mutual advantage."

"You wish a prolongation and enlargement of the cease-fire we have granted you, then?"

"Yes, a temporary cessation of all hostilities, for the purpose of enabling us to discuss your peace terms. And we ask your help in arranging an immediate meeting of our new government, here in Berlin."

It was time to remind them who was the victor. "Why should we agree to a cessation of hostilities?" Chuikov said. "Why should we engage in peace talks, when your troops are surrendering of their own accord?"

The German's face stiffened. "What?" he said. "Where?"

"Everywhere," Chuikov said. He waved his hand broadly. "Our men are advancing. Yours are surrendering. Do you deny this?"

"Perhaps in some isolated cases," the general said lamely.

Chuikov picked up a field telephone and said, "Get me Marshal Zhukov. And prepare tea for our visitors, will you? We may be here for a long time." He put his hand over the mouthpiece and said, "I will relay your proposal, General, but I believe I can tell you in advance what our position will be: unconditional surrender. Unless you are prepared to surrender immediately and unconditionally, the destruction will continue."

The German general raised his eyes bleakly and shuddered.

3

The armored car gained on him. It wasn't that the car moved any faster than he expected. If anything, it moved slower. For the first hour, he kept it in sight, never more than two or three blocks ahead, weaving through flattened houses, creeping across intersections, worming its way westward.

But Bascom made even slower time. The big Russian guns were still largely silent, but sharpshooters, both Russian and German, took potshots at anything that moved in the open streets. The armored car was largely immune to their lethal sting, but he saw a small band of civilians, six women and a pair of elderly men who were trying to get through to the west end of the corridor, shot to pieces before his eyes in the middle of a small avenue north of the East-West Axis. Most of the shots came from the Russian side of the Spree, but even after the first two women dropped and the others scattered, more shots peppered them from nearby German-held buildings, where sleepless German infantrymen saw ghosts in every running form.

So Bascom sought the darkness, moving from shadow to shadow, hedgehopping through gardens and courtyards. The Puma relentlessly pulled ahead. He caught glimpses of it for the next two hours, always a block or so farther along than the last time, creeping onward. When the occasional sharpshooters' bullets richocheted off its steel sides, it would spurt ahead, driving recklessly through the deeply gouged streets until the sharpshooters fell behind, then slowing again to seek the safest possible route.

After a while, he lost sight of it entirely. No matter how hard he tried, it was always just a little too far ahead, too many blocks beyond, for him to catch up. Fatigue finally forced him to stop for a rest.

He sank to his knees in a small courtyard and leaned back against a canted bird bath. His heart pounded in his chest. His lungs ached, and his legs felt rubbery. Dawn was rapidly approaching, and he had managed only to put himself somewhere along Charlottenburger Chaussee, not far from the Tiergarten Rail Station and the flak towers. He stared at the slowly lightening sky. He had hoped to make up lost time once he cleared the narrowest part of the corridor, where he was a tempting target for any marksman.

But now that he had reached its edge, gasping for breath in the predawn gloom, he realized that the armored car would surely pick up speed as well.

A noise touched his ear and sent him rolling to the side. It came from the darkness beyond the courtyard wall. A squeak. Ungreased metal rubbing against tired ball bearings. Someone out on the street, winding slowly through the rubble. Soldiers? He'd seen a number of abandoned gun emplacements along this side of the Spree, facing the far bank and the Russians. Most of the guns seemed to be intact but out of ammunition. Perhaps their crews were returning with fresh rounds.

He listened. No, not soldiers. Small voices, whispering. Almost childlike. He raised his head cautiously over the wall. Two girls in uniform, young teen-agers, walking a pair of bicycles toward the river. Möhnke girls, according to their sleeve devices, girls drafted into service during the early days of the Russian Oder offensive to help deliver supplies and messages within the city. Each of the bicycles still had a pair of *Panzerfäuste* lashed to the handlebars. They were obviously trying to move quietly, but a dry squeak from the rear wheel of one of the bikes chirped every few seconds, marking their progress.

Bascom eyed the bikes hungrily. Wheels. It could make all the difference in his pursuit of the armored car. Not only could he move faster, but it would also save wear and tear on his panting body. He eased himself over the wall.

The girls apparently realized the Russians were on the far side of the river, for they approached the near bank carefully. They propped their bikes in the shadow of a fragmented wall. One of the girls, a chubby little redhead with a pretty face, slipped to the water's edge and reluctantly removed a small PPK pistol from her belt. She looked at it sorrowfully, then with a jerky motion tossed it into the sluggish water. Next she tore the insignia patches from her uniform and cast them after the gun. Her shoulders slumped. The end of a war. A cause lost.

Her companion, a skinny young blonde with thick eye-

brows, had come better prepared. Standing in the deepest
of shadows, she peeled off her entire uniform and threw
it away. Then she unstrapped a small canvas kitbag from
the rear of her bike and extracted a wrinkled print blouse
and a blue skirt. As she put them on, the redhead came
back up the bank, hiccuping with sobs she was unable to
smother. The blonde embraced her, comforting her.

Bascom held back. It suddenly seemed grossly unfair
even to consider stealing one of their bikes, no matter how
badly he might need it. Both girls looked so young, so
vulnerable. Then he remembered the gold coins still tied
in his handkerchief. He could buy one of the bikes. Reichsmarks might be worthless to the girls at the beginning of
a military occupation, but gold would buy food, clothing,
perhaps even protection.

The redhead, still crying, leaned over her bicycle and
started to untie the *Panzerfäuste*. Bascom groped through
his pockets for the Volkssturm armband and slipped it
on, then stepped into the open. The young blonde saw
him first and shrank back. Easy, he told himself. Poor
kids. "Don't be afraid," he whispered. "I won't hurt you."

They edged farther away from him.

Bascom indicated the armband above his left elbow. "I'm
a militiaman, on a mission. I need your help." He slipped
his handkerchief from his rear pocket and slowly untied the
gold coins, letting the girls see them. "I must deliver some
dispatches to the front," he said. "I need one of your
bicycles. I will pay for it, of course."

"Leck' mich am Arsch," the blonde said. Kiss my ass.

Bascom blinked. "What?

"You want to desert, like all the others," the redhead
joined in. "You're a lousy traitor. Well, fuck off. We won't
help you."

"Not only that, you dirty *Schleicher*," the blonde said,
"but you were standing back there watching while I un-
dressed, weren't you? I hope you got an eyeful."

So much for youth and vulnerability. Bascom eyed her
skinny frame and said, "All I want from you, princess, is

one of your bicycles. There's enough gold here to buy five replacements. You'll take it, if you're smart. I mean to have one of them whether you take it or not."

"We're not afraid of you," the redhead said. "We've seen plenty of your kind. All talk. Now slink away and leave us alone."

Bascom stared at them for a moment, then ungallantly reached out and shoved the redhead away from the nearest bike. He tossed the coins at her feet and started to push the bike away, but both swarmed him. He warded them off as best he could and pushed the bike faster. After a running start, he straddled the bike and began to pump.

They chased him for half a block, then slowed and stopped. They stood in the middle of the street, no longer caring about the Russians on the far side of the river, and cursed him at the top of their lungs until he was out of earshot.

"Yellow defeatist!" they yelled.

"Bolshevist dog!"

"Filthy Peeping Tom!" the blonde added.

Bascom pedaled away grimly, leaving them behind in the graying light. When their voices at last faded, he heard another sound following him. He glanced at the two *Panzerfäuste* flanking the handlebar post and shook his head. Bad enough that he'd been forced to steal from children; but worse, he had taken the bike with the squeaky wheel.

4

Martin Bormann and Goebbels came instantly to General Krebs when he returned to the Führerbunker at noon. How had it gone? they asked. His report was unadorned and to the point. The Russians were adamant. After hours of futile negotiations, the Russian position remained the same: They would accept only an immediate and unconditional surrender of the city, plus the personal surrender of all government functionaries now residing in the Chancellery bunker complex. A line had been left open for an official reaction to the Soviet terms. Bormann and Goebbels exchanged gloomy looks. It took only moments of quiet discussion to decide. Predictably, they rejected the one-sided terms. The Soviets were so informed.

Just as predictably, the Russians answered with an immediate order to all artillery commanders: "Fire to full capacity!" The big guns opened up again after their twelve-hour silence, and *Katyushi* salvos screeched into the air. From the thunderous sound and rocking walls, it appeared that every Soviet gun in the area had now been trained on the Chancellery. Most of the bunker inhabitants promptly blamed Krebs for this, certain that he had erred in disclosing to the Russians the location of the remaining members of the German Government.

Goebbels sank into a deep depression. Convinced that there was no longer any possibility of a negotiated peace, he made up his mind to follow in the footsteps of his beloved Führer. He would die before the day played out, he informed everyone who would listen. His children, also present in the bunker, would be poisoned by Dr. Stumpfegger that very afternoon; then Goebbels and his wife would climb the emergency stairs to the Chancellery garden, where a trusted adjutant would apply the *coups de grâce*. Their bodies, like those of Hitler and Eva, were to be burned.

Bormann met with Krebs, Dr. Stumpfegger, and young Captain Schedle in the Führer's anteroom. Knowing how tired and defeated Krebs must feel, Bormann had expropriated some of the liquor stores and now opened a bottle and passed it around. To his irritation, Krebs declined, as did Schedle. But Stumpfegger drank greedily.

"I must assume Dr. Goebbels still doesn't know," Krebs said.

"The Führer didn't deem it necessary," Bormann reminded him.

Krebs grimaced. "He's going to kill his children. Surely someone ought to tell him."

"Dr. Goebbels was always something of an exhibitionist," Bormann said. "To tell him now would rob him of his greatest moment. Besides, my instructions were to leave things as they stand."

"But children," Krebs said. "There are six of them. Heide is only four. Even the eldest, Helga, is only twelve."

"We are powerless to intervene," Bormann said. "If the man wants to be a martyr and take his family with him, let him. It's his affair. As for us, I've arranged our departure, timed for tonight. You are welcome to join us, General Krebs. The future Reich will have use for such as you."

Krebs shook his head. "Thank you, no," he said stiffly. "I prefer to remain here and die a soldier's death."

"You prefer a bullet to freedom?"

"Under the circumstances, I believe a bullet will be a great relief," Krebs said. He stood. "If you will excuse me, I think I will go to my quarters."

Bormann nodded him out with clenched jaw.

Captain Schedle sat glumly in his chair, deep in thought. His dour expression annoyed Bormann even further, but Bormann concealed his irritation long enough to ask, "What about you, Captain? Will you accompany us on our odyssey?"

Schedle looked up, startled. "You are offering me escape?"

"Loyalty must have its reward," Bormann said.

Schedle shook his head. "I would like to go," he said. "God knows, I really would. I don't cherish the thought of dying or going to a Russian prison camp. But General Krebs is right. Under the circumstances, there is only one recourse for a soldier."

"Ridiculous," Bormann muttered. "There is nothing honorable about a self-inflicted bullet to the brain."

"It would appear that there are those in high position who agree with you," Schedle said. He must have realized how bitter his remark sounded, for he swallowed and stood up. "My apologies, Herr Reichsleiter. It is not my place to judge the actions of my leader. I can only answer for myself. And I must respectfully choose, as did General Krebs, what I consider to be the only option left open to me. If you will permit me to withdraw, mein Herr?"

"Permission granted," Bormann said. He waited until the young officer was gone, then took the bottle from Stumpfegger's hands. "I'm glad," he said. "I didn't want that bastard along anyway."

"What do you have against Schedle?" Stumpfegger asked.

"Nothing in particular," Bormann said. He tilted the bottle and swallowed, then wiped his mouth. "Doctor, I have one last assignment for you: Please attend both the general and the captain this afternoon and see that they fulfill their 'honorable commitments' as soldiers. Make sure they do it soon."

"And if they have second thoughts?"

"Save some juice for that little needle of yours," Bormann said. "I want them both dead before we leave the Chancellery."

5

It was midday before Bascom caught sight of the armored car again. It was parked on Kant Strasse, about halfway between the Tiergarten and Adolf Hitler Platz. He came across it by accident. The Russians had crossed the Spree during the night west of the flak towers. It was only a minor pocket along the Spandauer Chaussee area, but it bulged into the corridor almost to Kaiser Damm, forcing him to stop thinking of the armored car and to concentrate on a safe avenue of escape. His body made its own demands. He fell asleep in an alley briefly, dozing for several minutes before a distant mortar explosion rattled him awake. He dug out a handful of radishes from a rubble-strewn allotment garden and pedaled onward, munching. He was pushing his bike carefully through the battered streets of Charlottenburg, advancing a few feet at a time,

stopping, waiting until he could be certain the blank windows overlooking the street held no hidden dangers, when
he turned onto Kant Strasse and saw the Puma, motionless
under a barren linden tree, about three blocks ahead.

He wheeled his bike hurriedly to the side of the road
and paused, his heartbeat quickening. Even as slowly as he
had traveled, he should have known the Puma would also
have difficulties. Not only had the Russian bulge created the
same problems for it, but also the armored car driver would
have the task of finding roadways sufficiently clear for
passage. That would mean a lot of dead ends, backing and
weaving, like winding through a complicated maze. The
proof was there ahead of him. Almost twelve hours, and
yet the Puma had advanced no more than five or six
miles on a straight line.

He dithered a moment, wondering what to do now that
he'd caught up with it. It occurred to him that the two
Panzerfäuste tied to his handlebars might offer him an
aggressive course of action, assuming he could get close
enough before the gun turret swung around to face him.
But the wolf, still with him, whispered a warning. Why was
the Puma just sitting there, not moving? Surely not a rest
stop. Even though the driver was certain to be damned
tired after wrestling that awkward vehicle through all but
impassable streets, he wasn't likely, considering the importance of his passenger, to stop for catnaps until he was
in a well-defended area. What then? Danger of some kind?
Bascom held back, puzzled, and scanned the distance.

And then he saw it. Farther up the road, about a half
mile ahead of the armored car, a Russian tank sat lurking
in an intersection near the railroad tracks south to Grunewald. Only the front end was visible, great gray gun barrel
protruding into the street. Lying in wait. Not necessarily
for the Puma, or it would have pulled into the street by
now and opened fire. No, it was waiting for anything or
anyone who happened to come along. It had exceeded the
limits of its own lines, and was playing a dangerous game.
The Puma driver knew it, and was waiting the tank out, a
deadly war of nerves in miniature.

How long had they been like that? Hours? Minutes? How much longer would the tank stay there, knowing that someone might sneak up at any moment with grenades or a *Panzerbuchse?* Bascom looked down at his own two *Panzerfäuste* and welcomed the germ of an idea. Quickly he began to untie one. He was too far away from either vehicle to do any damage. At most, his effective range was sixty to seventy meters. But if he could fire one of them, even from here, the blast might catch the tanker's attention and pull him out into the roadway. Once the tanker saw the Puma, his heavier gun would do the rest.

But even as Bascom struggled with the cords, the big Russian guns, which had stayed strangely quiet through most of the night and the morning, suddenly resumed their thunderous symphony back in the center of the city. The Russian tanker's nerve quickly broke, and the heavy diesel engine cranked up. The gray snout backed slowly out of the intersection and spun around, and the tank rumbled rearward toward its own ill-defined lines. Bascom groaned. Moments later, the Puma was moving again, heading west toward Adolf Hitler Platz.

Three hours passed without another glimpse of the armored car. He saw practically no one. A few Germans. Two small bands of civilians heading, like himself, toward the west. A few baby-faced soldiers, mostly Hitler Youth with adult helmets that almost swallowed their child-sized heads, sitting in slit trenches with their backs to him, waiting for the inevitable Russian tanks. Many of them were asleep, the rest totally exhausted, and they scarcely spared him a glance as he rode past. The few who did noted the Volkssturm armband and ignored him.

Bascom was so tired that legs like concrete, lungs like bellows, seemed old friends, something that had been with him always. But the adrenaline of the hunt pumped afresh, and so did his feet on the bicycle pedals. By midafternoon, he was approaching the Olympic Stadium, less than two miles from the Pichelsdorf Bridge and the westernmost reaches of Berlin. Every revolution of the pedals called for

superhuman effort. The fact that he'd lost all traces of the
Puma didn't help.

He stopped briefly on a small rise and rested, half
hoping to see the armored car somewhere below, but it
wasn't there. The stadium itself, a giant amphitheater
situated below the Spree at the western extremity of the
city, had been left oddly untouched by the war. It rose out
of flat fields north of Kaiser Damm, only a couple of miles
short of Spandau and the Havel River. Built to accommo-
date a hundred thousand people, it was the showcase in
which Hitler had intended to prove to the world the su-
premacy of the master race during the 1936 Olympics, only
to be humbled by a young American black named Jesse
Owens. Surrounding the stadium was the Reichssportsfeld,
a sixty-eight-acre complex of game sites. But the game
now being played within its confines was a grim one.

Civilians on the last leg to the west and possible escape
had gathered within the shadows of the stadium walls to
gain courage, to despair, to pray before braving the gauntlet
of Russian guns trained on the Havel. Bascom could hear
the booms coming from the direction of the bridges. So
could the civilians. Their faces, drawn and spent from long
treks through the heavy fighting along both sides of the
corridor, sagged longer as they rested and contemplated
the terrors still to come.

There must have been hundreds of them. He couldn't
help but wonder where they had all come from. He hadn't
seen more than forty of fifty civilians all day, and most
were making such slow progress that he would have been
willing to bet that not one out of five would get through.
Yet here they were, scattered along the entire length of the
stadium. They must have been coming here for days. There
was no other possible answer.

As Bascom coasted down the rise, he spotted a unit of
Hitler Youth, strengthened by a few veteran soldiers, encamped at the western end of the stadium. A haggard
Army officer with an empty sleeve where his left arm had
been came up the line of refugees, trying to convince them
that it was useless to go on without military escort. Bascom

tried to detour out of the man's path, but the officer hailed him. "You there," the officer called. "You with the bicycle. Turn back. There's no escape for you here."

Bascom stopped. "I'm not looking for escape," he said. "I'm a courier, delivering messages." He gestured at his armband.

"Good Lord," the officer said. "To whom? There's no one left but us. The Russians closed off the bridges yesterday. Their tanks are across the Havel there, on Heerstrasse, less than four kilometers away. They've zeroed in on the bridges, so if you've a mind to pass through, you might as well forget it. Casualties have been damned high most of the day."

Bascom hesitated, then said, "I'm not interested in the bridges. I've been sent to catch up to one of our officers from the center of the city. You might have seen him. He was in an armored car, one of the big eight-wheelers. Green and yellow."

"Good Lord, man, you needn't describe it. It isn't as though we have armored cars and tanks coming and going at will. Your armored car was here, right enough. A wonder that it got through at all. It's the only one we've seen in three days."

"It was here?" Bascom's heart began to beat faster again.

"Yes, it came dragging in an hour or so ago and stopped for a rest. Damned peculiar, if you ask me. The driver insisted on parking down by the west exit. Wouldn't let any of us come near it. Pair of SS men stood guard the whole time until they were ready to leave."

"Which way did they go?"

"Toward Pichelsdorf," the officer said. "I tried to tell them the bridge was under fire, but the driver ignored me. He requisitioned one of my boys as guide. They left ten, maybe fifteen minutes ago. Who is this officer of yours? A foreigner?"

"Why do you ask?"

"Your accent," the officer said. "I figure you're one of the Nordlanders or something. What are you, Norwegian?"

"That's right," Bascom said. "What's the best way for me to reach Pichelsdorf from here?"

"Down across the Sportsfeld," the officer said. "Frankly, I'd give it up if I were you. One of our officers has turned loose all his Volkssturmers and sent them home. I've got barely two hundred boys down there in foxholes and trenches, and they won't last any time at all if the Russians decide to cross over. It could get bad."

Bascom shrugged. "Duty," he said. "I've got to."

"Well, you're a braver man than I am," the officer murmured. "I don't know why we're still fighting anyway. One of my older boys was monitoring radio transmissions this morning. He picked up a bulletin. According to the Army, the Führer has fallen in battle. Did you know that?"

"No, I hadn't heard," Bascom said.

"Yes. There were no details, but the rumor is that he led a Panzer detachment in a counterattack on the Potsdam rail yards. Damned Russians got him, I guess. We can't last much longer. Morale is pretty low since we got the news. I just wish those damned politicians would realize how hopeless it is and sue for peace." He looked at the huddles of refugees and said, "These poor *Narren*, running from God knows what, going to God knows where. Even if they make it, I doubt the Americans will treat them any better. I hear the Americans are turning people back, handing them over to the Russians."

"I must go on," Bascom said. "Will I need special permission to get through your lines?"

The officer waved his good arm. "Nothing," he said. "There's no no way we can stop people, anyway. Too many of them." He hesitated, then said, "Look, a piece of advice: If you have to cross the bridge to catch up to your party, wait until the tanks fire at someone else, then ride like the devil. There's usually a pause between shots. It would be better if you avoided the bridge entirely. You might try the point down below Pichelsdorf. There were still many pleasure boats tied up there last time I looked. Take one and row across. It's safer."

"Thanks," Bascom said. "I might do that."

"Good luck," the officer said. He continued up the line, telling the women to turn back, or at least to wait until dark. Some of them listened, but most seemed too weary to comprehend.

Bascom started to push off, but a painfully hobbling woman in a black cloth coat with a ratty fur collar, leading a sleepy little girl with a dirt-streaked face, called to him, "Please. Please, sir. Are you going to the bridge? Please, sir, take my daughter with you."

The woman's eyes were frantic. Bascom averted his face, but he couldn't force himself to start pedaling. "I can't," he said. "I'm on official business."

"Oh sir, please! Please! Her grandmother and grandfather are there, waiting for us. They have my older daughter with them. I told them I would catch up, but I've turned my ankle. She won't be any trouble. She's light as a feather. Here, feel her arms. See how light she is."

"She'd be better off with you," Bascom said.

"No one would be better off with me," the woman said. "I can't go any farther. If you don't take her, my mother and father will come back, looking for us. They might miss their chance, as well. We'll all die."

Bascom looked unwillingly at the little girl. Four, five years old at the most, and as thin as a starving sparrow. Her eyes drooped, and she almost fell asleep on her feet, leaning against her mother's leg. He thought of Freddy and Anne-Lise. And Erika. He knew he shouldn't, but he couldn't help himself. He sighed.

"All right," he said. "Put her on the handlebars."

6

Everything suddenly seemed to go wrong at once for Martin Bormann. He had planned carefully for his own escape, meticulously covering all contingencies, but as night fell on doomed Berlin and the hour of flight drew near, his entire framework began to collapse.

The major misfortune was the cataclysmic bombardment

rocking the Chancellery grounds. The Russians had thrown the full weight of their heavy artillery on the Wilhelmstrasse area now that they knew where the German command post was hidden. Bormann tried to counteract it. At nine o'clock that evening, a radio message was transmitted in Russian, saying: "Hello, hello! This is the LVI Panzer Corps, calling the Soviet High Command. We ask you to cease fire! We ask you to cease fire! We are sending envoys to the Potsdamer Brücke under a white flag to parley with you. Please cease your fire!"

The Russians, no longer inclined to be lenient, decided once more to permit a German request for a peace parley, but this time the guns fell silent only on a localized basis, in the area where the envoys were to meet. The guns trained on the Chancellery and elsewhere continued to blaze, and the streets continued to erupt.

Next, Bormann discovered that the scout car he had ordered to stand by in the Chancellery underground garage was nowhere to be found. The driver, unnerved by the increased tempo of the Russian artillery assault, had driven off earlier in the day to save himself. No other vehicles were available.

Bormann tried to contact the Müncheberg Division, fighting in the Tiergarten near the Zoo Bunker, for assistance, but learned that they were down to five tanks and four artillery pieces, and that they had only a sprinkling of troops left, not even enough to fight their way to the Chancellery, much less to fight their way out again. Dr. Stumpfegger suggested that Bormann arrange a linkup with the 18th Panzer Grenadier Division, which he understood was planning a breakout of its own. But when Bormann attempted to locate the Grenadiers, no one could say where they were. Either they had been wiped out, or they had already retreated to the west without waiting for orders.

While Bormann frantically tried to track down a military unit still strong enough to provide cover for a withdrawal, the rest of the bunker occupants gathered in one of the crowded underground chambers for last-minute instructions on how to manage their own escape through the exploding city. Brigadeführer Wilhelm Möhnke, in nominal command of the bunker breakout, had divided his charges into six groups. The first, consisting mainly of female secretaries and Hitler's vegetarian cook, would be led by Möhnke himself and Hitler's adjutant, Colonel Günsche. The other teams would follow at set intervals. Hitler's chauffeur, Erich Kempka, was put in command of the second team, also primarily women. A third, mostly men, was given over to Dr. Werner Naumann, one of Goebbels' close associates. And so on, down the line. Möhnke's suggestion to all teams, once they were clear of the Chancellery, was to head underground, to the subway system, and try to make it through the Russian lines. If they succeeded, they could proceed west, toward the Americans, or north to join Admiral Dönitz in Schleswig-Holstein. The panic-stricken men and women attentively absorbed every word, but nothing the solemn-faced General Möhnke could say helped to relieve their tensions.

By the time the first breakout group crowded up the bunker stairs to venture into the holocaust outside, Bormann and Stumpfegger had given up. There was no transport, no available escort. An officer of the Kampfgruppe Bärenfänger had offered to meet them with two Tiger tanks, if they could make it to the Weidendamm Bridge, near Invalidenstrasse, but he could do no more. He and his men were fighting for their lives already.

With no better options left to them, Bormann and Stumpfegger withdrew dejectedly to the underground anteroom where the breakout teams were assembling. A second group was on the verge of leaving. Bormann noted that the group was made up mainly of women, and held back. As soon as they were gone, Dr. Naumann called the third group together. Men this time. Bormann questioned Stumpfegger with his eyes and got an affirmative nod. Gloomily, Bormann asked Naumann if he and Stumpfegger could go along. Naumann agreed.

They waited until the second group had time to clear the area, then scuttled up the stairwell to the old Chancellery building. The walls creaked and groaned as they crept to

a breach in the front wall. Nonstop explosions boomed outside. One by one, they ducked through the opening and
ran into the street. Most of them had been below ground
for the past several days, and though they had heard
numerous reports of the destruction above, nothing in their
imaginations could possibly have prepared them for the
scene that now greeted them. It was like running into hell.

7

A vehicle lay just ahead, a dark outline against the water's
edge. The black Havel shoreline stretched endlessly before
him, miles of broad lake meandering south through the
still night. Heavily wooded slopes rose up on his left, with
legions of birch and pine trees whispering in a breeze not
detectable at ground level, somber sentinels against a distant, flaming sky. He was at the upper rim of the Grunewald forest, fifteen square miles of thick natural parkland
which sprawled like a green apron down the western lap of
Berlin, draping the edge of the city from Spandau at the
waist to Potsdam at the toe. Except for the fire-red glow
in the distance and the heavy *thump-whump* of Russian
artillery pieces, this could have been another world. An
almost peaceful world.

Bascom spared a weary thought for the caprices of
chance. Could it be the Puma? Could helping the little girl
possibly have brought him to the end of his search? It was
hard to make out much about the vehicle in the dark. No
sound coming from it, no movement. Had he finally re-
located the damned thing after all these hours?

The child had slowed him badly after all. He had
reached Pichelsdorf quickly enough, cycling across fields
with the little girl nestled between *Panzerfäuste* warheads
on his handlebars, but reaching and delivering had turned
out to be two vastly different things. It was getting on
toward dark when he approached the bridge. The child's
grandparents might have been there, just as the mother
said they would be, but so were about six hundred other

civilians, cowering, crouching, dotting the landscape, waiting for a chance to cross the bridge in darkness.

The Russians held the far side insecurely, only a few tanks standing off on Heerstrasse, murky shapes in the gathering twilight, but they were more than a match for the refugees. The tanks simply waited there, a mile away, dumping shells on the bridge whenever anyone got nervy enough or panicky enough to make a try for it. The tanks would have been more than a match for the Puma, too, Bascom saw immediately. It could never have crossed here. But then where had it gone?

At first, Bascom had to stifle impatient curses to avoid frightening the child he had saddled himself with. The waiting civilians were too scattered for him to check them all. He wheeled the bike among the more closely compacted groups, hoping someone would see the little girl and claim her, but bursting shells from across the river soon drove him back. He finally parked both child and bicycle in the lee of a shattered boathouse, out of harm's way, and returned on foot to the approach to the bridge. He hadn't thought to ask the woman at the stadium for a name. With growing agitation, he wandered from group to group calling, *"Grossmutter? Grossvater?* Is anyone here looking for a grandchild?" All he got in return were blank, terrified looks.

The sky steadily darkened. He'd covered no more than half the groups before it grew too dark to see. In despair, he turned back for the boathouse, wondering what he could do. He couldn't afford the wasted time, not if he really hoped to catch up with the armored car. Catch up. That was a laugh. He didn't even know where to start looking. There were Russians to the north, across the Spree; the all-but-impenetrable Grunewald forest to the south; and, back to the east, the city blazed and exploded. So whither his quarry?

He found the little girl asleep, curled up limply beside the bicycle, oblivious to the sporadic crash of explosions coming across the Pichelsdorf span. He stared at her, and bleak reality stared back at him. He would have to abandon

her. Just ride away and leave her. There was nothing else
he could do. But even as the thought formed, she awoke
and raised her eyes, so large and liquidly trusting that he
felt he could have fallen into them. Rotten kid.

"All right," he said, "time to go." She stood sleepily.
She showed no fear of Bascom, no confusion, just instant
obedience.

More civilian refugees were creeping into the area now
that darkness covered their actions, and Bascom wheeled
the bicycle and the girl among them, this time asking if anyone would be willing to take the child in tow. He repeated
himself over and over, fragmented phrases about the injured mother, about grandparents lost, spoken in haste to
passing faces. Few even stopped to listen. They had problems of their own.

He had almost given up hope when three people rushed
out of the darkness behind him. The first was a beshawled
old woman who snatched the child and hugged her close.
Next came a thin, bent old man, and a girl in her early
teens. "We heard a lady from Steglitz speak of you," the
man said. "Where did you find our Geli?"

"Thank God. You're the grandfather?" Bascom said.
"I've been looking for you forever. A woman passed her
to me. Her mother. At the Olympia-Stadion."

"What?" the man said. "Why did she not bring the child
herself?"

"She turned her ankle. She can't walk."

The man straightened his bent frame. "Then I shall have
to go back to fetch her."

Bascom shook his head. "You should cross the bridge
to safety before the tanks move closer. That's what your
daughter wanted. She says you are to save yourselves."

"Nevertheless," the man said, "I shall have to go back
for her. I thank you for your assistance." He glanced wistfully at the bridge, then told the young teen-ager to stay
with her sister and grandmother on this precise spot. If he
wasn't back in two hours, he said, they were to cross alone.

Bascom thought about the Puma and how hopelessly
ahead of him it must be now, but also about the time he

would lose if he allowed himself any further distractions. He sighed. "You'll need my help," he said.

The old man looked appreciative, but shook his head. "No, please. You've done too much for us already. It was the act of a hero, to delay your own escape for us."

Bascom grimaced. "Anyone would have done as much," he said. "Besides, I'm not planning to cross the bridge. I'm only a messenger, looking for an armored car."

To Bascom's chagrin, the old man looked at him with even greater respect. "I saw the very car," he said, "well before dusk. It stopped short of the bridge, then turned away. I greatly regret that I cannot assist you by telling you its direction, for I was so distracted, I—wait. There is a small thing we can do for you." He pulled the teen-ager over and instructed her, "You go with the Herr messenger and question other refugees among these people who may have noticed the armored car. Find out which direction it went. It's important military business."

"Yes, Grandfather," the girl said.

"I appreciate it," Bascom said. "But she'll have to ask the questions alone." He sighed again. "You'll still need my help. It'll take both of us to bring your daughter back to the bridge."

The man nodded wordlessly, too grateful to trust his voice. He embraced his wife and the two girls, and started back up the road beside Bascom, against the flow of refugee traffic.

Now the wolf's turn had come again. With feet that identified and catalogued every stone, every fallen limb they stepped upon, with even the hairs of his unshaven growth of beard registering each shift of air pressure, each whiff of wind, Bascom crept closer to the dark shape on the Lake Havel shoreline. By God, it *was* the Puma. Even after the time it took to help the old man find his daughter and make the long walk beside the bicycle, rolling her awkwardly back to the Pichelsdorf, he had still caught up with it. He blessed the teen-ager, nameless, who had pulled herself from her mother's arms to report that the armored car

was said to have turned south toward the Grunewald. He
hadn't believed it. But he'd had nowhere better to look, so
he pedaled into the woods anyway.

Now that he had actually found the vehicle, he was as
surprised as he was gratified. No, puzzled was more accurate. Why had the driver headed into the Grunewald?
It offered no avenue of escape. The wide waters of the
Havel blocked the west, and the Russians were undoubtedly
encamped on the far bank. Potsdam had fallen in the
South, so there was no safety there. It didn't make sense to
him that the Puma would leave the protection of the
German-held corridor merely to enter an undefended no-
man's-land like the Grunewald. All those elaborate movements from the center of the city, and now this. An empty
armored car sitting by the lake.

No, wait. Not empty. There, through the open panel, a
figure. He could see moonlight touching an arm and shoulder. Not moving. And there, by one of the rear tires, another figure dimly seen, lying on its side, head nestled in
the sand. Also not moving. Careful, the wolf warned.

Bascom circled to the far side of the Puma, away from
the open panel. He paused and listened. No sound inside.
His hand reached up and touched the metal cowling above
the engine. Cold. It had been here for a couple of hours
at least.

Slowly, carefully, he rounded the ungainly nose of the
armored car, slipping beneath the long 50mm gun barrel.
The figure by the rear tire was one of the Puma crewmen,
probably the gunner. Dead. Gunned down at close range
by an automatic weapon. Blood had seeped darkly into
the sand.

He looked inside. The moonlit arm and shoulder belonged to the driver, also dead. Shot in the back. Again, an
automatic weapon. The SS men with the Schmeissers, most
likely. Leave no witnesses. Had the crewmen seen it coming? Did they have any warning? Not the driver, from the
looks of it. The gunner, perhaps. He was lying as though
he had tried to run.

Bascom backed away from the open panel, and his gaze

fell on a third body, face down in the sand about fifteen feet away. It was a small, slim body. He rolled it over. A youthful face, no more than thirteen or fourteen years old, eyes closed peacefully beneath tousled blond hair: the Hitler Youth they had requisitioned back at the stadium as a guide. A bullethole, neat and precise, behind the right ear. A pistol wound, medium caliber. Perhaps the SS men didn't have the stomach for this one. Who then? The high-ranking Gestapo officer?

Bascom stood and peered through shimmering moonlight, searching the sandy soil for footprints, and spotted them, heading south along the damp shore of the Havel, four sets. The two remaining SS men and the two men in greatcoats. Where were they headed? Could he catch up with them? Probably. Though they had a good head start, they were now on foot.

He retreated to the trees for his bicycle.

The shoreline wriggled south for several kilometers, and Bascom wriggled with it, riding where the ground flattened enough for him to mount the bike, walking when it turned too rocky or the trees crowded too close to the lapping waters. Gatow slipped past on the far bank, with Russian campfires dotting the shoreline, then a small island close to this side. Some two miles ahead, faintly visible in the receding moonlight, the narrow neck where Kladow on the east bank and the Schwanenwerder Peninsula on the west bank squeezed the Havel back to river width before opening up into the Wannsee, a deep bay toward the lower end of the city.

The Grunewald, as it turned out, was not the no-man's-land Bascom had expected. True, the trees marched off as thickly as ever and it was no place for tanks or mechanized units, but the Russians had apparently infiltrated it with infantry patrols. He hadn't actually seen any of them, but he had heard them. Twice. Once when the shoreline dipped back close to Havelchaussee, a road that wound through the western edge of the forest. The Russians must have set up a roadblock in the trees, just in case any of the Germans trapped to the north tried to slip through to Potsdam. Evidently the Russians weren't expecting much action, for they made no attempt to keep quiet. He could hear them clearly, deep voices talking and joking in the darkness. He heard voices again a kilometer or so below Gatow, when his tracking carried him within a few hundred yards of a Russian field encampment. He even smelled hot food warming near the second group.

If he had heard them, so had his quarry. Their footprints each time detoured out of the trees and closer to the shore-line, as though they were trying to stay as far away as possible. Bascom briefly considered approaching one of the groups for help, but he knew he couldn't. He spoke no Russian, and they weren't likely to sit still for any panto-mime games. They would have to assume he was German himself. And that could get him shot.

There were also signs that the four men ahead of him were slowing—more frequent trampled spots where the footprints halted, two sets striding outward to stand guard while the other two sat and rested, leaving *Sitzmarks* in the dirt. Perhaps they were wary of the Russians, or perhaps the length of the journey was beginning to tell on the older members of the party. Bascom thought dully of rest for himself, but the wolf told him simply to accept the punish-ing weariness, without the human's mental complaint or protest, and by acceptance to endure it more easily.

It was almost midnight when he finally spotted them. He was about halfway down the winding twelve-mile shore-line, according to his own estimation, and he had just topped the rise that gave him the indistinct view of Kladow and the Schwanenwerder Peninsula to the south, when a slight movement below his rise alerted the wolf.

At first his mind objected that it was just a wavelet wash-ing against the bank, but when he looked more closely, he saw the two SS men bending over something in a sheltered cove, sweeping pine boughs aside with their arms. It ap-peared to be a small boat, perhaps five feet long. A few feet away, barely visible in the fading moonlight, waited the two men in greatcoats. One sagged weakly, as if ill or dead tired or both.

Bascom crouched. A boat? But the Russians held the far side of the Havel. The four men might be able to sneak across and land unseen, but they wouldn't get far. Not after sunrise. And if they tried to paddle south, following the water between the Russian ground forces, they were sure to run into a Russian boat trap somewhere along the line. So where could they possibly go?

The boat was free now, and the SS men flipped it over. It was a small rubber dinghy, painted flat black. Two sets of oars were strapped inside, beneath the seats. The SS men hurriedly worked at the tie cords. They kept looking out toward the water, as though they were running behind schedule.

As the two SS men fumbled with butterfingered haste, a low drone approached from the north. No more than a slight buzzing at first, hardly noticeable above the distant booming guns, it soon grew louder. The sound seemed to be drifting in from the water. Bascom scanned the broadening river vainly from his perch on the rise. Nothing. Only a flat, throbbing engine sound. No, more than one engine. A pair of engines. Perhaps three. Patrol boats?

The SS men heard the engines as well and worked more frantically. As soon as they had the oars loose, they picked up the dinghy and ran with it to the water's edge. One of them peered into the darkness, then tossed his Schmeisser into the dinghy and gestured for the two men in greatcoats to come. He leaned over to steady the boat, and his partner rushed back for the oars.

Bascom could hear the engines clearly now, but he still couldn't see them. The water stretched unbroken in both directions. No surface craft of any kind.

A flat pop, like a large firecracker going off down by the water, startled Bascom, and he swung his head back to the cove. One of the SS men fell to the sand. A foot behind him, with a smoking Luger in his hand, stood the high-ranking Gestapo officer.

The other SS man, knee-deep in the water beside the

boat, lifted stunned eyes and opened his mouth, but the
Gestapo man took aim and fired again. A brief flash illuminated the cove. The second SS man reeled away from the
boat and splashed under. The delayed firecracker sound
rolled up Bascom's hill.

The Gestapo officer calmly holstered his pistol and
scooped up the oars. He helped his companion into the
boat and handed the oars in, then climbed in after them.
Both men began to row, and the boat bobbed slowly away
from the shoreline, pulling past the partially submerged
body of the second SS man.

The engine sounds, forgotten for the moment, throttled
back and skimmed in out over the center of the water. It
was a trimotored Junkers seaplane, coming in without
lights, gliding toward the near-motionless surface. It seemed
to hang for an instant, then it touched, and a spume of
white foam washed back in its wake.

Bascom leaped to his feet. The cove, howled the wolf,
and Bascom's eyes stabbed at the man lying motionless in
the sand. His Schmeisser was still strapped to his shoulder.
The ground dropped steeply to the cove, and the path was
filled with rocks and trees, but Bascom flung his leg over
the bicycle frame and pushed off. He clung to the handlebars, weaving back and forth as he picked up speed.
Branches slashed him in the face. Rocks jolted him high
into the air. The bike shuddered with each lurch, and he
fought to maintain control. By the time he reached the
bottom, he was going much too fast to brake, so he yanked
the handlebars to the side and skidded in the sand, like a
baserunner stealing second. His right arm doubled backward, and he heard something pop. A sharp pain screamed
through his bicep and into his shoulder. For a split second, everything went black.

It couldn't have lasted long. When he opened his eyes,
the bicycle frame was resting across his waist, and the front
wheel was still spinning. His shoulder hurt like hell. He
must have cried out when he fell, for the two men had
stopped rowing. The dinghy was out about a hundred feet,
wallowing silently, and the two men were peering back

through the darkness, straining to see what had caused the noise. The seaplane, at the end of its power landing, had settled in the water and eased over to port, taxiing toward them.

Bascom kicked the bicycle away and crawled to the dead SS man. He tried to tug the machine pistol loose, but pain shot through his right arm. He touched his right shoulder and winced. He yanked the gun loose with his left hand. The men in the dinghy had seen him now. As he fumbled with the Schmeisser, wasting valuable seconds trying to locate the cocking bolt one-handed, the Gestapo officer half rose and gripped his Luger in both hands. Bright pimples of light blossomed across the water as he fired. Bascom heard the bullets *fizz-z-z-z* overhead. Twin firecracker pops echoed out of the darkness.

With the bolt pulled back, Bascom swung up the Schmeisser left-handed and braced it on his knee. He squeezed the trigger, and the unfamiliar weapon roared and bucked. Spray chopped up around the boat. The two men ducked and grabbed for the oars. Bascom fired another burst. More wild bucking, more spray. Then the damned thing jammed on him.

He rolled back in the sand and frenziedly checked the gun. The cocking bolt was stuck, for some damned reason. He tugged at it, hit it with the heel of his left hand, slapped it. Sand, maybe? A cartridge casing stuck in the chamber?

The boat was pulling away, but moving erratically. Neither man was much of a hand with an oar. The plane was drawing closer though, its big rotary engines wheezing softly as it rocked across the water toward the dinghy. A few more moments and he would lose them.

He flung the frozen Schmeisser away in frustration and crawled to his bike. They were still in *Panzerfaust* range, if he could get one loose in time.

Something ticked in the darkness above him. A pebble, dislodged from the side of the hill, rolled lazily down the slope and came to a rest in the sand. He looked up. Four or five dark figures moved from tree to tree across the crest. Uniforms. Rifles. Russian infantrymen. They must have heard the pistol shots, or the Schmeisser fire, or the sea-plane engines. Whatever had attracted them, they were coming down Bascom's hill.

He hesitated, good hand still tugging at the thongs on the handlebars. Hide while he could, or stand his ground? They hadn't seen him yet. They seemed to be looking out toward the plane. If he were to fire one of the *Panzerfäuste* now, they would almost certainly see the backflash and spot him. But if he didn't fire, the plane would pick up its passengers and be out of range before they reached the bottom of the hill.

No choice. He clamped his jaw and wrestled the two *Panzerfäuste* loose. Hugging them under his left elbow, he crawled as close to the water's edge as he could get and pushed to one knee. The Russians were slipping and sliding now, coming down the hill fast. He dropped one tube to the sand and shifted the other painfully under his right arm-pit. Someone yelled in Russian along the shoreline, closer than he expected. More soldiers, creeping along the shore-line from the south, coming toward his cove. He lifted the aiming mechanism with his left hand, arming the tube. The plane waffled to a stop, engines idling. The dinghy was only a few feet away from it. A man leaned through a loading hatch, holding out his hand.

Bascom depressed the spring trigger. With a great *shoosh*, a tail of fire flared out of the *Panzerfaust* tube, and the projectile arced through the air, streaking through the night sky. It fell short and to the right, sending a geyser of water shooting upward. The dinghy quivered in the blast, and the two men threw their arms over their heads. Water rained down on them.

Bascom cursed and fumbled with the other tube. As he awkwardly primed the aiming mechanism, both men lurched from the dinghy and scrambled into the plane. The engines quickly revved up. Bascom locked the *Panzer-faust* under his armpit, sucking air at the pain, and aimed at the plane.

"*Stoi! Stoi!*" someone shouted.

He glanced up to see a Russian crouching on the ledge

above him, rifle pointing down. Another soldier crashed around the point and jerked to a stop a few feet away. More came crashing through the trees. Someone yelled something that sounded like, *"ROO-k'ee V'EHRKH!"*

"Wait," Bascom shouted. "Amerikanski! Don't shoot!"

"Amerikanski?" the soldier on the ledge said. His rifle barrel drooped. The plane swung around slowly toward deep water.

"Yes, Amerikanski! Amerikanski!" Bascom yelled. "We've got to stop that plane! Adolf Hitler! Vroom! Get away!"

"Amerikanski?" the Russian repeated. "Eh-dolf Hitler?" He sounded deeply confused.

The Russian nearest Bascom took a cautious step toward him. His eye fell on Bascom's left arm, and he muttered something to his friend that included the word Amerikanski, but it didn't sound like a confirmation.

The plane was facing the lake now and beginning to move. Some of the soldiers on the hill, too far away from the cove to know about Bascom or what was happening, opened fire on the plane independently, rifle shots that plinked the water and the fuselage. The scattered shots confused the soldiers around Bascom even more, and they gaped at the plane uncertainly.

"Hitler!" Bascom yelled. "Forget about me! Shoot it!"

The plane was moving out of range. It had to be now. Bascom shifted and triggered the *Panzerfaust*. The projectile shooshed from the tube and ripped across the sky. It seemed to be on a good trajectory, aiming for the tail assembly. But Bascom never saw whether or not it connected. A rifle butt slammed into his ear, and he fell into the sand.

For another instant, rockets exploded. His ears roared. He listened to thunderous noise, sinking, sinking, wondering if it was the sound of the impacting *Panzerfaust* round, or the plane's engines carrying the two men aloft, or just the blood rushing through his temples. Someone tugged at his left arm, wrenching something from his elbow. His vision dimmed, and the roar subsided.

The last thing he saw before he blacked out was the soldier with the gun butt, holding aloft a piece of cloth for his friend on the ledge to see. It was the damned Volkssturm armband.

15

СМЕРТЬ ФАШИСТСКОЙ ГАДИНЕ!

"Death to the Fascist reptile!"

—slogan on Soviet military poster

1

Alexei Volkov cast a yearning look at the cot in the corner. A new day was dawning outside, and here he was, stuck in an office, no sleep, no respite in sight. How many more of these German fakers would they bring him? A steady stream of prisoners all night, young men, old men, sullen men with clenched teeth, men with erect military bearing, servile men with frightened eyes, all caught in civilian clothing while trying to slip through Russian lines, unable to produce the proper identity papers, all claiming *not* to be what they so obviously were—officers, petty political leaders, stewards of the German Third Reich.

The door swung open, and Lieutenant Ivanov poked his head through. "I think you'll find the next one interesting," he said. He handed a preliminary interrogation report to Volkov and summoned the guards.

Volkov eyed the folder without opening it. "They're none of them interesting," he muttered. "Not one has been able to tell me a single credible thing about Hitler or his hierarchy."

"Ah, but at least they're imaginative," Ivanov said. "What about the one in women's clothing?"

"Him least of all," Volkov said. He had to smile. "Who could possibly mistake a six-foot-two Wehrmacht major with hairy legs for a woman?"

He was still smiling when the two Russian infantrymen ushered in a youngish man with head swathed in bandages and right shoulder heavily taped, right arm cradled in a sling. They pointed the man toward the chair facing Volkov's commandeered desk, still cluttered with leftover Nazi memorabilia. The man sat stiffly, something in his posture signaling pain or deep exhaustion or both, but also signaling some urgency that goaded him, kept him going.

Volkov slipped his glasses on his nose. Ivanov waited expectantly while Volkov flipped through the preliminary interrogation notes. Volkov read carefully, absorbing it all, then readjusted his glasses for a closer look at the prisoner. Ivanov was right. This man spun a very entertaining, though absurd, story. Could he possibly hope to get away with it?

Widely spaced greenish eyes stared back at Volkov. Broad forehead beneath the white wreath of bandages. The prisoner was in his late twenties, probably, though the pain and weariness were deeply etched into a prematurely lined face, making him look older. Volkov found his expression interesting. Not surly or sullen, like some of the others. Not frightened. The urgency, and an element of impatience, perhaps. That was a good touch.

Volkov leaned on his elbows and made a steeple of his fingers. "So," he said. "You claim to be an American?"

"I *am* an American," the prisoner said. He spoke forcefully but with tight control, as though husbanding his strength. "My name is Henry Bascom. I'm an officer, a captain. That can easily be verified. I told your man," he nodded at Ivanov, "all about it."

Accented German, but anyone could affect an accent. Volkov decided to make him talk more, to see if he would unconsciously slip into a more fluent use of the language. "According to these notes, you were caught at the Havel, trying to escape by seaplane."

The prisoner shook his head. "I was trying to *stop* the plane. Reread your notes."

Volkov opted not to take offense. "Ah yes," he said. "Some outrageous story about Herr Hitler trying to escape. What do you expect to gain by claiming Hitler was on that plane?"

"I know he was on the plane. I saw him."

"But General Krebs himself has told us that Hitler died

at the Chancellery. Do you wish to dispute your own leaders?"

The impatience leaped like green fire in the prisoner's eyes. "Not my leaders. I'm an American officer, on loan to the British. I've given your people name, rank, and serial number. You can check with both OSS/London and SOE/London. They'll verify my identity."

"An American officer working with British intelligence," Volkov mused. "I suppose you think that explains why you are in Berlin, dressed like a laborer. With a German military paybook in your possession, I might add."

"The paybook doesn't mean a thing. It's issued to a phony name."

"As to that, I have no doubt," Volkov said. "You aren't the first German officer to try to escape by issuing himself a spurious paybook. Who are you, really?"

"I'm an American officer," the prisoner repeated. "I've been hiding in Berlin for the past two weeks. Haven't you got anyone around here who speaks English?"

"I'm sure your English is perfect," Volkov said. "You wouldn't be so eager to show it off, were it otherwise. But tell me, if you've really been in Berlin only two weeks, what was your mission here?"

"That I am not able to divulge. I have only divulged the fact that I am an intelligence officer, your ally, I might emphasize, in order that *we—can—by—God—get—some—action.*"

Really excellent, that tooth-gritted delivery, Volkov decided. Good stress. Good tone, especially. Not arrogant. He was already accustomed to the habitually superior manner of German prisoners. But impelling. Surely the man was indeed an intelligence officer. German, of course, but who but an experienced intelligence man could capture just the right tone that way?

Probing further, Volkov said, "Well, then, tell me this: If you've really been hiding, in fear of your life, how is it that you were well behind Russian lines and yet made no effort to contact us?"

"I was never anywhere near your lines until last night,"

the prisoner said. His façade wasn't perfect. He looked uncomfortable. Something in the eyes said he was lying.

Ivanov leaned over and whispered in Volkov's ear. Volkov nodded and said, "Perhaps it would be easier to believe you if we hadn't found you wearing an armband of the people's militia. I assume you have an explanation for that?"

"Yes," the prisoner said. "It was a ruse. I wore it to make my journey easier through German-held territory. I didn't want to answer too many questions."

"I see," Volkov said. "And the medal? Was that also part of the ruse?"

"Medal?"

"A German Iron Cross. The soldiers who captured you found it in your trouser pocket."

"I can explain that," the prisoner said.

"I'm sure you can. But let's return to the seaplane. Why did you fire on it? Was it out of anger that they tried to take off without you? Or was it merely to make your story more plausible once you realized you could not get away?"

"I fired on it because I saw Adolf Hitler climb into it," the prisoner said emphatically. "Surely your people reported the presence of a boat and two men near the plane?"

Volkov looked up at Ivanov.

Ivanov shook his head. "No, no one mentioned a boat," he said. "But they did report the presence of two SS escorts in the cove, both dead." To the prisoner, Ivanov said affably, "You must be a very important man to be given two SS men as an escort. Why don't you tell us now who you are? We'll find out eventually."

"I'm counting on it," the prisoner snapped. "If you'll just contact London, as I asked, we can straighten this out immediately."

Volkov leaned back and whispered to Ivanov, who pointed to a paragraph in the interrogation notes. "Ah yes, I see," Volkov said. "An SOE factor named Mr. Mumford and an OSS officer named Holley. And this is the proper code routing to reach this Holley?"

"It is," the prisoner said. "You might ask yourself how I happen to know the communications procedure and the officers' names if I'm not who I say I am."

"I'm sure German intelligence tried to provide you with everything you might need, although it was careless of them not to research the SOE routing as well," Volkov said. "But what I really don't understand is why you have elected to use it. If we were to follow through on your request to query either the British or the Americans, you would surely be exposed, would you not? Or can it be possible that you're telling the truth?"

"Well, thank God for that," the prisoner said. "It's about time someone admitted the possibility." His eyelids sagged, as though his body sensed the additional possibility of rest, of long, satisfying sleep.

"Possibility, yes," Volkov said. "Probability? No. Frankly, it is more than difficult to swallow your story. But I'm willing to check it out. You will be kept in custody, of course, until we get a response." He gestured for the guards to take the prisoner away.

"May I ask a question?" the prisoner said. "Your subordinate refused to answer me, and it's of extreme importance."

Volkov shrugged. "As you wish."

The prisoner turned to Ivanov. "What happened to the plane? I mean, after your people hit me. Did it get away?"

Ivanov queried Volkov with a raised eyebrow, and only after Volkov nodded permission did he reply, "We aren't sure. According to the men who brought you in, the plane was damaged by your last shot. But it managed to get airborne. It disappeared to the north. We've asked patrols to keep an eye open for wreckage."

"You're sure it was still flying?"

"The last time it was seen, yes."

The prisoner, his face a perfect picture of a man in deadly earnest, turned back to Volkov. "Then you must hurry to verify my identity. Please. It seems to be the only way you'll believe me. There may still be time if we hurry. What if the plane didn't go down? It might still be trying for a submarine rendezvous, or some other way to escape. And even if the plane did crash, what if Hitler is still alive? Hobbling off looking for aid? He'll find it. The Germans, damn their poor souls . . . it's . . . it's hard even for some of the best of them to stop believing in him. I know. Who does the stopping doesn't matter. But we've got to stop him."

Astute student of human nature that he was, Volkov found himself admiring the man. "We'll see to it as quickly as we possibly can," he said.

The prisoner's whole body sagged this time, and he let out a quiet sigh. "Thank you," he said. He shifted forward in the chair, anticipating the guards, and winced.

"What is it?" Volkov said. "Are you in pain?"

The prisoner nodded dully. He seemed to have lost all his focus and intensity. "My shoulder," he said vaguely. "Your doctor tells me it's broken. He sure must have done a sorry job of setting it. It hurts like hell."

Volkov's jaw muscles tightened at the criticism. That sounded exactly like the attitude he expected from a German. "Our doctors are very busy," he said stiffly. "I'm sure he did the best he could under the circumstances."

As soon as the prisoner had been helped from the room, Volkov shuffled the earlier interrogation notes together and handed them back to Ivanov. "I suppose you may as well send the queries," he said.

"I did," Ivanov said. "About two hours ago. We should have answers late this afternoon, if our sit-on-their-asses allies are still honoring our priorities. Do you believe him?"

"Not for a minute," Volkov said. "I've had three dozen Germans through here in the past six to eight hours, all lying through their teeth, trying to save their skins. I suspect this one is no different. He may even turn out to be a major war criminal of some kind."

"Then you don't think Hitler has escaped?"

"As to that, I'm not sure. Probably not in the way this prisoner suggests. It stands to reason that he would try. Or perhaps he committed suicide, just as General Krebs told General Chuikov. It's frustrating. We won't know for certain until the search teams can enter the Chancellery grounds for a complete investigation—and that, of course, must await a general surrender."

"I suppose you're right," Ivanov said. For a moment, he stared thoughtfully at the door. "Wouldn't it be odd, though, if it turned out that the man was telling the truth? What if we discover he *is* an American, as he says? We might have had Hitler under our guns and let him get away."

Volkov sat in stony silence for another moment, examining the possibility. Then he shuddered, like an animal plagued by a cloud of gnats, and said, "Bring in the next prisoner."

2

At the same hour on the morning of May 2, 1945, General Karl Weidling, commandant of the badly mauled and shrinking Berlin garrison, fully aware that further resistance was hopeless, crossed through the Russian lines under a white flag to offer an immediate and unconditional surrender of all surviving German troops. He was taken, as Krebs had been the day before, to General Chuikov. The meeting was short. Weidling had been left with nothing to negotiate. At Chuikov's instructions, Weidling wrote a brief proclamation describing the hopeless situation and ordering all Germans to cease fire and lay down their arms. He then read the proclamation into a Russian recording machine.

By noon, Russian sound trucks were in the streets, close behind the Russian lines. Weidling's voice, shaking with emotion, rolled out of the speakers: "Every hour of fighting adds to the terrible suffering of the civilian population of Berlin and of our wounded. Anyone who falls in battle is making a useless sacrifice. I order the immediate cessation of fighting." The message was played over and over.

Thus began a wholesale capitulation. Throughout the city, from bunkers, from behind jagged walls, they emerged, blood-stained white handkerchiefs tied to gun barrels, limping, crawling, stepping over the bodies of their comrades to give themselves up to the Russians.

By two in the afternoon, the last of the guns fell silent. A strange and awesome quiet spread like a cloud over the destroyed city. Civilians who had not seen daylight for a week ventured timidly from underground shelters. Red battle flags whipped in the wind from the top of the Reichstag and from the battered Brandenburg Gate.

A titmouse, hopping from twig to twig in one of the few remaining trees in the Tiergarten, cocked its tiny, gray-crested head at the unusual silence and suddenly burst into tentative song.

The battle for Berlin was over.

3

When the Russian query came through about a Captain Henry Bascom, Adrian Courtney retired for a moment to his office window and stared out past the spider web, examining both his credo and his options. From the beginning he knew what he should do. In the end, he did it: He put in a call for Bascom's tweedy superior, only to be met by a horrified yelp.

"What?" Holley actually shouted. "How did you learn about that? By God, don't you do a thing. Not one thing. I'll be over there in ten minutes."

Sidney Longland limped in as Courtney was hanging up the phone. "Was that Holley?" he demanded. "What did he say about Bascom?" He looked predictably excited. And tense.

The security in his office was becoming extremely lax, Courtney concluded. Ordinarily, one would have to speak sternly to Colonel Norman about that, but, given that one's ancient aide had handed in his resignation, effective June 1, with a look of steely disapproval in his faded eyes, one rather hesitated.

Courtney knew he should also deal with that demanding

tone of Longland's, but there were more important things
to think about. "Colonel Holley appears to have received
his own query about your indestructible Captain Bascom,"
he said quietly, "just as you seem somehow to have been
informed. I suppose I can thank Colonel Norman for filling
you in."

Longland had the decency to redden to the tips of his
pointed ears. But, as demanding as ever, he asked, "Then
Holley has already confirmed Bascom's identity to the
Russians?"

"He didn't say. He's coming here directly."

Longland hesitated for the first time. "Right to your
office? Openly?"

"That's right. Does that mean anything to you?"

"Bloody hell," Longland said, "I didn't think he'd dare.
At least not until he gets that promotion he's been angling
for."

Good. He was learning. Courtney started to nod ap-
provingly, pondering some word of praise for Longland's
obvious ingenuity in ferreting out Holley's possible promotion, but Longland slumped into a chair without being
invited, and Courtney remained silent. Discipline was fast
going to pot now that nothing remained of the war but formal surrender. But Courtney's own species of war went on
forever, and, disciplined or no, Longland seemed to know
that. Good, again.

At least Longland stood when Holley burst in, smelling
disgustingly sweaty in his heavy tweeds. Courtney checked
his watch. It had taken Holley only six minutes, not ten.
Courtney rose, too, having decided to feint. "What splendid
news, Holley," he tried for openers. "Young Bascom—"

Holley's words of greeting cut him off. "Don't hand me
that crap!" the American said. "That goddamned amateur.
He's broken his cover! How could he do this to me? Now
the Russians will learn everything! By God, if my boat gets
rocked, you'll go down with me, Mumford. They'll cut off
your head at the Tower of London when I get through
with you."

Always so melodramatic. Courtney looked forward to

the day when the shifting of allegiances—and national allegiances always shifted—might pit him against this particular vulgar American. But that day, if it ever came, would be far in the future. The Russians, as he had known for twenty years, would come next.

"See here, Holley," he said, "the Export operation need never come into this. If you are unable to devise some acceptable alternate mission on which we might have sent your man into Berlin, I assure you I can. The Russians will never be the wiser."

"Are you out of your mind?" Holley gasped. "Bascom has probably already blabbed every damned thing he knows about Export. If we acknowledge the sonofabitch, they'll hang us by our thumbs. Jesus, no! There's only one alternative: We've got to deny Bascom. We've got to keep the lid firmly in place. We've never even heard of him, understand? Then anything he says, by God, at least they'll never be able to prove it!"

Courtney watched Longland's foxy face turn pale. Odd how that red hair made the white face look even whiter. Longland looked to Courtney, not Holley, and said, "Are you going to let this sod get away with this? He's protecting his own neck, you know."

"I'm *not*," Holley protested. "It's political and military policy. A direct order."

Courtney sighed. "There's the rub," he said. He addressed the words to Longland, hoping he'd understand.

"Besides," Holley said plaintively, "who's going to miss the bastard? He's a goddamn orphan. He doesn't even have a family. And don't tell me you're going to miss him either, major. That girlfriend of yours—"

Longland shredded him with a single glance.

"Well, anyway," Holley muttered, "I say fuck him. We never heard of Bascom. And that's the way it's going to be."

Longland's jaw tightened. To Courtney, he said, "Do you agree?"

"Do I have a choice?" Courtney said.

The jaw drew tighter, and the pale face studied him. Not

an expression one would care to see over a dueling pistol at ten paces, Courtney realized. Without another word, Longland limped to the door, and closed it behind him. Quietly. Courtney's uneasiness deepened. He wished that Longland had at least slammed it.

"Well," Holley sighed, "thanks, Mumford. Thanks a lot. I owe you one now, and, well, I may be in an excellent position to return favors one of these happy days. It was a difficult decision. I mean, even a Bascom, you hate to junk one of your own people. It helps a lot to know that you agree with me that it has to be done. I guess the Russians will shoot him or something, won't they?"

"I wouldn't count on it," Courtney said. "Captain Bascom seems to be a survivor. You may be hearing from him again one of these, um, happy days."

Holley's eyes shifted. He glanced at the door, eager to leave, and said, "Hell, I'm only doing my duty. Like you. And listen, Mumford, I'm really serious about the favor. Call on me any time."

The remark about Bascom's possible survival had been a petty revenge, Courtney thought when he was finally alone, but it helped. Maybe Holley would sleep less well for a few nights at least. Courtney went to the window, restlessly, still feeling as uneasy as he hoped the American felt, and he regained no composure in noticing that Longland was limping along the edge of St. James's Park, apparently deep in thought. Longland's shoulders were straight. He stared straight ahead. There was something in the set of the shoulders that made Courtney suddenly wonder if he had tutored his newest pupil too well. Would he himself be hearing something less than pleasant, thanks to Longland, some future day?

There, he was gone. Stepped into a cab, which, ominously, had appeared almost by magic. There was something definitely ominous about yet another deeply disapproving subordinate with so commanding an air that he could attract a cab the moment he wanted one in cab-short London.

Attracted by some slight movement, Courtney's eye fell on the spider web in the window. He bent to inspect it more

closely and found a certain sign of ripening spring. Some
might look for fritillary butterflies, peacocks, red admirals,
but Adrian Courtney spied a young recently hatched house-
fly. It was caught in the web, struggling. Struggling with
considerable vigor, in fact, but obviously helpless.

Houseflies were pesky creatures. Courtney started to
turn away, but impulse turned him back. With an impatient hand, he knocked down the web and destroyed it.

4

En route to Ann Christy's flat in the cab, Longland tried
not to notice the gaps where buildings had been, the wood-
en barricades that shielded pedestrians from unfilled bomb
craters, the "Dangerous Walls" signs on other precariously
tilted structures, and he tried not to think of anger, betrayal, endings. He concentrated on finding the best words
for telling Ann. Though he and Bascom may have regarded themselves as rivals, he had come to know that she
cared most for Bascom, and he feared he would have to
hurt her dreadfully. It was against the standing security
orders for him to tell her at all, of course, but she had a
right to know. And if he didn't do one small thing in immediate protest, he feared he might boil over and jeopardize the ultimate protest against Mr. Mumford that was
slowly formulating in his mind.

Ann's stairs smelled of cabbage. They always did. Her
small building was occupied by two sisters, a pleasant
homosexual with a fondness for Abyssinian cats, a Polish
countess who had refugeed to London in time for the
Blitz, and a thirtyish woman who performed pantomime
in the music halls, and not one of them would have been
caught dead eating cabbage, but there it was. The smell was
almost nauseating this afternoon. Longland's spirits had
plummeted so low that he could barely summon a foxy
smile for the countess when he passed her on the stairs.

He felt absolutely rotten when he knocked at Ann's

door. She took her time answering, and, although he wouldn't have believed it possible, thus gave him time to feel more rotten still. Then the door opened partially, revealing Sergeant Ann Christy dressed in a man-tailored, midnight-blue silk robe that he had never seen before, and although the soft, loose silk of the robe revealed quite a lot of gorgeous Ann Christy, he couldn't even respond with pleasure to that.

Ann's matching eyes opened widely, but the door opening stayed narrow. "Oh Sidney," she said. "Darling, I just got home. Why didn't you tell me at the office you were coming over? I'm afraid I—"

Best get it over with. "Ann, something has come up. I've got to talk to you."

"Darling, can't it wait? Really, I was just stepping into the shower."

"I'm sorry," he said. "It's really important." He pushed the door open.

"Whups," a male voice said from behind her.

Longland jerked back, but too late. He'd always thought Ann's flat was poorly laid out, what with no foyer. The pilot whom they had enlisted to search for Bascom's sorry submarine, dressed only in a bath towel, retreated rapidly toward the bathroom. It looked as though Ann hadn't planned to shower alone.

"Sorry," Longland said promptly, but in an entirely different tone.

Ann made a moue and opened the door the rest of the way. "Oh well, you may as well come in," she said.

"Never mind," Longland said. "It isn't as important as I thought."

She called after him as he limped swiftly down the cabbagy stairs, but Longland didn't answer. The countess was returning to her own flat, carrying something carefully cradled in her hands, and he barely thought to stop when she hailed him by name.

"Look, Major Longland," the countess said happily. "See what the greengrocer at the corner has succeeded in getting for me. Early artichokes. They're tiny, but so dear. Somehow he managed to bring them in from the vicinity of Nice."

"Lovely," Longland said politely. "Looks as if the war is really over."

"Oh it is, with artichokes back again. I shall celebrate the fall of Berlin by devouring them. Where are you off to in such a hurry? A victory celebration of your own?"

Longland gazed up the stairs at Ann's closing door. "Something like that," he said. "Good-by, Countess. I hope you enjoy your artichokes."

A celebration? Not exactly, but the countess was on the right track. Longland limped out the door and turned right, remembering a pub in that direction.

There was nothing for it but to get roaring drunk.

5

They came for Bascom shortly before midnight, another pair of Russian infantrymen who smelled of vodka and sweat and whose eyes still glittered with the heady ambrosia of victory. They led him silently down a littered corridor, walls already scrawled with Russian graffiti, and into the street, where an array of German officers, some wounded, some seemingly whole but dazed, stood waiting. One of the infantrymen showed a written order to the chief guard of the small detachment of prisoners, then prodded Bascom into the circle. A rigid Wehrmacht colonel with bandages wrapped tightly about his stomach turned suspicious eyes on Bascom's dirty, tattered civilian clothing, but moved over to make room for him.

At a command from the guards, the group started moving. They marched away from the building and through the wasteland that had once been a street. Somewhere ahead of them, perhaps two or three blocks away, a massive shuffling sound rose through the ruins. Thousands of feet, like an army on the march. Not the quick, lively tramp of victorious troops. Rather, the slow, dull scuffle of defeat.

They wound through the devastation, getting closer to the sound, and turned onto a broad, wrecked avenue heading south. A long gray column of massed humanity stretched in both directions as far as the eye could see, perhaps as many as twenty thousand ragged men, shambling along the avenue with leaden feet and downcast eyes.

An American Lend-Lease Jeep was sitting at the corner, and in the rear, a Russian officer. As though by prearrangement, the small group of German officers was brought to a halt, and two of the guards came back to fetch Bascom. They nudged him toward the Jeep. As he drew closer, he recognized the officer. It was Volkov, the man who had interrogated him earlier.

"We have an answer from London," Volkov said.

Bascom tried to read his face in the moonlight. Nothing was there. No emotion. "What did it say?"

"You lied, as I expected," the Russian said. He didn't sound disappointed or angry. Just resigned.

Bascom stepped back involuntarily, one step, as though an abyss had just opened at his feet. "Are you sure? Sometimes, with all the red tape, they make mistakes."

"There is no mistake," the Russian said. "The answer came directly from one of the men you told us to contact. The one you called Holley. British intelligence later confirmed it."

Time froze, but Bascom's brain raced through the corridors of memory, seeking to understand. So that's how it was to be? Holley and Mumford had disowned him? Abandoned. The realization detonated like a bomb. Abandoned, a life's ending, as it had been his life's beginning. Then the wolf's red rage and raging tenacity flooded the pale jelly of the brain, and Bascom's teeth clamped shut. Perhaps there was a reason. For Holley's sake, especially, he hoped so.

"We will find out who you are eventually," Volkov said. "We have many prisoners among your higher echelons.

Sooner or later, one of them will recognize you and tell us, in exchange for his own safety."

"You'll have to wait a long time for that."

"We have time," the Russian said. He gestured at the waiting prisoners. "They are ready to join the march. Go along."

"Where are we going?"

"East."

"To Russia?"

Volkov nodded. "It will be a long walk for you. There will be no time for niceties. Because of your injuries"—he shrugged—"many of you will not come back."

The subtle, resolute animal that had come into existence inside Bascom stretched itself at full length, testing its strength thoughtfully. "I'll be back," the wolf said.

Perhaps it showed itself through Bascom's eyes. Volkov's shoulders drew up with a hint of inexplicable apprehension. Then Volkov gestured curtly at the two guards, and they returned Bascom to the covey of waiting officers.

The chief guard gave an order, and the officers were herded into the main artery of shuffling thousands. They moved slowly with the current, putting one foot ahead of the other as though it required great concentration. Though all knew this could well be the last time they would ever see their homeland, most of them walked with their eyes down, unable to stomach the sights around them. Whole blocks had disappeared. Bomb holes and shell craters yawned everywhere. Most of the canal bridges had been blasted to bits by bombs and artillery or destroyed by retreating Germans. Sewer lines strung beneath the bridges had collapsed and now poured filth into the stagnant waters. Fires still burned. Bodies, covered with flies, lay where they had fallen. Berlin had been turned into a massive cemetery.

"How could it happen?" a young German lieutenant murmured to himself. "How in God's name could this happen?"

The rigid colonel with the stomach wound stared bleakly at the heels of the soldier in front of him. He looked weak from loss of blood. As if in answer to the lieutenant's question, he intoned, " *'Gebt mir zehn Jahre Zeit und ihr werdet Deutschland nicht wieder erkennen.'* "

Bascom looked up in surprise. He recognized the quote. It was from a speech first uttered by Adolf Hitler in 1933. He'd seen it many times during his prewar days in Berlin, whitewashed on walls. In English it meant:

"Give me ten years, and you won't be able to recognize Germany."

EPILOGUE

Friday—March 12, 1954

The war in Europe ended six days after the surrender of
Berlin, at the stroke of midnight on May 8, 1945. After
six and a half years of catastrophic fighting, thirty-five
million soldiers and civilians were dead or missing, and an
estimated six million Jews had been exterminated in what
Hitler had foully called "the final solution to the Jewish
problem."

Russian search teams had begun the search for Hitler's
body almost as soon as the guns fell silent in Berlin. They
found it not once, but three times. The first Russians to
enter the Chancellery grounds accomplished little. The
surrender of the city was still in progress, and the silent
walls of numerous buildings overlooked the garden. Fearing
diehard snipers, the Russians hurried in, conducted a quick,
superficial tour of the grounds, and hurried out, reporting
only that the underground Führerbunker had been set afire
and abandoned by all occupants at least twenty-four hours
before the surrender. A number of bodies were visible to
them, some in the buildings, some in the garden, others at
the top of a water tower where a few SS guards had taken
their own lives, but the team stopped to look closely at
none of them.

A more thorough search group came the next day, on
May 3. They located the bodies of General Krebs and
General Burgdorf, slumped in their quarters, bullets
through their heads. They also found the bodies of the six
Goebbels children and the burned remains of Joseph Goebbels and his wife. Later in the day, poking through the
ruins of the garden, they uncovered the charred body of a

man in uniform whose features resembled those of the Führer, but who was wearing darned socks. They tentatively proclaimed the body to be that of Adolf Hitler, but the socks were worrisome. How could a man who moved nations and triggered the greatest holocaust in history be reduced to wearing darned socks?

Another search team returned to the scene on May 4, and discovered two more Hitler corpses, one burned and the other unburned. Perplexed as to what they could possibly do with two additional sets of Hitler remains when one was already in hand, they reburied both.

On May 5, the third day after the surrender of Berlin and three days before the over-all surrender, a final search team came back to the garden. The first Hitler had been rejected because of the darned socks, and since General Krebs had insisted before his death that Hitler had been cremated, they had been instructed to reclaim the May 4 burned corpse. But it had disappeared. Frantically they searched the grounds, digging and redigging the same trenches. Then someone located it in a hallway of the Chancellery building, laid out among a string of corpses, where presumably it had been placed by Russian soldiers who had been probing in the garden.

The body was badly disfigured by fire, but the teeth were still intact. Russian investigators rounded up two technicians who had worked as assistants to Hitler's dentist, and instructed them to make drawings from memory of the way Hitler's teeth had been bridged. The drawings and the teeth of the corpse were a fairly close match. After an exhaustive but inconclusive autopsy, the body was secretly transported to Moscow and the dental technicians imprisoned, one for nearly eleven years.

Heinrich Himmler never did get to meet with General Eisenhower. After the final surrender, Himmler traveled to Flensburg to offer his services to the rump government of Grand Admiral Karl Dönitz, but was turned away. With any chance of postwar power denied him, nothing remained but to go into hiding. He shaved off his mustache,

replaced his wire-framed spectacles with an eye patch, and
began to roam the countryside with his aides, looking for
safety. He stayed out of Allied hands for three weeks, until
May 21, 1945, when he was arrested by a British patrol.
Outfitted as an enlisted man and bearing papers that identified him as one Heinrich Hitzinger, he might well have
survived the war with no more than brief incarceration, but
his ego once more got the better of him. He announced his
true identity to a stunned British officer, and minutes later,
during a routine medical examination, bit down on a concealed cyanide capsule and died almost instantly.

The Russians had Berlin to themselves for two months,
months of starvation, disease, and terror for the defeated
Berliners. Red soldiers, drunk on victory, wreaked a stern
vengeance on the population for the savage excesses of the
German armies in the Ukraine and the Caucasus.

Then, between July 2 and July 4, 1945, fifty thousand
soldiers of the British 7th Armored Division and the
American 82nd Airborne Division rolled into the city to
join the occupation, and Russian behavior modified almost
overnight.

Slowly the city began to breathe. Clean-up crews of
women formed lines and passed rubble and bricks to
waiting trucks. Heavily damaged buildings were demolished. Streets were repaired. The city was stricken, even
gravely wounded. But it did not die.

As the years passed and the city slowly rebuilt, some of
the captive German soldiers and members of the people's
militia, taken prisoner in the final battle for Berlin, began to
trickle back from Russia. Enlisted men and Volkssturmers
came first, some only a year or two after the war ended.
Officers and members of the German General Staff were
released much later—seven years, eight years, some ten,
eleven, or twelve years after the surrender. Many, as Volkov predicted, never came back. General Weidling, for
one, died while still in captivity, ten years after the fall of
Berlin.

A number of prisoners, never properly identified but suspected of being either high-ranking officers or possible war criminals, were placed in isolation and hounded by interrogators day after day. Some were executed. Some died of injuries and disease. Others were questioned brutally until the Russians lost interest in them, then were casually repatriated to Germany.

It was one such prisoner, a man who had resurfaced after nine years in a Russian prison camp, whom Sidney Longland had come to meet on that March 12, 1954, in a city where the broken tower of the Kaiser Wilhelm church still stood among shiny new buildings, its clock perpetually frozen at seven-fifty, as a grim reminder of the terrible destruction brought upon Berlin.

Looking warily at Bascom, Longland found himself thinking of the ruined clock, drawing an almost unconscious parallel. Then, chiding himself for being shallow, he deliberately supplanted the thought with the image of the Tiergarten as he had last chanced to notice it. All but denuded in those final days of the war and stripped clean of wood by freezing Germans during the harsh winter that followed the peace, the great park had been replanted with one million new trees and was turning green once more. As for fauna, the zoo was open again at the park's western end, and newly populated by appropriate inhabitants for its rebuilt Elephant House, Monkey House, Small House for Beasts of Prey, and Great House for Beasts of Prey. Regarding the two-footed beast of prey who sat across a restaurant table from him, Longland realized he couldn't be sure that Bascom, like the city itself, hadn't undergone a regeneration, changing into something new and strong.

Bascom continued to sit in silence, warming himself in the sun, but the long silence made Longland edgy. There were still so many unanswered questions. Perhaps if he strived for a friendly note . . . He cleared his throat and said, "I should have brought Formoy with me to welcome you. He's been eager to thank you in person for a good many years now."

It seemed to work. Bascom came out of his reverie with a start. "Formoy's alive?" he said.

"Very much so, old lad. It seems he was spirited from cellar to church to house by some German women until your Americans finally entered Berlin, and then they bore him to the Yanks in triumph. Wouldn't give him up to the Russians, or even to us British, I understand. But, of course, he was still in pretty bad shape. Couldn't tell us a great deal about what had happened to you. I've had to piece things together pretty much for myself, though there are points I'd still like to get clear on."

Bascom apparently chose to ignore that opening. "Is he well?" he asked.

"Quite well. A few creaks and groans, but we all have those, eh? I don't see him much. He's been off on some nasty little volcanic island off Greece, puttering with shards again. Thinks he's discovered lost Atlantis, in fact, only the real thing, you know, some prehistoric Greek city or other."

The green eyes showed momentary interest, but Bascom had no questions beyond the key ones. His lapse back to silence made Longland feel like an idiot. Unable to stop himself, Longland plunged deeper. "You'll be wanting to know what's become of Ann, as well. She's married. Not to me. Some fellow who owns a coal mine. They've children, dogs, all that. I was invited down one weekend, but I had a little too much on my plate just then. The office keeps me awfully busy these days."

Still no reaction beyond mild interest. How damned exasperating. Well, try the direct route. Change the subject. Get to the point. Quickly. "I'm really sorry about what happened to you, Bascom. Unlike your Mr. Holley, I always thought you must have had a bloody good reason for abandoning your cover back then. I did a bit of probing. Even though the Reds are no longer our own dear allies, a little co-operation is sometimes possible in intelligence circles. I managed to finagle a copy of the Russian file on you."

"Oh? What did you find out?"

"More than I expected to. Is it true, what you told them about—"

He paused. He started to glance at the other tables, but Bascom's eyes alone told him no one was eavesdropping, no one was near but two shirtless, sun-worshiping, and thoroughly indifferent Germans. Just a flick of the eyes, animal-like, and a wordless communication that leaped across the table into Longland's surprised awareness. How had he done that?

Flustered, Longland continued, "This business you told them about Hitler. Some of us have never been completely comfortable with the official reports dealing with Hitler's suicide, but it wasn't until I bagged your file that I realized what your last message meant about the sub. We got three or four knocked off for you, but we could never be certain we caught up with the specific one you referred to."

A hint of puzzlement came over the quiet face, as though Bascom wasn't sure what Longland was talking about, but just as quickly subsided. Bascom had obviously turned into a man who discarded nonessentials.

"There've been rumors," Longland said. "One rather wearies of trying to chase them down, but since you've been . . . away . . . they've been rather numerous. Hitler is in Mexico. Hitler is in Spain. Or Saudi Arabia. Or just about all of your South American countries, at one time or another. But this story you told the Russians is the only piece of concrete evidence I've encountered. Do you really think he got away? That is: Did you really see him? Alive? Escaping?"

"Why do you want to know?" Bascom asked.

"Good lord, who wouldn't want to know? We all have an interest in Hitler. If he's alive, we've got to run him to earth."

The lean, calloused hands across the table caressed the almost untouched glass of schnapps but didn't pick it up. "I wonder," Bascom said, as if idly, "why I feel I've been through this before. Your Mr. Mumford, now, he wouldn't have objected to a feather in his cap, and my nice Mr. Holley would have worn one in his ass if he could have latched on to it. Do you want a feather, Longland? Is that it? Is that why you came to meet me today? Have you been thinking all these years about finally capturing Hitler? Cap or ass, take your pick."

Longland cursed under his breath, then caught himself and decided to curse aloud. "Bloody hell," he blustered. "It wasn't my fault you lost nine years. There wasn't anything I could do to change the situation."

"Did you try?"

"I did what I could," Longland said lamely. Then, angry once more, "Look, you can think what you want about my motives. I don't give a damn. There's only one reason I'm here. And that's to give you the bloody money and the bloody passport. I don't know why in hell I ever decided to worry about you in the first place. Keep your bloody secret. As far as I'm concerned, you can take the money and passport and go back to the bloody States, or you can bloody well go to hell. It's all the same to me!"

Bascom surprised him yet again. "Not yet," he said mildly. The killer's eyes inventoried the roll of bills and the forged American passport still lying on the table. "I have a few things to attend to first. Before I can go either to America *or* to hell."

"Such as what?"

Quietly, "Do you think you have a right to know?"

With resignation, "Well, I would have hoped so."

Bascom's hand wrapped around the glass, touching it, as if he enjoyed the mere glassy surface. Poor sod. Had he drunk only dubious water from a community tin cup for nine solid years? The killer's eyes turned merely greenish again, perhaps in response to the momentary and unwilling sympathy reflected in Longland's own face.

"You really want to know about Hitler?" Bascom asked.

"Of course I do."

"The Russians didn't believe me," Bascom said. "Why should you be any different?"

"I'm willing to try."

Bascom nodded. "All right, I'll tell you the truth. I used

to think about it almost every day. First I wondered why nobody would listen to me. Then I wondered where he was, whether he slept well nights. Then I thought about going after him, if I ever got out." He twisted the schnapps glass thoughtfully, making wet circles on the table top. "But that was all another lifetime ago. Now I'm not so sure whether I really saw him or not."

"But you surely have an opinion," Longland urged.

Bascom shrugged. "I saw someone. I had a friend, a German girl. She's dead now. She was with me that night. She was certain it was only someone who looked like him. Maybe she was right. I don't know."

Longland was disappointed. "You're recanting your story?"

"Not recanting. Just admitting some doubts. I thought I knew at the time. But now . . . hell, let's drink up." The hand firmly grasped the schnapps glass. "A toast? Something mutually agreeable? How about to Formoy and his lost Atlantis?"

The sod was lying, of course. Wasn't he? Bascom seemed content just to sit there outside the little workingman's bar with an empty glass in that emaciated yet muscular hand, and although Longland had no other appointments this trip in a city that still fermented with conspiracy, treachery, and wolfish plans for vengeance, he claimed such an appointment and signaled for a bill.

He rose, favoring his gimpy knee. He'd never found time to do anything about the knee, but, given the Cold War and his own personal affrays, he'd never found the time for any walking tours either. Standing above Bascom, he asked a penultimate question. "Truthfully, is there anything more I can do for you?"

"No, I think not," Bascom said. "Not yet." The greenish eyes looked up with something approaching a real smile in them. "Although it might always be handy to know someone who's a big shot in intelligence circles."

Longland grinned back, his foxy grin. "I don't suppose

you want to tell me what you're planning to do, do you?" he said.

"Rest awhile," Bascom said. "Then . . . who knows? Go hunting, perhaps."

Go hunting?

Longland didn't ask, but, limping away, he wondered. Mr. Yapp, his chosen *nom de guerre* in this new war, the chilly one, would surely have asked, but the man who had been Sidney Longland before ambition and his own targets for revenge had dulled his eyes with disillusionment said, no, don't ask what you once forfeited the right to hear.

He could have done something nine years ago. Couldn't he?

He could have forfeited sudden, flaring ambitions and allowed Mr. Mumford the pleasure of having his head, instead of vice versa. Couldn't he?

If Bascom was right, if Hitler had truly escaped, the former Führer would be living out his life in lonely seclusion, fighting nightmares and the depression of lost glory. Wouldn't he?

If he was still alive, that is. Was he?

But as Longland regained Friedrichstrasse and looked automatically for the black embassy limousine, then muttered, "Bloody hell!" because he remembered he had dismissed it, the real question in his mind was: Hitler or Holley?

If Longland himself had lost nine years of his life, would he go after the man who murdered those years, or the man who tried to murder a world?

A mere Holley?

Or a Hitler?

Or both?

Longland discovered that he was standing stock still on the sidewalk and that two German teen-agers were staring at him coldly from a motorcycle over which they were leaning.

He smiled at them without rancor and went on his way.

No need for rancor. No need for regrets. He knew which was to be the first prey. He had put the beginning tools in

Bascom's hands himself: money and a passport. Perhaps he had helped in some small way. He would help again, if asked.

And a stalking wolf was loose upon the land.

Dell Bestsellers